International acclaim

ADELE PARKS

—who delivers "cleverness to spare"*
and sharp, savvy portrayals of relationships, sex,
and marriage in her sensational bestselling novels!

LARGER THAN LIFE

"Parks has scored another surefire hit with *Larger Than Life*. . . .
Expect to see it peeking out of handbags near you soon."

—*Heat*

"Entertaining and moving."

—*OK*

"An engaging read."

—*Independent*

PLAYING AWAY

"Compulsively addictive!"

—*Elle*

"An affecting first novel . . . a cheeky first-person narrative. . . . A
balanced exploration of the rules of marriage."

—*Kirkus Reviews*

"*Playing Away* is a very edgy book. It's also wickedly funny and
very sexy."

—*Publishers Weekly**

Also by Adele Parks

Playing Away

Available from Pocket Books

Larger Than Life

a novel

ADELE PARKS

New York   London   Toronto   Sydney   Singapore

An *Original* Publication of POCKET BOOKS

A Downtown Press Book published by
POCKET BOOKS, a division of Simon & Schuster, Inc.
1230 Avenue of the Americas, New York, NY 10020

ISBN: 0-7434-5760-9

First Downtown Press printing August 2003

10 9 8 7 6 5 4 3 2 1

DOWNTOWN PRESS and colophon are
trademarks of Simon & Schuster, Inc.

For information regarding special discounts for bulk purchases,
please contact Simon & Schuster Special Sales at 1-800-456-6798
or business@simonandschuster.com

Designed by Jaime Putorti

Printed in the U.S.A.

For my son, an indescribable, unrepeatable splash of colorful, wonderful joy. And for my nieces, Claudia and Felicity, and my nephew, William. With love.

Acknowledgments

This book is dedicated to mams, mummies, mums and mothers everywhere. Especially the mums of the following indescribable, unrepeatable splashes of colorful, wonderful joy: Claudia, Felicity and William Dent, Harry James, Olivia and Charlie Buckley, Calum Butler, Megan Woods, Billie and Emily Rudolf, Patrick and Rhys Davis, Miles and Helena Weatherseed, Molly Isaac, Laura Wheatley, Carly Downes, Ruby Bond, Joe and Ben Geller, Polly Hodges, Joshua Harkness, Eliza Lander, Virginia Hickey, William Taylor, Jamie Hewitt, Imogen Harwood-Matthews, Hector Crosbie, Conner and Jasmine de Trafford, Megan MacDonald, Sally Moore, Zuli and Leo Stannard, Amelia Boyle and Ethan Danielle-Brewer.

Larger
Than
Life

Prologue

Are you good enough? Are you? Are you thin enough but not too thin? More Elle Macpherson than Kate Moss? Do you go to the gym? But do you starve yourself? Think of the Africans. Don't you? Don't you have a social conscience? Of course you recycle your bottles and your newspapers, but do you recycle your tins too? I know it's a nuisance and you often cut yourself washing them out and the recycling unit is miles away, but really you should make an effort. Where do you get your hair done? Really? Is it expensive? Because it should be expensive, you ought to take pride in yourself, but it shouldn't be too expensive, being flash isn't attractive. Are they new boots? Oh, you chose tan. You do know that olive is the new tan, the new brown, the new black. Black is a classic, of course, no matter what the magazines say. You do read the magazines, don't you? It is important to keep up. How's work going? Been promoted recently? Have you asked for a pay raise? Well, don't let them exploit you; it's important to know your own worth. But it doesn't do to be greedy. What time did you leave the office last night? Crazy, isn't it. The Brits work longer hours than anyone else in Europe, only the Americans do more. No wonder they're all in therapy. It's important to get time to yourself. I could never leave before seven o'clock, though, they depend on me. Your hands are very chapped. I know a good manicurist. Yes, it's the weather and the transport strikes, but what can you do about it? I know a fabulous girl who does a fabulous manicure and pedicure as well. It doesn't do to let yourself go. No time. Make time. Do you get out much? Did you see the Tracey Emin? They said she's become appallingly mainstream. Do you go to the theater often? Did you catch that one, oh, what's it called? I forget, the latest one with the ex-soap star, she takes her clothes off. Oh, it doesn't matter what it's called, you ought to go, everyone is. Have you visited Tate Modern? Who did you go with? Who did you see? Who were you seen by? Did you ever do that Dome thingy? No, me neither, I rather regret that now. Are you studying? Well, everyone is doing a night class nowadays, aren't they? De rigueur. Modern Spanish history, IT, film appreciation, the semantics of women's literature, it's so useful to have something to talk about at dinner parties. Which book are you using at the moment? Are you still with Jamie Oliver, or have you tried anything from the latest Nigella Lawson yet? Melissa's doing very well. Yes twins, yes one of each, so that's the set. Clever girl. She's planning to be back in the gym a week on Monday. I don't know what I'd do if I had a baby. Which hospital? Which nurseries? Which schools? And you would have to go back to work; it doesn't do not to have anything to say to the hubby when he gets home from work, exhausted. The nurseries are all full, you know, from now until the year 2005, well at least the desirable ones are. There's always childminders. Yes, a nanny is probably the answer in terms of stimulation for the child, but you hear such stories, don't you? A really good girl is the very devil to find. It's so important to give them the very best start. Baby Beethoven, Lamaze, Montessori, organic diapers. Part-time might be the answer, but then you'd hardly earn enough to cover the childcare costs and buy your sandwich. Well, I must be going. It doesn't do to be late. By the way, you've spilled something down your shirt, is that silk? Is that olive oil? Oh dear, it won't come out. I do hope that stain hasn't been there since lunchtime. That wouldn't be good enough.

January

1

I don't go back to the office but instead drive to Hyde Park. I park and then walk. And walk. And walk. Stopping only to barf and retch unproductively en route. It's an icy cold January afternoon. There's hardly a soul around, unlike the summer when the park is heaving with revelers. The occasional tramp shuffles by, and I see the odd figure dashing home through the twilight, probably clerks who religiously leave their office at five. Not paid enough, or motivated at all, to stay a minute after clocking-out time. Oblivious to their surroundings, they don't glance left or right—the park is simply something that must be passed through on the way to centrally heated rooms and hot cups of tea. The odd mother rushes by with her toddler in a pushchair. The kids are invariably ugly, tired and dirty. The mothers are all that, and also harassed. I suppose that pushchairs, previously beneath my notice, will soon become significant to me.

Pushchairs and high chairs and baby baths and cots and diapers and it's impossible. It's alien. It's wrong.

Where is the unquashable exhilaration that, surely, should be the order of the day?

I'd settle for a faint flush of enthusiasm.

I walk on. I walk past the Serpentine, the desolate, deserted bandstand and around the Round Pond. I walk up and down. I circle. I walk so much that I'm actually warm even though it's freezing and late. My feet and legs ache. I'm starving. And I feel sick. How's that possible? On balance the hunger is more com-

pelling than the nausea. I'm so desperate that, for the first time
since I gave up watching *Black Beauty,* I buy a hot dog from a sus-
piciously filthy man pushing an off-white cart. The cart, man and
hot dog would fail all health and hygiene regulations with spectacular success. I try not to think about it. He piles greasy onions into
the bread bun and then smothers the hot dog with mustard and
ketchup, which squelch onto his fingers and down his arm. He
wipes his dirty hands on his dusty trousers, runs his hand through
his hair and, the final flourish, wipes the back of his hand over his
mouth. I don't care. The hot dog looks delicious. I'm that hungry
I would eat the man, dusty trousers and all, if necessary. Without
even stopping to check if anyone can see me I gobble down the hot
dog in approximately three bites. For about seven seconds I feel
almost normal. My hunger is satiated and I don't feel sick, an
exceptional state of affairs for the last month or so. On the eighth
second my stomach lurches uncontrollably and I am hoying for
Europe. The undigested hot dog, with onions, mustard, ketchup
and trouser dust lies forlornly on the pavement. It's accompanied
by two digestive biscuits, and I think that other thing is rye bread
from my sandwiches at lunchtime.

"Ya fackin stupid bitch," says the hot dog seller. "What the fack
did ya do that for? That ain't good for business, is it?"

I scrabble in my handbag and locate some tissues with which I
wipe my mouth, sick-splattered trousers and boots, and then I walk
away, too weary to fling back a clever retort, never mind reapply lipstick. I walk around the park again until I'm convinced that my boots
are worn through. Finally, I throw myself onto the nearest park
bench, not bothering about the bird excrement or chewing gum.

The park seems joyless. Littered with filthy vendors, rushing
faceless people, dog muck and broken glass bottles.

I am growing a baby.

There is a baby inside my stomach. Or womb, or uterus. Or
somewhere.

I try to think about that for a moment.

And can't.

It's so big. The thing, it . . . he or she is probably about the size of a single grain of couscous, but the *fact* that I'm pregnant is big. Too big.

Do I want to be pregnant? Do I want a baby (the natural conclusion)? I have no idea. My mind is completely blank. I rummage around a bit but there is only space, a yawning gap, a brilliant, dazzling, gleaming, glossy whiteness where a reaction or a response should be.

What will Hugh think? What will Hugh say?

Oh God.

I pull out my mobile and flick through the menu. Who to call? Hugh? God no. No. Not until I'm calmer, more certain. Of what? Certain of what to say, of how I feel. The idea of calling Drew, Karl, Brett or Julia, the people I work with, the people I've spent upward of ten hours a day with, five days a week, for several years, makes me laugh, or at least it would if I didn't feel so much like crying. While each of them is certainly sexually active, alert, even aggressive, I don't think any of them have ever connected the thing they do every Friday and Saturday night with making babies. In fact the primary concern has always been making sure sex didn't have anything to do with making babies. Sam? No point. Not unless I can somehow spin my pregnancy story so as to relate to finding her an eligible bachelor; she talks of nothing else. I dismiss a dozen or so other names, acquaintances that will trill that this is marvelous news. The thought terrifies me because I'm not certain that I'm ready to hear that.

Because I'm not certain it is.

There's Jessica, of course. She *is* my mother. Albeit the type of mother who insists I call her by her Christian name, as she hates to admit that she has a thirty-two-year-old daughter and she hyperventilates if I reveal our relationship in public. She is so much the epitome of a "lady who lunches" that my father ought to have placed a copyright upon her when they married. She's all suntan and surgery, diets and drama. Her life's work is turning back the hands of time. To give credit where it's due, she's very successful in realizing this ambition. She looks about forty-five whereas she's nearly twenty years older than that. My parents live in Cannes in the summer and Cape Town in the winter. My father is a very silent man, more notable for the things he doesn't say than for the things he does. He is a retired diplomat, a career that suited him; he finds that the skills he developed in his professional life are still extremely useful as he negotiates his way toward his fortieth year of marriage. And Jessica, for her part, is the perfect wife for a diplomat. She knows things like how to address a bishop or a lord, which flowers last the longest in hot weather, and how to write an utterly charming thank-you note. She is at all times extremely practical and clear-sighted. To date, her maternal advice has ranged from which sunblocks are indispensable to the recommendation of personal trainers; I figure it's time to use my joker card.

"Darling, how lovely to hear from you. Oh God, it's not your birthday, is it? Have I forgotten your birthday?"

"No, Jessica."

"No. Of course not. You were a summer baby. It's not mine, is it?"

Jessica hasn't celebrated a birthday since I was eight. Instead, she goes into a darkened room on the actual day and wears black for a week.

"No," I assure.

"So why the call?" A sad but fair testament of our mother-daughter relationship.

I consider talking about the weather but realize it's pointless. "I'm pregnant."

There's a wail of horror. "Oh darling. How could you do this to me? That will make me a—oh God, I'm going to have to sit down—a *grandmother.*" She hiss-whispers the last word, as though articulating a curse.

"I didn't do this to you," I splutter, resisting the urge to scream, "Bugger you, what about me? What about me!"

"I've been dreading this call since you were fourteen. Oh darling. You didn't plan this, did you?" She's incredulous. We are, in many ways, very similar.

"No."

"Is it Hugh's?"

"Of course." I try not to sound offended.

"Well, that's something, I suppose," she mutters. "It will, at least, be good-looking." This is typical of my mother. Untouched by the traditional concerns, such as the facts that the child is unplanned, illegitimate and fathered by a married man, she focuses her attention on the aesthetics. I don't know why I was expecting her to be supportive or cheering. Since absolutely everyone's first question on seeing a baby is, "How old is he/she?" my mother views children as little more than giant, depressing egg-timers. She's always made it clear that she finds it hard enough to understand how planned pregnancies are met with delight, so she thinks falling pregnant accidentally is one of the worst things that can happen to you. Obviously not as bad as finding out you are seriously ill or someone you love is dying. But certainly up there with losing your job or your lover, worse than being gazumped on a house sale or pranging the car.

"Do you want it?" she demands, unabashed. I don't have the chance to reply before she adds, "Unlikely. I mean, who in their right mind actually wants a baby?" I try to forget the fact that this woman is my mother. "They are highly inconvenient and not in the slightest bit rewarding until they are old enough to make one feel *ancient*." She stretches the word ancient for an unfeasibly long time. "And, goodness, the damage they do to your figure." I have by now completely lost sight of the reason I chose to call my mother. "It's irreparable. Darling, have you considered the stretch marks, the weight gain, the varicose veins?"

"It's good of you to remind me," I snipe dryly.

"So, you don't want it?" Finally, I detect something like sympathy, or at least concern, in my mother's voice.

"I don't know," I wail.

"Shush, darling. You mustn't cry. You'll get awful wrinkles, crying dries out the skin terribly." She coos this instruction and it's soothing. It's vain and faintly ridiculous but soothing.

"I don't actively not want the baby. Or at least, I don't think so."

"Goodness, so many negatives, does that make a positive?" Forever the grammarian.

"I don't know," I mutter weakly. I deal with facts, data, information, and certainties. Agonizing over and trying to understand everything from my psyche to my G-spot has always seemed positively farcical, but now I'm considering, debating, procrastinating, *feeling* left, right and center. All this not knowing is exhausting. I have always *known* things. I know the importance of identifying a single-minded, strategic focus. I know that standing orders are an efficient way to pay bills. I know the importance of owning at least one piece of jewelry from Tiffany. I know that the Burberry bandana has been done to death, I'm over it. I knew I wanted Hugh. I knew he didn't want me, but I knew I could make him want me and I knew how to do it.

"Well?"

"I'm not ready for this, Jessica."

She sighs. "No one ever is. Even the couples who have spent years trying with IVF. They are not ready. They may want it more. But they're not ready either."

Job. Lover. Home. Friends, all star quality. I have it all.

Including a sneaky suspicion that this is a little bit more than I bargained for. This wasn't part of my plan. "Having kids seems like the end of life as I know it," I mutter.

"It is exactly that."

We both fall silent. I study the park bench. The graffiti reads *Andy Luvs Angie 4 Ever.* Will they? Forever? It seems such a long time. The time I have left is forever. *George Feels Sick 4 Ever. George Changes Diapers 4 Ever.*

My mother interrupts my musings and asks quietly, "So are we talking gin and hot baths?"

It's admirable that she does not shy away from the issue. I

am, and always have been, pro-choice. Abortions are an option for teenagers, mothers of half a dozen children in increasing, overwhelming debt. They are an option for anyone who finds out that their baby is seriously ill. They are an option for rape victims. Abortion is not an option for me. I'm thirty-two, solvent and I love the father of my child. "No. No gin or hot baths."

"Oh good." Jessica sighs with relief, although she hadn't betrayed her viewpoint until she'd heard my decision. This is her greatest strength—she never passes judgment. "Well, darling, I hope you know that your father and I are always here for you." She adds the caveat, "Providing you never, ever use the Granny word. By the way, Georgina, when I said the damage to your body is irreparable, I wasn't being entirely honest. I can give you the name of a marvelous surgeon at Bart's. The very essence of discretion. Visit him within three months of the birth and everything will be as good as new, if not better."

I know she's trying to be a comfort.

I hang up.

It's raining, and I wonder how long it has been doing so. It's the dark, relentless type of rain that offers no compensation or joy. Wind snakes its way into my coat and licks my back. Circles appear in puddles and disappear almost as quickly. It nearly always rains at commuter hour. I think of the sweaty tube carriages, damp and steamy with dripping people, bags and umbrellas. Irritated and exhausted shoppers tutting if someone opens the window, tutting if no one does. Tutting if someone stands on their toes, or they on someone else's. I imagine harassed office workers irritably fighting for an extra square inch of space, and drunks who sing and smell of streets and urine. In my mind I see the groups of Japanese girls who giggle quietly and relentlessly, neat and identical in their designer clothes. They are oblivious to the fact that all the other women in the compartment are glaring their resentment at the slim hips and advantageous exchange rate. I know all this life is happening right now, as it did yesterday, and as it will tomorrow. Everything going on as it went on before. No one aware that my life has changed, irredeemably.

I pull my coat an inch further around me and walk to the park gates.

Time to go home and tell Hugh the news.

2

I fell in love with Hugh Williams the first moment I saw him. Sam and I were first-year students at university and we couldn't believe Hugh was too. He appeared so much more mature. It turned out that he was twenty; he'd taken a couple of years out, to find himself, in India. Which he did in record time—he was there only about six weeks and spent the rest of his gap years stacking shelves in his local Sainsbury's. I always think this is why he's so good with people.

Just over thirteen years ago. Nearly half my lifetime. In all that time I've never loved another man. This all sounds *über*-romantic. People are generally bowled over by my story. Love at first sight and the idea of such constancy, etc., etc. Faces fall slightly when I mention that he was seeing someone else at the time, whom he subsequently married and had two children with. To be honest, I wasn't exactly thrilled either, but, hey girl, life's not a fairy tale.

A fairy-tale scenario goes something like this. Their eyes meet across a crowded room, she chastely looks away and then looks back again; he's still staring at her. He moves toward her holding two bottles of beer. They start talking, discover they have masses in common, he asks her for her phone number and tells her he'll call the next day. *He calls.* They meet several times over the next few weeks; each date is better than the last. He doesn't push for sex (she's marginally disappointed by this because she's gagging for it; why else leave home and go to university?). Eventually, after a respectable period of a number of weeks, after he's bought her flowers, poetry books and tastefully mounted Rothko prints, they fall into bed. Lovemaking is explosive, better than anything either of them has ever come across before—although, admittedly, their repertoire is rather limited (he is her first partner; she is his second or third, definitely not more than fourth). And, as they are smoking a post-coital cigarette, he tells her he loves her and that she's *the one.* At this point she is so besotted with him that she would happily agree to eat his pongy socks for the rest of her life, let alone wash them. They agree to finish their degrees, but set a date for their wedding to be soon after they've graduated. Then they live happily ever after.

My real-life scenario was almost identical, except for at the bit where they're smoking the post-coital. He didn't set a date, but instead flicked open his wallet and showed me a picture of his girlfriend. Girlfriend! And I know that makes him sound like a bit of a shyster but, really, he's not.

He is divine. A genuine god-like specimen. The most attractive man I've ever clapped eyes on, including anyone who's ever appeared on *Top of the Pops,* and all of the men in the Levi's ads throughout the '80s. Which, I suppose, were the only men I'd had intimate relationships with pre-university. Well, you don't get much opportunity to meet boys, let alone men, at all-girls boarding schools. I left my school with high hopes of what uni would offer, and though I went to Sheffield, not Oxford, I was expecting the experience to be entirely *Brideshead Revisited* revisited. On sight Hugh fulfilled all my expectations and my fantasies and my dreams, and then some. Tall, blond, chiselled—classically handsome—with broad shoulders and a tight butt. He's the kind of bloke that when you see him in the distance you almost hope that, up close, he'll be a bit of a disappointment. Perhaps his eyes will be too close together, or he'll have blackheads nestling on his nose. Because, if he is as gorgeous as his distant silhouette promises, he'll be overwhelming.

Up close, he doesn't disappoint.

He was then, and is now, staggering. His eyes are huge, sparkling, green, dramatically offset by long lashes and perfectly arched eyebrows. He has high, jutting cheekbones and a square jaw. An eleven, on a scale of one to ten.

And they matched.

Becca's photo was testament to her above average beauty. Details? Think creamy, flawless skin, huge, laughing, blue eyes, long, blond, curly tresses (the only time I've ever found an appropriate use for the word tresses is in relation to Becca), permanent, broad smile, revealing pearly-white teeth, big boobs, minute waist, hips, thighs, ankles, etc., etc. In short, irresistible.

Thank God it turned out that she didn't understand him.

And me? Well, even disqualifying British false modesty, facts have to be stated, and the fact is, or rather was, when Hugh and I met I was more of a five or five and a half—out of ten.

I also had long hair, but it didn't fall in long, blond tresses—more brown, tangled rats' tails. I've got two crowns, you see. Not two heads, that really would be bad, but two crowns, and so my hair never parts properly, but sticks out at angles perpendicular to my head. My teeth could be described as straight(ish) and white(ish), but then again they could be described as crooked(ish) and gray(ish), and, let's face it, I didn't have a huge amount to smile about at the time. I didn't have a waist at all. I was the shape of a rather chunky toilet roll, which probably gives you an accurate enough picture of my thighs and ankles too.

It wasn't as though I could even take consolation in her being stupid or uninformed. No. Becca was one of those who sat for endless hours in the student union bar nursing warm beer and packets of cheese and onion crisps. Not that she ate the crisps. She always made a great show of buying and opening bags and bags of them and putting them on the tabletop and shouting, "Dive in, dive in." And while mere mortals like me, with excess fat and deficient self-control, did dive in, she held back and discussed "issues."

She had opinions on sanctions on Cuba, on whether Soviet troops ought to vacate Afghanistan, and on the environmental consequences of using CFC aerosol hairspray. She protested against apartheid in South Africa and wanted some answers about China's human rights record. She debated the intricate politics of Iran and Iraq, whereas I spent all my time trying to remember who was on which side. She'd even read *The Satanic Verses,* for God's sake. I had "issues" too, but they were less lofty—mostly clothes, music and makeup. Regularly reading *Hello!* and knowing how much Marilyn Monroe's blouse was sold for at Sotheby's were as near as I got to current affairs (£7,150, if you're interested).

Becca was mesmerizing.

Everyone was captivated.

Even me.

I admit that if we had met under other circumstances, in another life, maybe we could have been friends. Maybe I would have liked her sense of humor, admired her compassion, conceded that she had impeccable skin and a pair of legs to die for. As it was, I simply loathed her.

I couldn't get over him. I couldn't let him go. I couldn't chalk him up to experience or carve a notch in my bedpost and move on. I really couldn't.

I sometimes wish I had been able to.

Our relationship makes the Grand Old Duke of York look spectacularly sedate and single-minded. *When they were up they were up, when they were down they were down,* just about has us in a nutshell. In the past thirteen years we've metamorphosed through all the possible boy/girl incarnations, including pen pal. The only consistency is that he's always been essential to my adult life. We've been "just good friends," anguished lovers, not-so-good friends, the person with whom we had a drunken fumbling at the end of a party, anguished lovers again, and finally live-in lovers.

And—er—now parents to be.

Wow.

It was the beginning of December. Hugh had just been head-hunted as MD for Rartle, Roguel and Spirity, renowned as one of the most creative agencies in London. A desperately coveted role throughout the advertising industry, the industry that we both work in. As a matter of fact, we'd both been approached and asked to apply for the position, but as soon as I heard that Hugh was seriously interested I stepped out of the running. Well, I didn't have a chance against him, and anyway it wouldn't have been good for our relationship. I firmly believe the best man won. To show my absolute support I went along to his welcoming party. It was a very tasteful affair starting with champagne and canapés in the boardroom, and then dinner at Nubo's. As is our way we drank a lot, partied until late and then made frantic, fervent love on the breakfast bar, the dining room table and the rug in the sitting room. He asked, "Is it the right time?" And while I was desperately trying to count the days on my fingers, well, let's just put it this way, by the time I'd done the math he'd done the deed.

And as I lay awake in bed that night, gently doing my Pilates exercises while trying not to wake Hugh, I reasoned no one ever gets caught out the first time they take a risk.

No one.

3

I've read about telling your partner that you are pregnant, I've seen the films. I know how it's supposed to be. The champagne is supposed to be on ice (which immediately strikes me as unfair because I know that alcohol is already a long-lost friend to me). I'm meant to dress up in something that is at once feminine and intriguing. But this is out of the question, as I seem to have put on five pounds just in the drive from the doctor's to the park, and another five on the drive from the park home. I know I'll feel bloated and uncomfortable in all my favorite outfits. Besides which, I don't own anything in a floral print. He's meant to arrive home tired but handsome.

I say, "Darling, you are going to be a father."

Then I faint. Except in this case I might have to be more specific and say, "Darling, you are going to be a father *again.*" He's then supposed to shrug off his tiredness long enough to gather me into his arms and whirl me around and around. It's essential at this point that he doesn't lose eye contact but gazes adoringly, while repeatedly telling me how clever I am.

I pour a great deal of concentration into visualizing this scenario but, try as I might, I simply cannot see Hugh and me in this state of domestic bliss. I guess ringing Becca for some tips is a little inappropriate. Besides, I know how Hugh felt when Becca became a mother.

Devastated.

He ran.

Directly into my arms.

Oh God.

It's fair to say becoming a mum didn't do Becca any favors. Quite the reverse. I'm rational enough to calculate that perhaps Hugh would have stayed with Becca if she hadn't fallen pregnant and become mind-numbingly boring. Plus fat. Yes, of course, it hurts knowing this. No one likes to think they won their man because his wife lost her sexual appetite and her ability to talk about anything other than baby poo and Winnie the Pooh. But kidding yourself is just that. It's wisest to understand, genuinely understand, where the other woman went wrong. In that way you can avoid making the same mistakes.

Or not, if you are haphazard with a calendar.

I mooch around the flat trying to submerge that last thought. *Think good stuff, think nice thoughts.* I instruct myself in the same way Jessica used to instruct me when, as a child, I woke up from a nightmare and couldn't fall asleep again in case the scary dream found its way back into my mind. O.K. Good thoughts:

Hugh arriving on my doorstep eight months ago. I beam to myself remembering the exquisite mix of relief, breathtaking excitement and sheer, unadulterated joy. He's chosen me! After nearly two years of undignified sneaking about and before that eleven years of frustrating silence, Hugh and I were able to declare our love for each other, to each other *and* to the world at large. Good thought—it doesn't get better than that.

What was so utterly wonderful about that day was that Hugh didn't sneak up to my flat with a battered suitcase and heart, he arrived with a flourish, with pizzazz. The doorbell rang, which made me think it was a courier from work as Hugh had a key; Sam never arrives without calling first and who else would pop by? I opened the door, and lying on the mat was the most enormous bunch of starburst lilies; there must have been thirty stems. The bouquet was undoubtedly the most beautiful bouquet I had ever seen, or have seen since. It was a frenzied mass of colorful flowers and ribbons, with arty twigs jutting out at jaunty angles. It was a bouquet that declared celebration. At the very center there was a yellow toothbrush. A toothbrush! Did this mean? Could this mean? I hardly dared hope. Giggling to myself I looked left to right but couldn't see any sign of a florist or Hugh. I picked up the enormous bouquet and, taking care not to brush the flowers—heavy with staining pollen—against the hall wall, I took it to the kitchen.

The card read, *I choose you.*

Yes. Yes. Yes. I punched the air, I screamed out loud. I literally jumped for joy; over and over again I jumped, pounding my feet on the floor until they hurt. He chose me. *Me. Chose* me. He did. My unrestrained delight was brooked (but only momentarily) when Hugh knocked on the kitchen window. He was laughing, it was clear he'd witnessed my entire response. Heart racing, I ran to the back door, pulled it open and flung myself into his arms. We kissed and kissed and kissed until he scraped my chin away, and my knickers.

That was eight months ago.

By the time Hugh arrives home I am trashed. Not woozy, not merry, not pleasantly inebriated, but trashed. Plastered. Wrecked. Far from becoming a long-lost friend, alcohol is my closest intimate. And while I know I absolutely should not be drinking now, let alone drinking enough to become legless, I simply can't stop myself. I might as well admit it: I am smoking my eighth cigarette of the day, too. I argue that if I hadn't found out about the pregnancy until tomorrow I'd probably be at some wine bar right now, smoking and drinking myself into oblivion in happy ignorance.

I know it's a shoddy argument and I already feel guilty.

"Hello, gorgeous. Can I join you?" Hugh kisses me on the lips and nods toward the nearly empty bottle of Merlot. He throws his jacket over the back of a chair, it's a really simple action. But this simple, domestic action makes my heart zoom to my mouth and then ricochet to my knickers. He, at least, has fulfilled his part of the bargain; he does look handsome and tired. I really regret my lack of floral prints. I love him. Every tiny bit of him. From his disheveled hair, which he has so obviously run his fingers through numerous times today, down to his immaculate, shiny shoes. He takes great care of his shoes. He has a shoe-tree for every pair he owns, and he never puts on or takes off a shoe without the aid of a shoehorn. This practice, although undeniably old-fashioned, endears him to me anew every time I witness it.

I love him so much it hurts. I love him so much I feel sick with it.

But then that could be the pregnancy.

"How was your day?" I ask.

He treats me to a half-grin, a half-shrug. We both know that the other's days are, as a matter of course, busy, stressful and political. We wouldn't have it any other way. He pours himself a glass of wine and tops up my glass. He joins me on the gray buckskin settee and we shuffle into our usual position—him upright, me slouched lengthways, with my feet resting on his legs. He absentmindedly starts to rub my ankles.

"I like the nail varnish." He nods toward my pedicured toes. "So what's up?" he asks. While I'm gratified that he knows me so well that he's immediately sensed that something is wrong, his question blows any hope I had that I'd kill time with polite small talk.

"I went to the doctor's today."

The pressure of my foot massage increases marginally.

"You didn't tell me you were going to the doctor's. You're O.K, aren't you?" And all that he wants to hear is a simple, "Yes, I'm fine." I'd like to oblige.

"Blooming," I sigh, not able to keep the drunken weariness out of my voice. Bull by the horns: "I'm pregnant." The comforting circular motion on my feet draws to an abrupt halt.

"Pregnant?"

"Yes."

"You're having a baby?"

"I don't know any other type of pregnant." Unless you include the pregnant pause which follows. I watch him closely. But he's too much of a professional to rashly betray any emotion.

"How pregnant?"

"Nine weeks." Which is something else that's been bothering me. I have no idea how the doctor came up with this date. It seems that it's nothing to do with when the deed was actually done. Apparently, it's a scientific calculation taking into account the date of the first day of my last period, whether or not there was a full moon that night or an "r" in the month, and if Hugh was wearing blue socks.

"How?"

That's an original one. I bet the Treasury would like a pound for every time a man has asked a woman, "How could this happen?" We'd probably clear our national debt.

"I guess we played Russian roulette just once too often." I try to smile, but the muscles in my face are behaving treacherously and I'm sure I'm grimacing.

"You said it was your safe time."

"I was wrong." I know it seems odd to him. It does to me, too. I'm thirty-two, hardly at my fertile prime. I started successfully repressing my reproductive organs over thirteen years ago. Besides which, sperm counts are supposed to be down—there are always articles saying as much, and what about the stuff they put in London water and the effects of pesticides on our food? I watch Hugh compute the information, consider it, balance it, and then finally react to it.

"Well, that's big news."

"Yes."

"I never expected . . ."

"No."

"And you want to keep it?"

"Yes."

The caution that we are both exuding stains the air. It's a yellowish color. I know what he's thinking. He's wondering whether we'll be any good at it. Parenting, I mean. Obviously he's at an advantage, he's already had a crack at it, but Becca had never allowed Hugh too much active involvement. I'm sure she limits his access so that she has the opportunity to bemoan his lack of commitment. He's nervous—what if the child is stupid, or ugly, or even beautiful and clever but depressed and a drug addict? And one child, more often than not, leads to another, doesn't it? Pregnancy, and ultimately a small person, will restrict our freedom (dinners out, holidays, entertaining, gym visits, etc.). Ditto sex life. Ditto our relationship generally. Ditto our careers. Well, probably just my career. Hugh's career will be unaffected by this, or possibly enhanced. Fertile men are still held in high esteem by their colleagues, visions of passing cigars around come to mind, as do conversations about golden bullets. A family man—however many families he has—is seen as stable and reputable. By contrast, a procreating woman is seen as unreliable, dizzy and a liability. He's thinking about sickness (mine), fatness (mine), lank hair (mine), spots, piles, skin flaps, skin coloration, loose vagina, uncontrollable gases escaping from the body (all mine). He's contemplating loss of sexual desire (both of ours!). He's considering the indignity of maternity clothes and the possibility of the eradication of adult conversation and foods. And, finally, there's the pain of labor (mine).

"Marvelous! It's marvelous news."

Oh, the relief.

I thought that—well it seems stupid to even mention it now but I thought, no, not as strong as *thought,* but certainly *feared* that he'd . . . leave.

That's all I've thought about.

He flings his arms around me, hugs me very lightly for over a minute, then pulls away, takes my cigarette out of my hand and stubs it out.

"Well, that's the last one of those you're having. And of those." He pours the remaining wine from my glass into his, goes to the kitchen and returns with a large glass of milk. I am so stupid! How could I have worried about Hugh's reaction? How unbalanced. How unnecessary. Of course Hugh's delighted. He's a wonderful man and he's bound to be delighted to hear he's having a child. What kind of man wouldn't be delighted?

What kind of woman?

4

After our one night of passion back in 1987, Hugh went back to Becca and I settled for becoming Hugh's best friend, or at least posing as such while disguising my more lascivious motives for wanting to spend every waking moment with him. Whenever he and Becca had a spat, he'd pop by my hall of residence and tell me all about it. Then we'd have a terrific time, eating garlic bread in cheap Italian restaurants, standing freezing and cheering on the sidelines as Sam played hockey, and drinking countless cups of coffee and eating countless slices of buttery toast in our bedrooms or the communal kitchens. The best times I had at university were definitely those times we spent together, and I treasure every single wonderful memory.

The more time I spent with Hugh, the more intensely, insanely, incurably I fell in love with him. It wasn't just his stomach-churning good looks, it was the fact that, by quite some way, he was the most vibrant, alive person I'd ever met. He had a sort of animal energy and a phenomenal curiosity in everything and everyone around him. His mind was a labyrinth and appeared insatiable. He was good at sports. He played the guitar and wrote his own songs. He could drink anyone who dared to challenge him under the table. He had a big dick. Becca obviously wasn't impervious to his charms either because she would always turn up a couple of days after their rows, all red-eyed and penitent, and I'd watch as with nauseating inevitability they kissed and made up.

Actually, *those* memories don't rank among my fondest.

Throughout my time at college Hugh was polite and friendly toward me. But then he was also polite and friendly toward Sam, and all of the hockey team, the first and second eights, all the reps on the student union, the librarians, the entire end-of-term ball committee and every female fresher—among others. He is just a polite and friendly sort of guy. Polite and friendly as in no flirting, no accidental touching of hands across the table or banging of knees underneath, no shrouded references to our night of hot sex. Hugh seemed to find me as gender specific as a teddy bear. And quite a lot less appealing.

I quickly came to realize that Becca was a better proposition than I was. Tragic but true. She was prettier, sportier, cleverer, more interesting and interested. She could leave half a Mars Bar uneaten for months. But, I argued, *I* didn't owe Becca any loyalty. O.K, so she saw him first and said *bagsie,* but that hardly seemed reason enough for me to throw in the towel. My undergraduate self reasoned that Hugh was still up for grabs until Becca had a ring on her finger. And the answer to wetting his whistle was that I'd have to become the better proposition.

Come on, I'm not the first, nor will I be the last, woman to try a homespun, crash-course, Pygmalion-like transmogrification with the aim of netting something delectable in the staminate department. Haven't you ever dyed your hair just to see if blondes do have a better ride? Haven't you ever pretended you've read a book that you'd only looked at the cover of—just to appear more interesting and informed? Do you honestly like football?

I began to read newspapers and I joined the debating society. I went out of my way to meet as wide and varied a group of people as possible. Naturally, this meant I squandered numerous evenings with bores and weirdos, but slowly I also began to build a base of knowledge on issues cultural, financial, historical, economic. I didn't waste any more of my vacations slouching around my parents' home, but instead visited a kibbutz in Israel, restoration projects in Naples, holiday camps for socially deprived children in the Bronx. And, while up until meeting Hugh I'd viewed studying as something to do when the bar closed and attending lectures simply as a means of checking out my mates' new clobber, I suddenly started to take my degree seriously. I worked hard. Very hard. I was able to quote Keynes, Einstein and Euclid at the drop of a hat; even now I can tell you anything you want to know about Benazir Bhutto, Manuel Noriega, the poll tax or De Klerk. Go on, test me.

I did all that walking-up-the-stairs-instead-of-taking-the-lift thing. I cut the fat off my ham when I made ham sandwiches, but I didn't melt away into a pre-pubescent nymph, so I cut out ham altogether, and other meats, too, pretty soon after. In fact, nothing ever passed my lips unless it was nutritionally valuable and had been interrogated in terms of fat and calorie content. I obliterated my couch-potato persona and reinvented myself as a fitness freak and, most particularly, as "very outdoorsy." The illusion I created has been so effective that I have subsequently found myself on skiing holidays in the winter and sailing holidays in the summer. The free time in between has been punctuated by hikes, treks, Saturday and Sunday afternoons standing on the touchlines of rugby and football pitches, crossing the London Marathon finish line—twice—jogging, swimming, serving, volleying, batting, running, biking, on one occasion kick-boxing, and the undisputed low point, pot-holing. Hell. Undoubtedly that's what hell is. A cold, damp hell, as opposed to the more traditional fiery hell. But hell. I suppose, sooner or later, I should tell Hugh that the only type of sweating, panting and grunting I want to do in front of him is, in fact, under him, and even going on top is more athletic than I'd ideally opt for.

I followed a strict regime of cleanse, tone and moisturize with exclusive La Prairie products, even though the products cost a term's rent. I had my hair cut every six weeks, and colored every twelve. I used toothpaste that bleached my teeth. I paid to have six of them capped, and I wore a brace for several months and—this might sound extreme—I had a boob job. Why not make the best of yourself? If you have the money. Actually, I didn't have the money but I took out a loan.

Everything I read, I read to impress Hugh. Everywhere I visited I stored up stories to repeat to Hugh. Every purchase I made, I made with him in mind. I didn't stop to wonder whether any other man would do instead. I knew, simply knew, as clearly as I knew my own name, no other one would. All other men were gray. They seemed finite and unreliable.

For three long years I was always "there" for Hugh. Helping with essay crises, his election campaign as president of the student union, being a shoulder to cry on when his parents divorced, running out to buy hangover cures after very heavy nights. Well, isn't this what best friends do for one another? In fact, it is because I did so much research for his milk-around interviews in advertising—studying every IPA paper and scrutinizing every issue of *Campaign*, the advertising industry's weekly bible, memorizing the business performance league tables and the names and faces of all the players—that I didn't have time to think about another career, one for myself, so we both interviewed. We were both accepted on a graduate trainee course with Saatchi and Saatchi, and I got a place with Q&A and JWT as well. Which was a bit freaky; I think the industry was discriminating positively in favor of women that year—why else would Hugh get only one place and I get three? I chose Q&A because they offered a four-month training course in New York and Hugh said I'd be mad to turn down that opportunity. I'm still with them almost eleven years on, although Hugh has worked at Saatchi and Saatchi, Leo Burnett, Lowe Lintas and now Rartle, Roguel and Spirity.

So I went to New York for no other reason than the fairly ignoble one that it would impress Hugh. And while I was there the worst thing that could happen did happen—as usually is the way. Becca and Hugh got engaged.

The news scalded my ears and tore at my heart. I ached. Every fiber of my body revolted as pain bounced from my kitten heels to the tips of my Paul Mitchell–conditioned hair. I felt as though my bloodstream were infected and polluted with grief, as my hopes, dreams and plans collapsed like a straw house, defeated by the breath of the huffing and puffing big, bad wolf. I bobbed like a bottle at sea, vacuous, without bearing. And the hardest part of all was admitting that I wasn't even surprised that Hugh chose Becca. I knew that despite my superficial reconstruction I wasn't good enough for him. Elevens marry elevens; they don't marry five and a halves masquerading as eights. That would be against the natural order of things. Darwin probably wrote a paragraph or so about this exact subject.

What can I say? It is not better to have loved and lost, as anyone who has ever lost will confirm. I felt raw and exposed. I missed him, or at least the chance of him, with a breathtaking, ferocious intensity. For a time I tried alcohol, drugs and pizzas—none of them soothed the agony. But after several weeks the wretchedness did dull to a quiet (although persistent) ache and I pulled myself together sufficiently to try a new line in survival.

I didn't go back to London in January as planned, or indeed for another five years after that. I couldn't. It represented all that I had lost. I persuaded Q&A to give me a full-time position in New York. I threw myself into my work, vowing to put Hugh out of my mind for good. I concentrated on gaining a reputation for dedication and professionalism. I also dated, constantly and unsatisfactorily, but often rather glamorously (my conquest list included several up-and-coming politicians, minor actors and one of the Kennedy cousins—distant). It was the ultimate frustration that so many other men believed in my reinvention while Hugh had not. Which just proved that Hugh was more discerning, more sagacious, more judicious. By rejecting me he showed himself the better man and became even more attractive to me. I dressed in designer labels, worked my ass off both in the gym and in the office, I holidayed on the West Coast, learned to scuba-dive and to drive a Harley-Davidson. Slowly I built up the reputation I longed for: I became a serious professional with great tits.

By the time I returned to London in late 1995, Becca and

Hugh were married and living in Highgate, while Sam was only in the infancy of her search for the love of her life.

They all came to meet me off the plane at Heathrow. I had planned my emergence from behind the sliding doors for weeks, and to every last detail. I had neatly stacked my Prada luggage on a trolley (anything that wouldn't conveniently fit into these suitcases had been sent on ahead so as not to ruin the effect). I was wearing a black, halter-neck catsuit, which made my legs look longer than the reality, and exposed my now ferociously toned, muscular arms. My hair was immaculately styled and, despite the transatlantic flight, still hung in the sleek drop it was newly trained to; my Gucci sunglasses sat jauntily on top of my head. I wanted to look carefree. I wanted to prove, not least to myself, that I was over Hugh, that he'd been nothing more than a crush, escalated in my head by eight years of longing, which had *surely* been adolescent. As the doors swept back the gang let up a cheer and waved flowers and a ludicrous cuddly toy. I took one look at Hugh and knew that my self-imposed exile had been pointless. Far from diving, dating and dealing him out of my system, I loved him more.

My post-graduate self reasoned that Hugh was still up for grabs despite the ring on Becca's finger.

In 1996 Becca gave birth to Kate, and eighteen months later she gave birth to Tom. Six months after that I became Hugh's mistress. It's ugly, I know. I wish I could make it, the situation, or, more honestly, me in particular, sound more noble or at least less ignoble, but the fact is that in 1998 I became his mistress. And even if I tell you that she didn't appreciate him, that she's never worked since they married and has depended on him entirely for an income (while professing to disapprove of his career choice) . . . Even if I explain that she didn't like him going to the gym and she nagged him about the fact that he played rugby once a week and trained another evening . . . And she grumbled because she didn't think he did enough for the children and that she said he didn't pull his weight around the house . . . If I divulge that there is a serious probability that she had an affair with her tennis coach . . . Or if I elucidate by saying that she never read the books he read, she never laughed at his jokes, or noticed when he'd had his hair cut, or asked how his day had gone . . . It would be pointless; none of this would alter the fact that being a mistress is not a very heroic position, whichever way you look at it. I can't justify it. I can't make it seem right. I am still a mistress. *Still*, because technically he's still married to Becca, although he moved in with me eight months ago. Annoying, isn't it? One of life's little irritants. Colossal irritants, actually, because I am so tired of being apologetic. The truth is nice people (me) do not very nice things from time to time (sleep with other women's husbands, for example).

He should have been mine right from the beginning, he really should have.

But he wasn't, and when some things go wrong you can never, ever put them right.

5

There are lots of unwritten rules in the advertising profession; besides what to wear, eat and drive, you have to know how to conduct yourself from day to day. It is of paramount importance to be perky and productive at all times; no one wants to network with a dormouse. Getting from reception to desk in the mornings should be a social occasion. Smile at all times. Wide, toothy smiles.

"Watcha Georgie, you're looking gorgeous."

Karl hasn't looked at me. He says the same thing every morning, to everybody. He's a very popular man. If he had looked at me, he might have noticed that the jacket of my Armani suit is swinging open, as opposed to fastened as is usual, and the top button of my trousers is also undone. Although I am now only nine weeks pregnant, I'm already struggling to find clothes that fit. It's not that I am fatter (I am, but it's not that); as unbelievable as it seems, my hips have widened. They've been aching for days, and now I can hardly fit any of my trousers over my hips, not even my emergency-fat-period trousers. Hips widening! I can only assume it is to make way for the baby's head, giving me a tiny insight into the torture which is ahead of me. And my ribcage has moved. No one tells you that; indeed it's probably better that they don't, otherwise I'm pretty certain the human race would die out.

"Why thank you, Karl," I *smile,* barely glancing his way, and I add, "And you. Have you been working out?" Karl is—get this—

an Assemblage Account Director (meaning he manages a group of suits).

"Thought you'd be interested in this report, page nineteen hits the issues," says Drew, the Emporium Strategist (basically a planner).

"Cheers," I *smile,* taking the paper from him without breaking my stride toward my desk (that's another rule, never walk if you can stride, but never, ever run; it's cool to be busy but not frantic).

"Georgie, are you coming to the opening of Champagne Charlotte's tonight?" asks Brett, the Officiating Creative Director (the one with the crayons).

"Certainly, I'll be there," I *smile.*

The boys and I are all ranked at the same level. Our current positions are mutually dependent upon one another's success, so we all frequently, loudly and, if necessary, insincerely expound on each other's talents and profess adoration. Our relationship smacks of "friends close, enemies closer." It's not that I don't like them; they are all smart, savvy, sexy and cocksure. They operate in a homogeneous mass; if they ever had individual personalities, they've long since been erased. They are the advertising world's equivalent of a boyband. I *do* like them. I just don't trust them. Experience has shown there's no advantage to being sentimental.

"Georgina, can you read this and give me your opinion on the IPC situation by close of play?" says Dean, the MD, everyone's boss, as he tosses an inch-thick report onto the already towering pile of papers I'm carrying.

"Sure thing." I broaden my smile an incredible fraction further. I think my face might split. He's American, so I find myself sounding like a Wild West settler whenever I speak to him; it's entirely deliberate.

My title at Q&A is President of Neoteric Enterprise. Brand enhancement is our way of life; hence the overly grand and misleading job tides. While my job is important to me and at times exhilarating (when I'm talking to a headhunter, for example), it does fall slightly short of the title imported from the U.S. If I didn't work for an advertising agency I'd probably have a more modest title, such as New Business Manager. But then we are talking about an office culture that calls cleaners Industrial Waste Executives, and the woman who doles out the slop in the canteen is a Protein and Vitamin Execution Executive (pronounced Vite-a-min).

My job essentially boils down to endlessly trawling through personal contacts, newspapers, annual reports, etc., in an effort to identify companies that don't currently advertise but might be persuaded to, or, rather more lucratively, those that currently advertise and spend heaps of money, but with another agency. I then put together a team and we plot, persuade, coax, cajole, entice and impel said companies to part with large amounts of cash in the hope that we can help them make yet larger amounts, which in turn we help them in spending. I seem to have quite a knack for this. I like to see it as a virtuous circle.

In truth, I often see it as a fairly undignified way to earn a living.

"Doughnut, Georgina?" offers Julia, my number two in the office, but also my mate after hours.

I shake my head and repeat the old adage, *"A moment on the lips, a month on the hips."* I sing this through my smile, while mentally calculating the calories and fat units in a doughnut. Julia immediately throws the doughnut in the bin, which I wish I hadn't seen. I'll spend all day thinking of it, languishing there. Uneaten. My smile falters momentarily.

My usual practice is that I positively bounce into the office every morning, fired up for debating the brand properties of loo bleach or "refreshing" versus "thirst-quenching" as the unique selling position for the latest carbonated drink. But today I feel wiped out, low, feeble, exhausted. I am a used bin liner, as rubbish as that. My head hurts, I feel sick. Think pernicious hangover combined with worst period pains ever. Bingo. The important thing is no one must know this. I finally reach my office. I slump into my chair and lay my head on the desk. I usually conduct my entire day's business standing up; it's more intimidating for the audience and good exercise for the calves. Sod that, I'm exhausted. Without lifting my head I rummage inside the top drawer of my desk, where I keep a collection of remedies for all ills. Spare pair of tights in case of ladders, clear nail varnish in case of laddering spare pair (a little blob at the top and bottom of the ladder does the trick). Tippex to be used on ladder in spare pair of tights when I can't unscrew the lid of the clear nail-varnish bottle. Toothbrush, breath fresheners, comb, an assortment of Boots 17 cosmetics (anything more expensive would be nicked), nail file, tweezers, spare battery for my mobile, modem line, roughly £20 of change in six foreign currencies, a variety of pens, pencils, elastic bands, paper clips, string, business cards and, finally, aspirin. I reach for the packet of aspirin then read the instructions and discover I can't take any.

Because I'm pregnant.

I try thinking about butterflies and freshly squeezed orange juice but the visualization technique fails miserably. It's bollocks, actually. I feel even more nauseous and quite extraordinarily ravenous. The doughnut in the bin is the only thing that I can imagine will help. But only if I eat it now. *Now, now.* Not now as in how long it will take to nip out and buy another one. I *have* to eat *the* doughnut that is in the bin and I *have* to eat it *now.* I turn around and see that Julia is standing by the scanner, leaving her desk and, more particularly, the bin-languishing doughnut unguarded. Moving like James Bond on blades, I speed back to her desk, retrieve the doughnut, hide it in between my files, dash toward the privacy of my own office, which thankfully has a door—a perk negotiated with my last promotion, along with a beechwood desk and a dry-cleaning allowance—and then I eat the doughnut. To put this into context, this is the first cake I've tasted since my twenty-first birthday. This 007-like operation takes me about four seconds. I feel well for a further four seconds and then I throw up into my bin—the white one, which is for paper. I suspect this is a little more than the office administrator was bargaining for in terms of recycling materials. I move the bin outside my office door, but I have the feeling that the stale smell of spew will linger all day.

The indignity is staggering.

I don't have time to spray perfume around the office before the phone starts to ring. I pick it up. Someone wants to know something about portfolio planning. My second line is ringing, a question about relative market shares, and then Julia is suddenly by my side, trying to get me to sign a pile of papers, which I do—with my free hand, while reading them with one eye. A coffee appears on my desk. I cradle the phone under my ear and then take a sip. I finish the call about commissioning market research into teenage girls' views on digital TV, put the phone down and it immediately rings again. My lead-like limbs are operating in their own time zone, refusing to keep pace with my mind, which, anyway, is lagging behind the required canter set by my job description. I knock back the plastic cup of coffee, hoping the caffeine will take effect a.s.a.p.

Yuk.

"Julia, have you switched coffee houses?"

"No, it's the same old, same old," Julia replies.

Julia wears her hair cropped short and spiky, a look which really only suits elf-like girls, which Julia is not, in fact, but she considers herself to be so. I am jealous of her misplaced confidence. It's odd, isn't it, that some girls who aren't naturally beautiful become intrinsically beautiful once they believe they are. And other girls, like Sam for instance, are gorgeous but can never really believe it. I'm somewhere in between. I know I'm beautiful when Hugh says I look "good," then I'd happily sunbathe in a bikini next to Miss Universe. I disappear altogether when he doesn't notice my new outfit. Yes, I do realize that this is unhealthy. Every self-help book I've ever read has violently condemned over-reliance on other people's opinions and praise. I've given all my self-help books to the local Oxfam.

Julia changes her hair color every week; this week it's plum. Her hairdresser's bill must run to thousands a year. She has huge, brown eyes (so laid-back they're insolent), which she frames with trendy, square, yellow Calvin Klein glasses. I'm not sure if she is genuinely short-sighted, or if the glasses are a fashion statement. She wears skimpy, clingy designer T-shirts with things like *roger me senseless* printed across her breasts. Diesel jeans and the latest, trendy, must-have sneakers from the States. She always looks cold and bored. But cool. At a guess I'd say she spends 90 percent of her wages on clothes; the remaining 10 percent is spent on newspapers and style magazines. Her father pays her rent and her "friends" pay for her gigs and drinks; she doesn't eat. Julia has a low boredom threshold so the words "same old, same old" are her anthem. She's been known to use them when referring to an outfit she purchased fifteen minutes earlier, or about a guy she's accepted her first drink from. I see a low boredom threshold as the sign of a lively mind, so while I don't mind her response, I do doubt it.

"Are you sure that you didn't get this from the vending machine?"

"I'm certain. I know how you feel about your double espresso from CaféCafé. Although your predictability in such matters does surprise me."

Traditionally my life has lacked certainty, therefore sticking with a coffee brand is disproportionately important to me.

"Why, what's wrong with the coffee?"

"It tastes bitter and smells odd," I complain.

Because I'm pregnant.

Of course, I shouldn't even be drinking coffee. I'm saved from explaining the fickle nature of my taste buds as my landline screeches at me at the exact same moment that my mobile pings to let me know I have a text message. I'm pretty certain that both desperate attempts at communication are from the same source.

"Hi, it's me. Have you got time to talk?"

I say no but Sam talks anyway.

I love her dearly; remembering her antics during Freshers' week still brings a smile to my face and a tear to my eye, and makes me wonder who her lawyer is. Yet her scatter-gun approach to her love life is irritating in the extreme. Oblivious to the fact that I may be very busy (which is normally the case), or that I am very pregnant and therefore feeling more filthy than a dog's arse (which is admittedly news), we, yet again, reenact a conversation we have had several times a month for the last thirteen years. An endless, directionless flow of self-pity about her being very nearly thirty-five and "half her life being over." I point out that with extended life expectancy Sam can reasonably anticipate living into her nineties. She counters that a long life will be torturous as the best bit is already over, and then she starts comparing quality of life: rollerblades vis-à-vis Zimmer frames, blooming new bosoms and sagging tits, university and retirement homes. She has a point and she makes it well but my patience is stretched. Sam is not suffering from a deadly disease or redundancy, her flat hasn't fallen into negative equity, nor has she broken a nail. The source of her desolation is, in Julia's phrase, "same old, same old." Last night her date stood her up. Her life's over.

I hope my silence is condemnation enough. Sam knows I think she's pathetic. She thinks she's pathetic too—it's this refreshing honesty that makes me love her; everyone else our age pretends to like being single.

Sam's original life plan has gone way off course. According to it, by now, she should be a corporate wife, lovingly supporting a dynamic husband as he thunders his way up the corporate ladder. She should be mother of two adorable children, one boy, one girl—dark and blond respectively. She should be living in a large detached house somewhere in the green belt, with a huge manicured garden and perhaps even a pool. She should be heavily involved in the PTA and organizing a weekly rota for the school run. Ideally, she'd be driving a Land Rover.

Need I go on?

Sam's current position—lying under the duvet with nothing more than a box of Kleenex for company—is a situation that is horribly, depressingly familiar. Her life achievements to date (has made junior partner in a huge firm of management consultants;

has swum with dolphins off the coast of South Africa; can fly a helicopter; has bungee-jumped from Victoria Falls; owns a racing-green MG) are forgotten. What grieves and shames Sam the most is that she could have lived without all that stuff if only she were surrounded by silver-plated photo frames displaying testaments to her success as a wife and mother. I can't think of any heartfelt words of consolation, so resort to the comfort of the cliché and mutter, "Still. Never say die." Sam complains that I've worked too long in advertising if I think an old saying like that is any help at all. This is hilarious coming from Sam, who speaks almost entirely in terms of "fish in the sea," "a change is as good as a rest," "all that glitters," "a stitch in time" and other such non-profundities. Anyway, what choice do I have? I can't tell her that she wears her desperation as conspicuously as most other people wear Vivienne Westwood—and, to men, it smells more intrusive than Poison perfume—although this undoubtedly is the case. Besides which, I simply can't see the mild embarrassment of being stood up as anywhere near as serious as the issues I'm currently facing—i.e., the embarrassment of the stench of regurgitated stolen doughnuts drifting condemningly through my office. I want to tell her that I'm pregnant, but don't know how. In the past it's been our habit to share our lives, entirely. We've always confessed to every love affair, emotion, victory, loss, piece of luck, joyless fuck and paranoia going.

But suddenly I'm stuck for words.

The thing is, I'm sure she'd tell me this is brilliant news and I'm sure it is. I know it is. Hugh says it is. I'm just waiting to feel that it is, or, more accurately, to feel that it is for longer than ninety consecutive seconds. I'm bound to get excited soon, aren't I? I'm bound to go gaga about little socks in babyGap. I wonder if they come with instructions on how to get them from the packet to the foot? It's just so new and unexpected and unplanned that I haven't had time to digest, process and react appropriately.

And I'm nothing if not appropriate.

I'm a slave to the magazines that tell you how to file your nails, buff your skin, wash your hair for optimum shape/silkiness/shine. I know which shoes go with which length skirt. I know which denier stocking to wear for every occasion. I know how much to tip taxi drivers, bellboys and waiters in every European country, Canada and the States. I have an appropriate response to a discussion on any election—local, national or international. In fact, I have an appropriate response to just about any conversation: the arts ("fascinating"), food ("This is delicious, is that cinnamon I can taste?"), football ("I'd like to see it become a family sport again") and politics ("it's a serious matter"). For the record, I can discuss a number of other subjects in depth. I know an awful lot about Renaissance literature, Helmut Newton's early work and the history of Punch and Judy shows, among other topics. You'd be surprised how rarely an in-depth knowledge of anything is considered appropriate. My adult life has been a series of goals, which I've set, then achieved. I've always known the direction I was traveling in, even during those long years while I waited for Hugh—at least *I* had decided to wait for him. It was my choice, my decision. I have always been unquestionably, undoubtedly, assuredly, 100 percent in control. The thing is, I don't make mistakes. I don't make blunders, miscalculations, slips. The only "err" I've ever made is to err on the side of caution. I haven't so much as made an impulse purchase in a sale that I've later regretted.

And now this.

I decide against mentioning it over the phone and instead tersely advise Sam to get showered, get dressed and get into work before anyone notices her absence. I promise I'll ring her tomorrow and then I hang up quickly to avoid hearing her cry.

6

The morning passes in a smudge, not even a blur. A blur would at least suggest activity. I wonder if I appear to be exactly the same George to everyone else? Probably. Which is odd—in fact, I am entirely different.

At lunchtime I nip out to buy a maternity book, as it strikes me that while I have some vague notion that being pregnant means my periods stop and I'll get fat, this is all I know. I'm spectacularly uninformed on the subject.

The wet London streets are teeming with shoppers, hoping to take advantage of the dregs of the sales. I watch them scuttle from shop to bus trying and failing to avoid the rain. The shoppers are the only things moving. The rest of London is at a standstill, partly because of the pouring rain, and partly because the truck drivers are protesting against something or other, they have a taste for it. I think that today they are objecting to the French exporting French cheese. A point of principle that evades me.

On the way to the bookshop a strange thing happens to me. I swear I have never, ever seen a pregnant woman in London. Not one in all the years I've lived here. But on the short walk from Golden Square to Piccadilly, which can be no more than a few hundred yards, I see three. *Three.* And two women with babies strapped to their front in those sling things, plus countless women with pushchairs (and therefore babies). I keep expecting Jeremy Beadle to jump out from behind a lamp-post and tell me that I've been framed, that this is all a joke, that the waddling women are really extras with cushions stuffed up their dresses for my benefit.

Although their misery looks real enough.

And they are miserable-looking. Tired, uncomfortable, fat. Not blooming, blossoming or benign as promised by prevailing myth.

Sigh.

It takes me about thirty minutes to locate the relevant section in the bookstore. It's on the third floor, which leads me to believe that a man, or a woman who has yet to discover her reproductive capacity, designed the store. I huff and puff my way up the stairs doing a good impersonation of Dawn French running the final mile of the London Marathon. Odd to think that not so long ago I prided myself on sprinting up stairs all over London, including that double set at Piccadilly tube station because the damn escalators are never working.

It's an eye-opener to discover that there is a whole industry devoted to the thus far invisible army of women that give birth. There is shelf after shelf after shelf of books about pregnancy. Straight books, funny books, medical books, books that look at the emotional, psychological, sociological, economic and political aspects of having a child. Books with diagrams, books with photos—black and white and *color* (aahhh)—and books that rely entirely on text. There are books about conceiving, carrying and labor. There are books about the first days, weeks, months and years of childhood. The choice is overwhelming. I have no idea which book to buy. Despite the choice, all the books have two things in common. One, they all picture women with dodgy 1980s haircuts and sailor-collar dresses, and two, they are universally terrifying and depressing. In a near trance-like state I finally grab the two nearest to me. One is a week-by-week guide to pregnancy. I flick over some pages until I come to the section on the baby's development at week nine.

Week 9
Your baby's arms and legs are longer. Hands are flexed at the
wrist and meet over the heart area. Your baby now moves its
body and limbs.

I look at the diagram expecting to see something that could audi-
tion for a Huggies ad. In fact, there is a diagram of a small alien-
like thingy. Its eyes look evil. The second book I choose is a light-
hearted text detailing the things a best friend should tell you about
pregnancy. Since I haven't actually managed to tell my best friends
I am pregnant as yet I hope that this book will be a good enough
surrogate.

There's another book, one that acts like mercury spilling into
my nervous system. I can hardly bring myself to glance at the title
on the spine. It's about dealing with miscarriage and stillbirth. So,
for the first time since I was a Brownie, I say a prayer. A sort of
prayer. I don't drop to my knees in the middle of the shop, but I
sort of ask whoever is out there that if at all possible could (s)he see
to it that the little grain of couscous grows to be a howling, mewl-
ing, spewing baby.

I want this so much that I think I've stopped breathing.

What does that mean? Could that be the first hint of an appropriate response? It feels right. In fact, it feels much more right than
many of my other appropriate responses—for example, raving
about *Pulp Fiction;* I'm aware I'm supposed to love the film, I just
didn't but best we keep that to ourselves. It's definitely more
appropriate than describing beds in galleries as informative and
sophisticated, as opposed to wanky.

Exhausted from the effort of climbing three flights of stairs, I
decide to stop for a quick coffee. I reluctantly remember that I
should no longer be drinking coffee, and so order a banana milkshake instead, another habit I kicked in the Brownies, but my
churning stomach is threatening revolt yet again and is more or
less demanding something creamy and calorific. I patiently queue
in the bookshop café, nervously eyeing the only free table and

wondering if it will be my stomach or my legs that will let me down first. I notice some guy walk into the café, put his bags on a chair at the free table and then join the queue behind me. Let's face it, we've all done it. The bagsie thing. So I'm not perturbed. I take my milkshake and sit on the other side of the table.

Have you ever read one of these books? Have you? I am carrying an alien! A puke-inducing, body-deforming, breast-engorging, amniotic-fluid-drinking (whatever that is) alien!

And the book I've chosen has an obsession with food, too. How tactless is that? Apparently the crown-rump length of the embryo is just over 2 cm; they liken it to an olive, and my uterus is a little bigger than a grapefruit. Yuk, yuk, yuk, yuk. Olives. Now there's a thought. I fancy an olive and some of those cherries they served in really naff drinks in the 1970s. I think I'll nip to Tesco Metro on the way back to the office.

The bagsie guy joins me, I smile, and for the sake of good form I add, "Hope you don't mind me squatting, there was nowhere else to sit."

I turn back to my pregnancy book, thus making it clear that I have no intention of talking to him and that my sitting at his table is entirely driven by necessity and not an attempt to leapfrog the lonely-hearts column.

The introduction reads: "Whether this is your first pregnancy or whether you've already had a child and you are expecting for a second, third or fourth time"—get real—"this is a very exciting time for you. Having a baby developing inside you is an incredible experience."

Incredible is a word I can agree with. As in unthinkable, unimaginable, suspect.

Turns out that pregnancy is not nine months but nearer ten, well at least forty weeks, a device to prolong the agony. Sorry, obviously I mean to prolong the excitement. And apparently, like the Queen, my fetus has two birthdays, fertilization age and gestational age. By page six, I'm dizzy with confusion brought upon by words such as mucus, cellular debris and endometrium.

"I do mind, actually," says the bagsie man.

"Sorry?"

"I do mind you sitting here. I have some friends joining me."

Somewhat taken aback I look up from my book. I doubt the friends bit—this chap looks like a lonely techie nerd, the only friends he'll have are virtual—but I can't very well call him an out-and-out liar.

"Besides I was here first," he adds, quickly metamorphosing from a techie nerd to an awkward git.

He wasn't, strictly speaking, but I'm too sick and tired to argue; I simply reassure him, "Don't worry I'll move when they come." I ought to point out that this level of tolerance and compromise is unusual for me, and unprecedented in London.

"No. That's not good enough. I want you to move now," says the miserable turd. He's glaring at me with fish-like eyes. Cold and wet.

"Well, I'm not going to, there's nowhere else to sit." I wave my pregnancy book about a bit and try to stick out my stomach, hoping he'll pick up on my *condition* and feel shamed into leaving me alone. I feel appalling and don't think I could stand up to drink my creamy, gunky drink even if I wanted to. And actually part of me does want to, the part that doesn't like sitting with weirdos, but the other part, the stubborn, I-know-my-rights-you-miserable-twat part, is not prepared to budge.

This guy has glasses and a struggling goatee. He's wearing M&S jeans and a beige sweater. He weighs about nine stone. At a guess I'd say he went to university and studied geography. He reads the *Guardian* and tries to pretend he gets the jokes in *Private Eye*. His mother probably has her hair "set" once a week at the local hairdresser's, and his father spends most of his day on the allotment. He hasn't got a girlfriend. He's not a threat. I'm prepared to ignore him, to overlook his obvious hostility, to drink my milkshake quickly and leave. But he has other plans.

"You're one of those fucking assholes, aren't you?" he says.

He says that to me. *To me.*

Look, I live in a cosmopolitan city, I work in advertising, I am not unaccustomed to colorful language. We all know who he means when he says "fucking assholes." He means the Sunday drivers who drive below the speed limit, he means the boy racers who cut you up at traffic lights, and he means traffic wardens who give you a ticket even though they are still writing it when you return to your car. And *he,* apparently, means *me.* I cannot reply. Literally cannot. I know if I speak I will shower the man with every expletive I know (many) in a way that would make a sailor run for cover.

Or I will cry.

Torrents.

It takes every ounce of self-control I possess to reject both these responses. Instead, I quickly finish my drink, gather up my books and leave. Hoping that he can't tell that I'm shaking.

Question: what kind of world is it that I am bringing a baby into? Answer: one where brutal words are said aloud, in a bookshop, by a middle-class, *Guardian*-reading man to a middle-class, milkshake-drinking woman.

7

We fall out of the lift, a rowdy crowd desperate for a drink, tobacco and irreverent chatter. I try not to resent the fact that only one of those three is still a viable option for me. We often have a drink after work—the theory is that this drink is to help us relax; the reality is that we often carry on discussing office politics and, rather than helping us to unwind, our drunken evenings only serve to wind each other up. Still, these nights out are irresistible. If we're drinking on expenses we visit trendy watering holes such as Mash, Attica and Titanic, but if there's no client spondulicks then we usually go to the Crown and Sceptre. This is the grotty local that sells warm, tasteless, overpriced beer; it has carpets splattered with cigarette burns, blood from brawls and vomit from those who can't understand the concept of "one too many." It has nothing to recommend it except that it's next door to our office. You can find us there most evenings. Tonight is different again. Brett has a friend who is opening a bar and he's blagged us invites, and although I'll be drinking fizzy water I'm still looking forward to it. Champagne Charlotte's has had the rare and dubious honor of being positively reviewed in *Time Out*. Everyone who is anyone will be there. The boyband is on a mission and I'm in remission. It's been a long day.

"My balls are aching, it's a necessity that I get laid tonight," comments Karl.

"Darling, you are all charm," I muse.

"Not getting enough, you effing shirt-lifter?" asks Drew sensitively. It's the only way they know how to communicate.

Karl snarls some retort, but I miss it because at that moment I notice Hugh in reception. I'm thrilled—it's been a while since he's surprised me by meeting me after work like this. He's obviously being doubly thoughtful since I've told him that I'm pregnant. A fraction of a second later I notice Kate, Hugh's lovable little tyke—except she isn't in the slightest bit lovable—and Tom, who is still so tiny that he is a non-person without any personality at all, not even an offensive one.

My heart sinks. Obviously, I've forgotten some commitment or other. "You guys go ahead, I'll catch you up." I sigh.

As they walk toward the door Hugh exchanges a few pleasantries with the lads. They congratulate him on his job move and they all discuss football and bottled beer. They're nearly bosom buddies. In the background I'm beaming. I can't help it, he *is* proud-making. He fits so easily into any social situation, happily chatting and passing the time of day, and yet he's so much cleverer and more distinguished and remarkable than other men.

Although I think Karl is in exactly the same shirt, and Drew is wearing the same suit, but in a different shade.

"Babe." Hugh turns to me and kisses me full on the lips, holding my face between his hands. I adore the openness, especially after the months of skulking. I cast a cheerful, victorious glance at the boyband, but it's wasted because they've already scooted out of the door, in pursuit of that first drink.

"Babes, you are looking hot," murmurs Hugh.

"What do you want?"

He grins and I'm grinning too because seeing through his blatant flattery is another sign of our being a legitimate, established couple.

"Buggered up the childminding arrangements, haven't I?" Hugh shrugs and then bangs his hand against his head, managing to leave his hair helplessly ruffled. He plays the little boy lost to his advantage frequently, and while it's no longer quite as charming and endearing as it was thirteen years ago it is now quintessentially him and therefore irresistible. "Becca's at some night course, I said we'd babysit. After all, the sooner she's retrained and back in the workplace the better it will be for us."

This is undoubtedly true. Becca doesn't work, so Hugh still pays the mortgage on their place and lives rent-free at mine. Well, it would be ridiculous to ask him to contribute toward a mortgage that I can easily afford. We both earn serious salaries and we don't go short on luxuries, never mind necessities. Besides which, Hugh quite rightly points out that Kate and Tom shouldn't have their lifestyle compromised because of the choices that the adults around them made. They're used to having their mum at home. Having said all that, I sometimes wish that she was more financially independent, the emphasis being on independent.

"Fair enough," I comment as I scoop up the wriggling Tom. Oh God, his diaper needs changing. "What course is she doing?"

"Furniture restoration."

I don't see this as a practical choice for a fully trained accountant trying to get back into the workforce. Surely, she should be updating one of her qualifications on tax fiddles. Furniture restoration! A bloody delaying tactic if I ever saw one. She's hardly likely to find employers queuing up to offer her a job bringing a Louis XIV chair back to life. A surge of irritation washes over me and I battle to suppress it. Deep breaths, deep breaths. Bloody Becca always seems to use the children to get what she wants. This reminds me of Christmas, which was difficult. Naturally, Hugh and I had wanted to spend time together as it was our first official Christmas as a couple and, naturally, Hugh had wanted to spend time with his kids. Naturally, Becca had wanted the kids to be at home over Christmas and, naturally, she did not want to spend any time with me. The feeling was mutual. Besides these immediate warring factions, various grandparents, uncles and aunts had a claim on the kids' time too. If they continue to be so much in demand, they'll be on *Tatler*'s "most wanted list" before they start prep school. From about August onward all the various interested parties argued as to where and when they could spend an hour with the monsters. I really couldn't see the appeal of watching them carelessly rip open their carefully wrapped presents, eat the paper, squash the box and break the toy, but it seemed that I was the only person in the Western world that had no such urge.

Finally and unsatisfactorily Hugh spent Christmas morning with the children, at Becca's. I stayed in bed sipping champagne and deciding what underwear to put on for his return. I'd planned that we'd spend the rest of the day making love, only venturing out of bed to eat the amazing and exotic delicacies that I'd prepared. Delicious in a low-key way—ginger and lemon grass risotto served with mustard and black pepper crackers, homemade chocolate soufflé with violet and rose creams, a small *panettone,* and plenty of port. In truth there was absolutely nothing "low key" about the twelve hours it took me to prepare the food, not to mention the time it took me to plan, source and purchase the ingredients. But, as I'd been waiting for this Christmas for years, nothing was too much trouble. I'd thought that the contrast between such a sensuous and indulgent Christmas and the raucous, chaotic household he'd just left would delight Hugh. But when he finally arrived back from Becca's (three hours later than agreed) he explained that he'd already eaten as the children were expecting it of him.

Which was good of him, because it wouldn't be fair to disappoint Kate and Tom.

I do a quick calculation in my head and realize that by next Christmas I'll have my own mini-vandal. I believe it less than I believe in Father Christmas.

"Oh well, we can pick up pizzas on the way home." Resigned, I move reluctantly toward the revolving glass doors. Tom nips my earlobe and Kate swiftly kicks my ankle. I can see we're in for a good night.

Hugh hangs back. "Er, the thing is, my love, I can't stop. I'm meant to be meeting some clients for dinner. It's the whole intro thing, I can't very well let them down at the last minute like this."

"Hugh." My expression speaks volumes of irritation and I

would complete the picture by putting my hands on my hips, but I'd drop Tom. I can't say too much in front of the ever-vigilant Kate. She's nearly five going on fifty and repeats everything I say back to Becca. She twists my words in a way that the editors of some of Britain's scummiest tabloids would be proud of. I'm not giving Becca the satisfaction of knowing she caused a fracas.

Hugh walks toward me and puts his arms around my shoulders and rests his forehead on mine. He tries to stare into my eyes but I won't look at him. Instead, I'm staring at the floor—not a very violent protest but my resources are low. There aren't any handy railings that I could chain myself to.

"If you knew how much I'd prefer to spend the evening in with you . . ."

"Really?" I immediately lock eye, forgetting my protest.

"Do you have to ask?" He's using a low, groany voice, the one that indicates that I'm sending him wild with desire. Despite the fact that Tom is pulling my hair clip out of my hair (effect created being chaotic rather than tousled) and I have vomit on my jacket, I am sending Hugh wild with desire. The thought instantly cheers me up. Poor Hugh having to work at night. Reinvigorated, I try to locate Kate. She's terrorizing the security guard; he's trying to shake her off but losing the battle. I try to pry her fingers off his legs but she has a vise-like grip, and the moment I loosen one finger she clamps another one down again.

"I knew you'd be cool with this. You are so good with the kids, you can tell you love them." Hugh is not so much outright lying at this stage (although what he says is a lie), he's simply deluded. In fact I don't love them. They bore me at best. However, I've made a superb impression of being besotted with them since their births. I suppose I do feel a bit responsible for them. Even though I make their daddy happy (and nothing on this earth makes their mummy happy, so I've given up caring that I *may* have been responsible for some of her unhappiness), I do admit it would have been more textbook, from their point of view, if their parents had stayed together. That's why I'm generous with the mortgage payments and patient with the fact that Becca's lawyers are tardy with the decree nisi. That's why I encourage Hugh to spend as much time as possible with them, and I always drag myself along on their trips to Planet Hollywood or the Disney shop, even though there are other places I'd prefer to be on a Saturday afternoon, combing Bond Street or Harvey Nicks fourth floor, for example.

That's why I'm biting my tongue now, though Kate is biting my thigh. I drag her toward the door with one hand, while using the other to carry my files and laptop, and balancing Tom on one hip. I wonder if Kate's violent tendencies are because she's from a broken home or because she's intrinsically genuinely awful.

"It's not a problem," I assure Hugh brightly and falsely, while mentally and reluctantly kissing bye-bye to my noisy night at Champagne Charlotte's. "Come on, Kate, we'll walk your dad to the Tube and then go and buy a Häagen-Dazs." She scowls—I might as well have offered to pull out her toenails or torch cute puppies. I reassure myself that the only person who is less enamored with this childminding arrangement than me is Kate.

We set off toward the Tube station, dodging left and right to avoid large umbrellas belonging to harassed office workers who are dashing to the nearest pub or fighting over available cabs. I glance through the window of Champagne Charlotte's. It looks warm and inviting. It's already heaving with boisterous boys and girls. I look away quickly before Hugh notices my longing. Although he probably wouldn't notice anyway, because he's excitedly telling me about things that happened in the office today. He loves his new job. He's always been extremely driven, but I've never seen him quite so enthusiastic about work in years. He likes the people who work there, he likes the clients, he likes the creativity. He's never been happier and I'm really happy for him. We reach the Tube station. Hugh strides toward the ticket machine. It salves his social conscience to travel by Tube now and again rather than always by taxi. Bugger that, once he is safely on the Northern line I'm going to hail a cab. It's bad enough having to be responsible for Kate and Tom, there's no way I am going to attempt to be so on public transport.

Two of the ticket machines are out of order; two are not giving change; the fifth is surrounded by jubilant Italian teenagers who can't read English and, even if they could understand the instructions on the machine, would feel that it was unpatriotic to hurry. We stand in the miserably long queue, with people with miserably long faces. Kate lies on the floor and screams that she hates me. Hugh doesn't react to this antisocial behavior ("don't pander to her, that's what she wants"), but grabs his ticket, kisses Tom and the space near my left ear and pushes his way through the ticket barrier.

Kate screams on. This she-devil is the half-sister of the being I'm carrying. That must count for something. I dig deep for some reserves of patience and understanding, while sighing silently and hoping to God Kate takes after her mother. I drag her along the dirty tiled floor while fruitlessly pleading with her to stand up. Besides the fact that I'm in serious danger of losing my balance and dropping Tom, I can't take any more tuts of disapproval. I want to shout at passers-by that she's not mine, that I'm just shagging her father, but I don't think it will help. God, I'm tired, I'd love to go home right now and hide away under the duvet. Still, there's no chance of that for the next several hours. Scrub that, the next several years. I rally and think of my grandmother's motto, "Make do and mend." Of course, she was referring to a ripped shirt or frayed basket; I'm battling with shredded patience and tattered nerves.

Surprisingly, we all do make it to the Häagen-Dazs store in one piece. I hand Kate and Tom cones stuffed with tutti-frutti and strawberry ice cream. I know that Becca wouldn't approve of me feeding them ice cream, which secretly motivates me. Kate's cone sways precariously for a split second and then the tutti-frutti hits the deck, leaving evidence of its fall on Kate's school coat and my trousers. She lets up an enormous wail; the horrifying pitch is such that it prompts at least three other customers to consider calling the police and the social services. I quickly buy her a replacement, which she accepts ungracefully, shooting me looks that clearly indicate she holds me responsible for the catastrophe. I have a distinct feeling that it's going to be a long evening.

8

It's Kate who first notices Sam camping on my doorstep. I live in Clapham, and there are often down-and-outs rolling around my neat residential street—it's one of the many colorful juxtapositions that make up London life. However, the vagrants are rarely dressed in Karen Millen and hoofed in L. K. Bennett. Sam and her sadness stand out like Scary Spice on a Saga holiday. Her red-rimmed eyes tell me everything I need to know at a glance. She explains that she couldn't face either checking out ancient names in her Palm Pilot or going home to her empty flat, which offers little more in the way of company than a bottle of wine and a box of microwave chips. She adds that there's only me who understands "because we are so alike." I'm extremely shocked and offended by this comment. It truly terrifies me. Does the outside world see me as such a dismal throwback? Sam thinks the suffragettes were a 1970s pop band. She's a pushover where guys are concerned. It's embarrassing. I may have bemoaned a lack of Hugh in my life in the past, but the difference is I've only ever bemoaned the lack of *Hugh* in my life; Sam has bemoaned Alan, Bart, Clive, Doug, right through to Zachary, all with equal vehemence. It's a big difference. Her inconsistency is maddening, and threatens any real sympathy I might be persuaded to muster.

There again, she found my consistency absolutely bewildering, yet she was always the other end of a handkerchief.

(G&)tea and sympathy are the order of the day.

I try to view her presence as a blessing; at least she always knows how to entertain Kate and Tom. And it's a good thing Hugh had to go out; he wouldn't have seen Sam's presence as anything other than an irritant. Listening to Sam's stories of her countless near misses is some way away from his idea of fun. He claims that her stories depress me and that she causes me to be irritable. This simply isn't true. In fact, the reverse is the case. It's not very nice to admit, but Sam's stories of her hapless love life make me mentally jump with joy that I have Hugh and that I'm in such a great relationship—I mean, there but for the grace of God. Anyway, whenever Sam comes around for a debrief of her unromantic liaisons, Hugh grabs his car keys and mumbles something about "taking it for a wash" and leaves me alone to the job of superglueing together Sam's shattered heart and self-esteem. I wonder if I could pull the same stunt and leave Kate or Tom in charge of Sam; looking at the state Sam's in, there is only a minuscule chance of the more conventional alternative being a viable option.

Kate falls through the door and runs directly to the sofa. She picks up the remote and tunes in to Cartoon Network. I know that the only way Hugh can ever persuade her to stay in with me is with the bribe of cable TV. Still, I'm not complaining; one down, two to go. I change Tom's diaper (there really isn't anything more disgusting in the entire world and I simply don't believe mothers who say that you get used to it) and I pop him to bed in the spare room. Finally, I deal with Sam. I pour her an enormous G&T and while the kettle is boiling I eat three slices of toast.

"Kate, give me a hug," demands Sam. I'm amazed to see Kate actually skip across the room into Sam's open arms.

"Can I have one too?" I ask. I can only assume this request is hormone-driven. Kate tuts and sidles reluctantly toward me. Too well drilled to actively refuse, too much of a four-year-old to pretend to enjoy complying. I wish I'd never asked. Her second journey across my coir matting floor leaves another set of muddy

Wellington-boot prints, and as she hugs me she blows an enormous gum bubble that pops in my hair.

I'd say it was deliberate sabotage but I have no absolute proof.

"I'm sure I've heard your daddy say that bubble gum is not
allowed," says Sam, through her smudged mascara and sniffles.
"Take your wellies off and go and wash your hands before you
touch anything." It amazes me that even a distracted, heartbroken
Sam is more capable of babysitting than I am, especially since I'm
trying hard. However, the instructions, although well-intentioned,
come too late. I can already see sticky fingerprints on the B&O
stereo, the aluminium coffee table, the TV, the remote. I'll have to
go to the hairdresser's to get the effects of the burst bubble cut out
of my hair and, for some reason, logical only to a four-year-old
brain, Kate has chosen to take off her muddy Wellington boots
while sat on my white goatskin rug. I sigh but say nothing.

I pour Sam another large G&T (lordy, she got through that
one quickly enough) and I try to silence Kate's demands for
peanut-butter sandwiches, Coke and Twiglets. I can supply the
Coke and Twiglets, as I bought them especially for her, but I don't
have any peanut butter. When she visited last week her undisputed
favorite sandwich filler was Nutella. Last week I hadn't any
Nutella, this week I've stocked up heavily on it, but Kate simply
stares at me as though I've suggested poisoning her.

"Yuk. Never touch it," she yells categorically. "It's so calorific."

I'm tempted to tell her that peanut butter is more calorific, but
realize that this is not a dignified argument to have with a four-
year-old. I offer her avocado and mozzarella, a banana or French
plum jam. It appears that neither my fridge nor my life are particularly child-friendly. She finally accepts the banana, pulling a face,
which clearly communicates her belief that I am trying to poison
her. I wait, expecting her to demand that Sam act as food taster,
rather like Queen Elizabeth I. Finally she settles back in front of
the TV.

I decide to concentrate on cheering up Sam, at least I'm practiced in that skill, but I realize that I am doing a fairly poor job

when I can't even remember the name of the guy she's been seeing. Nor do I help myself with my defense—that it isn't my fault; I've only met him once and they've only been an item for five minutes. Sam struggles to hide her irritation and points out that they've been seeing each other for three months. To be pedantic, they've been seeing each other two months, two weeks—she always rounds up. Coincidentally it's the same length of time I've been pregnant. I tell her that she doesn't need a man to define her. She tells me that she *knows* she doesn't *need* a man, and if she had a pound for every time someone has said that she'd stop applying for a slot on *Who Wants to Be a Millionaire?* She just "*wants* one."

Sam is thirty-five. Her life story is roughly as follows. From the age of nought to fifteen she spent looking beautiful and imagining being Cinderella, or similar (it is my personal belief that this is the reason behind Sam's shoe fetish—in her mind pretty shoes are intrinsically linked to the happily ever after). Aged sixteen to twenty-four she latched onto a specific boy or man for a period of two to three years in the hope he'd propose. This strategy was so extreme and followed so strictly it even led to her delaying her university entrance for three years as she was "so close" to a proposal from some guy or other. The proposal didn't come, so she changed track and went to university to meet more men. Turned out to be more of the same men because, despite an impressive array of candidates and considerable effort on Sam's behalf, a diamond ring never materialized. When she graduated, aged twenty-four, she heard her body clock ticking so loudly that she thought the wake-up call was coming from Big Ben. In response she shortened the probation period she'd allow for prospective husbands to demonstrate their commitment. Her boyfriends were given anything from a month to six months, maximum. If at that point there was no indication of serious intent (at the very least the suggestion of a weekend break in the Lake District) she dumped ruthlessly. Problem is, Sam attracts commitment-phobes like Winnie the Pooh's pantry attracts wasps. As time passes and Sam panics, she swaps one hopeless case for another with increasing, and alarming, rapidity. The result is that despite being gorgeous, funny, kind and generous, she's still alone.

She's lonely.

Becca is doing a night class in furniture restoration.

And I'm pregnant.

We all have our crosses to bear.

It's a melancholy evening, which bizarrely recommends itself to me. Between us we consume (besides the G&Ts and toast) four pots of tea, an entire packet of chocolate-covered Hobnobs and a fish-and-chips supper (two and a half weeks' calories in less than two and a half hours). Sam also smokes twenty Marlboro Lights and drinks a bottle of Chardonnay.

"You're not drinking?" Sam refills her own glass. She is so absorbed in her own problems that she barely pauses for my response.

"No."

"Not smoking?" She offers me the pack for a brief second and then lights up and inhales deeply.

"No," I mutter.

"Another detox program?"

"Sort of."

"But you are eating chocolate?" she insists.

"Yes."

"Odd detox program. Whose is it?" But she doesn't wait for a reply. It's quite depressing that an absolute reversal of thirteen years of ruthlessly strict habits draws no more attention than this from my best friend, which makes me wonder if we are on different planets. At the very least we are operating in different time zones.

Melancholy tips into maudlin, slips into depression and finally nose-dives into full-scale despair by about 9 P.M. and after the second bottle of Chardonnay. I am actually relieved when Becca arrives to pick up Kate and Tom, as she interrupts Sam's monologue about how she feels incomplete and if that's so wrong, saying a man completes her, then come the revolution put her against the wall and shoot her. I am tempted to shoot her there and then when she crashes into my telephone table, knocking over a vase of flowers, breaking it and spilling water onto a pile of papers that Hugh has left in the hallway.

"I'm not saying all girls are incomplete without guys." She still calls women "girls," even though nearly everyone she knows is in their thirties; some would think this endearing. "But I am saying people, human beings, are incomplete without other human beings, and having one special human being to love me above all others is my nirvana. I'm always the bridesmaid, never the bride." And so she spews forth her words of wisdom as I encourage her to put on her coat and pashmina and fold her into a waiting taxi. "I know it's not a fashionable point of view, but it is *my* point of view. I want someone to buy a house with, celebrate birthdays with, have kids with and"—she hesitates—"recently I've begun to feel fed up that 'someone' is always a 'different one' or, worse, 'anyone.'" She grabs my hair and stares at me with an intensity that can only be achieved if you have consumed more than half a dozen units on an empty stomach (you can't count Hobnobs as food) and a dozen more after some fish and chips. "You understand, you felt just this way about Hugh."

Yes I did, do.

9

*H*ugh finally comes home some time after one in the morning. He wakes me up as he gets into bed but I don't let on. If I admit to being awake I'll have to ask where he's been until this time of night. And I don't want to have to do that. He probably persuaded his clients to go to his club after the dinner, which will have undoubtedly been a success (Hugh's charming most of the time, and when he makes the effort he's irresistible). They'll have been bowled over by the fact that he has a private membership at Monte's, especially as Jamie Oliver was actually cooking tonight. It's worth staying late because the lovely Jamie often pops out front after he's hung up his oven gloves. Hugh knows how to show his clients a good time.

Probably.

What am I thinking? Of course he's been with his clients. Bloody hell, I'm becoming really paranoid. If I asked him now he'd tell me all about it.

I think I will ask. Just to prove to myself how stupid I'm being.

On second thought, best not, I don't want Hugh to think I'm mistrustful. Besides which, he's unlikely to say, "Actually, I've been having wild sex with Scandinavian nymphomaniac twins." Instead I lie very still, trying to ignore the fact that I feel nauseous again. Hugh falls asleep immediately. The smell of alcohol seeps from his pores and his snores reverberate around the room; weirdly I find this comforting. I've never minded his snoring. This is what I wanted. It's intimate. It's us. The street light is leaking through the roller blinds, illuminating the room in parts, and casting shadows in other parts. I can just about make out the silver frames on the Klimt prints, but not the detail of the pictures. Not that I actually need to see them, I know them all by heart. *The Kiss* and the one with the pregnant redhead. Hugh bought me them for my twenty-first birthday. They're just posters bought from Athena but I was thrilled; at the time every other student room was decorated with black and white photos of women wearing big hats and too much make-up or men with bare chests holding naked babies. I had the Klimt posters framed in silver, which the guy in the shop advised against, he was pushing us toward the more traditional gold frame. But Hugh pointed out that gold was such an obvious choice, everyone framed Klimt in gold. So I held out for what I wanted.

Looking at them now I think they might have been better with gold frames.

Still, no point losing sleep over a decision I made donkey's years ago.

I can see the chair at the end of the bed. It's wooden, with a white seat. Hugh has carefully folded his trousers and left them on the chair back. The trousers and a small pile of loose coins next to his side of the bed are the only obvious signs of his inhabitance. Naturally, his other clothes are hanging in the wardrobe and his CDs dominate the rack, his razors are in the bathroom and he has some travel books on my bookshelves—he's not a great reader of novels—but it doesn't seem to add up to very much. Suddenly it doesn't seem very permanent.

God, girl, get a grip.

Talk about middle-of-the-night heebie-jeebies. Of course Hugh's permanent. He was delighted when I told him about the baby. *A baby.* Our baby. That's more permanent than anything we've ever done before. More permanent than touring Mexico, or trekking in China, more permanent than choosing Christmas presents together or visiting aged aunts, more permanent than anything, full stop. And permanency with Hugh is all I've ever wanted. I need the loo. I really, really need to wee. My bladder is groaning. It feels exactly like a balloon stretched to its limit and full of water. And I feel sick. I thought it was supposed to be *morning* sickness. The strain I've got is obviously insomniac and has no regard for time of day. Right now, in terms of permanency, I'd have settled for Hugh putting his name on the deeds of the apartment.

Joke.

I've already been to the loo twice tonight and it's freezing on those bathroom tiles. I lie still for a few more minutes and will the inflated balloon to go away, but it doesn't. In fact, all I can think of is Victoria Falls. I get up, brave the icy tiles and then decide to read a brief Julia has drafted. It's all about odor control in shoes. It's a good paper, and I only have to mark one or two amendments in red ink, like a teacher correcting an essay. One of Brett's team already has the creative solution anyway, so it doesn't much matter what Julia's brief says. He wants to use Moby's song "Why Does My Heart Feel So Bad?" and change the words to "Why Do My Soles Smell So Bad?" I'm torn. It's a really beautiful, gravelly, soulful song. If Moby (or more likely, his agent) gives us permission, we'll probably make a great ad that will render odor eaters cool and undoubtedly send the record back up the charts; but I can't help thinking that it will be a shame if Moby's agent does accept the offer. I mean, what lyricist can seriously want their song associated with pongy feet? Just as I am contemplating getting back into bed and fighting Hugh for my half of the duvet, the phone rings. I dash to it, heart pounding; I hate middle-of-the-night calls. They invariably spell trouble.

"George, George. It's me. It's happened!"

"What has, Sam? Are you O.K?"

"Never better. George, *it's* happened. Gilbert's proposed!"

"Who?"

"Gilbert."

Is she still drunk? Isn't he the one we've been questioning the parentage of all evening?

"Gilbert, as in the one who stood you up the night before last?"

"Well, yes, but he explained all that."

"He was working late, right?"

"No, his tire blew."

"And he couldn't get to a phone?" I ask skeptically.

Sam ignores my question. "George, he's proposed!"

"Right. Yeah. God, how embarrassing, you hardly know him. How did you get out of that?"

Silence.

I suppose I should want to eat my words, but I've only said what everybody must be thinking.

"I didn't want to get out of it," says Sam, trying desperately to keep the offense out of her voice. "I accepted."

"Oh."

"He's lovely."

"Good."

"Seriously lovely."

"Oh, seriously good, then."

"Aren't you going to congratulate me?"

I stare at the carpet that is still wet with the water from the broken vase. It seems an indecently short amount of time since I was spooning a sobbing Sam into the waiting cab. Admittedly, I'm not good with sudden change. I'm known to be a creature of habit but this strikes me as the opposite extreme.

"It just seems a little sudden. It would be a mistake to accept the first proposal that comes along, you know, Sam. Just because you want to get married."

"Oh, and do you suggest I wait for a second one? At the current rate that will be when I'm seventy," she snaps. "I love G and he loves me."

"Who's G?" I ask, momentarily confused.

"Gilbert. I've decided to call Gilbert 'G.'"

"To make him sound more twenty-first century?"

"No, because I want a pet name for him," she defends.

"How about G-spot? I mean, he must have hidden talents that you're not telling me about."

"That's very nasty, Georgina." Besides which it's stupid, because she's told me everything about G. Me and everyone else for that matter.

"So you love him?"

"Yes. He's reliable and honest." Except when he stands her up and tells lies about it.

"Those are the reasons you employ a plumber or buy a car," I point out.

She ignores me. Of course she loves him. Nearly every woman would agree that to be a single woman in London after the age of thirty is not pleasant and when you're tipping thirty-five it is distinctly uncomfortable. Sam thinks it's absolute social failure.

I weigh it up. Should I continue my honesty policy? Which is obviously as popular as a naked Keith Chegwin. Or do I tell her what she wants to hear? I hear myself mutter an apology and I do my best to sound sincere. That is the problem with saying what you think, it's rarely popular. Better to stick to the appropriate responses. Sod honesty.

"Well, congratulations, Bird. I'm really happy for you." I struggle for something nice to say about him and finally come up with, "Good bridge player." I'm referring to a tiresome evening Hugh and I spent with Gilbert and Sam last month. We had dinner at her place and, naturally, got very drunk during the evening. I suggested we play cards. A light and easy game of "Aces High" was what I had in mind, but Gilbert was tediously competitive and insisted that we play bridge instead.

"That was a fun evening, wasn't it?"

"Hilarious," I lie.

"To think I'll be married by the end of the year. I've always wanted to be a winter bride." This at least is true. Inasmuch as she's always wanted to be a spring, summer, autumn or winter bride.

"Have you told Julia?" I'm interested to hear what Julia has to say about the hasty engagement. I introduced Julia and Sam to one another a year or so back. As they are both single they took to going out together, ostensibly to be independent and go clubbing, patently to find men. However, while Sam was hunting for some-one to glide down the aisle with, Julia was looking for something altogether less churchy. Her idea of permanency is two dances in a row. Julia, the queen of treat-them-mean-keep-them-keen, does however have a far greater success rate when it comes to follow-up calls. They both regularly treat me to (radically different) accounts of their exploits. Sam is dangerously romantic, poetical and ideal-istic; the three things that are most notable about Julia are that she is spiky, funny and a bigger bitch than Bette Davis. Therefore she is an excellent gossip; I can't wait to hear what she has to say about this engagement.

"No. I haven't called Julia yet. I thought you should be the first to know."

I'm itching to swap notes.

I sit down on the floor and settle with my back against the radiator; I sweep the skirting boards with my little finger in an attempt to eradicate all dust.

"O.K, so tell me everything," I instruct, summoning every molecule of enthusiasm in my body.

And she does. She tells me how when she got home from my flat he was waiting for her, armed with bribes (a bouquet of red roses, a magnum of champagne—not that she needed anything more to drink—and a reservation at the Ivy).

"They let you in?"

"Yes."

"But . . ." But she could hardly stand. I can hardly say so.

She reads my mind. "They've seen worse."

I suppose they have. The Ivy is famous for its lush celebs; the alcoholics count is second only to the Groucho club. Besides which, it will have been late. Ten o'clock maybe. Those who go to the Ivy to see and be seen go for eight-thirty.

She tells me that when they got to the Ivy, they didn't eat any-thing from the menu because he had already prearranged a bespoke selection. He'd chosen all his favorite foods that he wanted to introduce her to. Wasn't that sweet? They started with oysters, which actually Sam hates but she ate them anyway, she's swallowed worse things. Then they had foie gras and water biscuits. It's a good job that Sam had already eaten a fish-and-chips supper, that way she could pretend to have the appetite of a bird, an impression every woman feels compelled to give. And the waiters made such a fuss of them. Gilbert is a regular, and Sam thinks they'll both be dining there frequently in the future. They had such a fun time, neither of them stopped laughing and there wasn't a single pause in the conversation. The food just kept coming, as did the champagne. And it is so elegant. Proper linen tablecloths and decent-sized tables. I let her repeat every word, gesture, inflection, several times, and largely I manage to stay awake.

"Well, I'm very happy for you, Sam," I say, trying to bring the conversation to a close. Bored to death, I wiggle my toes; my legs and bum are so numb I fear that rigor mortis has set in. I check my watch—Sam has been on the phone for an hour and a half.

"How are you?" she asks dutifully, obviously feeling a teensy bit guilty that she's neglected this social nicety for ninety minutes.

"Fine." Instinctively I know that this isn't the "I'm pregnant!" moment either.

The tedium of Sam detailing the entire contents of the Pronuptia catalog overwhelms me. I congratulate her again, then I hang up. I'm not sure she notices.

10

I've been in the office precisely ninety seconds. Julia and I don't bother with niceties, but cut to the chase.

"What do you think?" I demand.

"Astounding."

"At first I didn't have a clue who she was talking about."

"How could you fail to recognize the hallmark of 'G', the International Man of Mystery?" sniggers Julia. (It's natural that we should be a tiny bit bitchy.) "I bet that pissed her off."

"Well, I recovered by pointing out that she had called me at three A.M.," I defend myself.

"I'm glad that you're known for your enthusiasm and that I'm known for my lack of it, because otherwise I'd be the one receiving the excited calls at ungodly hours."

Am I? I consider "being known for my enthusiasm" for a moment. Is it a good thing? Enthusiasm strikes me as a bit amateurish. Not very cool. Why can't I be known for my sound advice? Or my level-headedness?

"She just called me. I made a huge effort to summon up the proper amount of delight. Should I be delighted?" asks Julia. "What's he like? It's all happened so fast that I haven't even met him."

The thing is, we both love Sam.

"Gushing is not my thing," I lie, trying on a level-headed persona that is alien to me. "But, yeah, I think we can be happy for her. He seems nice enough. I've only met him once but, unusually for a man of Sam's, he seems genuinely interested in her, her friends, family, job, et al." I'm saying this partly because it's true but mostly because I want it to be true. "And he's certainly willing to commit."

"Definitely a point in his favor as far as Sam is concerned."

"A necessity."

"Don't you think the speed is a bit suspect? Could he be a psychopath?"

"Well, he's getting on a bit. Mid-forties, he doesn't have time to hang around."

"She said that the proposal was everything she ever wanted and more."

I find that hard to believe. "Good."

"She said he looks like a film star—does he?"

I consider. "Well, not any particular film star that I could name. Not a Ben Affleck or Jude Law, not really a Tom Cruise either, but thinking about it" (generously) "he does have a generic film-star quality. Perhaps Cary Grant—before we knew he was gay—crossed with Errol Flynn."

"He wears green tights?" chortles Julia again.

"Stop being mean. He's other-worldly, decent and charming."

"Dull, then?"

"As ditchwater," I confirm. "Still, she's happy that he's so other-worldly, because most men that she's been with have been so 'of this world' that their main hobby was downloading porn from the Internet."

"And she did say that the ring was the one she'd have picked out herself if she'd been given the choice."

"Oh, my God, the ring, I forgot to ask. It must be the square solitaire from Tiffany."

"No. I thought that, but it's an emerald cluster."

"Oh."

"Still."

"Still."

"She seems happy."

"That's the main thing."

"Hmmm."

Having said very little it's obvious that we are in total agreement.

I ring Jessica to tell her about Sam's engagement.

"How lovely for her. I hadn't realized she was seeing anyone seriously. You girls are so secretive."

"No, we're not."

"What did she say about your pregnancy?"

"Er, I haven't mentioned it yet."

My mother chooses to think better of me than I deserve. "Didn't want to steal her thunder?"

"Something like that," I mutter.

"Well, what's he like, this Gilbert?"

"He's a forty-seven-year-old, nice enough guy who is a cautiously efficient MD of a small, reasonably successful firm that writes mildly interesting computer programs," I say bluntly. I resist adding that he reminds me of everyone's father.

"You don't sound very enthusiastic."

"I hadn't realized until today that my enthusiasm was so conspicuous," I grumble.

"And now you have noticed, you're trying to eradicate it?" I can hear exasperation leak into Jessica's voice.

"Sort of."

"Why? Being enthusiastic isn't a bad thing. Just because you are it, it doesn't necessarily mean it is a bad thing to be. Why do you insist on always trying to be something you're not?" Jessica scolds. I wonder if she's being ironic when she turns the conversation and mentions that she's considering liposuction on her thighs.

February

11

Hugh ruins my Saturday morning almost the instant I open my eyes by asking, "Are you coming to the gym?" I wish, and not for the first time, that I'd wake up to an offer that we go to the King's Road together or, better yet, out for lunch. Ever since I met Hugh, or more accurately ever since he showed me the photo of the elegant, elongated Becca, the gym has been my torture chamber. It represents all that is evil in the world, i.e., the fact that my genetic make-up veers toward rotund, and the fact that naturally skinny is simply a cruel myth perpetuated by people who starve themselves. I find little comfort that for almost fourteen years I have been one of those perpetuating the myth. My natural state of slothfulness is further exaggerated as during the night someone has poured cement down my throat and now my legs are ton weights. My back and boobs ache, gold-medal style.

Hugh repeats the question about the gym but, before I can answer him, I have to make a dash to the bathroom to throw up last night's supper. A ritual that has become as intrinsic to my morning routine as applying Estée Lauder moisturizer, or fishing around in the cereal boxes to find plastic models of dinosaurs.

It's almost impossible to think that this is the same bathroom that used to be a zone of erotic pleasure. Hugh and I used to have frantic, fantastic sex in the shower and long, loving bubble baths. The numerous candles and sensuous massage oils are being neglected. I can hardly bear Hugh being in the same flat as me when I puke, so the chances of him getting into the bathroom are microscopic; he's having to grow a goatee.

I am seriously considering suing the publishers and authors of all the maternity books I've read for printing incorrect information. Information that raised my hopes and allowed me to believe that pregnancy was in some way a bearable, if not a desirable, state to be in. The books warn me that a "small amount of nausea is normal." Ha! Nausea. It strikes me that nausea is a pitiful word, woefully inadequate, far too refined to describe the reality of the state I'm in. "Ill" is also a euphemism, because ill suggests that there will be a recovery. "Queasy" is insultingly mellow, considering there is a huge and constant ball of bile and vomit swelling in my gut. A ball of spew that is insidiously leaking into my nervous and capillary systems, infecting every part of my body. Nothing helps. Not dry biscuits, nor ginger, nor sucking lemons. I consider explaining this to Hugh, but decide there's no point—he gets squeamish if he sees me putting bikini-line wax in the trolley at Tesco's. Instead, I stick to the facts.

"No, I'm not coming to the gym. My personal trainer was a bit shirty when I threw up on the stationary bike last week."

"You threw up on a stationary bike? How embarrassing."

"It was. And I threw up in an umbrella stand in Harvey Nicks. The accuracy of my aim cost me £180. Nothing's sacred."

"Poor you."

Yes, poor me. I climb back under the duvet and wait, hoping that he'll offer to stay with me and while away the rainy Saturday. He could help me find something to satiate my hunger and at the same time calm my churning stomach. So far I've come up with pickled onions and tinned pears (simultaneously).

"Well, come for a sauna or a session on the sun bed," suggests Hugh cheerfully, oblivious to my telepathic plea for company and sloth.

"I can't use the sauna or sun lamps anymore," I reply, not trying too hard to keep the self-pity out of my voice. Pregnancy, I've found, isn't simply about washing vegetables and giving up raw meat.

"Well, it is much more fashionable to use fake tan," Hugh says.

It's not. It's much more vogue to say you use fake tan but still use sun beds; they give a more even cover. I don't say so. Nor do I comment that some of the maternity books I've been reading suggest it's better to avoid fake tan as well for the duration of the pregnancy. The books are American; I can't take them too seriously. Hugh doesn't offer to stay with me, but simply comments, "Perhaps it's a good thing that you're throwing up so much if your workouts are going to be restricted." I can't be bothered to point out that even if I do more tactical chunders than a supermodel, between now and the delivery, I'll still be obese.

"Well, if you're not coming to the gym, can you pick up my suit from the dry cleaner's?" asks Hugh, as he starts to pack his sports bag. He sweeps the bathroom shelves, collecting up deodorant, shampoo, shower gel, shaving cream.

"Yes," I mutter, although I had planned to hide in bed all day. I ought to buy him a double set of all his toiletries; then he could keep one lot in his gym bag and one lot in the bathroom—it would make things much easier for him.

"And buy a birthday card for my mother."

"I already have, you just have to sign it."

"Oh, great. Well done." He starts to search his drawers for something. As he becomes more frantic he scatters socks and T-shirts onto the floor like confetti.

"What are you looking for?"

"Sports socks."

"Second drawer down on the left."

"Oh, right, thanks. And my blue Nike shirt?"

"In the dryer."

"Great." He rushes downstairs, leaving a Hansel and Gretel trail of clothes behind him. He comes back into the room with his squash racket but no Nike shirt.

"Your shirt," I remind him.

"Absolutely. Right." He grins and runs back downstairs. "What would I do without you?"

"You'll never have to find out," I shout after him. Which is true, and a much nicer thing to say than, "Just leave, just go and play squash!" which is on the tip of my tongue.

The door bangs behind him.

Bye, then.

Even under the duvet I can see that there's regurgitated Weetabix on my shirt. Without surrendering my horizontal position I wiggle out of the shirt and throw it in the general direction of the dirty-laundry basket. Then I sleep.

The telephone ringing wakes me up. I feel around for the handset.

"Hello." I try and project an alert and jolly tone into my voice, so that whoever is calling can't tell I was asleep.

"Were you asleep?" demands Hugh.

"Er." Truth or tiny, little, white lie?

"It's midday," he adds, his tone betraying exasperation and disgust.

Lie then. "No, I was just by the telephone, dusting."

"Oh. Isn't that what we have a cleaner for?"

Maybe I should have said painting my toenails; dusting gives off all the wrong vibes. It's too domestic. Also, it implies I don't manage the cleaner properly.

Luckily Hugh has much bigger things on his mind. "I've had a brilliant idea."

"What?"

"Let's throw a dinner party to tell all our friends about the baby."

"That *is* a good idea." Sweetie. He's so pleased about this baby!

"Knew you'd think so. How about tomorrow?"

"Bit short notice, isn't it?" We often throw lunch or dinner parties, and in my experience they cannot be pulled together at the last minute. At least, not if you serve a minimum of three different nibbles with the four different cocktails, a starter, a main course and a pudding, mints, coffees and cognac. Handmade pastry, hand-whisked soufflé, hand-ground coffee. And we always want to do all this.

"You like a challenge," he urges.

I don't like to look incapable so I stall. "Not the cooking." I manage to hit a note which implies, "Ha, cooking, that will be a breeze." "Short notice for the guests. Everyone will be doing something."

"Don't worry. I sounded out a couple of the chaps at work yesterday. They said they could make it for seven-thirty."

Right.

"Did you ask Sam or Julia?"

"Babes, I thought you'd want to tell your closest girly friends the big news in a more personal way, not at a dinner party. You should call them."

True. I should. It's odd to think that when I got my job at Q&A Sam knew within hours of my signing the contract. When I first kissed Hugh, illegally, I called her within minutes to give her the details. In the past neither of us would have considered it odd if I phoned her to ask her opinion on whether I should buy "the red one or the blue one" (dresses that she'd never even seen). I'm eleven and a half weeks pregnant; according to the scary books, this being I'm carrying is close to 0.18 oz (5 g), and is the size of a small plum. (The food obsession continues.) It has eyelids and clearly defined fingers and toes and yet Sam doesn't even know of its existence. Sam who knows how many lipsticks I own and the precise shades of all thirty-seven handbags in my wardrobe.

Perhaps that's why the handbags still seem more real.

I call Sam and Julia and get them to agree to meet me at the Bluebird Café, on the King's Road. I think that the service is dire and the food is overpriced, but it is terminally trendy and I'm a sucker for the glamour. Besides, the supermarket there stocks the most gorgeous delicacies. I'll be able to pick up some "cheating" groceries for the dinner party.

12

It's a dark, February Saturday afternoon. Shop windows, sporting vast displays of red nylon underwear and faded boxes of Milk Tray, are the only interruption to the grayness of the streets, the weather, the people. The hope is that these Valentine's window displays will rekindle the flagging passion of the British public. Not so much a long shot, more an Olympic challenge. Thank God Hugh has more style. He's not a curry and a couple of pints type of guy; the lingerie he buys me is always silk, wrapped in enough tissue paper to cover the Empire State Building. I imagine that he'll whisk me to the George V, in Paris, for a weekend.

Not that he's mentioned anything, and Valentine's Day is now less than two weeks away. Still, I love surprises.

Julia arrives first.

"God, you're looking rough, another hangover?"

I wish. She immediately points out that my trousers are held together by a complex engineering feat involving safety pins and a belt belonging to Hugh. I try to convince her it's high fashion.

Sam arrives in a halo of happiness. Her first words are, "I can't stay too late, G is expecting me." This isn't necessarily true, but it allows Sam to introduce Gilbert into the conversation within seven syllables. Then with suitable aplomb she orders champagne. It may only be mid-afternoon but she hasn't drunk anything else since she got engaged. I order a mineral water.

"So, why the council of war?" asks Sam, as she takes a sip of the champers. I can only imagine how good it must taste. Dry, crisp, off-limits.

"Problem at work?" asks Julia, as though I'm single-minded.

"I've some news."

"Oh, my God, *you are getting married,*" yells Sam, jumping up and spilling her drink. She flings her arms around my neck and starts to sing the wedding march. I stay utterly still. "That's absolutely *the* most fantastic news I could have hoped to hear," she giggles.

"You're pregnant," says Julia, identifying the look of bemused vulnerability and desperation that I'm sporting as something other than pre-wedding jitters.

"Yes," I confirm, "I'm pregnant." I am sure there are more elegant ways of breaking this news. But, "I'm blessed" or "the stork is going to be making a delivery" must have seemed ridiculous even in the nineteenth century. "I'm up the duff" or "creek without paddle" may be more accurate but are more emotive than I want to be at this stage in the conversation.

Sam stops dancing around me. For a moment she is lost for words. She rallies and says, "That's the second best piece of news I could hope to hear." Then, because she's not entirely ensconced in cloud-cuckoo land, she adds, "Isn't it?"

I try to pull my face into an appropriate celebratory expression and I try to nod, but I think the gesture ends up looking like a shrug.

I should be ecstatic, shouldn't I? Because Hugh is, isn't he? We are going to be a family, how perfect is that? Although I hadn't really envisaged the culmination of all my dreams as me spending days cleaning puke off the bathroom tiles. While I'm sure ecstasy is waiting in the wings, my immediate response is considerably less gung-ho.

Sam and Julia stare at me expectantly.

Maybe I'll just tell them that some of it unnerves me. Some of it has left me a little out of sorts.

Surely they'll laugh and tell me that lots of their friends/

cousins/sisters/neighbors felt exactly like this. That they too were held hostage by their emotions and were victimized by their bodies in the same way. We always have consoling counter-examples to hand to comfort one another, whatever the situation:

"So he said he wanted more space and can only see you one night a week, don't worry. A friend of mine had a boyfriend who wanted more space so he trained as an astronaut."

"Not giving you a house key is not an inability to commit. My cousin was dating this guy for three months and he wouldn't give her his telephone number. Now that's an inability to commit."

"I've been feeling quite ill," I mutter, the crowning glory of understatement. "I still don't quite believe it." My luck, or lack of it, that is. However, neither of them rush to make me feel part of the human race. Instead Sam giggles disproportionately and asks, haven't I ever heard of the old adage, "If you can't be good, be careful." I nearly argue that, "It's easy to be wise after the event," but then I catch myself. She's really going to have to stop resorting to these pathetic old sayings, not least because they're infectious.

They ask the same questions as my mother and Hugh did.

"How long have you been trying?" (Sam). Oh, *pleeease.*

"How far gone?" (Julia). Too far.

Sam adds a new one. "Well, accidents will happen. So when will you be getting married?"

"No plans as yet," I comment breezily and make a pretense of trying to catch the eye of the waiter.

"But you will be getting married," insists Sam.

"We're not really the type of couple to be tied down by all that conventional stuff," I bluff.

"So he hasn't mentioned it, then?" asks Julia.

"No," I admit.

"But Hugh's pleased." It's half statement, half question, from Sam.

"Oh, yes," I assure them. I consider telling them about the dinner party he's throwing to celebrate the news, then I remember that neither of them are invited and so I keep quiet.

"That's what all the flower business was about," adds Julia.

"Yes."

The day after I told him, Hugh sent the most enormous bouquet of pink roses to my desk at Q&A. An hour later I received irises. An hour after that pink lilies, and then cornflowers. He alternated pink and blue flowers every hour for the entire day.

Sam almost wets herself when I tell her this and I know she's making a mental note to instruct Gilbert that he must do the same when the time comes. This makes me feel dreadful, because my reaction to Hugh's generosity wasn't as enthusiastic. The gesture was ridiculously generous; I couldn't carry them all home and had to give most of them to the secretaries. But besides being ridiculously generous it was in fact just plain ridiculous. Karl guessed that I must be pregnant and cranked the rumor machine into operation, within twenty minutes of the second bouquet. Brett suggested starting a whip-around to buy me a carrycot. I'm surprised Julia missed the furor; she must have been doing some serious drugs the night before and sleeping it off in the boardroom, as is her way. It was all slightly embarrassing, because I hadn't had a chance to discuss my pregnancy with Dean, my boss. He sent me an e-mail demanding to know whether he had to "write me off to the great pool of gaga women on maternity leave." This is probably against some European employment law, and when I pointed out as much to him he succinctly replied, "Bollocks to the garlic-eaters." In the advertising industry a sympathetic employer is one who puts a Tampax machine in the loos.

Besides which, I know that Hugh did exactly the same for Becca when she fell pregnant with both Kate and Tom. I remember her telling me.

"And you are pleased, aren't you?" asks Julia again.

There is a slight, almost indiscernible tension in the air. I should be. I know I should be. I want to be. But can "want" and "should" combined counter the distinct feeling that I'm not?

"Because your car only has two seats," Julia prompts.

"Joseph doesn't do maternity wear," adds Sam.

"It will be the end of your exotic holidays."

"And sex on the stairs."

"And sex, full stop. So, are you?" prods Julia.

And I barely hesitate before I answer, "Absolutely. Thrilled. Absolutely thrilled."

The girls beam at me, reassuring me that I've just hit upon the appropriate answer. And it's probably a good thing that the voice that said I'm "thrilled. Absolutely thrilled" sounded more committed and cheerful than I really am.

13

We spend the rest of the afternoon talking about Sam's wedding, a safe topic for me, the only topic for Sam, and a foray into a foreign country for Julia. Sam is sky-high. Bugger drugs, this is her answer: an emerald and a cluster of diamonds on the third finger of her left hand. She holds her ring up to the window for about the zillionth time today and then turns back to us with a smile as wide as the Eurotunnel.

"Can you believe that I've been engaged for two weeks and two days, a whole three weeks next Thursday."

"Really." Seems a lot longer.

"Where has the time gone? Not so much flown past as rocketed."

I wipe the steamy window of the café and lose myself in the world outside, leaving the burden of conversation to Julia. I don't expect Sam will require too much active participation.

I'm glad I chose the Bluebird because the King's Road always cheers me up. The shops are divine, as are the people who frequent them. Admittedly, they aren't often very polite or smiley, but they look amazing. I'd wager that there's not a man who earns less than £60K, nor a woman who is bigger than a size 10, on the King's Road today.

Except me, of course.

Suddenly the thought isn't as cheering as it usually is.

What is Sam saying now?

"The last couple of weeks have been awash with champagne and goodwill. It's true everyone loves a lover. You only have to drop the slightest hint to your hairdresser that you are newly engaged and suddenly it's all free honey and primrose conditioner, coffees and magazines."

I can always buy my own.

"It's the same in shops—assistants positively crowd around my ring, sizing it up and admiring it."

Wondering how much he thinks she's worth. It's probably just my hormones that won't allow me to be as happy for Sam as she'd like.

As I'd like.

I wish I knew Gilbert a bit better. Perhaps I can persuade her to have a long engagement.

"Would you like to try on my ring? It's lucky, you know; if you twist it around your wedding finger three times you can make a wish," Sam offers.

I notice Julia is looking as sick as I feel. Macabrely, I find this a comfort. I do wish Sam'd stop all this "Wanna be in my gang, my gang" stuff. If I wanted to be married, I would be married, but I wanted Hugh and Hugh's already married. My head suddenly fills with cotton wool. Why would I want to be married? Marriage comes with in-laws, and, in this case, stepchildren. Isn't marriage synonymous with endless sock-washing and family teas? I've never imagined myself married.

But then I've never imagined myself not married, either.

And I already wash his socks.

"I'm almost worn out with celebrating. I wish you'd seen my parents' reaction."

"Pleased, were they?"

"Delighted. Daddy never says much at all, but I could tell by the way he opened his malt whiskey and offered G a cigar that he approved of my choice."

"I bet they have loads in common," says Julia. I snigger and try not to catch her eye as I catch her oblique reference to Gilbert's age. Sam, wrapped in dreams like tissue paper, doesn't catch it either.

"I *was* rather annoyed with Eddie when he commented that Mummy and Daddy had probably spent the money they'd put aside for my wedding as they must have 'given up hope of anyone actually proposing.' " While Sam is doing her best not to appear troubled by her brother's insensitivity I can see indignation burns in her eyes. Quite right. It may be an open secret between her family and friends that she's always been extremely keen to marry and have a family, but it does seem in rather bad taste to mention it in front of Gilbert.

"What did Gilbert say?" asks Julia.

"Oh, G was the perfect gentleman, assuring Eddie that he imagined that 'Samantha must've been fighting off suitors for years,' " and anyway he'd be more than happy to pay for the day of my dreams."

"Samantha?" I ask.

"He calls me Samantha, he prefers it, he thinks it's more sophisticated than Sam."

He's trying to make her sound older, she's trying to make him sound younger—is there hope that they'll collide somewhere in the middle? I feel like a bit part in *Back to the Future*.

"Good for him. I bet that shut baby bruv up," comments Julia. "Who are you having for bridesmaids?" She is obviously angling for an invite. Bloody cheek, she can get in line. Julia's only known Sam a year or so, I've known her a lifetime.

"Well." Sam is suddenly and unusually reticent. She obviously finds this question excruciatingly difficult to answer. Her reticence ensures my absolute undivided attention much more easily than her earlier recital of the order of service had. "Well, there's Connie who I used to work with, my friend Daisy, because I was bridesmaid for her, and I was going to ask both of you," she says, looking at Julia but without looking at me. "But . . ." The but is loud and clear.

"In light of my news."

"Exactly."

"Now, I'm pregnant, it's out of the question." I bite out the words, furious with myself for making it easier for her to slight me. I try to smile and try to look unconcerned. It's not that I desperately want to be a bridesmaid. Just because I'm her oldest and bestest friend. I mean, who wants to dress up in fuchsia and frills?

Me.

Me.

I do.

That's how irrational I am. It's not my fault, it's my hormones.

I smile a brittle smile that is all teeth and that definitely hasn't made it to my eyes. O.K, so there would be a serious possibility that I would look like an Easter egg staggering up the aisle, but I'm her best-friend Easter egg. Sam might want four identical size-10 bridesmaids, but it's not very real, is it? Couldn't she get married after I've given birth? Or not care that I'd look like an Easter egg? She shouldn't see it as me ruining her photos, she should think of it as enhancement—she'd look like Kate Moss in comparison.

Julia tactfully picks up one of the many bridal books that Sam has taken to carrying around with her, *How to Create Your Perfect Wedding Day,* and asks whether it's any good. I know that she couldn't care less, but Sam answers the inquiry as though it was genuine.

"It's very helpful. It tells you all about the order of service and wedding lists and civil services. It's terribly modern, suggesting seating arrangements if the bride or groom's parents have divorced and remarried, up to three times each. And there's a section that you might find useful, George—it outlines the proper etiquette as to whether the groom should mention the unborn child in his speech. It seems to depend upon whether the bump is desperately obvious. It also has suggestions as to where stepchildren should sit. All very interesting stuff." Yeah, right. "And there's a handy wedding planner at the back of the book. It's tear-out, so you can carry the planner around in your handbag. It's extremely useful, timetabling when to send out invites, book cars and order almond favors. There are neat little boxes where you can tick off each task as you complete it, which I've always found very satisfying."

I bet Julia wishes she'd never asked.

My mobile rings, saving me from having to slice out Sam's tongue. It's Hugh. When he hears that we are at the Bluebird Café, he says he'll swing by and pick me up. I'm delighted and don't try very hard to keep the smugness out of my voice when I tell the others his plans. Sam might have the ring but where's Gilbert, hey? At least Hugh actually wants to spend time with me. The wind is somewhat stolen from my sails when Sam announces that Gilbert is busy taking *her* mother to *her* great-aunt's, and she didn't even have to go along. Whichever way I look at this (soppy, wet creep or amazing, gentle man), I have to admit it's the action of a devoted lover.

I leap ahead again on the silent "I have the better deal" poll when Hugh arrives. He looks sweaty and relaxed from his game of squash and unquestionably knicker-dropping gorgeous. I know for a fact that when Sam looks at Gilbert her first thought is not that she must dash to Agent Provocateur and stock up on scanty panties. The sexiest thing that Sam has ever said about G is that "there's many a fine tune to be played on an old fiddle." This is the only reference that Sam has ever made to their sex life. Which is odd, when you think that in the past Sam has always told us about her conquests in such gratifying and gratuitous detail that after her debriefs I always felt like going to confession, and I'm not even Catholic.

I turn my lips to Hugh's (which always look bee-stung tender). He kisses me on the forehead and asks if I've told everyone our news. Establishing that I have, he orders a bottle of Bolly, shunning the house champers that Sam and Julia have been drinking all afternoon. Then he engages Sam in a conversation about bridal magazines. I feel ridiculously smug, even if I can't enjoy the Bolly.

"Aren't they all the same?"

"Not at all. There's *Brides, Brides and Setting up Home, Bride and Groom, Bridal Beauty, Beautiful Bride, Just Brides, For Brides,*

Wedding Day, and *Beautiful Weddings.* You've only flicked through them; if you read them properly, you'd realize that each and every one has its own individual style."

If he read them properly I'd have him committed.

"Doesn't it make you want to take the plunge?" asks Sam. She playfully pokes Hugh in the ribs, and at this point I'd cheerfully kill her.

"What, tie the knot?" he asks.

"Yes."

"Are you oblivious to the connotations? Tie the noose, more like. If you looked up knot in a thesaurus, you'd find 'snarl,' 'tangle,' 'web,' 'difficulty,' 'conundrum.' " Hugh laughs. "Once was enough for me."

I've always thought it's best to know where you stand.

Julia diverts the conversation, but I don't think her intentions are entirely altruistic toward me, more mischievous toward Sam, whom Julia finds too easy a target to resist ridiculing. "It must be a relief for you to actually be able to purchase one of these, sorry, several of these, magazines, Sam."

Sam, bless her, doesn't take offense, but takes the comment at face value and nods enthusiastically. The truth is that for years Sam has visited newsagents and surreptitiously flicked through the glossy pages, fantasizing about flowing white dresses, debating tiara or flowers, agonizing over the cut of the bridesmaids' dresses. She'd almost wear the pages thin with handling. I know this because she once told me that she felt bad about leaving the mags in less than pristine condition for real brides-to-be to buy; but then she comforted herself with the thought that *they were real brides.* Whereas she used to have to wear a ring (that she'd bought for herself in Turkey) on her wedding finger to convince the shop assistant there was serious intent to purchase.

We stay in the Bluebird until Hugh, Sam and Julia are guaranteed hangovers tomorrow, which worries me a bit because I haven't started to prepare for tomorrow's dinner party. I have garlic to peel, chilies to chop and deseed, prawns to marinate . . . Still, at least I won't feel as isolated when my body is convulsed with nausea in the morning. I pay the bill, hail cabs for Sam and for Julia, and then help Hugh back to his car.

Hugh wraps his arms around me, trying to find the place where my waist used to be. I make a small maneuver to avoid his grasp; I'm too podgy to touch. As he's obviously in no fit state to drive, I take the keys. I'm beginning to feel queasy again; which seems unfair, because I haven't eaten anything rich and I've only drunk water all day.

"Kate and Tom are coming over tomorrow," he says.

Whoopee do.

"Really? Had any ideas as to what we should do with them?" I ask, as I lower him into the car. We always do something. I usually arrange tickets for the London Eye, or a visit to an aquarium or the London Zoo, etc. Hugh's kids never sit in and simply watch *Little House on the Prairie,* like I had to when I was a kid. What I really fancy is an ice pop or a Yorkshire pudding.

"No," comments Hugh, "any suggestions?"

"I'll put my mind to it." Between skewering and chilling and chopping and sautéing. I sigh. Tinned peaches with salt and vinegar crisps might help. I don't mean for the dinner party, I mean now.

"Did you buy Kate any Nutella?" asks Hugh.

Ah, Nutella, that's the answer. I screech the Boxster to a halt outside a Cullens, flick on the hazard lights and dash in to buy a jar of Nutella. I'm parked on a double red line but, after all, this is an emergency—I can't wait to get home to eat the jar in the fridge. Hugh initially assumes I'm being particularly solicitous of Kate and his face oozes pride and pleasure, but as soon as I'm back in the car I open the jar and scoop a large dollop onto my finger and cram it into my mouth. Hugh says nothing, but his look of approval dissolves and he stares with open disgust as I continue shovelling.

"Kate prefers peanut butter," I mutter by way of a defense.

14

So, what's on the menu?"

"Coriander-marinated prawns, chili and lemon olives, seared and marinated tuna, and herb-chicken skewers as nibbles. Linguine with sardines to start, monkfish baked with crème fraîche and panzanella for main, and a chocolate soufflé to finish."

"Hope no one is allergic to fish. Have you bought flowers?"

"Yes, but I haven't had chance to put them in vases yet; they're still in a bucket of water in the utility room."

"Oh, George, isn't it a bit warm in there for flowers? They'll open prematurely."

"Yeah, sorry," I mumble as I quickly rub moisturizer into my neck. How old do I look? Twenty-eight? Fifty-five? I can't decide. I looked about twenty-eight this morning, but after a day with Kate and Tom I could probably apply for a bus pass and no questions would be asked. I snatch a pair of tights from my top drawer and start to examine them for runs.

"What are you wearing?" asks Hugh.

"Er, maybe my gray hipsters from Joseph." If I can still get into them.

I rattle through my extensive wardrobe in a hapless attempt to locate a pair of trousers or a skirt that will negotiate my spreading hips and protruding stomach. I gather up four or five outfits and take them into the bathroom. I want to try them on where Hugh can't be a witness. I have a horrible feeling that none of my clothes, selected to emphasize my normally board-flat stomach, will now zip up. Oh God. Stop the sushi bar, I want to get off. Hugh is unaware that I'm trying to carve out some privacy and follows me into the bathroom. He sits on the loo and chatters. This intimacy is lovely, obviously. But I would much prefer it if I could simply *emerge*, dressed, made-up and accessorized. I don't want him witnessing my undignified wrestle with fashion; besides he'd be much better employed in the kitchen. I haven't made the champagne framboise or the manhattans yet, let alone stoned the dates or chilled the mascarpone for pudding.

Eventually I find a Cerruti skirt, which I am able to bribe and tease my corpulent flesh into. It looks O.K with the Carolina Herrera shirt, providing I don't tuck the shirt in but leave it hanging over the groaning zip. I look in the mirror and try to decide whether I'm presentable enough.

"How do I look?" I ask, as I nervously run my hands over the skirt in a pointless attempt to flatten it.

Hugh stands behind me and looks in the mirror at my reflection. He doesn't answer, but starts to kiss my neck and his hands weave their way to my breasts as though on autopilot. In a matter of weeks I've grown from a very attractive 32C cup to a 36DD. Personally, I think my big bosoms are farcical, it's a look that should be confined to postcards sold on Blackpool pier. Luckily, Hugh is more enamored but, less luckily, he shows his appreciation by constantly lurching at his new toys. The thing is, my swollen breasts are so painful that I swear if he tries to touch them again I will not be responsible.

Knifing him is too humane. Why should I be the one left alone to cope with the baby? Kneeing him in the groin or hitting him with the nearest blunt instrument are options. I've often wondered why there's always a copy of the Gideon Bible in the bedside drawer in hotels; now it's clear.

Just kidding.

I check my watch. The guests are due in forty minutes. The wine is still under the stairs and not in the fridge. Hugh kisses my neck and then he turns me toward him and starts to unbutton my shirt. If we make love, the seared and marinated tuna, the herb-chicken skewers, the coriander-marinated prawns and the chili and lemon olives will not be ready in time for the guests' arrival. Hugh's kisses become increasingly intense. Well, we do have some Bombay mix in the cupboard. I could put that in little bowls. That always looks nice.

Forty minutes later the doorbell rings; Hugh is in the shower and yells to me to answer it. There hasn't been time for me to get showered so I greet the guests feeling distinctly shabby. I suppose that it is some consolation that the just-shagged look is undoubtedly better than the just-vomited one I've been wearing so openly of late.

Hugh had said this supper was an opportunity to announce the pregnancy to our friends, so I'm a bit taken aback when I open the door to six smiling faces, none of which I recognize. I comfort myself that everyone seems pleasant enough and I try to think that strangers are just friends not yet made. The strangers who are friends not yet made beam at me and shout out all at once, "Seth," "Piers," "Hedley," "Jasmine," "Eve," "Viv." It's not easy to know who owns which name. I beam back and offer to take their coats. The embarrassment increases substantially when the first chap through the door makes the mistake of assuming I'm Hugh's wife. Hugh canters down the stairs in time to explain, "This isn't Becca, this is George." Which seems to clear the matter up.

"Oh, I am sorry," says Seth/Piers/Hedley, coloring, but the others help him out of the excruciating moment by laughing raucously at his mistake. Which is nice of them.

Hugh leads his guests through to the sitting room and I try not to dwell on how Seth/Piers/Hedley could mistake me for Becca. Indeed, how they even know about Becca's existence. Why would Hugh have a need to talk about Becca to his new work colleagues? Becca is history. I pass around the Bombay mix and then go to the kitchen to pour drinks and check on the food in the oven. Hugh follows me through.

"Have you come to help? You could mix the dressing for the salad," I suggest.

"Oh, I'd best not." He smiles and pulls a face that clearly communicates "Christ-no-don't-let-me-near-I'd-mean-well-but-undoubtedly-cock-it-up-so-sorry-old-thing." Honestly, I think Hugh Grant copied it off my Hugh. "Best leave the cooking to the expert," he adds, then he smiles and pats my bottom. Before I get chance to bask in the glory of the compliment he adds, "Bombay mix, though, darling—what's going on?"

"Well, you distracted me." I smile and try to catch his eye so we can share the joke, but it's hard because he's concentrating on opening a bottle of wine. He shakes his head in genuine bewilderment, then comments, "You need to blend in your foundation along your jawline." And, while it probably isn't relevant, I can't help but remember that, besides the indiscretion with the tennis coach, Becca made the fatal mistake of "letting herself go." Too many coffee mornings and finishing up the kids' plates.

I feel as though I've just been shown the yellow card.

Despite the inauspicious start, the dinner party turns out to be a relative success. I say relative insomuch as the monkfish is delicious and the soufflé is perfect. And I suppose it is a good thing that I can't drink—I'm certainly more efficient when it comes to pouring other people's drinks; in the past Hugh has often mentioned that when I've had one too many I forget to pour the guests drinks and just keep refilling my glass. Which is unforgivable.

But perhaps understandable if our guests are always so mind-numbingly boring.

How can Seth, Hedley and Piers possibly think that talking exclusively about advertising is interesting? I know we are all "in the business," as advertising people like to say (as though there were only one business to be in), but surely their interests extend beyond this single topic. More perplexing still, how could Jasmine, Viv and Eve think that not talking at all, but simply smiling and simpering, is a valid contribution? I cooked for them, didn't I? The least they could do is bring a bottle of wine and an entertaining anecdote. Despite having to keep one eye on the oven timer I try a number of different topics, all to no avail. It's pretty clear, within the first twenty minutes, that a conversation about UN law is going to be a stretch, but they stare equally vacantly as I recall a particularly amusing sketch in the last episode of *South Park*. I then try something more hallowed in the hall of comedy fame and start to recite Monty Python scripts—not a flicker. They don't have opinions on West End plays, whether Posh is too thin, or even the current *Coronation Street* story line. All of my usual conversation starters are met with polite but firm rebuffs.

I'm not sure what I'm doing wrong.

Hugh obviously knows how to communicate with them. Eve laughs at every word he utters, including, "Refill?" and Jasmine practically has an orgasm when he passes the cheese board and asks, "Can I tempt you?"

Still, accepting the fairly dire company I cannot help but wait with bated breath for Hugh's announcement. I've waited throughout starter, main and pud, but he's made no hint. I pour the coffee and pass the brandy, and I'm almost giving up hope that Hugh has remembered what this dinner party is supposed to be about when, suddenly, he goes to the kitchen and comes back with a magnum of champagne. I rush to find the glasses.

"I'd like to make a small announcement." He grins, naturally basking in the fact that he has everyone's attention. He fills the glasses and passes them around. Hugh raises his glass and the light from the candles dances giddily with the bubbles in the champagne. Everyone waits—the chaps are genuinely interested, as they are probably assuming that Hugh is about to announce that R,R&S have won a new account, the girls are affecting polite interest while desperate to feel the champers hit their throats, as champagne always represents an explosion of possibilities.

"Please raise your glasses to toast the beautiful Georgie, who is about to become the mother of my third child."

There is a fractional pause before Seth/Piers/Hedley find their manners. "To Georgie, congratulations," they affirm. I think that as they've had a fair bit to drink it took a moment for the news to sink in, and perhaps it would have been better if Hugh hadn't mentioned that this is his third child, although obviously the first one with me. But then again I can't expect him to ignore Kate and Tom's presence. Viv giggles but does manage "fabulous news." Eve and Jasmine barely mutter "congrats" before quaffing the champers and holding out their glasses for a refill.

"Are you having it privately? At one of the 'too posh to push' hospitals?" asks Hedley.

"I haven't thought about it," I confess, and I turn to Hugh to gauge his opinion. He doesn't comment as he's busy pouring drinks.

"Names, had any thoughts?" asks Eve.

"I like Lizzie," I offer tentatively.

Eve turns to Hugh. "What do you think of Lizzie?" she demands.

"Don't know her, what does she look like?" asks Hugh.

And everyone laughs loudly, as though his joke was absolutely the funniest thing anyone's ever said.

15

Darling, how are you?"

"Fat, sick and tired."

My mother ignores my answer because it's not what she wants to hear, and I'm left wondering if I spoke at all.

"Guess where I am." Before I can take a breath to reply, she continues, "Heathrow. Quick stop before I go to New York. I *have* to shop."

She says that she "has to shop" with the same seriousness that other people reserve for "I have to pass these final exams" or "I have to battle this debilitating disease."

"Cape Town does a marvelous sunset, but it's rather dire when it comes to retail therapy. Let's meet up."

What will I wear? It was a depressing day when I could no longer button my jeans all the way to the top, but it was nothing on today. Today I couldn't tug them past my knees. Every bit of me has metamorphosed. I knew pregnancy was about getting a big stomach; if only it stopped there. It's about big stomachs, big legs, big arms, big bum, big cheeks, big ankles, big bosoms.

And small self-esteem.

I've religiously read the pregnancy book and followed, with some trepidation, its obsession with comparing the fetus to food. It grew in size from a small lime to a peach, and is now the size of a grapefruit. It's puzzling, therefore, that I am the size of a baby elephant.

I look down; my present garb could hardly be described as high fashion. I have resorted to wearing Hugh's clothes because they are the only things in the flat that fit. However, he won't let me wear anything half decent (not since I was sick on his Nicole Farhi flannel trousers), and so I am forced into wearing the stuff that has lurked at the back of his wardrobe since his student days. This morning I was underwhelmed with the choice between a sweatshirt embroidered with his college crest or a Meatloaf T-shirt. To be twinned with tie-dye trousers (purchased in India during his years out) or a green suit with a double-breasted jacket (apparently it was his first interview suit and he kept it for sentimental reasons). I opted for the sweatshirt and hippy trousers and then called in sick—it was easier than washing my lank and unmanageable hair or trying to conceal my sallow skin under layers of foundation. The bags under my eyes are bigger than Posh carries home from Bond Street.

I can't let Jessica see me like this. She has standards.

"I have an invite to an art exhibition at a gallery in Walton Street. Some ghastly new artist. Hermia something or other, I forget. Unlikely to be her real name anyway. Probably be dismal but I have to go, it's Clarissa's daughter's gallery."

Clarissa and my mother have known each other longer than either of them care to remember. Clarissa's daughter Freya and I are roughly the same age and therefore we have endured a lifetime of being compared and contrasted by our highly competitive mothers. Jessica had always been perfectly happy to enter into this comparative game, providing I won. I passed my piano and violin grades before Freya, I thrashed her at gymkhanas, exceeded her marks at school and, while advertising wouldn't have been my mother's first choice of career, she takes comfort in the fact that I earn shed-loads of cash. Things were fine until the mid 1990s, when Freya netted herself a count or duke, or something or other. Jessica never really forgave me. Freya then went on to have three bouncing babies in quick succession. Not that Jessica was in a great hurry to be a grandmother; she wasn't. But she hated, on principle, my coming second to Freya. To add to my mother's irritation, Freya never put on more than eighteen pounds for any one of her pregnancies—I've already put on twelve, even though I'm just fourteen weeks pregnant. Nor was she sick or spotty; she positively glowed and no doubt made shampoo from the placenta. I can't imagine ever being able to retrieve my position.

"Are you having lots of beautiful thoughts to help your baby's karma?" asks Jessica.

"Mostly murderous."

"Darling, I thought you said you wanted this."

"I do want it. I just didn't want it to be so hard."

"Well, you can't have everything."

Apparently not. Even accepting that the pregnancy has left me—what were my words?—"Thrilled, absolutely thrilled," I can't help but think there's a design fault somewhere along the line. Why can't I just go and pick up a baby in John Lewis? The fact that giving birth is supposed to be the most exquisite, enriching, natural and substantive thing a woman can do has passed me by. Zoom, straight by. I don't feel mother-earthy; looking at me no one in their right mind would "give it up" for the fertility gods, or high-five for Aphrodite. And while I concede that it is a miracle that you can hear the baby's heartbeat at this point, I'm less thrilled about the fact that the small intestine had developed and is now capable of producing the contractions that push food through the bowels, reducing me to little more than a public convenience.

"Are you listening to whale music? Freya listened to whale voices throughout her pregnancies and then had water births. Personally, I find that rather gimmicky but from all accounts the children are angels. They all slept through for eight hours by the third night."

"Really."

"Gospel. So I recommend whales."

Well, this little bugger should be all right then, as it's being born to a whale.

"And plenty of exercise, darling. You are still visiting the gym, aren't you? At least three times a week."

Yes, I'm exercising—I've nearly worn through the carpet en route from the settee to the fridge and the loo. I avoid answering the question directly by agreeing to meet at the gallery at six-thirty. This gives me roughly five and a quarter hours to transform myself from grungy hippo to something that she may recognize.

My first stop in the search for my former self is the bathroom. I know that it is paramount to wash and style your hair before you visit the salon. If you go in looking dire the stylist assumes you have low standards and then proceeds to disappoint them. If you go in looking good you have a chance of leaving looking spectacular. In fact, I have a hair-salon league, and it has been known for me to visit a division-two stylist in the morning, just as prep for an afternoon appointment with a premier-league stylist. The same is true of clothes- and shoe-shopping. I've learned that it's vital that you wear your current best outfit to shop for new clothes, and always polish your shoes and check your hosiery is in order if you are shoe-shopping (time permitting have a manicure and pedicure as well). My problem today is that in my present state I look too awful even to visit my beautician, so I resign myself to home treatments. This demands a battle with my lethargy, but will save me the humiliation of being seen by my beautician.

I shower using my Aveda body polish and moisturizing gel. I try to lose myself in the fragrance and strive not to notice that the power shower feels like pins and needles being jabbed into my tender boobs. When I do have thoughts like, "Whose ankles are these?" (mine are slim, toned, worked out and for—the ones on the ends of my legs are podgy, puffy and distended), I attempt to push them from my head. I endeavor not to get too depressed when I finger the place where my hip bone used to make an appearance; the bone is now safely shielded behind inches of flesh. I comfort myself that, while at the moment I simply look fat, in a couple of months I'll look pregnant and that will be a genuine improvement.

Which just goes to show how bad things are.

After I have cleansed, toned, moisturized, loofahed, exfoliated, brushed and pummelled every inch of flesh I have (side benefit: this is a really good upper-arm workout) and shampooed, conditioned, brushed, blow-dried, serumed and rebrushed every hair (including my eyelashes and muff—you really can never be too well-prepared), I am beginning to feel vaguely human. I carefully apply my make-up (to a stranger's face—even my eyes have changed color; the emerald green is now more of a Thames-river-sludge color; surely that's my paranoia).

I consider what to wear. I root through my lingerie drawer, ignoring the flimsy little bras with cups that would no longer support my nipple, never mind a complete breast, and locate a clean boulder-holder. I'm tempted not to bother with knickers at all, on the grounds that, at the moment, they are about as comfortable as sitting on a cheese grater; I'll have to buy the next size up as soon as I have an opportunity. I wish I had a tent to wear but I don't, so I root through my summer clothes, which tend to be less tailored than my winter wardrobe. I try on a number of cashmere cardigans and cotton T-shirts, but the cardigans won't fasten and while some of the T-shirts do stretch across my Pammy Anderson tits, the hem rises at the front, so I look farcical. In the end I opt for a button-up shirt of Hugh's, which is outsize enough to make me look still not quite elephantine. And I settle for a pair of linen trousers. Unsuited to the climate maybe, but they are a step up the sartorial ladder from the tie-dye number or the green interview suit. I grab the car keys and my credit card and set off.

My second stop, in search of my former self, is Bond Street. I automatically dismiss the smart boutiques that sell sexy, skimpy numbers (which are normally the staple of my wardrobe) and I walk right past the large designer stores that don't stock anything bigger than a size 4. Effing fashion fascism. The retail environment may be more relaxing if you don't have to encounter heaving women in the changing rooms, women that are universally depressed about their cellulite thighs and post-pubescent figures, but it's not very real, is it?

I head for a small maternity-wear shop, the stock of which has been described to me as "adorable, perfect, divine," so I'm quite hopeful that I'll be able to buy something glam and appropriate. I'm feeling surprisingly upbeat. It's been a couple of months since I've indulged in any retail therapy and my credit card is feeling as under-exercised as my inner thighs.

After five seconds in the shop I realize that the description of the clothes as "adorable, perfect, divine" omitted the all-important caveat, *"for maternity clothes."* The disappointment is breathtaking. There are row after row of machine-wash trousers with elasticated waists. Of course machine wash is essential, as I discovered by week ten of my pregnancy, when I deposited no fewer than thirty-six outfits at the dry cleaner's. The bill on collection could have bought me a week's holiday in the Caribbean. Of course the trousers have to be elasticated, but does elasticated have to mean ugly? Apparently, yes. There's nothing sheer, fun, flirty or exciting. There's not a single tailored garment. There's nothing high fashion (or even mid fashion). There's nothing catwalk or statement. In summary, there's nothing to get my libidinous glands secreting.

The shop appears crowded. In fact, there are only four other women in the store, but three are pregnant and therefore space is at a premium; it feels similar to Harrods on the first day of the sale, except without the optimism. We don't look at each other, but can't peel our eyes away from one another's bumps. The biggest dollop of resentment rests on the neat bump owned by the woman who is telling the assistant that she really *is* seven months pregnant, and, yes, everybody says that she looks tiny. It's the yoga! The shop assistant also looks genuinely cheerful, but then she's a size 8 and hasn't spent the last few months staring at limescale on the inside of the toilet rim. I take a deep breath and push toward her. I explain that I need something special for a reception plus, with a sigh, I concede that I need some work suits and shirts, casual clothes and nightwear. Why do I feel like I'm losing the school trophy?

The assistant bundles me into a changing room (small) together with a pile of clothes (large and occasionally large enough). The biggest shock is the pouch of material hidden in the front panels of the trousers; surely my stomach will never fill those excess yards. I try the trousers on and discover that they are too snug already and I need the next size up. The colors are drab, mostly beige, which I presume is selected for its camouflage properties; I suppose I should be grateful that there are no polka dots in sight. The "special" outfit the assistant suggests is a black Empire-line, on-the-knee dress. Despite the fact that it has sequins around the neckline, it appears promising. And, while these clothes are obviously not a patch on anything Alberta Ferretti, Givenchy Couture or Marc Jacobs would produce, in the end I buy all the things she gives me to try on—just because they fasten right to the top. Relieved, I wait for my credit card to clear. It astounds me that while the fabrics, tailoring, designs and names don't match my usual purchases the prices are about the same. The assistant smiles as she hands me the bags; obviously she has no conscience about fleecing the deformed.

My third stop is the hairdresser's. My stylist is very sympathetic. "Darling, lank, greasy hair is to be expected. Be thankful you don't have a mustache." The floor stubbornly refuses to open and swallow me up, so there is nothing I can do except accept a herbal tea and sit through the catalog of horror stories about pregnancy that the shampoo girl, my color technician and stylist all insist on relaying.

At six-thirty on the dot, my mother's cab pulls up outside the gallery. I watch her hand over the correct money for the fare and tip, pull a comb through her hair and snap open a compact case so that she can check her reflection. I quickly turn to the gallery window, to check (as taught at the breast) that my teeth aren't smeared with lipstick. My reflection isn't bad, *considering I'm pregnant*. It's been a lot of effort, but the outfit and blow-dry works, I think. I look . . . pleasant. Jessica will be pleased.

Jessica hops out of the cab and almost walks straight past me. I stop her by leaning in for an air kiss.

"Georgina?" she demands, lifting her sunglasses onto the top of her head (an unnecessary accessory as it's February and the chance of seeing the sun in the U.K. within the next five months is slim). "Georgina," she repeats, not quite believing her own eyes.

I smile hesitantly.

"We'll have to do something with your hair."

16

It's the kind of party that I adore, or used to. It's obvious to me from the moment I walk through the door that I'm not going to enjoy myself. The gallery is huge and white, with a polished wooden floor. There are two or, tops, three pieces of art hanging on the wall. They are very modern, mostly solid blocks of color. If they have a meaning it passes me by. Heaving crowds of shadowy people try to compensate for the empty walls and empty pictures.

"What did you say the name of the artist is?" I ask Jessica.

Jessica shrugs. "Some Italian woman—I forget."

"Well, she is certainly very well connected." I nod around at the guests. "All of London's Great and Good are here."

"Or at least those who like to consider themselves to be so," adds Jessica haughtily. She prides herself on never being impressed.

"Isn't that Jemima Khan?" I ask, genuinely thrilled.

"Yes—don't stare. Note, Georgina, she has two sons and has retained her figure."

I sigh, and point out someone who looks a lot like Elton John; no one can accuse him of keeping his figure. To describe the guest list in the vaguest terms, there are a number of politicians, TV celebs, journalists, and a liberal scattering of lords and ladies, marquesses and marchionesses, barons and baronesses. To be specific, there is every wealthy, powerful, jowly man in London and every beautiful, scarecrow-thin, peroxide woman. My black sequined number suddenly seems woefully inadequate. Between us, my mother and I know, at least by sight, nearly every guest, and we are intimately acquainted with a respectable number. So why am I standing alone with only the peanut bowl for company?

I survey the champagne-swilling and vol-au-vent-eating room (the vol-au-vents are filled with goat's cheese or Parma ham, so I can't indulge), and wonder who I should speak to.

"This one represents the legitimacy of death." A platinum-blond, skeletal woman is staring at a red square and a black rectangle. Her companion, equally skinny but with titian hair, nods and comments, "A superb depiction, the very epitome of the lawfulness of dissolution."

Actually, it's still a red square and a black rectangle. I ponder their words, trying to make sense of them and then I decide I can't; they don't make sense. The words, like the pictures, mean nothing. The skeletal women may or may not know that their words mean nothing; they may or may not care that their words mean nothing. I suspect their real reason for being at the gallery today is to be seen, and if they can also manage to spout a bit of nonsense, which is mistaken for a profundity, all the better.

I could talk to Patsy Kensit's agent; he's always good for a natter. I suppose I should congratulate the artist and tell Freya how beautiful her gallery is. I decide against this when Jessica announces Freya's expecting her fourth child.

"Really. Is she due much after me?" I ask.

"Six weeks before you," says Jessica, not even bothering to hide her flames of fury (ignited by her competitive streak, and well and truly fanned because it's a competition she's already lost). "You can't tell, can you?" she adds.

I glance in Freya's direction. No, you can't tell. Her stomach is flatter than a two-day-old bottle of Veuve Clicquot. Why does my mother want to torture me in this manner? Why does she hate me? Why did she give birth to me? Why did Clarissa give birth to Freya? Why did Freya have to get pregnant at the same time as me? Why am I fat? Oh, back there again. I note that, as with Freya's other three pregnancies, her skin is amazing and her hair is growing madly, I've never seen it so long. She looks terrific.

"I chatted to her on the phone earlier today," comments Jessica. "She was so calm about this party and the exhibition. She's definitely more serene than I have ever known her to be."

We can assume a comatose state, then, because Freya is normally so cool that she can chill a bottle of Chardonnay with a single glance. But why? Why isn't she hostage to the roller-coaster ride that leaves me feeling delighted, bitter, blissed, blistering, all in as many minutes? I can't resist twisting the knife. "Was she sick a lot in the first few months?"

"If she was she didn't mention it," Jessica admits.

"Listless? Unable to concentrate?"

"No."

"Sweaty feet?"

"Georgina! As if anyone ever talks about such things." Actually pregnant women do, and about excess hair growth, and skin flaps and loose vaginas, among many things. I've forgotten what passes as an acceptable level of familiarity.

"Hemorrhoids?" I ask, hopefully.

"What are hemorrhoids?"

"Piles." I blush. The English term is much more disgusting than the U.S. one.

"Oh, goodness, Georgina, is there any call for you to be so bestial? Don't tell me you have piles."

"Not me, no. But some women do get them," I lie hastily.

"Oh, there was one thing."

"Yes?" I hope for a grim morsel of consolation.

"She says her nails are growing at an extraordinary rate and she's spending a fortune on extra manicures."

Big shame.

It's obvious that Freya is having the pregnancy that was intended for me.

I can't help but think that pregnancy is some sort of device to expose me. To show me up for what I am (a five and a half out of ten), not what I've become (the quintessential twenty-first-century woman).

Desperately, I try to find someone else to talk to who will serve as a diversion. Is that thingy? Oh, what's her name? She won the Barclays Businesswoman of the Year Award last year. I went to her wedding, so I should be able to remember her name, it's err . . . thingy . . . It can't be her, can it? Has she lost weight? She can't have, she had none to lose. I smile at her. It's the smile I've perfected to ensure that if she does cut me dead then I can catch the eye of a passing waiter and take a glass of champagne, thus not losing face. She throws back a half smile, betraying that she can't quite place me, then quickly (but not quickly enough) breaks into a genuine grin.

"George, darling, how lovely to see you." Air kiss, air kiss.

"You know Jessica." It's as near as I can get to an introduction, as I still can't remember her name. Bloody pregnancy spongie-brain.

"Of course."

They smile and shake hands.

"I almost failed to recognize you." The words are out of Ms. Barclays Businesswoman of the Year's mouth before she can calculate their damage. The thing is, she's quite a decent woman and wouldn't deliberately hurt me. She blushes. "You're blooming." We both know this is a lie, especially when she adds, "A spring baby, how adorable. I think you are so brave coming out. When I was reaching the end of my pregnancy I wouldn't be seen dead."

The baby isn't due until the end of August. I don't say as much but instead mutter something unconvincing about water retention.

"But you are well, generally?"

"Oh yes, absolutely fine. We're thrilled."

She nods, smiles, looks over my shoulder and then makes her excuses and goes on to find someone more useful to talk to.

"Slept with one of the judges to get that award," comments my mother loyally but untruthfully.

It's not accurate to say that everyone fails to recognize me; some do, and these ghouls take great delight in swarming in for a closer look—my size can be established from a distance, but the poor condition of my skin can only be vouched for on near inspection.

"Darling." Air kiss, air kiss. "You look so well."

Everyone knows that "well" is a deliberately facile code to crack. It means anything on the scale from plump, fleshy, corpulent, chubby, obese, right through to lard-ass.

"I didn't even have an inkling that you were married, let alone pregnant," smiles Mindy, a vague acquaintance of mine whom I have bumped into at several parties over the years.

"And, Mindy darling, how is your husband? Remind me, is this number three or number four?" asks Jessica, the very picture of innocence. She draws Mindy to one side and whispers, "Tell me, do you recycle your gowns?"

"George, sweetie. I see you are pregnant. How very year 2000. It's not like you to be so appallingly behind the times," smiles Dulcie. It's true. At least if I'd had a baby in 2000 I'd have been in good company. Last year everyone was at it—Madonna, Cherie Blair, Catherine Zeta Jones, even Zoë Ball managed to make the deadline. Having a baby in 2001 obviously isn't a fashion statement; it's simply a contraceptive gaffe and no amount of insisting on my part that we are thrilled will convince otherwise.

"Dulcie, darling, have you seen the 'art,' that's with an 'f.' Absolutely appalling, entirely emperor's new clothes, don't you think?"

Dulcie looks furious. "Actually, you may not be aware, but Hermia Vicci is my partner."

My mother flashes one of her most charming and flirtatious smiles. "Oh, I do apologize." The Machiavellian smile almost convinces me that she's sorry. Almost. "What do I know? I'm sure she'll be an enormous hit." We move on.

My mother is reassuringly rude throughout the evening, she sends back the champagne, insisting it is Asti Spumante, orders Krug for herself and cranberry juice for me. On my behalf she bats back the slights, the snubs and implied insults like the true pro she is. She also insists that we circulate constantly and fires instructions at me such as "chin up," and "don't let that smile falter, not for a nanosecond."

I repeat, no fewer than fourteen times, that I'm "thrilled, absolutely thrilled." It's an exhausting evening but I'm grateful.

We find the time between vol-au-vents and catty comments to catch up on the family news. I establish that my father is accompanying Jessica on this shopping trip to New York and is currently preparing himself and his credit cards for the inevitable battering by spending a restful evening at his gentlemen's club. My brother is pursuing the unlikely profession of DJ; Jessica comforts herself with the fact that it is no more unlikely than all the other professions he's tried since being sent down from Durham ten years ago. He's been a film extra, a musician, a car mechanic and a gardener, to her certain knowledge. A "courier" in South America, and an "escort" in Las Vegas, to mine.

"And that thing with the cameras, how did that go?" I have no idea what Jessica means. She elaborates, "What's it called? The scan."

"Oh, it's tomorrow."

"Do you want me to come along?"

"I thought you were flying out tomorrow."

"I am, but I can change it if need be."

I'm touched. "No, don't worry. I'm sure Hugh will be coming along."

"I hope it's all good news. Not twins." My mother grins mischievously.

At eight-thirty Jessica concedes that I've done enough. She puts me in a taxi and comments, "Now that wasn't too bad, was it?"

It was bloody awful but, because we both know it, neither of us is prepared to admit it. I wind the cab window down and ask, "Did I ever like those people?"

"I doubt it," she smiles.

I catch her hand and squeeze it. "Thanks, Jessica."

She returns the squeeze. "That's what mothers are for, George."

17

Week 12

It is important to involve your partner in the miracle that is happening in your body. He can be a big support to you. This can be a time of communication and growth in your relationship. But you may have to work a little to make your partner feel that he is part of what is happening to you.

More jobs, I sniff resentfully.

Hugh can't join me for the scan; he's too busy. I try to understand, he is very important. And, anyway, who needs all that hand-holding nonsense?

Every other pregnant woman in the room, apparently.

I hate doctors' waiting rooms. They are so embarrassing. The lack of reading matter forces you to notice the other patients. (I don't count dog-eared copies of *Hello!* magazine as reading matter; was there ever anything charming about puff-ball skirts?) A number of the patients are in an even more distressing state than me. Their arms are hanging off, or they are sneezing so much that they've obviously got bubonic plague. I try not to sit too close to anyone else in case I leave the surgery with something awful. Really, couldn't they have made an effort? I have. I've put on a pair of trousers that fasten and I've wiped the puke off my shoes. After all, the poor man has trained long and hard to get where he is now,

and he doesn't want to have to look in more dirty or badly presented crevices than absolutely necessary. Couldn't they have
brushed their hair, taken off their slippers, closed their mouths?
What does it take to apply a little bit of lipstick? Also, I find those
posters of rotting vages completely offensive.

I had my tonsils taken out privately. In Harley Street everything is a little more discreet. The walls are white, and the only
things hanging are tasteful reproductions of Monet's waterlilies.
All the patients were immaculately presented and wore the uniform of the rich: white shirts tucked into dark jeans, lots of gold
jewelry, flat navy shoes, and sunglasses resting on top of recently
highlighted hair (this was just the men).

It's a straightforward procedure, the scan. Once you're past the
full bladder/empty bladder dilemma. The books say a full bladder
is necessary for best pictorial results. As usual, the books are woefully out of date. The doctors now use cameras that prefer not to
have a filter of urine between lens and alien, but I only discover
this after having kept my legs crossed for three hours in the waiting
room. Then I endure the indignity of emptying my bladder in an
aluminum loo while the midwife waits for me next door; she has
nothing more to do than listen to my wee splash against the pan.
Oh joy. Then she puts a freezing cream on my stomach and rubs a
microphone-like device over the Mount Everest bulge.

It's amazing.

The alien thingy, it's *amazing*. I'm surprised that, at the right
angle, the alien thingy looks recognizably human. I can definitely
make out its head bent over its chest, and I can see its arms and
legs.

It can swim.

And mine is particularly athletic.

18

Increasingly, work is hell. I work in a glass office that looks out onto long rows of desks, piled high with PCs, identical except for the screen savers. The thirty-odd account handlers sit, stand and shout at each other from these desks for eight hours a day and more. This used to be my idea of heaven. I can see who and what is coming and going on, up and down. However, now that the thing coming up is my breakfast, the open-plan structure is a disaster.

Brett, Karl and Drew charge into my office and catch me stuffing a cream-cheese bagel into my mouth.

"You shouldn't be eating that," comments Brett. I'm not sure if he means because it's unpasteurized cheese or because I'm the size of a house.

Ostensibly, we're meeting to discuss the agenda for our strategy meeting for our pitch meeting, for a toilet-tissue account. It's a high-profile pitch as this business is worth a media spend of an astounding six million: the agency would take approximately 10 percent of that in revenue.

However, the boys have little interest in "Puppy Salience," "Puppy Love" or "Puppy Metaphor," the attributes the existing incumbent agency exploits so magnificently. They're irked that I won't play Fantasy Football but insist on sticking to the point instead.

"The client says he considers the current ads to be strategically sound," I offer.

"He means boring," Karl dismisses.

True, he probably does; traditionally this is a business where one thing is said and something altogether different is meant, but the ritual of at least appearing to believe what is said must be observed.

"And well branded," I add.

"He means very boring," dismisses Brett. As Creative Director he sees branding as a heinous crime—"Intrusive branding is diametrically opposed to creativity." The others make noises of agreement.

"It's imperative that we remember that creating, fashioning, forming a brand, a mark of ownership, a seal, a *name*, can be a near-religious experience. A veritable adventure," comments Drew, as he nods sagely.

Everyone in the room nods too, except me. I feel as though I'm back in Freya's art gallery. I'm not sure he's said anything at all but, if he has, he's just said the opposite to Brett, so why is Brett nodding? There's a board at one end of the room on which Karl has written the words *Prominence, Commotion, Style, Elegance, Divertissement, Well-being, Negotiate, Personal, Amour, Culture* and *Accessibility.* We all stare at the wash-down whiteboard and nod some more. The words are not relevant to our discussion. It's an old trick—whenever we meet we write some hocus-pocus on the board. In this way we are free to discuss the fact that Dave in production is shagging Cindy, the receptionist, or whether a Stella Artois is a cleaner drink than a Budweiser Budvar, while giving the impression that we are brainstorming the brand's properties. I wonder why Dean has never noticed that it's always the same words, irrespective of whether we are supposed to be branding an insurance company or a loo roll.

"Look, this pitch doesn't have to be so hard," grumbles Karl. "We'll end up doing what we always do. Show a few of the ads we've made for other clients, make some short, pithy generalizations, show some dull charts demonstrating that we've done the number-crunching, add a line or two "in summary," and then present the creative solution, which is all anyone is ever interested in anyway."

I sigh a lament at his cavalier attitude, and a little bit of me also sighs because he's probably right.

"Don't you miss the days when we just sent George in, and she so set their rocks on fire that it didn't matter what she said?" teases Brett.

I treat him to a weary look.

After about fifteen minutes, it's decided that the best plan is to have a *pre*-meeting to discuss the long list of possible agenda items and narrow them down and *then* have a meeting to discuss the agenda for our strategy meeting for our pitch meeting, for the toilet-tissue account. It's agreed that the best time for this meeting is tomorrow lunchtime, and the best venue is Mezzo restaurant. The current meeting is adjourned and the boys go back to their offices feeling that they've done a good day's work.

I'm less confident.

I often think that I chose the wrong career. Well, rather, I ended up in the wrong career. "Chose" is far too active a verb to describe how I ended up in advertising. I suppose I should be grateful that Hugh wasn't interested in joining NASA or the armed forces. Although there would have been an undeniable cachet telling people at parties that I was an astrophysicist and Hugh certainly would have looked cute in uniform. Advertising is meant to be a laugh, everyone in the industry knows that. The only people that ever take advertising seriously are the moral brigade, who regularly object to ads for underwear. Everyone else sees the job for what it is; a great way to avoid growing up but at the same time making more money than you would make if, say, you'd stayed on at university to do a PhD.

Not me.

I haven't got the *je ne sais quoi*. I'm simply not chilled. I try to be (which is certainly my first mistake). I really *wish* I could perfect that fly-by-the-seat-of-my-pants-write-the-strategy-in-the-lift-on-the-way-up-to-the-clients'-office-put-the-whizz-in-spin-doctor-bullshitter approach. But I can't. I really do think it's immoral to fill in your own questionnaires as a basis to recommending a creative direction to the client, call it research and charge them thirty grand for the pleasure. I can't agree that the only work that is ever "on strategy" is the work created by those who can advance my career. Nor is my best friend Alberto, the office administrator, just because he has the keys to the stationery cupboard and the corporate drinks fridge (to be honest, he's a git).

I work really hard to keep my head above water. I am the only person I know in the industry who has actually read Levitt, Kotler, Ansoff and Porter. I know the difference between sales volume, net sales volume, sterling sales at RSP, gross contribution, net contribution and break-even point. Moreover, I do care about our clients' profit margins. I've worked on creative award-winning businesses. I've worked with the world's best photographers, directors and film editors. I've helped create brand equity on a number of household names. I don't simply use acronyms such as ECR, FMCG, FMPG and KVI as a way of confusing the person I'm presenting to; I use them because these words are basic currency. I understand the importance of agency culture, a fat expense account and a big Christmas party. I'm firm but fair with all my staff and I never resort to political shafting. Yet, despite all this, I live every day thinking someone is going to find me out.

Find out that I'm not effortlessly chic, but that I spend half my salary on face creams and half my life in the beautician's. That my personal trainer terrifies me, that my personal shopper exploits me, that I don't even like avocado, never mind caviar, and, worse still, I don't even know the proper pronunciation of Renaud Pellegrino. I mean, is it "green-o" or "grin-o?"

It's a terrifying way to live.

The people I work with are entirely Jekyll and Hyde. Affable and amusing company at dinner parties, unscrupulous, greedy and insecure during office hours. A noxious cocktail. It strikes me that some of the most dangerous people in London work in advertising. It's populated by those who were born at the end of the baby boom and then suffered over a decade of Thatcher rule—how can they be anything but self-centered and overly ambitious? Therefore my falling pregnant, and suddenly doing convincing impressions of a dizzy Sigourney Weaver from *Alien,* is seen by most as a huge opportunity to supplant me.

Returning from my lunch hour (spent in the bathroom), I find the office deserted.

"Where is everyone?" I ask Julia. I notice that there is a huge box of Jelly Belly Beans on her desk. Without waiting for an invitation I start to hoover them up, red ones first.

"Help yourself," smiles Julia. Immediately guilty, I try to resist by clasping my hands behind my back. I last about four seconds before I start to eat the lime ones. The thing is, all I want to do is eat. Eat and eat and eat and eat. Anything. Everything. I just want to stuff food into my mouth and chew it very quickly so I can stuff something new into my mouth. I eat as though I want to compensate, in the next fifteen minutes, for nearly fourteen years of starving.

Thinking about it, this is absolutely the case.

"Didn't you get the memo? Some speaker is over from the U.S. office. A three-line whip that everyone attends."

Funny, no one mentioned an imperative meeting when we were discussing diaries this morning, not Brett, nor Karl, nor Drew. Or maybe not so funny.

"No, I didn't get the memo." I resist adding that, as my number two, it is Julia's responsibility to see that I do get memos and that important meetings are put in my diary. It's so tricky managing a colleague/friend relationship. She's unconcerned, more involved in applying another coat of nail varnish. Julia is not ambitious. She's "in advertising" simply because she spent so long in bars in Soho that a number of people assumed she already had a job in some agency or other and eventually she was "headhunted" from a job she didn't have into this one, a job she barely does. She's extremely bright, but has a trust fund and is too wealthy to care about actually doing the job well.

"You should have gone, there's free sandwiches and champagne," she comments.

Besides the free lunch I should have gone. It turns out that the "speaker" from the U.S. office is none other than the new Global Chief Executive, Philip Marx. He recently inherited the role after a rather savage and sleazy power struggle. The entire corporation was split into two rival camps of supporters. Anyone with any commercial and survival instinct knows that it's career suicide not to be seen to be endorsing, and celebrating with, Marx. The war cry of the office is "the best man won." Not because Marx is the best man for the job, but because he won. *Fuck.*

"Why aren't you there?" I demand. Her absence combined with mine will be interpreted as departmental mutiny.

"I offered to man the phones." At that point a phone rings. Julia ignores it, as she is busy blow-drying her nails.

"Any messages, then?" I ask but I'm not hopeful.

"Er, yeah, there was one." She roots around tentatively on her desk; it's a mass of cosmetics, but there are one or two pieces of paper interspersed with the mess. "Here."

She waves a Post-it note triumphantly. However, on reading the message it's about as clear as the Enigma code.

"Who's Gar?" I ask. Apparently he wants me to call him.

"AAR," she clarifies.

The Advertising Agency Register. The AAR contacts me when Q&A have made it on to a pitch list. This is good news, I suppose, although frankly I'm so stretched with my current workload that getting onto another pitch list is a mixed blessing. To be accurate, it's not that my workload has increased at all, it's just that I can't tackle my in-tray when my head is down the loo.

I sit at my desk and hope that no one has noticed my non-attendance. Fifteen minutes later everyone starts to file out of the boardroom and back to their seats.

"Oh, Georgina, you *are* here," says Karl. "We thought you'd gone shopping."

Bastard.

"When have you ever known me to go shopping at lunchtime?" I smile.

Karl raises his eyebrows. A gesture that succinctly implies, to anyone taking an interest, that women simply can't help themselves and, important business meeting or not, we will be out abusing the plastic. I adore shopping but I've never, ever shopped on company time.

"I was expecting an important phone call, I couldn't leave my desk," I lie.

"Really," smiles Karl. "Shame. Interesting meeting. You were missed. Marx even sent someone to look for you."

Bugger. I mutter something about being in the loo at the time and decide not to tell Karl that he has a cress seed stuck between his teeth.

Things go from bad to worse when that afternoon, unable to fight the overwhelming fatigue of pregnancy, I twice fall asleep at my desk, only being brought back to consciousness by banging my head on my computer screen. Dean notices my fiery ambition has been dampened to smoldering embers when during a team meeting I lose my train of thought three times. On the fourth occasion he leaves the room without even excusing himself. By doing so he makes it clear I'm wasting his time.

I call Hugh because I need to be soothed by his sympathetic tones.

"Can you talk?" I ask, as I know how irritating it is to be called at work when you are right in the middle of something tricky.

"Not a good time, Babes, is it important?"

To me, yes. "Nothing that can't wait until this evening," I mutter and carefully place the phone back in the cradle. I pick the phone up again, just to check, but the line is dead and the dead tone isn't in the slightest bit sympathetic.

At six the computers are slowly switched off as thoughts turn toward cool lagers. Most people are bushed with the exertion of trying to impress Philip Marx. I'm bushed with the exertion of trying to stay awake.

"Drew, fancy a beer?" asks Karl.

"Ever known me to say no?"

"Brett?"

"Damn right, I do."

"Where are we going?" I ask. The silence can be heard in Asia.

"Look, Georgie, no offense, Babes, but we're planning on a bit of a lads' night. No skirt," explains Karl. "I'm sure you understand."

"Sure," I smile, "I understand." And I do. It's crystal clear. "I have plans, anyway. I'd have had to rearrange."

"Of course you do. See you tomorrow. Enjoy. Take care."

He throws out a couple more facile, insincere comforters and they leave. Karl knows I haven't got plans tonight as plainly as he knows that I always attend the boys' nights out in the local pub, where all the real wheeling and dealing is conducted. He doesn't give a damn if I enjoy my evening or if I take care. These platitudes are spun to the losers and no-mates simply as a conversational salve. Finding myself abruptly excluded from the high-powered meetings in the boardroom is serious; exclusion from high-jinks meetings in the pub is the signing of my death warrant. If I don't receive the latest hints and tips, as I have always done in the past, my job (as much dependent upon rumor as on share-of-voice reports) will become increasingly difficult. Just fifteen weeks pregnant and already I'm history.

I should fight back. I should rally, reassemble, charge and counterattack. And I would. I certainly would. I've done it before. Only now I can't think how. My mind is a fog.

The best thing is for me to have an early night and to get in at the crack of dawn tomorrow morning to strategize. I mustn't get this out of proportion; after all it's not as though I've received my P45 in the internal mail.

Julia is reapplying her lipstick. It's unlike her to stay a minute after five-thirty. She must be going somewhere special.

"Going somewhere funky?" I ask, half-wondering if she'll invite me along. We haven't been out together for a couple of weeks, in fact since the afternoon at the Bluebird. While I do feel a bit guilty for neglecting our social life (it's always me that arranges the nights out), right now clubbing is so low down on my agenda it doesn't even make it to AOB.

"Nowhere special. Just out with Karl and the boys for a drink." She snaps her bag and her smile closed.

I see.

19

I can't consider waiting at a bus or Tube stop so I decide to jump in a cab. I know this is a big mistake when I have to endure a solid twenty-minutes monologue on foreign and domestic policy according to Mr. Cabby. None of it is original or enlightened; most of it is offensive. Although when I think about it carefully, he's not saying anything I haven't heard before and it's never bothered me in the past. But, suddenly, I object to the barely disguised bigotry; it's not made any more acceptable just because it appears in most of our national newspapers. The cab driver puts me in mind of the difficult man in the bookshop. He makes me think that however much Milton sterilizing fluid I use this world will never be clean enough to bring my baby into. I'm not in a good mood. It's not my idea of fun to crawl through town at about three miles per hour, breathing in toxic fumes. It amazes me that even at this speed he can manage to brake so suddenly that I am flung from the backseat and only just prevent bashing my head on the glass partition by rolling into the brace position. While there I fall asleep; when I wake up the meter reads nearly forty quid, even though ordinarily the journey home costs me seven. I know the cab driver has been driving around in circles, taking advantage of my chronic fatigue. I tell him so but he argues that the traffic was bad. I know he knows I don't believe him but I'm too strung out to argue. The only form of protest I have available to me is to refuse to leave a tip.

I tip him.

And then stumble out of the cab and into my flat, dazed with the humiliation of being so weak as to accept his bullshit.

I don't bother to hang up my coat but fling it over the back of a chair. I pull myself up the stairs and into the bedroom. I start to take off my suit and shirt. My breasts ache and then bounce about as I release them from my boulder-holder bra. There's a limited range in maternity underwear—big knickers, big bras and not a suspender belt to be had, not for lust nor riches; all of it is less aesthetically pleasing than the Hunchback of Notre Dame's vest. My boobs finally settle down long enough for me to examine the red welts where my engorged flesh, swollen to unrecognizable proportions, has chafed against the generous elastic straps.

Oh God, I forgot to call AAR. I must do that first thing tomorrow. Sod it. There's nothing for it. I can't fight it. I struggle out of the rest of my clothes, rummage around Hugh's drawers for a roomy T-shirt and, although it's not yet seven, I slip between the cool cotton sheets.

To sleep.

I wake up to see Hugh rip off his tie; too impatient to unfasten the buttons on his shirt, he removes it by seizing it at the back of the neck and hauling it over his head in one swift efficient movement. It's almost as though he doesn't like having his face covered by the shirt in case he misses anything. The muscles in his back and shoulders flex tantalizingly. My heart leaps to my throat and I have to swallow it back down again. He pulls off his trousers and boxers, throws his socks into a corner of the room and slips between the covers.

"This is a nice surprise. What are you doing home so early?" he asks.

I'm a no-mark, a has-been, a loser. I say that only in my head because if I say it out loud it might ring too true. His hands are already running up my thighs; he encounters the T-shirt and halts. "Oh."

Oh indeed.

I'm a girl with serious aspirations to glamour. In all the time we've been together, Hugh has never seen me in anything other than designer underwear. If I bother with nightwear at all, it is always silk. This is not because I keep my best underwear for the nights when I think we'll have sex; I simply don't have anything other than sexy stuff. My wearing an outsize cotton T-shirt in bed is the equivalent to other women leaving a note that reads, "Your dinner is in the dog." Finding me in bed early of an evening, Hugh had obviously thought I was requesting a steamy session.

Wrong.

Very wrong. My libido has absconded. It is possibly nestling under my many acres of stomach. How can I feel sexy when my body is a pincushion and a professional producer of urine?

I grab his wandering hand and force him into conversation. "How was your day?"

"Fine; yours?" He doesn't care. He wriggles so that he can start to caress my hair with his left hand. I consider clutching his hand in my vise-like grip, but then I notice that the caresses feel nice. If only he'd leave it at that, then I could relax. But I know that the hair-caressing stunt is just to lull me into a false sense of security, then he'll move in on my tits.

"Terrible." I start to tell him about missing Philip Marx's introduction meeting and then the scene with my boss during the team meeting. Ours is a small industry so Hugh knows Dean and therefore tries to reassure me.

"Dean is known for conducting his meetings like that, leaving before they are over, taking calls in the middle, it's a way of reminding everyone how important he is."

"No, it was more sinister than that, he was marking my card."

"You're overreacting, it's your hormones. Your body is going through a lot of remarkable changes right now. That's why you are being so extreme, tearful, overly sensitive and moody." Suddenly he's turned into Dr. Hilary Jones, but even more patronizing.

I glare at him but don't reply. Instead I reach for my week-by-week guide. I almost find it funny when I read that in week fifteen "growth continues to be rapid, but the skin is very thin." I can't help but be concerned that the skin may have to toughen up, with Hugh as a father. Both mine and the baby's. Apparently its entire body is covered in a fine hair called lanugo. Yet more similarities. I nudge the duvet surreptitiously and try to quickly appraise my body without drawing Hugh's attention. Besides the great mass that is my stomach, the other obvious sign of my pregnancy is that my bikini line has hit my knees. This entire process is designed to humiliate.

Hugh starts to massage my neck. It's pointless, I'm so tense it feels like he's nipping me. I tell him about barfing on my keyboard. His eyes glaze over and I don't blame him, I'm boring myself. In an effort to rediscover the woman I consider myself to be I put down the book and give way to his caresses. I'm pretty sure a really substantial orgasm will make me feel at one with the world again.

Sex is unworkable.

Hopeless.

However hard I try I cannot summon up the tiniest residue of desire. Even when I try to stay absolutely still my stomach thinks it's competing in a gymkhana. I feel entirely separate and alone. Hugh's hand runs up and down my thigh but it feels as though he is peeling off my skin. He tries to kiss my stomach, which causes me to shudder; I don't want him to touch the squelchy bits. Bastard lying maternity books say I "might be suffering some slight discomfort in the breasts, a tingling sensation"—in reality they feel as though they're being tackled by the entire national rugby team, so they are entirely off-limits. He interprets my brushing him away and dismissing foreplay as an indication that I want a quickie. I suppose I do, in as much as I certainly don't want to prolong this.

I'm ashamed of my loss of desire and so hide it by faking orgasm. This is the first time in my life that I've ever faked and it's with the man I love more than myself. Where's the sense in that? I'm not even very good at faking it. I find myself impersonating people on TV pretending to orgasm and not imitating my own.

"God, yes, yes, yes. Oh that's it. Don't stop. Oh wow. Oh angel."

Hugh sees through me and this hurts both of us equally. He rolls away from me, picks up a packet of cigarettes and then puts them down again. He does this in an extremely pointed manner. He wants me to note his huge sacrifice. But I don't feel grateful that he's restricting his smoking because I know he can still drink whiskey.

"Is this still about Valentine's Day, Georgina?"

He means the fact that he forgot Valentine's Day and had to resort to buying me a bunch of carnations from the local garage, the type of bouquet that makes a dusty box of Milk Tray look positively thoughtful.

"I just don't feel in the mood, that's all. I'm not well," I mumble. "It's ironic that I feel permanently premenstrual when in fact that's something I simply am not." I try to smile.

"Well, that's something to be pleased about, isn't it?" he says encouragingly. "No more periods for months. You've always grumbled about your periods. You said that they were the worst plague inflicted on womankind."

I'm now having a rethink but I don't say as much.

"I'm sorry about Valentine's Day. And I'm sorry I've been working such long hours. I'm very involved in . . ." I tune out. Again, it's unprecedented but I'm not sure I care what's going on in Hugh's office. I only start to listen again when I hear the words, "You need a holiday."

Love.

Incredible, wonderful love.

Yes, yes, I do. Somewhere glamorous, somewhere peaceful, somewhere hot. The Caribbean? The Maldives?

"We should go away with the kids." Hugh turns to me, enthusiasm oozing out of every pore. "Why didn't I think of it earlier? We can tell them about the baby."

Pig.

Misogynistic, chauvinistic pig.

No, no, I won't. However, because I'm pregnant my brain appears to be operating in reverse and I can't formulate an excuse quickly enough. Holiday and kids in the same sentence is an oxymoron.

Hugh interprets my silence as an assent. "Not abroad but somewhere in the country. We could take long bracing walks."

Holiday and long bracing walks is another contradiction. Holiday equals white, private beaches and long days lying in the sun. However Hugh is too approving of his own idea to notice my doubts. I can only hope that Becca vetoes the suggestion.

March

20

Becca thinks it's a brilliant idea for Hugh and me to take the kids away. She even suggests that we team up with Hugh's brother Henry and his family. I'd have never credited her with so much spite.

Henry is a pleasant enough guy, but his wife, Penny, and I don't see eye to eye. She's Becca's friend and, as such, is never going to be mine. Their three children, whose names escape me, are devil's spawn. Suddenly I'm noticing how many badly behaved children I know. I wonder if there is any other variety. Ideally I'd like one that comes with a volume-control button and self-clean surfaces.

To avoid the weekend away being an unmitigated disaster I suggest that Sam and Gilbert join us. Hugh has enough sense to realize that, in this case, dilution is desirable and readily agrees. Moreover, when Sam rings up and asks if Gilbert's brother James can join the party too, we fall over ourselves and agree.

"Will there be enough room?" she asks.

"Yes. The cottage we've hired is more of a country house. It has four bedrooms and a caravan. That's a bedroom for Henry and Penny, you and Gilbert, Hugh and me, and the kids can bunk in together. James can have the caravan. Do you think he'll mind?"

"Can't say for certain, I've never met him, but I don't expect so. He lives in Africa. He's some sort of safari guide. He's probably used to sleeping in odd places. He's taking a season off and coming to England. G's delighted. He obviously adores him."

"Older or younger?"

"Younger, quite a bit. And, from what I can gather, very unstable."

Oh, I hope so. I could do with the excitement. "What makes you think that?"

"Well, what sort of a job is a safari guide for a thirty-six-year-old? Why can't he get a boring job like everyone else? I'm sure he's only coming home to watch his old mother into the grave."

"Sam. How unlike you to be bitchy. Isn't it great that you can get to know him before the wedding? You must be excited about meeting Gilbert's nearest and dearest?" The subtext is, of course, that in the normal course of events this nicety would have been observed before the engagement ring was slipped onto her finger.

Sam is silent for a minute. "Suppose. Sorry." She isn't. "It's just that G has been behaving so strangely since he heard that James is coming home."

"Really." I'm very interested. I wonder if it will turn out that Gilbert is more interesting than assumed thus far.

"Like a cat on a hot tin roof. He is so keen to make a good impression on James, it's ridiculous."

"I thought it was supposed to be the younger brother that hero-worshiped the older one."

"Exactly. Get this, last night G tried on three different outfits in order to choose which is the most suitable to wear to meet his brother at the airport."

"Odd, but not a hanging offense," I point out reasonably.

"He wouldn't agree to this weekend away unless his precious brother came along too. Apparently he 'doesn't see enough of James as it is.' "

So, nothing sinister in Gilbert's past then. The mystery is solved. Sam is having a bout of the green-eyed monster. She's used to having G's attention, full and devoted. It seems her pique against James is nothing more than a reluctance to share the stage.

"Be nice, Sam," I warn her.

"O.K. I suppose there's 'nowt as queer as folk.' " She falls back on a cliché. "Er, by the way, should have asked, how are you feeling?"

Hugh and I have agreed to make a supreme effort to leave work at a relatively reasonable time this Friday. We plan to collect Kate and Tom and then head down the M4 (with about half of London's population) for a "relaxing" weekend in the country. The relaxing bit starts after the four-and-a-half-hour traffic jam.

However, I'm the only one who sticks to the bargain. I get home early, pack for both of us, make supper, eat my half, put his half in the fridge, shower and change clothes. It's seven o'clock and he hasn't called. I eat his supper and try to comfort myself with the thought that we will have missed the worst of the rush hour. I open the post and am irritated to see that Sam has sent me a package of magazines, a tactless mix of bridal and maternity. There's a note attached: *Wouldn't a double wedding be a scream?! Hint, hint!!*

As subtle as a brick through a glass window. Cow, she would never have suggested a double wedding if I'd still been a size 10; the dates she's picked for her ceremony mean that I'd be waddling down the aisle in a mound of organza, praying that the contractions didn't start.

It's surprised me that so many people have assumed Hugh and I will now announce a wedding date. Unsolicited, friends, family and colleagues launch into the debate as to whether we should have a shotgun marriage immediately, or whether it would be better to wait until after the baby is born so that I'll have my figure back. Last week my mother called to express an opinion, or more accurately, to give directions.

"Darling, I'm assuming that you'll want the family christening robe."

"Haven't given it any thought."

"It's in storage somewhere. I'll locate it and forward it to you." Without pausing for breath she added, "It would be tidiest if you could marry before the baby is born. How much weight have you put on?"

"Sixteen pounds," I muttered sulkily.

"In as many weeks!" she yelled. "Well, in that case, a wedding is out of the question until after the baby is born. You have to live with the photos for a long time."

I repeated the conversation to Hugh, hoping for a dose of sympathy about my weight gain. "I know that she thinks I'm a self-indulgent, gluttonous slut. I can't expect her to understand—in her day they were allowed to smoke. Oh, the relief of putting something in your mouth that isn't calorific."

"How about my penis?" asked Hugh, completely missing the point.

Both points, actually.

Because while everyone from my mother to the local greengrocer has expressed a view on when Hugh and I should get married, the one contribution which has been notably lacking is Hugh's. It's not that I want to get married. I think marriage is an outdated, restrictive, misogynistic, one-way deal.

But it would be nice to be asked.

Although fairly impractical since Hugh is, technically, still married.

But it would be nice to be asked.

I pick up *Beautiful Brides*. There's a bewildering mass of photos of models with supercilious grins (which I find inexplicable—how can anyone feel supercilious dressed as an extra for a low-budget costume drama?). Those that don't look like a smug Mr. Whippy have obviously been instructed to appear beguiling or demure. Neither look appeals to me. There isn't a man in sight. If these magazines are to be believed, grooms are incidental to the whole marriage process. It's horrible, it's terrifying. It's the nastiest thing I've ever seen.

I pick up *Mothering* and instantly change my mind. This magazine redefines horrible and terrifying; in comparison *Beautiful Brides* is a walk in the park. There's picture after picture of fat women, followed by picture after picture of bloody, bawling, tiny William Hague lookalikes. There are pictures of hospital wards, which are grim and drab, with the women in the hospital beds looking exhausted and defeated; they're real, they aren't models, and so there's not a hint of serenity or superciliousness. I keep turning the pages, looking for cute gurgling bundles and blissed-out mums in white silk nightgowns—there are none. There are articles on pain relief (none of it appears to be foolproof), treating engorged nipples (ditto) and incontinence (ditto). There are a couple of articles on how to dress well during pregnancy, but the editor's tone isn't hopeful. The article admits disappointment even before it begins, because, frankly, how can anyone look good when she's carrying an extra three stones? Once again, there isn't a man in sight. The impression I'm left with is that it's perfectly normal for the male partner to make an efficient appearance at the conception, but he doesn't actively participate again until the child graduates or scores its first century playing for England. I shiver involuntarily.

The telephone rings and I dash to it. But it's not Hugh, it's some poor sod from BT trying to sell their latest marketing package—friends, family, vague acquaintances and dodgy chatlines, or something like that. I can't be bothered to listen to him so I pretend to be my Polish cleaner instead. I catch sight of myself in the mirror that hangs above the phone. My cleaner is better presented.

The doorbell rings, I fly to the door—Hugh!

"Becca."

"Hello, Georgina." Before she says anything else Kate and Tom charge past me into the flat. Becca starts to unload more baggage than Geri Halliwell travels with. "Hugh called me."

He didn't call me.

"To explain that he's stuck in a meeting. We agreed that it was best that I drop the kids off here. That way you can make an early start tomorrow." She doesn't pause but tells me these facts in a clinical, straightforward way. Becca and I have an unwritten agreement to be calm and polite with one another on all occasions but especially in front of the children—that is Kate, Tom and Hugh. If I were generous I would assume that she behaves in this reasonable way because she is a proud woman who loves her kids. The less generous side of my nature is more inclined to believe that her reasonableness is to do with the fact that she's financially dependent upon Hugh and me. I behave in this reasonable way because I won; winning creates capacity for refinement. We both recognize the need to be civil, but our motivations are so diverse that, naturally, the arrangement is an uneasy one.

"Becca, you've lost weight." I silently congratulate myself on this choice of double-edged compliment.

"No, I don't think so. Perhaps you've gained," she smiles, but only with her mouth—her eyes remain flint.

I find the comment quite droll, not least because of its unlikely source, but then I consider that it's true and don't find it in the slightest bit amusing.

"I understand that congratulations are in order," she adds.

So he's told her. Or maybe not; I'm kidding myself if I think this is the type of pregnancy you can hide. I summon up the sort of smile that my mother used to wear on her official duties, wide, exaggerated, all teeth, and I beam back. "They certainly are."

"Well, congratulations, then." Becca moves her head too quickly and I can't be quite sure how to interpret the look in her eyes. She seems genuinely pleased. But she can't be. Which woman would be pleased that her husband and the mistress he absconded with are having a child? Except perhaps if Becca knows something I don't. Like how unsuited I am to the task. Or Hugh is. Or we both are. Just at that moment Kate tips out the contents of my handbag onto the floor. Perhaps Becca simply knows how hard the task is.

"I don't think I've ever seen you without make-up," Becca comments. I don't tell her that I'm wearing the full quota but my face must betray me because, slightly more sympathetically, she adds, "Have you been very sick?"

"As a dog." I don't even consider lying to save face. It's that bad. "I was seventeen weeks yesterday. I'd placed a lot of faith in the idea that the sickness fades in the second trimester. But it doesn't seem to be easing. I'd heard that this is when I'll feel glorious and blooming and—" I'm about to add that, most importantly, my sex drive will come back, but I remember who I'm talking to so I simply say, "But . . ." and leave it hanging there.

"Don't hold your breath. I was sick for nearly six months."

Bitch.

"Seventeen weeks, so the baby must be about 100 g by now, that's 3.5 oz." Becca drops her eyes to my bulging stomach. She's obviously trying to account for the other 15 lb 13 oz weight gain.

It's typical that Becca would know stuff like this even though she's not pregnant right now. I try and demonstrate that I'm not altogether ignorant by parroting a fact I read just thirty minutes ago. "The crown-rump length of the baby is 11–12 cm."

"Really, it's amazing, isn't it." Becca holds her hands up in the air and estimates 11 cm.

I hope she's no good at measuring because 11 cm looks big to me. Very big. Eleven centimeters is about the length of a banana, but how wide? That's the pertinent question. How the hell does this thing get out?

I take the final bag from Becca and put it in the pile with the other 430. Why does she always pack as though the children were going on a year-long explorative trip to all six continents? We are only going to Wales for a couple of days. It's a hallmark of Becca's to make child-rearing appear as complex as possible; I'm sure she does it to intimidate me. She then begins to recite the list of instructions for the weekend. Yes, I'll remember to give Kate her penicillin. Yes, I do know that Tom is allergic to nuts and yes, I know he has an inhaler to treat his asthma. Wimps. I hope all these defects are on her side of the family.

"One more thing—Hugh asked if you've remembered to pack his walking boots?"

If I knife Becca, would a woman judge be more or less sympathetic than a male one? I wonder.

"Yes, I have." I glower.

"Goodo." Suddenly Becca checks her watch and then hastily

kisses the children goodbye, explaining she has to dash or else she'll be late for her date.

Date?

I know I shouldn't be surprised—Becca used to be a beauty and recently she's lost a bit of weight and started to smile again in a way that does bring to mind her past loveliness. But I am surprised. I've never considered the possibility of life after Hugh. There certainly wasn't life before him. Not for me, at least.

Date.

So this explains why Becca is so unexpectedly (and treacherously) compliant with regard to access. Historically, Hugh has always had to visit the children at her home (*their* old home, stuffed with poignant memories—a transparent tactic) or somewhere neutral, but rarely here in my apartment. Obviously, Becca tries to exclude me as much as possible. Now it appears she's happy to offload the kids onto me, the Wicked Witch of the West, at the drop of a hat. Although I doubt it's that she's planning on dropping tonight.

I close the door behind her and turn back to the children. Kate is crayoning on the dining room table. Literally. There is no paper involved in this creative endeavor. And Tom is kicking repeatedly the leg of a barstool, for no apparent reason other than that he can.

Enjoy your date, Becca.

21

It's not accurate to say that you can cut the atmosphere with a knife—you'd need a hacksaw.

Hugh finally rolled in last night at 11:15 P.M. I, in the meantime, had just got Kate and Tom to bed, after playing a seemingly endless game of jungles. The game was free play, there were no rules, boundaries or limits, but after playing for about twenty minutes I began to realize that there was an aim. It was for them to keep me tied up and on all fours for as long as humanly possible. Apparently I was a captured hippopotamus (a distressingly accurate analogy). I'd been ensnared by traffickers for an illegal zoo. I had to endure two and a half hours cramped under the dining room table, which I would have objected to but it seemed the safest place in the flat; they used the rest of the rooms to terrorize each other. They ran, jumped, wailed, fought, bit, kicked, screamed, nipped, cried and crashed their way toward oblivion, and eventually wore themselves into that state Jessica used to refer to as "past tired." I then gave them a glass of milk each, a reasonably successful operation as only Tom broke his glass, and finally ushered them into bed. Then there was the lights-on-or-off fiasco—which involved my trying out more illumination combinations than there are on Blackpool front: main light off, hall light on, door open; or main light on but dimmed; or main light off, bedside lamp and hall light on; or all lights on; or all lights off but the radio on. We settled for bedside lamp on but with a cloth over it so it wasn't too bright. Then at last they fell asleep.

Silence.

I've never appreciated stillness quite so much in my entire life. By this time it was 10:45 P.M. The effects of spilt milk, chocolate handprints and crawling on all fours for hours had obliterated any efforts I had made with my hair and clothes. I considered that at least the constant activity required to amuse and occupy Kate and Tom had stopped me thinking about my nausea. It must be this that cajoles a woman into having a big family; it appears that this particular strain of exhaustion is the only effective antidote to sickness.

Suddenly it struck me that at least the children were company of sorts; now that they were in bed the silence taunted me. This was possibly the most depressing thought I'd had in the last couple of months and, believe me, my thoughts have been fairly bleak.

Truth is, I'm lonely. Recently I've spent so many evenings at home alone that I'm beginning to think that I have something special going with the talking clock. In the eight months before the two blue lines, Hugh and I had probably less than a dozen nights in (if you include going to the gym as a night out). We were to be found at parties and receptions, in bars, restaurants, cinemas and pubs. In the last two months I've been out twice. Where the hell's Hugh? Whatever he's working on can't be this important, can it? I resent the bloating pregnancy. In the circles I mix in the only parts of the body that are meant to bulge are botoxed lips or silicone boobs. No wonder Hugh doesn't want to spend any time with me. That said, it was his bulging trousers that put me here.

When Hugh finally got home he tried to tell me he'd been working late, while the distinct smell of a good time—booze and fags and fun bars—wafted over from his suit and smile, betraying him.

"You bastard," I yelled, not waiting to hear his full explanation. And that was about the nicest thing I said to him for the following hour and a half. The energy that had been eluding me recently came flooding back with venomous, Incredible Hulk–like proportions. I screamed, ranted, hollered and raved, not allowing his entreaties—that yes, he had been to a restaurant but it really was work—to interrupt me.

"So why didn't you call me?"

"We were short on time."

"You had time to call Becca."

"Well, I knew she had to make arrangements for the kids. I knew she was going out."

"Oh, so you considered Becca's plans but not mine? You kept your promises to her but not to me."

Hugh's face was flooded with confusion, as well it might be; no one had ever accused him of that before. Hugh rarely makes me mad and on the odd occasion he does I never show it. Being angry is hardly attractive, is it? Screeching and crying achieve nothing but premature aging. If we do argue, the subject matter is never more serious than what we should watch on TV. We'd never had an actual fight. I shout infrequently, and I'm never jealous. Or, at least, if I am, I take care not to display it. This, our first proper row, was spectacular. Without allowing reason or rationale to direct my soliloquy I yelled about random things that had been niggling me. And, when I'd run out of those, I alighted on new things that don't really irritate me at all, but at least fueled the row, giving me the opportunity to vent further my ill-defined fury. Throughout my roaring Hugh remained irritatingly calm and tried to persuade me to lower my voice so I didn't wake the children.

"Oh, so suddenly you remember you have children?" I yelled, managing to sound accusatory, bitter and self-righteous in just one sentence—quite a feat. I didn't allow him to answer but demanded, "And what about the broken tile in the bathroom?"

"What *are* you talking about?"

"Didn't you notice the broken tile in the bathroom, near the sink?" I marched off in the direction of the bathroom and pointed at the broken tile triumphantly. "It needs replacing," I insisted. All at once it seemed like an atrocity. "Didn't you notice?" I demanded again.

"Well, no," he muttered, amazed at this sudden turn in the conversation.

"*No?*"

"Yes," he tried tentatively, but I could see from his face that he didn't think that this answer was going to be any more palatable to me. He was right.

"Well, if you noticed, then why didn't you do something about it?"

"I didn't notice," he yelled, finally breaking in the face of my persistent hysteria.

Perversely, I found his loss of calm rather soothing. "Ah." I smiled with morbid satisfaction. "And do you know why you didn't notice?" He looked around the room, obviously hoping to find the correct answer scribbled on a wall or graffitied on the shower curtain. "I'll tell you why not. Because it's too domestic, that's why not. It's nothing to do with you. The domestic arrangements of this home are nothing to do with you. You aren't interested."

"You're not interested either, that's why we have a cleaner," he pleaded.

While this was a fair point I was determined not to fold that easily. "And you're not interested in Kate or Tom or me either, because if you were you'd have come home at 6:30 P.M. as per our agreement." I hadn't realized I thought this, at least not until I'd said it. All I could think was, Thank God I'm not married to this selfish, thoughtless git. I'd sooner swim with crocodiles than shackle myself to this wanker.

But I am shackled to him. The baby that's growing inside me is more binding than a bloody wedding band, and although it only weighs 100 g it's more constraining than a ball and chain.

And he's not a wanker. He's Hugh and I love him and I've always loved him and I will always love him. There isn't any alternative. It was my own self-pity that finally broke me. The emotional hurricane that had whipped me into such frenzy passed, leaving me with the devastation wreaked by the words I'd used. I am not the sort of woman who behaves in an insane, illogical, pre-posterous way and then blames it pathetically (and disloyally) on her "time of month." I've never "absentmindedly" shoplifted, I've never cut out the crotch of my ex-lover's designer suits. I am in control of my body, my emotions, my future, and I'm responsible for my past. I would have told him all of this, but I was crying and couldn't get the words out between the sobs. Lying prone on the settee, two things crossed my mind: one, Hugh is no more used to seeing me cry than seeing me rant. Normally I really am the very epitome of rational behavior. I've often sobbed about him, but I usually employ a policy of stiff upper lip in front of him. Even when I watched him return to Becca, over and over again. Even when I watched him get married. Even when I drove Becca to the hospital to have Kate (there was no one else to do the honors). Yet, now, when I'm having his baby, I start to sob. Where's the logic in that?

The second thing that crossed my mind was that I was wearing pop socks.

I'm the size of a whale and my trousers are riding up to expose pop socks. This bout of histrionics would almost certainly have been more effective if I still weighed eight stone four and was wearing stockings.

With relief Hugh realized that the storm was over and gathered me in his arms, while making soothing, cooing sounds. I instantly forgot that it was him I was angry with in the first place and clung tightly, wrapping myself around him like a limpet.

So, naturally, the atmosphere this morning requires a hacksaw to penetrate through the confusion, regrets and fear. We are both being overly polite. Trying just a bit too hard to show that last night, our first-ever row, is forgotten, and by doing so we betray the fact that neither of us is thinking of anything but.

First ever.

Hugh and I often take weekend breaks. Usually abroad—Barcelona, Prague, Paris or Rome—but sometimes in the U.K.

too. Just before Christmas we spent a weekend at Babington House, enjoying the hotel spa, the countryside and the fact that we were miles away from Christmas shoppers. I can't help but compare that car journey to this. Then, as now, we sat in a seemingly endless traffic jam, but then it was distinctly fun. Our CDs were playing on the Boxster stereo and we sang along at the tops of our voices. I kept popping squares of bitter, dark Lindt chocolate into his mouth (although not into mine) and each time he sucked on my fingers. The traffic was moving so slowly that it was possible for him to lean over and kiss me or grab my thigh every now and then. And we chattered, nonstop, about our week at work, treatments we'd indulge in at the spa, our plans for Christmas, anything really. That was three months ago. It might as well have been three years ago or three million years ago.

I wonder if Hugh is remembering that journey too. I can't decide if I hope he is or I hope he isn't.

Hugh is bewildered. He often has to stay at work for impromptu dinners with clients; normally I don't mind and I do know that he is working on a big pitch for something or other. I can't remember which brand; it's definitely not Mothercare or Avent. I, more than anyone, should understand the pressure of big pitches; they demand copious amounts of time and energy. He is under a lot of pressure proving to Rartle, Roguel and Spirity that he's worth the six-figure salary his new job commands. He needs a couple of big new business wins under his belt. O.K., so he had time to make only one call, he knew that Becca would relay his position to me, and he expected me to understand because, as I say, it's a regular occurrence. I've always understood in the past. Because that's what mistresses do, don't they? They understand. It's the wife who traditionally has a comprehension problem. And mistresses don't do shouting; again that's the wife's domain. Still, I suppose I should find some comfort in the fact that I slipped into the role with a certain confidence, despite the lack of a ring on my left hand.

I'm confused too. Why should a regular occurrence, which has never bothered me in the past, suddenly annoy me with such a ferocious intensity? On the other hand, why can't he see how insensitive his behavior was? I'm also annoyed at myself for having presented my grievances in such a hysterical manner; my genuine injuries were washed away with the murky gripes that came to mind when I was playing the wrought-up shrew. The broken tile, for example—definitely more minor battle than war. I sigh, exhausted with trying to decide who was in the right and who was in the wrong.

I force myself to concentrate on the weekend in front of us. After all, it's supposed to be a holiday. I politely offer Hugh a boiled sweet and he politely accepts it. He comments on the weather, I mention that it's cold inside the car, he tries to adjust the heating, fiddling with unfamiliar dials. We've hired a saloon to accommodate the children; I know Hugh would have preferred a four-by-four. I'm afraid I didn't ring the car-hire place in time, this was all that was available. I ask him if he wants to listen to a CD or the radio, he insists it's my choice. The kids somehow sense that this isn't a good moment to misbehave and therefore do fairly good impressions of a couple of angels; there's so much caution swilling around in the car I think I might drown.

About half an hour into the journey, Hugh yells, "Oh shit."

"Shit," shouts Tom.

" 'Sit, sit still,' Daddy said 'sit still,' " counter Hugh and I in unison. We take a second to grin at one another, relieved that the formality has been blown away with Tom's expletive.

"What's up?" I ask.

"I've forgotten a file I need for work. I brought it home last night but I've left it on the breakfast bar. It's really important that I read it this weekend. I have to take a conference call on Sunday night and need to be up to speed. We'll have to go back for it. Sorry."

I don't mind in the least; in fact, I even remember (just) when I had the energy and inclination to work at the weekends. At the moment, it's all I can do to drag myself into the office to work conventional hours. I know I'm coasting; my hope is that I'm the only one who knows.

When we arrive back in London I jump out of the car and run up to the flat to save the time of Hugh finding a parking space.

"Got it." I smile, waving the file at Hugh. He takes it off me before I've even fastened my seat belt

"You were a long time," he comments.

Was I? It is so cute that Hugh guards my every moment so jealously.

"Becca rang to see if we'd set off," I say as I roll my eyes. Hugh smiles and leans forward to kiss me. Everything is going to be O.K. For the second time that morning we head off toward Wales.

22

We arrive at the cottage at about midday. It's not the Maldives, nor the Bahamas. There are no white beaches, no designer boutiques and no five-star restaurants. However, since I look more like a beached whale than a beach babe, since I can't fit into any designer labels, and since most restaurants have menus littered with dishes solely composed of soft cheese, raw meat, and soft-boiled eggs—all of which are off-limits—Wales is perhaps a more reasonable holiday destination.

Except, of course, we have brought the children with us. Becca's children. And there's Penny. Becca's friend.

I wonder if the facts that the cottage is thatched and has a working chimney, and that there are window boxes at every window, dribbling snowdrops and daffodils, will be enough to make the weekend a success. Pull yourself together, girl. I'm surprised at myself. Normally I'm so good at looking on the bright side. I'm here with Hugh, aren't I? And that's always been enough for me in the past; just being with Hugh guarantees I have a good time, no matter where we are.

Although it's mid-March, it is Wales, so spring has not yet sprung. Snow is still lying in thick rolls on the hills and there is a light dusting of frost in the cottage garden. The sky is electric blue and a frail but brave sun is seeping through the clouds that slice up the view. It is very different from the soggy and gray sight of Clapham High Street. I have to admit it's spectacular. I breathe in, deeply. Trying to budge the nausea.

I can see Henry around the side of the cottage—he is chopping wood, which I think rather quaint and endearing. Hugh and Henry look alike, or, rather, Henry looks exactly as Hugh would have looked if I hadn't rescued him. Henry is four years older and looks about ten years older. They have the same square jaws and strong Roman noses and they have the same laughing green eyes and sandy blond hair, but Henry is carrying an extra stone and a half and his laughing green eyes are invariably clouded with worries about promotions, parking tickets and pets with lice, issues that I shield Hugh from. In my opinion, Henry's overwhelming domestic concerns would be somewhat alleviated if only Penny would allow him to shag her senseless now and again; she'd look better for it, too. Her complexion would benefit.

Henry's eyes do light up when he sees us arrive. He is one of the few people who manages not to betray any signs of whether he approves or disapproves of Hugh and me. He simply chugs along with it, endeavoring to be civil and courteous to me and, no doubt, to Becca too when he sees her. Everyone else we know feels duty-bound to pass an opinion. Most mount a moral high horse (standards notably lacking in their own lives); this is extremely annoying. One or two try to be open-minded and encouraging, which is more annoying still. Henry's diplomatic silence makes him very relaxing company.

It turns out that there's another surprise guest, a friend of Penny's, Libby. I don't hold out much hope for her entertainment value, not if she's a friend of Penny's.

"She's really, really nice," assures Henry.

This doesn't recommend her. It turns me off. "Nice" means she'll be boring. "Nice" means I'll feel inadequate. Still, Sam will be delighted she can pair Libby off with James; since Sam got engaged her number-one pastime is matchmaking.

Henry is thinking the exact opposite. "We'll have to do something about the sleeping arrangements," he points out. "Penny suggested that Libby could take the caravan, and the single chap—what's the name of Gilbert's brother?"

"James."

"Yes, James, he'll have to make do with the futon."

"Very sensible," I say, nodding. I know Penny will have given the sleeping arrangements a lot of thought. I wonder if she'll insist that James wear a dressing gown at all times. Risqué, as far as Penny is concerned, is hanging underwear on the washing line.

I politely inquire as to where Penny is, although in truth I'm not interested, and as to whether the others have arrived. I'm told that Sam, Gilbert and James all arrived last night and they are currently out walking. Libby is due any minute.

"Penny's in the kitchen," says Henry. "Let's go and say hello."

Because it's impossible to refuse, I agree.

The kitchen is a hive of activity. The smallest child is squashed into a sticky high chair. I think it's a girl, but it's difficult to tell because it has so much organic and freshly pulped baby food on its face that it's rather hard to distinguish its features. I notice the racks of organic vegetables in the corner of the kitchen. Oh, another formidable criterion against which I will soon be measuring myself. I know I won't have the courage to use baby food in jars. The child smells. Not of diapers (thank God), but of regurgitated food, child sweat and tears. Henry ruffles its hair. I notice Hugh smile warily from a distance—I think he's waiting for Henry to rinse his hands.

We let Kate and Tom loose on the other two children (definitely boys, I can tell by their clothes) who are sitting on the floor, playing with large Lego pieces and small cars. I nearly tread on them as I cross the kitchen to air-kiss Penny. Penny endures my physical proximity because she's too polite not to, but I can tell she wishes that I'd disappear. She hugs Hugh because no one can help but like him. And while I love him, I am his greatest fan, it does cross my mind how unfair it is that I am seen as scarlet, positively radioactive, while he, the one who took the wedding vows, is seen as a victim. I never asked Hugh to leave Becca for me. Which I think is to my credit, since it was the thing I wanted most in the world. I never once suggested that we needed a resolution to our affair. I simply accepted whatever I was offered. I made sure that we had good times when we were together and I left Becca to destroy her own marriage. Which she did, very successfully.

Penny isn't wearing any make-up but she is sporting a healthy ruddy glow, and only the faintest film of sweat from the heat of the kitchen. She's been baking bread and fairy cakes. Hugh steals a cake and Penny playfully slaps his wrist. I ask if anyone wants a Bloody Mary, and even though I plan to have a Virgin Mary, Penny throws me a look that is intended to turn me to stone. I deflect it with a huge smile, which wins over Hugh and Henry, at least. I also steal a fairy cake. Penny shoots me another withering look and moves the baking tray out of reach. I hope I've sabotaged the catering plan.

"Have we missed breakfast?" I smile my inquiry. It's obvious that we've missed breakfast. For a start, it's after midday and while I don't know much about children I do know they demand their sugar-coated E additives at about seven in the morning. Besides which, the great pile of gleaming, newly washed pans shows that a large cooked breakfast has just been cleared away.

"Penny could knock you up some scrambled eggs. I think we have some salmon," offers Henry helpfully. He moves toward the fridge.

"The salmon is for a quiche for Sunday tea," protests Penny. Henry tuts as though she's being a killjoy. I know that it's more likely that she's simply concerned that if we eat out of turn there won't be enough food for the rest of the weekend. Which is sensible of her and therefore the tone *is* killjoy.

"Oh, don't worry, I'll nibble on an apple until lunch is ready," I smile, nicely making myself out as compliant and her as difficult.

I'm immediately ashamed of myself. Penny brings out the worst in me. I sigh, suddenly exhausted. Since Hugh and I got together I seem to have entered into hundreds of these small battles with first wives. All at once they tire me. I wish that Penny liked me more or at least loathed me less. I wonder if that will ever happen and what I can do to make it happen. I wish that the resentment and mistrust could be wafted away by the yummy, sweet smells of her baking. I look up hopefully at Penny. Of course she can't read my mind and doesn't see the olive branch. She sees a big sign that reads THREAT hanging over my head.

"Let me show you around, George," offers Henry. "Hugh, you two are in the front bedroom, kids next door, if you want to settle in." Hugh takes the bags up to our bedroom and lights a fire in there, while Henry shows me around the beautiful cottage.

It is textbook. There's plenty of room to house the tasteful rustic furniture and big Persian rugs. Every window boasts a stunning vista of rolling hills and possibilities. There are two big, noisy black Labradors playing in the garden, a fat, squelchy cat in front of the fire, piles of dusty old books and even a piano. Twee and clichéd, exactly what I want for a weekend break in the country. Hugh catches us up in the sitting room.

"The kids will love this big garden." I beam at Hugh to see if he's caught my enthusiasm, but he's not concentrating on what I'm saying; he's looking for somewhere to plug in his ISDN line.

"Libby's here," shouts Penny from the kitchen. Curiosity gets the better of me and I lean out of the window to watch the new guest get out of her car.

Libby is quite a surprise. I was expecting a Penny clone, plump and mumsy, but Libby is anything but. She's about five foot eight, slim, with long mid-blond hair, which is only just visible as she is wearing a large hat with flaps tied under her chin. She looks young, probably still in her twenties. She's wearing a knee-length sheepskin coat and a long multicolored scarf—I'd put money on it that she knitted the scarf herself or found it in a trendy little vintage-clothes store in Brighton. The effect is extraordinarily chic. Libby's look announces to the world that she is a unique combination of artisan meets trendsetter; yet, while she looks as though she's just stepped out of the pages of a style magazine, the whole outfit probably only cost a few quid. Just as I'm beginning to be quite hopeful that Libby's presence will tip the balance of the weekend away from conversations about jam-making and toward something a little more exhilarating, I notice another kid. A sticky girl, aged about seven, climbs out of the back of the car; the scales have just plummeted back down on the jam-making side. The young girl is tall, slim and blond. She's wearing hipster jeans from GAPKids and, despite the fact that you can see your breath, she's wearing a cropped top, emblazoned with pictures of Westlife. However, her sophisticated look is ruined because she is also sporting a milkshake mustache and she is sucking her thumb. Naturally, because she is a child, she's sulking about some disaster or other— I think it has something to do with the number of sweets she was allowed on the journey. She must be Libby's kid sister.

Penny does the introductions. "This is Hugh, Henry's brother. This is Libby and her daughter, Millie."

"Daughter?" I ask, not bothering to hide my amazement.

"Yes, daughter," says Penny, as though she were talking to an idiot.

"Millie's your daughter?" I ask Libby, just to be sure.

"Yes." She smiles pleasantly.

Libby is oblivious to the fact that she has just *ruined* my theory. Since I've become pregnant I've separated all women into two distinct categories. Non-mothers are easy to recognize. No baby sick dripping down their shoulders or clinging to their calves; they wear a jaunty, celebratory, carefree look, as distinguishable as the morning-after glow; in fact, interchangeable with that look, because this lot are the only ones getting the type of sex that makes you smile the morning after. Mothers, on the other hand, look harassed, defeated and traumatized. Their faces are set with grim determination as they battle with the will of a minor and the indignity of doing so. Weary with self-sacrifice, they walk a thin line between arbitrator, disciplinarian and comforter. They walk it in snagged tights and ugly clothes. They smell of sick and wee.

Except Libby smells of a Calvin Klein perfume. I'm stunned.

"I'm sorry, I didn't catch your name?" says Libby. That's because Penny didn't give it.

"Georgina, but call me George." I smile.

"Hugh's partner," chips in Henry for clarity, rather ruining Penny's chances of labelling me as the local whore. Henry pats Millie on the head, obviously mistaking her for a pet dog: she rolls her eyes and snorts her derision, but doesn't get the chance to say anything rude as Penny ushers us through to the dining room.

Throughout lunch (a generous and elaborate Ploughman's, with apple pie and cream for pudding) the conversation, rather tediously, revolves around what I should avoid eating. While I can't complain that being pregnant means everyone ignores me, I'm still not happy. I've read the books. I know what I should avoid.

"Raw eggs," says Penny.

"Peanuts," adds Henry.

"Pâté," adds Hugh.

"Goat's and sheep's milk," adds Penny.

"Caffeine," adds Henry.

"Saccharin," adds Hugh.

Pregnancy comes with lots of problems; varicose veins, swollen ankles and unwanted advice are but a few. I glare at them around the table and defiantly dip my finger into the melting Brie. I don't actually want to eat it as I'm aware of the dangers of listeria, but the bloody food-fascists have riled me into defiance. I don't like receiving unsolicited advice at the best of times; I've never bought into the theory that it's well intentioned, I consider it impertinent. Throughout my relationship with Hugh "well-meaning" friends have offered advice, which nine times out of ten could be boiled down to "forget it, he'll never leave his wife"—now, it's a good job I ignored that advice, isn't it? If you *ask* for direction you must roll with it, take it or leave it, but roll with it. If it's uninvited I feel almost duty-bound to be uncivil. Without doubt the most irritating counsel comes from women who haven't had children and men whose wives have.

"What are you doing?" demands Henry, when he sees the dollop of Brie resting on my finger, hovering between my plate and palate.

"You haven't even had a baby, Henry. What makes you think you're qualified?" I snipe.

"Yes, I have. I've had three."

"No, *you* haven't," I insist. I would have elaborated but, luckily for him, long before the steaming apple pie is placed on the table I have to dash to the loo to accommodate the pickle's second appearance of the day.

By the time I emerge from the bathroom, lunch has been cleared away and everyone is settled in the living room. There's nowhere for me to sit, and the after-lunch cigarettes (and in Henry's case cigar) make me feel queasy again. I'd rather hoped that we would go for a walk and get a bit of fresh air. But when I say this, mutters go up about arctic climes. I point out that Sam and Gilbert are out walking, but I know my reasoning is falling on deaf ears. From the number of beer cans and wine bottles on the coffee table it's obviously been agreed that the only march we are making this afternoon is the one toward alcoholic oblivion. Even Penny has a glass of wine.

I feel like a leper.

Even here, the ass end of nowhere, I don't fit in. I look out of the window.

It *is* a very pretty ass end. Maybe I should just go for a walk on my own, do my own thing.

But then that would appear churlish.

The children seem to recognize that I'm the only sober adult and pester me constantly.

"Why does water freeze?"

"I'm hungry."

"Where is my comfy cloth? Have you seen it, Georgina?"

I ignore most requests and demands and eventually the children turn their appeals to Penny and Libby. I wonder if kids have a radar system that identifies mums as being the people who are the most likely to replenish the cup of Ribena or wipe bottoms, noses and faces. If so, it's a pretty primitive system, it doesn't seem to identify fathers; neither Hugh nor Henry are much help. Hugh's effort to explain how water freezes is far too complex; it bores and confuses the children. While Henry does *offer* to make some sandwiches, his attempts are ham-fisted. Rather than shout out a constant stream of instructions—"the butter's out," "there's some chicken or jam," "the knives are in the top drawer on the right-hand side"—Penny, in the end, gets up to make the snacks. The snacks don't appease them and the children quickly start to snipe at one another. The adults are all a bit tipsy and so they start to snipe at one another as well. There's nothing on TV except an old black and white musical. Penny and Libby want to watch it, but Henry is the king of the remote and irritates everyone by constantly flicking between channels.

"We can't even look forward to *Brookside,*" comments Libby.

"Why not?"

"Get this! Wales doesn't receive Channel 4."

I notice Millie emptying the entire contents of my make-up bag onto the tiled kitchen floor. I watch helplessly as a twenty-quid mascara rolls into the black hole that is the space under the fridge and as she liberally applies my foundation to Kate's face, hands and T-shirt.

The initial holiday mood is fading fast. I fear that I'll suffocate in the dull domesticity that abounds.

Luckily, Sam, Gilbert and Gilbert's brother, James, arrive on the scene. I haven't seen Sam for nearly a month, we still talk on the telephone, but as I'm not a florist or a dressmaker it's nearly impossible to actually get to see her. Even before they've taken off their hiking boots, I notice that Sam has never looked more radiant. I'm not sure if it is the day's hiking or the stop off at the pub that has put the glow in her cheeks but she looks fabulous. I hug her, greet Gilbert and then turn my attention to James.

I'm immediately pleased that he's joined our party; James is instantly identifiable as a good laugh. He's obviously a bit of a flirt and immediately sets to charming Libby. Sam will be thrilled.

I'm not.

I can't help but notice that neither his face nor his trousers flickered with appreciation on greeting me. Not that I fancy James. I don't, not in the least. I'm with Hugh and there's never been anyone else for me.

But.

But when did I become invisible? Historically men have not been impervious. Even with the most decent man—who is absolutely besotted with one of my friends, who would never think of trying it on, who has no real interest at all—his eyes would always sparkle in appreciation for a fraction of a millisecond. And the majority of men make it clear they'd like to peel my knickers off with their teeth.

Something's changed.

Who am I kidding? Everything's changed.

I take consolation in the fact that James's eyes and smile do betray that he is bright, easy-going and entertaining. His insistence that we "get off our asses and get outside to play a game of rounders" confirms it.

"In this weather?" protests Penny.

" 'You can keep your hat on,' " sings Gilbert, giving a reasonable impersonation of Tom Jones.

I actually agree with Penny that it's far too cold for a ball game, but I'd rather pull out my fingernails than say so. I don't want to appear as miserable as she is, so I rush to the door.

The rounders game turns out to have been a brainwave. It involves everyone, kids and adults alike (except for Penny who excuses herself by insisting that she has potatoes to peel), and it blows away the cobwebs of an afternoon sat in front of the box, drinking and eating too much. We split into teams naturally. Libby, Hugh, Henry and I play against Sam, James and Gilbert (my presence is obviously seen as a handicap; once again I'm eleven years old and the last to be picked for the netball team). The gaggle of kids who are old enough to run stay involved by randomly fielding the ball for both sides. They are too young to be genuinely useful but at least they hamper each team equally.

Hugh and Henry immediately revert to their teen selves. Even though they are on the same team they jostle competitively with one another, often risking dropping a ball altogether rather than allowing the other the glory of a clean catch. Gilbert and James's approach is entirely different. They work with each other. Gilbert allows James to field a catch. James raucously cheers Gilbert throughout the game and Gilbert does move surprisingly quickly, for an older man.

We play until it is dark, and then we put on all the lights in the house and play a bit more. Eventually we have to give up because the electric light is proving inadequate and, anyway, none of us can stand Penny's constant harping about the waste of electricity. Sam checks her watch—it is 8 P.M. exactly. Her team is a single point ahead, so she throws her arms around James's neck and declares that the match is over and that they are the winners. If it's true that, "it's not the winning but the taking part that counts," why does she look so smug? Gilbert takes up the cheer and they are so noisy that it is impossible for our team to argue that we are each owed another bat. Instead we concede defeat gracefully, well, quite gracefully—Hugh keeps insisting that my performance was sub-standard due to my pregnancy, and while he's probably right I'm not sure it needs saying.

23

Libby and Sam bathe the kids, and James proves to be as good a sport off the rounders pitch as on by offering to read a bedtime story. By the time he reemerges Penny is just putting an enormous fish pie on the table.

"I put six kids to bed, is that right?"

Everyone falls silent and does the math. Kate, Tom, Millie plus Penny and Henry's three, yup, six in total. Bloody hell, so many. They're everywhere, and yet we still had fun, despite Millie cheating on the scores and Kate biting Josh. A lot of fun.

How odd.

Another oddity is that staying sober turns out to be O.K, quite interesting in fact; it gives me the opportunity to people-watch. Everyone else is drinking copious amounts and as a consequence becoming increasingly odious, flirtatious, argumentative or charming. By the time the pregnancy is over I'll have several months of embarrassing stories about my nearest and dearest. I could blackmail them for large sums of money and give up my day job.

Sam has obviously forgiven James for being held in high esteem by Gilbert and is making a huge effort to put him at ease among so many strangers. Not that he seems to require any particular care or attention. He's one of those blokes who quickly makes himself at home and he obviously expects to be popular, which he is, so fair play to him. He entertains Sam, Hugh and me with stories about safaris in Africa. The stories excite Hugh so much that he starts to make plans for us to visit Namibia or Botswana.

Sam points out that I can't take malaria tablets at the moment and that by the time I can take them again we'll have a baby. "Africa is hardly the place to take babies."

Her comment is accurate, but I can't see Hugh at Butlins. Henry and Libby are chatting merrily about music. Most people have Henry down as a Mr. All-work-and-no-play, and it's true his clubbing and gigging days are behind him but, rather sweetly, he still buys NME and therefore does have a reasonable knowledge of what's pop and what's not. They are exchanging views on who was the main influence on the Aloof. Turns out that both of them prefer the radio edit of Groove Armada's "At the River" (as opposed to what, I don't know, the non-radio edit?). I wish Henry wouldn't monopolize Libby; the more I watch her the more I want to get to know her. All day her conversation has interested me. A unique mix of high(ish) brow topics and a healthy interest in the tawdry goings-on of the rich and famous as reported in *OK* and *Hello!* She seems good fun; I want to know more. Is she married? Who is Millie's father? Where did she buy those jeans?

I notice that Gilbert is spending most of his evening talking to Penny, which is noble of him but can't be much of a laugh.

"Supper was marvelous, Penny," comments Gilbert.

"Oh, it was nothing, very easy, anyone could have done it."

"Ahh, but you did," he smiles.

"Really, it was nothing. In fact, I think it could have done with a hint of basil and perhaps a touch more salt."

"It was delicious."

"No, not at all. My friend Becca gave me the recipe." Penny glances in my direction. I affect to be fascinated by the candle wax melting down the sides of the wine bottles. I consider assuring her that I know how perfect Becca is. I've known since 1987, which is why my life has been one long struggle. But I stay silent and remind myself that Hugh is mine now.

"Now, when *she* bakes fish pie it really is something to write home about. I thought mine was a bit bland."

Gilbert sighs and gives up on the compliment. I don't blame him. For God's sake, why can't Penny simply say thank you and leave it at that?

Penny's next conversation non-starter is, "I know other people's dreams are the most boring things on earth, but I had the strangest dream last night." She's right, for once, other people's dreams are the dullest things on earth, but she starts to relay hers anyway. The story, something about a train and a fish, is lacking in humor, exoticism and eroticism; it doesn't even have an ending. Gilbert nods and smiles throughout, not betraying for a moment that he's so bored that his blood has ceased circulating to his brain. I can't decide if I admire his politeness or find him wet.

At a quarter to ten Gilbert suggests a game of cards. I've fallen prey to his tedious competitiveness as far as bridge is concerned before, so I decline the offer, as does Libby. Sam, Gilbert, Hugh and James make up a four, Henry looks on and Penny starts to wash up, despite everyone's entreaties to leave it until the morning (she really does know how to break up a party). So, finally, I get to chat to Libby.

"Is it too smoky for you in here?" she asks thoughtfully.

"To be honest, I am beginning to feel a bit queasy," I admit.

"Come on, let's go and have a walk outside."

I don't mind giving up the open fire, even though it's an outrageously cold night. I grab my coat, scarf and gloves and follow Libby up the garden path. The air bites at my skin and makes me doubt that spring will ever arrive.

"It's a shocker of a year weather-wise, isn't it?" I comment.

"Yeah, but you don't want a hot summer anyway, it will only make you feel more uncomfortable."

I could kiss her. It's not that I've suddenly developed lesbian tendencies, it's just that that comment is the first I've heard from anyone that suggests they know how difficult pregnancy can be. I was beginning to think that there's only ever been me, in the entire history of mankind (or, to be technically accurate, womankind) who has struggled with this pregnancy thing. Everyone else seems to imply that it's as easy as a lady of the night, as natural as the waves coming in. Libby hasn't said much about the pregnancy but, notably, she hasn't said that I must be "excited" or "delighted." She hasn't offered any advice on what to eat, nor has she asked me how much weight I've put on. I'm very, very grateful.

"You work in advertising, right?"

"Yeah, I'm a New Business Director at an agency called Q&A." I briefly tell her what I do. In my experience, people don't much care or understand what other people do for a living—it's just one of those questions we feel under some obligation to ask—but surprisingly Libby seems genuinely interested.

"And Hugh?"

"He's at another agency, R,R&S."

"What's with this initial thing? Why can't advertising agencies have proper names? I thought that was the point of advertising agencies, to make distinct brands."

I smile. "Good point. It's designed to confuse."

"Hugh was talking about pitching for new business too. But he's not a New Business Director, is he?"

"No. He's the MD." And I can't help myself, I shimmer with pride. "But the MD is always intrinsically involved in new business. I report into a guy called Dean, who's my MD."

"Is he a good boss?"

I think about it, perhaps for the first time, and find that my not very inspirational answer is, "Mostly good enough."

"Do you like your job?"

"Ditto. Mostly good enough," I admit. Oddly enough, I haven't ever really given it that much thought. It's what I do. I'm reasonably good at it, or at least I am when I concentrate. "What about you?"

"I work in an STD clinic, in the city. I deal with the bankers that are more than wankers," she grins.

"I bet you have some stories to tell."

"I do," says Libby, laughing to herself. I think that she's about to enlighten me, but we fall silent when Libby notices a fox. We watch it cross the path sleekly and glide into nothingness in the hedgerow.

"So, do you like your job?" I ask.

"Funnily enough, working as a receptionist in an STD clinic wasn't my ambition," admits Libby with a wry smile.

"What was?"

"I wanted to be a doctor; the surprise arrival of Millie put paid to that idea. I was in my third year at medical school."

"Where's Millie's dad?"

"Missing since action."

"Oh. That's hard."

"It was when I was alone in my bedsit, counting stretch marks, while my mates were out on the razz, chasing tequilas, but it got easier and now I see that Millie is definitely the best thing that ever happened to me."

Libby must be doing some weird drugs. I mumble that indeed it must be a relief now that Millie is out of diapers and can put her own bread in the toaster. Libby laughs, although I wasn't making a joke. I am so lucky. I am. At least Hugh isn't about to do a Houdini.

"What was Millie's father like?"

I know I'm behaving like a student again. Not just because I'm doing a credible line in asking, "Where do you come from?," "What grade A levels did you get?" and "What position on the UCCA form was this university?" There's something else very studenty about this conversation; it's direct and honest and seems drunken. I'm not asking Libby polite questions that I know would be socially acceptable (as is usually my way); I'm not asking pointless questions such as "what type of tree is that?," which would be safe and give the impression that I give a damn about stuff. I'm asking her the things I want to know. It's a relief, it's unusual. Libby doesn't seem fazed by my directness but answers me in the same straightforward way that the question was intended.

"What was Millie's father like?" She repeats the question to herself and then shrugs, "I can't *really* remember."

I don't think she means that she can't remember who Millie's father is; her tone suggests that time has eroded the memory of how he was.

"Quite funny and not entirely useless in bed. Millie has his smile," she adds.

I try to think of Millie's smile. Today, she has done a fair amount of scowling, snarling and sulking—have I seen her smile? Yes, I think I do remember her bestowing it at teatime. Suddenly her smile burns my retina. It's wide and sincere. A charming smile, although I presume her father had more teeth.

"How did you meet Penny?" The more I know about Libby the less likely their friendship seems.

"At prenatal groups. Josh is the same age as Millie."

"And you've stayed friends all this time?"

I obviously don't do a very good job of keeping the incredulity out of my voice, because Libby answers. "She can be a bit straight, but her heart is in the right place. She's been very good to me over the years. There are times when I'd never have managed without her. Girl friends really come into their own when you're pregnant, don't they?"

I don't reply because, to be frank, mine haven't. None of my friends have experience in this department. Ask them what you like about lymphatic drainage, calorie content, the effects of grape seed as an antioxidant and the advice is limitless. They can list over a hundred uses for Vaseline (thickening lashes, conditioning nails, a cheap lip gloss . . .) but I doubt soothing baby's bottom would be one of them. They don't do babies. Sam always asks, "So, how are you?" but before I can answer she comments, "Gilbert and I can't wait to start a family," and then she talks about Gilbert or, more accurately, the wedding. I don't spend as much time at work and I never see Julia after work now; even if I did I don't think she'd be interested in my pregnancy. In fact, I know she wouldn't. I'm beginning to realize that work was all we ever had in common.

The champagne-swilling, vol-au-vent-eating women who I used to meet at parties and receptions were never more than acquaintances. On hearing about the pregnancy, many of them have telephoned—once. Which is the correct thing to do. I've assured them all that I'm thrilled and excited, the correct thing to say, and I haven't mentioned my mood swings, hot flushes or frightening discharges, as these are distinctly incorrect things to discuss. I don't wallow, but return to the question of Libby's career.

"Maybe you could go back to uni and finish your training, now Millie's a bit older and at school."

"Yeah, I keep saying I will. The people at the clinic are really good about Millie's childcare arrangements, so I bet they would be flexible about study time, if that's what I really wanted. It's just that I've never quite got around to putting pen to paper to apply. If I ever have five minutes spare I eat chocolate or drink a glass of wine."

"Perhaps it's for the best."

"Why do you say that?"

"What year did you say you were in when you fell pregnant?"

"My third."

"Well, consider your basic grasp of biology—surely they'd done the birds-and-the-bees bit by then?"

Libby laughs out loud, as I'd hoped she would. It's a strong confident laugh that rings through the woods. She links my arm in hers and we walk back to the cottage, discussing whether Jude Law's arrogance is off-putting or gob-smackingly sexy.

24

At eleven-thirty I decide to turn in. I'm far too tired and sober to stay up to argue the pros and cons of Leo Sayer's voice versus Barry Manilow's.

"Where's Hugh?" I ask Sam.

"Dunno," she slurs back. To be fair, she is juggling her wine glass, a fag and a hand of cards, so I can't reasonably expect her to keep an eye on the whereabouts of my boyfriend as well.

"We whipped their hides," adds James, giggling drunkenly, then he turns back to Sam to make another toast to their victory. I almost pity them the hangover that is certainly scheduled for tomorrow. I wander through to the kitchen, where Gilbert is helping Penny dry the pots.

"Have you seen Hugh?" I ask.

"Yes. He and Henry are fetching firewood from the shed," replies Gilbert.

"They took the whiskey bottle," says Penny, not bothering to hide her irritation. It's code, of course, for, "They've gone for the night," but why is she being so testy about it? It's not a criminal offense.

I throw on my coat and gloves and scarf once again and brave the "arctic climes." It's such a clear, cold night; it really wouldn't surprise me if it snowed again. I hear Henry and Hugh before I see them.

"Congratulations," says Henry, and he bangs his whiskey tumbler up against Hugh's.

"Thank you," Hugh over-articulates, immediately betraying that he's more than a bit merry.

I turn a corner and spot them by the barn, although they can't see me as they have their backs to me. They are sat on a huge, neat pile of chopped logs, looking out into the black night rather than at each other. The sight is quite touching, brother sat with brother, shoulder to shoulder, so I pause to take it in.

"How are you er . . . managing with the . . . erm . . . pregnancy?" asks Henry. The question makes me smile to myself. Hugh and Henry are equally ill at ease with discussing anything remotely emotional or female. The mix of both pernicious subjects is crippling. They are archetypal products of a single-sex boarding-school education. They are charming, independent, witty emotional cripples. However, I'm sure that if Hugh is going to talk to anyone about how he feels about the baby it will be Henry, so I stand mute and still.

"Clipped your wings a bit, no doubt."

Now I really can't move, it's simply not possible. I'm rooted, waiting for Hugh's response. I'm not sure what it will be. It strikes me that I don't know how he's "er . . . managing with the . . . erm . . . pregnancy."

"In a way, but they can be rather fun, though, can't they? Children?" says Hugh.

Isn't that lovely? I start to breathe again, but I don't move, maybe I'll hear more lovely stuff.

"If only George was a bit more fun."

Or maybe not.

"She's not taking it too well, then?" asks Henry, and I can hear concern in his voice.

"You'd think she was the first woman on earth ever to get pregnant, the way she's going on."

Going on! I've hardly said one hundredth of what I feel. Going on!

"Don't you think she wants it?"

"She says she does, but she's behaving very strangely."

"Eating coal?"

"Spitting fire." They both laugh, "A total dragon."

I can hear whiskey glugging from the bottle into the tumblers, another drink, and then silence as they savor the woody taste. A total dragon! It's just not true. One row. We've had one row! I consider coughing and letting them know I've arrived on the scene because I am aware that people who eavesdrop never hear good things about themselves. I stay silent.

The giggling subsides and in a more serious tone Henry comments, "Well, it must have been a shock to her. You didn't plan it, did you?"

"Good God, no."

"And she's quite a career woman. That won't be easy to give up."

"No. I suppose not."

So I'm giving up my career? Or at least Hugh seems to think so. We haven't talked about it. I thought I'd be carrying on after the baby is born. We need the money and, besides that, I may not be saving lives but it is *my* career. I know that only half an hour ago, on this very spot, I described my job to Libby in the lackluster terms "mostly good enough" but it is *my* mostly good enough career.

"And you two have had a high old time living the fast life—holidays, parties, restaurants, bars—you can't do all that after the baby is born."

"*I* can," insists Hugh, and, scarily, I believe him.

"Shame that they all become victims of their hormones in the end." Henry shakes his head with genuine regret. I'm not sure what it is he's regretting; the fact that women have the vote, perhaps? "I always had George down as fairly rational, quite considered. In many ways, I've always thought she was more of a man than I am," chuckles Henry. "Certainly has a better car and stereo."

"Not very good at math, though, look at her blunder over her safe dates." Hugh starts to laugh at his own joke but I don't think it's very funny.

"She was unnecessarily sharp over the Brie this lunchtime," admits Henry. "She does seem a bit tetchy." His disloyalty inspires a rage in me that makes me think hanging is too humane a punishment for such treachery.

Which possibly proves his point. Possibly.

"Yes, she is," agrees Hugh.

"And she always used to be so—"

"Compliant, accommodating," Hugh fills in the gap.

"Yes," nods Henry.

"Such comfortable company," adds Hugh.

"Yes."

"But now she's always angry, tearful, neurotic."

"Yes. Well, I'm sure it's her hormones. They all get neurotic. I'm certain she's no more neurotic than any other pregnant woman is. Hormones are to blame. Things will settle down after she's had the baby," comforts Henry, with the sensitivity of a genocidal Neanderthal.

"I hope you're right, Henry. I do hope you're right."

I'm gutted. This is terrible. Absolutely irreparable. Hugh thinks of me as compliant, accommodating and comfortable. I thought he thought I was sexy, stylish and sassy. Not at this precise moment, admittedly. But generally.

My head starts to spin as I desperately try to compute what I've just heard. For once, I'm certain that the dizzy rush is nothing to do with plummeting sugar levels and the pregnancy. Compliant, accommodating and comfortable! Hugh thinks I'm docile, submissive and subservient! Which is just one step away from imbecilic. It's so insulting. My breathing is shallow and fast. I can see it on the chilly night air, which is a small comfort. Seeing my breath cloud the icy night at least proves that I exist. That I'm here. Hearing your lover say such things can obliterate your very sense of self. The physical assurance of my presence helps me to remain calm. I watch my breathing become slower and more regular. Deep breaths. Deep breaths. Maybe this is good news. Maybe I'm being too hasty and judgmental. Hugh probably means compliant as in kind and gentle. Gracious. And comfortable is a compliment. At ease. I put him at ease. Hugh thinks I'm gentle, gracious and tender. And as Hugh is with me because I'm gentle, gracious and tender, then it doesn't matter if I'm not sexy, stylish and sassy. Which I'm not at the moment. Oh joy, oh joy, he's not simply interested in my looks, he's interested in the core me.

Providing, of course, that the core me is compliant.

Meaning gracious. It's just semantics.

He did say that he was looking forward to having a child with me. That it will be fun. Which is a very positive thing to hear. I smile to myself. I'm thrilled, ecstatic, amazed. Hugh is interested in how I *am,* not how I look. Which is fantastic. What's he saying now?

"And she looks bloody terrible. She's piling on weight and she used to have the most amazing tits but now they are fast beginning to resemble cows' udders, decorated with veins and stretch marks that look like the Tube map."

"Big, though," Henry tries to be positive.

"Yes, great big boobies," says Hugh with audible disgust.

It's my own fault. No one ever hears good things about themselves when they listen to other people's conversations.

It's my fault.

It has to be.

Hugh finally comes to bed after 2 A.M. He starts to play with my breasts; obviously after a bottle of whiskey it's not always easy to tell the difference between "amazing tits" and "cows' udders."

I chase the bitterness out of my head and heart and I try to remind myself that I shouldn't have listened in to the conversation. It was a private conversation. And he wasn't sober. Nowhere near. We can't really be held accountable for the things we say when under the influence. We all say things we don't mean. He did say that he was thrilled to be having a baby with me and that he couldn't imagine anything being more fun. I can't help but think of Libby, who hasn't anything other than her bedsocks to keep her warm (unless she got lucky with James), so I cling to Hugh as though my life depended on it.

As indeed it always has.

We make love and, while it's not planet-scattering, it does have the advantage of being well rehearsed; it's warm and comfortable. I must make a bit more of an effort to be more "up" when I'm around Hugh. I always used to ensure that he only ever saw me at my happy best. And although it is much harder now that I see him every day, rather than on two week nights and every second Sunday, I simply must try harder. I have been unnecessarily snively recently.

I fold my body into Hugh's and murmur that the fresh air must suit me. "I haven't been sick for hours."

"It must suit Sam too; she hasn't mentioned her wedding for hours, either," he quips.

We giggle. I start to tell Hugh about Libby, but quickly discover that I am wasting my time. He's asleep. His breath gently pours onto the back of my neck, his left arm cradles my pillow, his right arm is thrown across my body, my back is toasted by his chest, and our legs are so entangled that it's nearly impossible to work out who is giving whom a cramp. It's only when we are wrapped around one another like this that I feel really warm and truly safe. It is at moments like this that I remember where and why I've been traveling all these years. This is it, I have arrived.

Haven't I?

25

I wake the entire house with my retching. The only consolation is that I'm not the only one feeling rough; those who are feeling vaguely human are in the minority. Surprisingly, Hugh is one of them. I can only assume his hangover is yet to kick in, because when I got up at seven—to empty my insides into the plumbing system—he got up too and went for a run. Penny obviously isn't hung over as she only ever drinks moderate amounts. However, pretty much everyone else is reaching for the Alka-Seltzer. I realize that I can't be a very nice person as I find being ill with company infinitely more palatable than being ill alone.

I wonder if that's something I should work on.

"I'm too old for such late nights," comments Henry.

Not for a second do any of us believe that his hangdog expression, pounding head and overactive sweat glands are the result of lack of sleep.

"I could make a cooked breakfast," offers Sam. There is a roar of unanimous approval.

"Good girl."

"Fine idea."

"Well done, you."

I catch Penny's eye. She's wearing rubber gloves as she's washing the kitchen floor and has just finished cleaning the bathrooms. Although she planned the menus, did all the shopping for the weekend's catering and has made every meal so far, she has not received as much praise as Sam gets for offering to stick a couple of rashers of bacon under the grill. I wonder if she's noticed. Libby obviously has, because when Sam leaves the kitchen to go and find her fag packet Libby comments, "I wouldn't waste your time cleaning loos if you want to get noticed." She drops three teaspoons of instant coffee into a mug. She does this in slow motion; it's obvious that she feels wrecked too. "Men don't see dirt, they don't notice when it's messy, so why would they care if you tidy up?" She shuffles to the fridge and pulls out a pint of milk. She sniffs it carefully, but of course it is fresh because Penny wouldn't have sour milk in any fridge that she's in charge of. "They notice drink. Pour them a glass of wine or fetch a can and a cheer goes up." And while she doesn't have to be explicit, it's obvious that Libby's next observation is that men notice the food that soaks up hangovers. Therefore, despite the fact that breakfast is the simplest meal to prepare, it's always the meal that earns the most lavish praise.

I think it's pretty good of Libby to share this advice with Penny, but Penny doesn't thank her, she doesn't say anything at all. She waits until Sam reappears from the sitting room and simply says, "Would you make breakfast, Sam?" (Although I do notice that the smile is a little stiff.) "Then I can take the children to church. I looked up the mass times yesterday. There's one at eleven."

"Do they go to church every week?" I ask.

"Most."

Religion. What will we do? Will I instruct my baby that there is a God (other than the modern-day ones, such as Amex and Robbie Williams) or will I admit that, as far as I'm concerned, the jury is still out? There's so much more to parenting than buying the latest Nike trainers and, not for the first time, I wonder if I'm qualified. Hugh and I have yet to discuss the God issue. We must, and soon. Maybe I'll broach the subject on the car ride home. And I'll find a way to bring up the fact that I am planning on going back to work after the baby is born. It strikes me that besides sex we haven't done much together to actually prepare for this baby's birth. We haven't even agreed on a name and I can't pin him down on whether he's planning on attending the birth or not.

"I'll come with you," I offer. It's so out of character that Penny initially thinks she's misheard me. It's true that I don't regularly attend church—in fact, I limit my visits to weddings and funerals. "You'll never manage all the kids on your own," I justify. I don't suppose Penny wants me to go to church with her but on the other hand she can't refuse my offer. It wouldn't be very godly; it wouldn't be very Penny.

I bully Kate and Tom into wearing something vaguely smart, or at least clean, and, as Libby has shuffled back to bed to take advantage of the, I assume, rare chance of a lie-in, I ask Millie if she wants to come too.

"Why should I?" she demands. Fair question.

"We're stopping off at the newsagent's on the way home to buy newspapers and sweets," I reply. It's a tough call. Millie will have to leave her Barbie and Steps videos or trust someone else to choose her favorite sweets.

"O.K., then, I'll come," she sighs, making it clear that her agreement is reluctant.

Millie won't put on anything suitable for church. To be fair, it soon becomes obvious that she doesn't actually own clothes that would be considered suitable. God is just going to have to accept her fluorescent-green mini skirt, silver halter-neck top and ruby-red sling-back sandals, worn (with undeniable flair and a dollop of unconventionality) with multicolored, stripy tights. To prove she knows she's going somewhere a bit special, Millie also chooses to wear about twenty friendship bangles; it looks as though the weight of them is going to make her tumble sideways. Penny is obviously horrified and if I'd realized that Millie's appearance was going to upset her so much I would have allowed Millie to put on her fake tattoos; as it is, we have to hurry.

By some miracle, we manage to get all children to the church on time and, by another, they all look set to behave impeccably throughout the service.

My motivation for coming to the service is ill-defined. I know for definite that I didn't want to sit among the smells of a fried breakfast, yet another trigger that my oh-so-sensitive stomach reacts to. And a tiny bit of me thinks that, however self-righteous and irritating Penny is, it isn't fair to expect her to manage all the children on her own all the time. Who would have thought that rubber gloves could unleash such sympathy?

And then again there is something more than that.

It may be curiosity. It's certainly a novelty spending a Sunday morning in church rather than simply spending it in the supermarket or on the King's Road. It's not that I want to pray or anything. It's not that I have anything particular that I need help with. My life is just fine. Hugh and I are having a baby and he speaks of me in glowing terms to his brother. Everything is fine. And, anyway, even if it wasn't fine, mumbling silently in my head, to a silent something in my head, is unlikely to be much practical help. Having said that, I find myself mumbling anyway. Something about "please, silent something in my head, let it be fine." Because it can't harm, can it?

There is no flash of lightning, no parting of the seas, no obvious sign of divine intervention. But, sat among the shiny wooden benches and smiley old women, singing hymns that I sang as a child, and watching the early spring sun filter through the stained-glass windows onto the worn marble floor, I feel peaceful. Supported. I lose myself to the sound of the choir and simply enjoy the confident, understated harmony of combined voices.

It's a relief.

The feeling of calm doesn't last as long as the sermon.

Penny has to take her youngest two outside the church—one is screaming louder than the tenor is singing, the other has peed his pants. A fact revealed to us during silent prayer, when Tom yelled at the top of his voice, "Naughty Marcus has done splashy wee-wee all over the floor." Penny's oldest child, Josh, has listened to more propaganda than your average Russian during the Cold War, and sees me as the devil incarnate. Given a choice of companions he'd rather spend time with Cruella De Vil. He eyes me warily and I know that I have only a matter of minutes before he starts to bawl. Kate and Tom are fighting because, apparently, Tom's coin for the collection box is shinier than Kate's. Millie is bored and keeps kicking the pew in front of her. Each time she does so she apologizes in a loud voice and explains to the angry occupants that she comes from a one-parent family and has never been in a church before, not even to be baptized. The entire congregation sighs communally for her poor lost soul and glares at me. The ones who still possess the majority of their faculties look at my ringless left hand and my swelling stomach. They mutter something about cushy number on the welfare state, tut their disgust and turn back to their hymn books.

I no longer feel supported.

I just want a fag.

And a stiff gin.

When the service is over I quickly usher the kids outside, trying to avoid the vicar's handshake and Marcus's pee. I'm delighted to see that Sam and Libby are waiting with Penny.

"We thought we'd come and meet you and we can all walk back together," smiles Libby.

"Or pop to the pub," suggests Sam. She catches Penny's eye and adds defensively, "For a lemonade, there's a garden."

"I don't think so," comments killjoy Penny.

"Well, I do," I assert. I'm in need of a drink, even if the only stiff thing about it is the straw.

Penny insists on taking Kate and Tom home with her. She exercises her right as auntie and I, common-law stepmother, have no rights at all. Oh, I don't care, let her take them. It can't be healthy that I've started to actively seek Kate and Tom's company. I am pleased that Libby opts to join Sam and me. It's understandable. As Londoners we are all deprived of fresh air and we think it's a luxury to sit on a bench near a tree, even if it is still chilly and we have to keep our coats on.

"Shame Penny didn't want to join us," ventures Sam. While I'm not losing sleep over her absence, I don't say as much. It's unnecessary to be mean to a woman whose idea of a good time is donning rubber gloves and cleaning loos. "Penny is awash with old-fashioned housewifery skills that are dying out. I feel I could learn a lot from her. She does her own decorating, hangs wallpaper and everything. She showed me some photos of the children's rooms; she's painted adorable stencil designs all around the walls and ceiling."

"Really?" I try to stifle my yawn behind a polite smile, but fail.

"She can ice cakes, arrange flowers. She knows stuff like the importance of turning a mattress." Sam sighs her adoration. "You'd find her interesting, too, if only you'd give her a chance. Remember, they say it takes all sorts to make a world."

This is the second time in twenty-four hours that I've been given this advice and still I doubt it. Indeed, I'm piqued beyond reason that Sam would even think so.

"What makes you think that just because I'm pregnant I want to turn into the type of woman who knows how to remove stains?" I demand. Libby and Sam look at me pityingly. My example was a bad choice; likelihood is I will want and need to know how to remove stains from shirts, dressing gowns, carpets, coats and car seats; all sorts of stains, sick, milk, milky sick, Ribena, squashed banana and worse. It's a dismal train of thought, so I change the subject and ask, "Where are the chaps? Didn't they want to join us?"

"James has gone back to bed," says Libby.

"Wise," I approve.

"Gilbert never drinks at lunchtime," says Sam.

"Old fart," I comment, but dilute the harsh words with my sweetest smile; my gesture is unnecessary as Sam doesn't seem to be listening to me. "And how are your heads?" I probe.

"I have to stop drinking so much," says Libby, laying her head on the wooden table and moaning. "It wasn't just last night; I had a very heavy session on Friday as well."

I *really* like Libby, more and more. This is more like it. Forget stenciling and turning mattresses. There's no need to assume that mums throw in the towel as far as having fun goes. It's obvious that Libby's life is no picnic, but I'm thrilled to note that she isn't letting her spirit, youth and beauty go to waste.

"Did you have a good time?" I ask.

"Millie, why don't you go and play on the swings?" suggests Libby.

"Don't want to." Millie can obviously sniff a good debrief from quite a distance and is not prepared to lose out. Libby glares at her daughter and, after a short but undignified battle involving bribes of a bottle of Coke and a packet of crisps, Millie slinks off toward the swings, which puts her out of earshot—although her mother warns us that she's quite good at lip-reading. Libby chooses to answer my question anyway.

"Kind of. Some of the gang from work invited me out for a few drinks, and as Millie was having tea at one of her friends' and I'd arranged for her to be picked up from there by her babysitter . . ." Self-justification elegantly mixed with guilt is possibly Libby's natural state.

"So you were young, free and single, as it were," I say, trying to hurry her along.

She nods. "Well, a quick one turned into a slow several. The works: beers, wine, tequilas, a nightclub and . . . sordid S.E.X. with a friend of one of the junior consultants." She whispers the last bit.

"Oh no."

"Oh yes," she assures, half cheerfully, half ruefully. We pause to open a packet of crisps for Millie; personally, I doubt whether this will be a robust enough distraction.

"And was it any good?" I ask dutifully. No one ever makes a confession of this kind except in the hope that they'll be asked for details.

"Not sure," whispers Libby. "When I woke up the next morning there were two things on my mind. One, who is this

P.E.R.S.O.N. L.Y.I.N.G. next to me? Two, how can I remove H.I.M. without attracting the attention of you know who." She spells it out quickly although Millie is at least fifty yards away; Libby obviously thinks she's currently in training for MI-5.

I smile sympathetically.

"Actually, there were numerous other questions springing to mind, vying for attention. What time is it? What day is it? If it's a weekday what shall I put in Millie's sandwiches? Is her school shirt ironed? How did I get home? How did my K.N.I.C.K.E.R.S. get stuck on top of the headboard? Who blew out the candles? Is that a red wine stain on the carpet? If so, will Fabriclean remove it? I decided that my rudimentary decision to concentrate on the original two questions was wisest."

Sam and I laugh and Sam asks, "Did you get rid of him without inciting the wrath of the scary . . ." She makes a movement that's a cross between a wink and a nod as she motions toward Millie.

I notice Millie tut. Obviously our attempts to preserve her childhood innocence are as ineffective as they are ludicrous.

"Yes and no. Getting rid of him was a doddle. He seemed rather too keen to make an exit, especially after he spotted the Pokémon stickers on the fridge door and the Mickey Mouse toothpaste in the bathroom. However, we didn't manage to accomplish his flit without being spied on by the ever-vigilant . . ." Libby points at Millie.

Millie breaks her sulky silence as she re-approaches our bench and comments, "My mother is a disgrace" in her best Mary Whitehouse accent, behaving as though she were Libby's mother, rather than her daughter.

"Show no fear," I whisper. Libby tries to smile but I can tell she's concerned. I don't know what to say to her to make her feel better. But I can't just sit back and watch her drown in guilt and responsibility. "O.K., so you slept with a handsome stranger. How bad can that be?"

"Not bad at all if I were simply single, rather than a single mum," mutters Libby. It seems that Millie is an albatross and a lifebuoy all at once.

"We've all done it," says Sam, patting Libby's hand comfortingly. "Well, except for George," she adds, which makes me distinctly uncomfortable.

"Haven't you ever had a one-night stand, George?"

"No, well not unless you count my first night with Hugh." I briefly fill her in with the background of my and Hugh's relationship. It takes a remarkable amount of self-control to stick to the broad brush strokes rather than give her the minutiae, but then I am restricted by time—we have to be back at the cottage for lunch in a couple of hours.

When I've finished, Libby asks, "Can I ask you a personal question?"

"Go on," I agree cautiously. It must be bad if Libby feels she has to ask to be personal; we've assumed a girly level of intimacy and honesty thus far.

"How many men have you slept with besides Hugh?"

I'm sure if we'd met in our early twenties this question would have been included in the first five questions on meeting one another. Name, age, occupation, which Tube line do you use to get into work and how many notches on the bedpost? The order of questions four and five is interchangeable. But meeting a little later in life normally demands more reticence; I'd hoped to avoid it altogether. "Besides Hugh?" I clarify.

"Yes."

"How many?" I stall.

"Yes."

"Err." I take a moment; my answer is frighteningly unfashionable. If Sam wasn't here I'd lie, but Sam knows the truth. "Em, well, none," I finally confess.

"None!" Libby is so shocked that she nearly drops her drink. "No one other than Hugh?"

"No," I confirm.

"But you work in advertising?"

"A few near misses. Quite a few. But no actual, you know."

"Hiding the sausage."

"Exactly."

She stops to do the math. She's so obviously aghast that I'm distressed for her. "That means you were celibate for roughly ten years, most of your adult life," she says, incredulous.

"Yes."

"But you give the impression that you are so worldly."

I shrug, what can I say? He was worth waiting for. I hunt for a fresh packet of crisps among the debris. At least the rustling breaks the silence.

"Why?"

"Why what?"

"Why just Hugh?"

"I love him. I've only ever loved him." It seems straightforward to me, but I guess mine could be regarded as a fairly complex moral code. I slept with Hugh although he was married to Becca, but I've never slept with anyone else because I've never loved anyone else.

"God, Hugh must be amazing to have kept you so . . ." she searches for the word, "focused." Libby can't take her eyes off me. In her mind I'm obviously akin to something that's just landed from another planet. I sometimes wish I were Madonna.

"Don't look at me like that."

"How am I looking at you?"

"As though I've wasted my life."

"How should I be looking?"

I can't think of an answer.

At great personal expense, Sam creates a diversion. Or maybe she just wants to talk about herself again.

"I'm giving up alcohol too. I feel as rough as budgie crap."

Millie giggles and seems to forget her mother's one-night stand and my lack of them as, this time, she skips off toward the swings, appearing every inch the adorable, compliant seven-year-old. I can only assume she thinks she's achieved her mischief quota in church this morning.

"I didn't get to sleep until after 5 A.M. this morning," says Sam.

"Show-off. Nooky in the early hours of the morning. I'm beginning to understand why you're engaged to Gilbert," I say, coarsely winking and elbowing Sam in the ribs. It's funny, since I've become pregnant I don't seem to be able to do anything elegantly, not even discuss the lurid details of my friends' sex lives. Actually, thinking about it maybe that's not so odd.

"I wasn't with Gilbert. He went to bed just after you."

"So what were you up to?" asks Libby, guffawing. If Libby knew Sam better she'd know *for a fact* that Sam won't ever be "up to" anything again. Sam is engaged now, which was her lifelong ambition and therefore that's that.

"I was up till late with James. We went for a walk, actually."
What?

"Just you and James?" I want to be sure of my data.

"Yes," Sam is talking to something at the bottom of her glass, and she suddenly seems to be extremely interested in the grain on the wooden bench.

"Gilbert's brother James?" I ask.

"There aren't two Jameses staying at the cottage," she points out, mildly aggravated.

"A walk? At night? Alone?" I persist.

"Yes. Yes. And yes." The irritation is mounting.

"Why?"

"I don't know," she admits. Suddenly deflated, the irritation disappearing in a puff of smoke. She tries to replace it with mock bravado. "He's a great guy. We get on well. He's going to be my brother-in-law. I'm just trying to get to know him. We've spent the week together, he's a great guy." She completes her ever-decreasing circle of reasoning.

And why shouldn't she? What's wrong with taking a walk with the guy who's going to be your brother-in-law?
Nothing.
Something.
Yes, something is definitely wrong. A vision of Sam falling

through the door of the cottage yesterday afternoon, laughing raucously, her entire demeanor radiant and luminous. I'd thought it was the fresh air. Another vision, this time Sam flinging her arms around James when they won the rounders match—why didn't she give Gilbert the victory hug? And last night she hardly said two words to Gilbert, she spent her entire evening in deep and often exclusive conversation with James. I'd thought she was simply being welcoming and polite, but now I'm not so sure. My misgivings are further fueled when Sam takes the unprecedented step of saying, "Look, if you don't mind, I don't want to talk about it. Best we forget all about it."

"Absolutely," says Libby.

I just nod. This is Sam! Sam who has been known to accost strangers in the street and force them to listen to the bloody details of her love life because she's running out of willing listeners.

We fall into awkward silence again. I feel I owe Sam for helping me avoid Libby's tricky questioning so I accept the conversational onus and try to provide some entertainment.

"Hugh and I had a huge row on Friday night," I confess.

"A row?" Sam doesn't try too hard to hide her surprise.

"Yes," I sigh.

"You and Hugh?"

"Yes. I was furious with him."

"Furious?"

"Yes."

"With Hugh?"

"Yes!" I'm beginning to wish I hadn't said anything.

Sam lets out a long, low whistle. She's so taken aback that she doesn't even ask what the row was about.

Luckily, Libby is on hand to fulfill this social nicety. "What about?"

"He was late. Five hours. I was stuck at home with his kids."

"Look on it as practice," comments Libby, then she drains her drink.

Funnily enough I don't see this as a comfort. "He's started to call my tits boobies," I blurt. The girls stare at me non-comprehendingly. "I hate it. There are so many awful connotations. It makes me think of *Carry On* films and booby traps, booby prizes." The girls both stare at me, obviously still not grasping the problem. I try to be crystal: "Tits are sexy, breasts are sensuous, boobies are indubitably ludicrous."

Their faces are vacant.

I give up. "Fancy another lemonade?"

26

We arrive back at the cottage at about five minutes to two. Penny is just about to serve up an enormous roast lamb. A small twinge of guilt nips me. Unassisted, Penny has managed to entertain five kids and cook what promises to be a delicious roast for fourteen. I consider skulking off to the sitting room to kill the last five minutes before lunch as a way of avoiding her cold gaze, then I think better of it. I think of the countless brunches, lunches, dinners and suppers I've prepared in the past that have passed by uncommented on. Plates cleared, glasses drained, napkins discarded without so much as a "Well done, George, very nice."

I lift the lid off a pot and peer in. "Looks very tasty," I comment, and then more warmly I mutter, "I'm sorry we left you on your own, Penny." Half of me hopes that she won't hear me.

"Oh, it's O.K., I'm used to it," she breezes.

Instantly irritated, I fume that this woman is devoid of social graces.

Almost as quickly I acknowledge that she's within her rights not to let me off the hook that easily. "I'll wash up afterward," I offer, then I quickly leave the kitchen before I change my mind.

Lunch is fabulous and everyone enjoys it, except for poor Sam who isn't eating; presumably she's dieting for the wedding. Apparently a must, irrespective of your size or shape.

"You're not dieting for a wedding, are you?" asks Gilbert as he spoons a generous portion of roast potatoes on to my plate.

"No." Sadly not.

"Nice to be pregnant and temporarily released from the tyranny of calorie-counting, isn't it?" smiles Penny, smoothing over any potential discomfort Gilbert's comment could have caused. All at once I'm glad I offered to do the washing-up.

"I suppose you're right. I've never looked at it like that." I smile back and nod as she piles the works onto my plate. Lamb, mashed potatoes, three different vegetables, Yorkshire puddings, mint sauce and gravy. I even chew on the crackling, something I haven't done in donkey's years. Hugh stares at me with barely disguised disgust but doesn't say anything openly, so I pretend not to notice his disapproval.

It's not so hard.

Crackling tastes fantastic. Chewy and crunchy at once. The mash is made with real butter, not a low-fat spread. It melts in a creamy delicious mush on my tongue. How did I ever give it up? And because I can't drink alcohol I have lime and lemonade with the children. The full-sugar version. It tastes syrupy and luscious, rather than acidic and caustic like diet lemonade.

"This is really gorgeous, Penny. I can't remember when I last had a full Sunday roast lunch."

"I don't know why you starve yourself."

"To stay thin."

"Well, it's not natural, we're supposed to eat. Do you know that your baby is sucking and swallowing by fourteen weeks?" says Penny.

"Really?" I probably have read that. But I hadn't taken it in. When I read the pregnancy books I tend to concentrate on weight gain; mine and its. Or abnormal fetal development, infections, the many ways in which this pregnancy limits my lifestyle. The bad stuff. I pause for a moment and consider the miracles Penny is talking about.

"And, incredibly, your baby's permanent teeth are already

forming as tiny buds behind the milk-teeth buds in its jaw by nineteen weeks."

"That's fascinating. Imagine how minute they must be."

"They can already distinguish between sweet and savory." Penny is on a roll; this is obviously her specialist topic.

"Better not have any of the bread-and-butter pudding then," advises Hugh, intercepting the plate that Penny is handing me. I look at it with longing. "You don't want to be teaching the baby bad habits this early on. A little restraint wouldn't go amiss." He laughs to himself but no one joins in. Nor do they comment when I quietly take the plate from him and firmly start to fork the sticky pudding into my mouth.

After lunch everyone settles down in front of the TV except Hugh, who finds a quiet room to read his file. It strikes me that we could all have been thus engaged in London and it seems a waste of Wales. I mean, there are hills and things, aren't there? We should be walking up them, or at least looking at them. Once again I'm sorely tempted to strike out on my own and go for a walk.

But I don't.

Instead, I offer to give Hugh a hand with his work, but he points out that he's pitching for an account that demands a certain level of confidentiality. He hints darkly that Q&A might also be pitching for this business and therefore we can't discuss our strategies with one another. He must be on about the Sun 'n' Sauce Hols account; both Q&A and Rartle, Roguel and Spirity are on the pitch list. As are WCRS, Ogilvy and Mather, Y&R, Saatchi & Saatchi—in fact most of the advertising agencies in London. MKJL already run the account, and it's my belief that they are doing a terrific job. Sun 'n' Sauce Hols have just hired a new Marketing Manager. He's called a pitch simply to flex his muscles; I very much doubt he has any real intention of moving the business, he just wants a few free lunches. He must be a very hungry man if the number of agencies he's invited to pitch is anything to go by. I think Hugh may be sulking because of the incident over the pudding—I can't believe he is genuinely interested in winning this pitch; it's not worth more than a few hundred thousand in a media spend. Perhaps he sees it as a potential creative-award winner. Arguably, any half-decent agency could create fun and attention-grabbing ads for such a cheeky brand. That said, our strap line at Q&A is a clumsy and unimaginative play on the words *Get off on Sun and Fun.* I think we've lost the pitch before it's even begun and so I'm not biting my nails. Oh well, if Hugh doesn't want my help it looks like I have no excuse for not keeping my promise to do the washing-up.

The pans are so numerous and so large that I estimate that the task may take me a week. I'm just musing on the fact that every idyllic little cottage with window boxes should come with an efficient little electric dishwasher when Libby follows me into the kitchen. She picks up a tea towel and quietly starts to dry the plates I've washed.

"So, are you attending all your prenatal checkups?" Libby is drying the dinner plates with slug-like speed. She stares at the little red rosebuds that adorn the crockery with such interest that you'd be forgiven for believing that they held the answer to the eternal questions, such as "Why are we here?," "Which is the one true religion?" and "Who will win the Derby?"

"Yes. I go to my checkups," I confirm.

"That's a good sign, well done," beams Libby. I look around for the child with learning difficulties to whom she is so obviously addressing her praise. "Some women in your position go into total denial. They don't attend their checkups, they continue to smoke and drink. They exercise fanatically and generally try to live their lives exactly as they did pre-pregnancy."

"My position?"

"Our position. Unplanned. Unmarried."

I'm not in Libby's position—she was also unsupported—but it doesn't seem polite to say so.

"Going to the doctor's is a nightmare, though," I confess, plunging my hands into the suds again.

"Why so?"

I look at Libby. There's something about her slightly harassed, shiny face that makes me realize that I'd actually relish a girly chat. Which is odd, because the only thing in anyone's face in the past that has inspired such a sentiment was something on the face, i.e., "Is that the new Chanel lipstick you are wearing? Does it last?" Libby's smile gives me permission to be a bit more frank with her than I am with, say, Julia or even Sam. Maybe it's because her face is unadorned (other than with a faint alcohol-induced flush), and her hair is carelessly tied back in a stubby ponytail. Last time I looked, Julia's hair was ebony with red streaks (signature Toni&Guy) and she was wearing a Stella McCartney T-shirt and Joseph jeans. Sam's look is quite different but, if anything, even more expensive. It's all Hermès, Escada and Chanel. I'm not sure why both looks prohibit a swapping of confidences about the safety or otherwise of douching, itchy flesh and bladder infections, but they do. I wonder when Libby last blew more than £25 on anything for herself (Dyson vacuum cleaners don't count). Knowing that it's much more likely that she has to spend her Saturday mornings in the Early Learning Center and then McDonald's, rather than in Jigsaw and a neat little French bistro, is somehow comforting.

"It's odd. I've never worried about demanding answers from doctors, nurses or other medical bods in the past. They're just people."

"Absolutely," agrees Libby. "I've slept with an anesthetist." The ultimate leveler. "It was a complete disaster, his technique was appalling, although as an anesthetist he was probably very skilled," she muses.

I giggle, allowing trust to flow into our relationship. I offer a confession to meet her own. "And at university I drank a number of medics under the table. I do know them for what they are. I've always considered it my God-given right—no, duty—to cross-examine them on exactly what they are prodding and why," I pronounce.

"Absolutely," agrees Libby again. And then she prompts, "But . . ."

The bubbles dance prettily around the greasy plates, oblivious to my difficulty. "But suddenly doctors and midwives have become deus-like. I'm convinced that no one other than the Virgin Mary could have ever looked her midwife in the eye. When talking to a midwife, my line of inquiry is something like this, 'Excuse me. I wonder if you can help. I don't mean to be too much trouble. I am *very* sorry for asking, but could you possibly explain why you are treating my private parts with a battering ram . . . Oh, it's procedure. Fabulous. Thank you. So sorry to be a bother. Thank you.' "

Libby is laughing.

I'm not.

I seem to have lost all my assurance, all my confidence, and it took me so long to collect it. For years I have tried to be better informed, wittier, sharper, more intelligent, more sagacious, more lucid and perceptive. None of the above adjectives have ever applied to the pregnant women or new mums I've come across. Nearly fourteen years of effort. It's demoralizing to think that fifteen minutes of duvet action have reversed all that.

"I remember the prenatal examinations being intimidating," Libby admits. "It's natural that you feel a bit apprehensive, you are sailing uncharted waters."

"There is so much to learn, and, however many books I read, or however many strangers stop me in the street to offer unsolicited advice, I don't seem to be any the wiser." I raise my eyebrows and Libby laughs again.

"But everything's O.K., isn't it?" she asks, suddenly serious. She asks the question without lifting her eyes, allowing me some privacy as I procrastinate about how honest I want to be. While I've never actually been in a confessional box I think this is what it must be like. Frightening, difficult and yet enticing. It would be a huge relief to be honest. To admit that I'm nervous, that I feel overwhelmed and underqualified. It might help to explain that I find it disconcerting that my body, which has always been just that, *my* body, for the exclusive use of G&Ts and Helmut Lang dresses, is now public property. It is peculiar that my vagina has had more tourists than the Dome.

It's not just my body; my life is not my own.

It would be a huge relief not to have to use "the voice" to tell her "everything is fine" and that "I'm doing beautifully." I'd like to say fuck "the voice."

"Absolutely fine," I smile. "I'm doing beautifully. Well, you know how marvelous it is to be expecting."

Libby stares at me for the longest time but says nothing. The moment passes, and I'm left with the distinct feeling that the only person I've let down is myself.

Libby hangs her tea towel to dry out on the back of a chair. "Millie and I are heading back to London soon. We want to miss the worst of the Sunday afternoon traffic. Here's my number—I thought we might get together for a coffee or something."

"I'd like that," I beam. And while it's true that I haven't exactly been inundated with invites recently I realize that her offer for coffee is the only social engagement I've actually wanted to accept in two months.

"Well, give me a call," she smiles. "Soon."

27

Hugh, Kate, Tom and I leave the cottage at about 5 P.M. after Hugh's important conference call and about two hours after the optimum time for departure; we catch the traffic and the children's Sunday evening blues. Still, on a more positive note, the long journey home does give me plenty of time to talk with Hugh. Until this weekend I hadn't realized how much we haven't talked about. I'd never thought of ours as a house of taboos.

I start with the question of childcare. "Do you think we should have a nanny or send the baby to a nursery when I go back to work?" I ask. I've considered this question for twenty minutes before I put it to him. I've decided it's best to rule out any ambiguity as to *whether* or not I will be going back to work.

"Oh, you are going back to work, are you?" His question isn't challenging the assumption; he merely sounds mildly surprised.

"Yes. Had you expected me to stay at home?" Of course I know he had, but I can hardly admit as much without revealing that I listened in on his conversation with Henry.

"Hadn't given it much thought." He smiles. "I suppose that because Becca didn't go back, nor Penny, come to think of it, I'd assumed you wouldn't want to, either. But, by all means, if you want to work, do so." He grins at his own benevolence.

"So nanny or nursery then?"

"Your call."

"Do you think the baby should be christened?"

"Up to you."

"If we do have it baptized we should go to church too, on a regular basis; there doesn't seem much point otherwise."

"Oh, I'm not sure about that, George. Sundays are very busy as it is. There's golf, rugby and the papers."

"Right." I pause and look out the window. Everyone is in such a hurry to get home. All three lanes of the motorway are cluttered. I peer into each car that passes and watch the occupants. There are lots of couples. Some happy and relaxed; some obviously rowing; some weary, hardly talking to one another at all but already thinking about the towering in-trays and endless e-mails that will greet them in the morning. I pay particular attention to the cars full of families. It surprises me that there is no noticeable disparity between the cars full of families and those with couples only. The families are also a mix of happy and relaxed, or weary and rowing. The only discernible difference is that the family cars tend to have boxes of tissues on the back shelf and hand prints on the windows, not such a monumental distinction. The light fades and it becomes more difficult to people-watch, as the car headlights are dazzling. I turn back to Hugh.

"Have you read that literature I gave you on epidurals?"

"Most of it."

"And you're happy for me to go ahead if necessary?"

"Well, it's up to you. Becca didn't have anything other than gas and air."

"I know." I bloody know.

"I feel sick," shouts Kate from the back of the car.

"Stop looking at your book then," I instruct. "Here, suck this." I pass her some boiled sweets. She doesn't thank me. "What do you say?" I ask.

"Thank you." She mutters this with all the sincerity of a *Big*

Brother contestant expressing regret that they have to pick a nominee for eviction.

"Have you given any thought to names?" I ask Hugh.

"Have you?"

"I like Jake for a boy, or Isabel for a girl."

"Not Jake," yells Kate. "There's a Jake in my class at school and he's horrible."

"Isabelly," lisps Tom, "really smelly."

Hugh laughs and says, "Not Jake or Isabel then; you'll have to think of something else. Now how about some music?" He turns on the radio and the children let out a squeal of approval as they hear the charts countdown.

Conversation finished.

I lie back and close my eyes. I know it will only be a matter of minutes before the motion of the car and the hum of the various indistinguishable songs will lull me to sleep.

I'll be asleep before the end of this track.

Or the next one.

I'll soon be in the Land of Nod.

I sit bolt upright, I'm not even drowsy.

After weeks of battling with killer lethargy, why, when I'm given this perfect opportunity to nap, can't I sleep?

I wish I'd been more frank with Libby. She appears entirely trustworthy—I should have been more forthcoming. I mean, that stuff about the midwife, while true, is only part of the problem. As indeed is the stuff about getting fat and missing fun and flirtation. So what's really bothering me? Why do I feel so desperate, so defeated, so despondent?

I glance across at Hugh. He's singing. He's got a great voice. And beautiful eyes. A wicked grin. His eleven-out-of-ten-ness shines brightly. I look down at my swelling hands and can't help but think that once a five and a half, always a five and a half. I've spent half my life at gyms and beauticians' trying to drag myself up to an eight. Don't make the mistake of thinking I'm vain. I'm not vain. The botox, the designer clothes, the bleached teeth, the diets, the gym, the implants, are not about vanity. The vain ones are the ones who go out without any make-up. I'd never have the confidence to inflict my nude face on the world at large. I admit I *am* finding the symptoms of pregnancy a strain; I sometimes can't imagine ever feeling human again, but that's not the problem. I don't resent the fatness, the spots, the lank, greasy hair per se. I fear them.

Hugh bought into the size-4, hard-body me who drank at the right watering holes, wore the correct Christian Blanken garb. He chose the skinny-ribbed, dainty babe. I was sharp, too.

As in funny.

That was what attracted Hugh, and I secured him by making his life as comfortable as possible. Feminists gasp, suffragettes spin, and my friends throw their arms up in the air and use words like "mug" and "doormat." But, the thing is, I know we are meant for each other. I am a better person because I met him. Without him I'd have an average degree and a dull job, I'd shop at Etam, and I'd probably get my hair cut at the local hairdresser's. I might not even know who Christian Blanken is. Wouldn't that be awful? So, yes, I fawn and flatter and fall into line. All relationships are compromises.

Things have been a bit wobbly recently. No one said a perfect life is easy to maintain. You need to put a lot of effort in. It is possible that by not going to the gym I've ruined everything— I'm not talking jinxes; it's more scientific than that. If you don't go to the gym, you get fat, you become unattractive—and your boyfriend leaves you. If you don't read the newspapers, concentrate at work, you become dull company—and your boyfriend leaves you. If you don't go out with your friends and keep up with the latest trends and gossip, you become boring—and your boyfriend leaves you. Being pregnant is just another ball I have to juggle. It's not an excuse. What would I do if he left me? I could not survive. I wouldn't even want to. Vicious and virtuous circles are entirely the product of the manufacturer. I just need to get back on track. I should have a manicure or read *The Economist.*

I can hold this together despite Mother Nature being a class-A bitch.

I'm sure I can.

April

28

Let's cast our minds back to this time last year when you came to us, to share your marketing objectives. Three simple objectives. Firstly, to take a 2 percent share of the fruit-flavored carbonated-drinks market by the end of year one—bearing in mind that this market is extremely fragmented and crowded, with no one brand taking even as much as a 9 percent share. Two, to minimize the cannibalization of our clients' extremely prestigious fruit-flavored portfolio." Karl pauses at this point to flash a winning smile at the young Brand Manager. She smiles back, succumbing to the blatant flirting. "And three—" Karl pauses again. Yes, and three?

I wait expectantly. Karl looks around the room in desperation and then I remember it's at this point I'm supposed to interrupt him and say, "Karl, I really don't think we need to teach Ms. Carter how to suck eggs; she knows her own brand objectives better than we do."

Actually, we didn't achieve the third objective, which was to come in on budget. A fact that we obviously don't want to dwell on. I manage to jump in just in time. Karl shoots me a look that would sour sherbet; I nearly dropped him in it. Drew is shaking his head, too. Whoops. I don't know why they are looking so stressed. Ms. Carter clearly has the hots for Karl and, if push comes to shove, I'm sure Karl will oblige to keep her sweet, all in the name of duty, you understand. Besides which, Karl has delivered his little intro perfectly. He commands the room and hijacks everyone's attention. This act *is* impressive the first couple of times you see it, but recently I've longed for him to drop the show; he uses it in his business and private lives alike and it bores me. I imagine that if he ever does decide to propose to his long-suffering girlfriend of nine years he'll use a PowerPoint presentation.

Point One: why I'm proposing, subdivided into three categories—a, Karl is an irresistible proposition; b, the demographic-trend data detailing average age of those tying the knot; c, financial considerations.

Point Two: why Jenny should accept . . .

I deliver the next part of the presentation and, luckily, Ms. Carter doesn't notice the fact that we overspent on her budget by about 17 percent.

I'm torn.

I'd wanted to come clean and explain to the client why we had overspent. The fact is, the repeat fees for the actress who starred in the ad broke the bank. The client was informed of the cost at the time and agreed to it, "providing we tried to cut back elsewhere." We did try, but not too hard. When we were preparing for this annual review, I suggested that we simply remind the client that she did sign this cost off. Karl disagreed and was annoyed that I should want to be so "naively transparent." Drew doesn't dirty his hands with anything as grubby as money, preferring instead to stay resident of his personal ivory tower, and Brett didn't support me much either because he'd been the one who had insisted on that particular actress. I hadn't the energy to argue the point of principle. To be honest, it surprised me how little I cared—it's only a fizzy drink. So we resorted to the one, two, but not three, set-up. I have to admit Karl was right—we got away with it.

I'm barely concentrating on my part of the presentation, but that's O.K., because neither is Ms. Carter—she's too busy playing eye tennis with Karl, the consummate flirt. I suppose Karl *is* attractive, in an obvious sort of way and, arguably, what other way

is there? He's just flashed her a smile that regularly causes melt-
down in the West End. He has Ms. Carter's undivided.

I stagger out of the room and am planning to slope off early
this evening to the chemist's to pick up some vitamins, but my
plan is brought to an abrupt halt when Dean catches me sneaking
out of the door. He calls me into his office. His tone is neutral, but
I feel like I've been caught smoking behind the bike sheds and
have been ordered to the headmaster's for a big bad bollocking. I
wonder what the summons is about. I rack my brains for things
I've forgotten or failed to do, or have simply done in a fairly inadequate way; I stop counting when I run out of fingers and toes.
Therefore it's a pleasant surprise when Dean turns to me with a
smile.

"Great news that we're on this pitch, George. High five."

I take the letter he's waving and read it. It's from the AAR and
says that a well-known luxury-car brand has decided to allow us to
pitch for their advertising business. I would tell you the name of
the car brand, but then I'd have to kill you.

"Make Project Zoom your priority," Dean insists.

"Project Zoom." I chortle at the unimaginative code name.

"My code name. Cool, don't you think?"

"Oh great." I conceal my snigger and cynicism under a pretense of enthusiasm.

For some reason that I am yet to fathom there is always a dark veil
of secrecy around pitches. The bigger the account the more tightly
that veil is drawn. And this is big business. We're talking a multinational account with a media spend of £80 million, which is worth £8
million in revenue for the agency. My target this year is to grow the
agency income by £3 million. Wow. Even in my half-baked-
pregnant-mind-for-mush state I can see the importance of this pitch.

"I've already met the Marketing Director. Nice chap," says
Dean. "He mentioned you. Apparently you met at the Marketing
Forum last September and then again at the IPA ball. Frank
Robson. Does the name ring any bells?"

"Yes, I remember." A shrewd enough guy. I was pleasant to him and did talk at length about the advertising strategy he is currently pursuing. I made him laugh with my summary on product life cycle. One, development: an expensive time that generates small revenues and little profit (we rarely muddy our hands at this stage). Two, a period of growth with rapidly rising sales and profits (count us in). Three, maturity, and then four, decline. I told him to call me when his brand hit Stage Two, but not a minute before. He laughed a lot and said he appreciated my honesty. It just goes to show it's worth being nice to everyone; you never know when your hens might come home to roost and it seems that this time the hen may be laying the golden egg. I feel almost excited. I almost feel like the old me.

"Well, apparently, he remembers you. You made a big impression, George." Dean sniggers, he can't help himself, he just has to repeat, "A *big* impression, although I dare say you'd make a much bigger one now."

I glare at him and he tries to rein in his buoyancy. "Well done. Attagirl. Just when I was beginning to think you'd lost your edge, you pull the rabbit out of the hat." He chuckles to himself and starts to root through his desk drawer for a cigar. "I needn't spend so much time wondering about your severance package now, ha, ha." He smiles, but part of me knows part of him isn't joking.

Lost my edge! Lost my edge! I want to say something cutting, but then I consider that the criticism is fair enough. A fact confirmed to me when I notice that at the bottom of the letter from the AAR there is a paragraph noting that they've been trying to discuss this pitch with me for over a month and I've failed to return their calls. Presumably Dean has overlooked this passage in his euphoria at Q&A actually having made it onto the pitch list. I hastily gather up the letter and say, "I'm all over it like a rash already, Dean. It's all under control."

"The client's insisting on absolute secrecy with regard to who's made it onto the pitch list. Even within the agency we should only discuss this with those who will be directly involved."

"Well, that code name will be a tough nut to crack," I comment. Luckily, Dean takes himself far too seriously to suspect that anyone else would do otherwise.

"We don't want to come across as a leaky ship. I want Chinese walls, not bloody Chinese whispers. See to it, George."

"Will do."

"Thought of a team yet?" he demands.

No. "Yes. Obviously, with such an important piece of business we need some heavy management guys. Karl, Drew and Brett should all be very much involved."

"Absolutely."

"Karl and I will discuss the finer points of who we should draft in to make up the best account-management team; we'll get back to you with details."

"Go get 'em, George."

Lost my fucking edge.

I'll show him. It will be the best pitch in advertising history. I'll wow them with the strategy; I'll schmooze the client to within an inch of his life; I'll pull together the sharpest, keenest, brightest the agency has to offer; I'll use the most innovative media yet—we'll advertise on waterfalls if we have to. I'll be galvanized, I'll be energized, I'll be motivated.

I better go and buy those vitamins.

29

*C*hemists' are awful places. The smell—a noxious mix of suffering and sanitation mingling to create the most unwelcoming aroma possible—is worse than fishmongers' or even pet shops. In addition the queues are always endless and, like doctors' waiting rooms, there is a serious possibility that standing in line will turn out to be lethal. I try to avoid the other customers' eyes and illnesses by studying the produce on sale—incontinence underwear, support tights and powders for athlete's foot. How can a chemist's be a pleasant retail environment if the nicest thing on sale is TCP throat pastels? I shuffle to the front of the queue and hand over the prescription.

O.K. The pitch is just another ball to juggle. I can do it. The vitamins will help with the pregnancy and I'll cook for Hugh tonight. Something special. Although I think he mentioned that he'd be late tonight. Never mind, I can use the time to read the brief for Project Zoom. I can do this.

"You can buy these over the counter," the assistant yawns. What does she mean? That's what I'm trying to do. "They're all the same."

"Whatever." I shrug noncommittally.

"Well, which ones?" she demands. The rest of the people in the queue begin to groan impatiently and glare angrily because I don't know the system.

"I'll just have whatever it says," I comment, nonplussed.

"Over the counter or from this prescription?" she pursues.

What's the difference? Do I care?

"Over the counter is cheaper if you pay for your prescriptions. Do you pay for your prescriptions?" she stalks her point.

"Yes." I'm shocked that she'd ask me. The rest of the customers seem shocked that I pay and tut their disapproval.

The pharmacist scrutinizes the prescription and then glares at my bulge. "Oh no, you don't. Not now that you are pregnant," she sneers.

Why does her tone suggest that she thinks she's caught me trying to defraud several governments so as to provide illegal funds to terrorists? My only mistake is that I tried to pay for a prescription that she wants to give me for free.

"Sit."

Her Barbara Woodhouse tone is extremely effective. I grab a seat and wonder when life became so complicated. I know the answer. I can date it back to the two blue lines on the baton. The lines that broke the camel's back. My surge of confidence at hearing we are on the pitch list begins to wane. What if I can't pull it off? What if being pregnant really has mushed my mind? After all, I can't seem to manage efficiently the simple task of buying vitamins. Has Dean really been thinking about my severance package? Damn, I've spent so much time worrying about how ugly and lonely this pregnancy has rendered me that I haven't been paying attention to the big stuff. If twenty-second jingles can be considered the big stuff, that is. I'll simply have to try harder. Try harder to be more efficient and effective at work. Try harder to be more pleasant company around Hugh. And try harder to be better presented.

I have a dull headache starting just above my right eye; it's irritation that I'm sat in a chemist's and yet there's no chance of any medical intervention. I look around to find something to distract me. There's not much choice—leaflets and posters about treating acne or demonstrating the correct application of an ankle bandage. The leaflet on acne makes me itch so I opt for the one on ankle-bandage application.

Although I've offered no encouragement, the woman sat next to me, who has a double buggy and a bump, decides to strike up conversation.

"When are you due?"

"August," I reply and return to the fascinating topic of ankle bandages. I'm not in the mood for chit-chat.

"Really? I thought you were further gone," comments the bump woman.

I'm halfway through my pregnancy and, although this morning I marked the milestone on my calendar and I felt O.K. about it all, suddenly I simply feel like a fat failure again. If only I could stop eating—I reach for a packet of breath-fresheners (the only "food" on sale in the chemist's), and start to munch them.

"I'm due in June," she tells me, although I didn't ask. "You must be having a girl as your bump has spread everywhere, even your arms," she chuckles. I shift uncomfortably in my chair. I have no idea if I am having a boy or a girl. I haven't given it much thought beyond the fact I'd like a healthy one, preferably with Hugh's eyes. I try not to become riled by the fact that this complete stranger has noticed that I have enough fat stored under my arms to feed a starving family of five for an entire drought season. I try and see it as something that could come in useful if, say, I find myself in Africa.

"No, it's a boy," chips in another woman. She's licensed to comment by the fact that sticky twins are clinging to her legs. "Stand up," she barks. Silently and stupidly I comply. "Look, she's carrying a lot of weight on her bottom—'A lazy boy is all behind,' they say."

Do they now.

"No," disagrees the first woman, with conviction, "a boy bump is neat and all upfront. Nobody could describe that bump as neat."

I sink back into my chair and a prayer that they will argue it out together without requiring any more input from me. I close my eyes and hot tears sting my lids.

This is worse than pot-holing. This is hell.

Bored by the guess-the-sex conversation (after all, neither of them can emerge triumphant in the immediate short term), the first woman turns back to me. "Are you using the microwave?"

I wonder if this is a trick question, but before I can work out the punchline I hear myself answer truthfully, "Yes."

"But what about the radiation and the fetus!?" she screams, and the odd thing is the other customers look at me as though *I'm* mad. I furiously blink back the tears; the dull headache is starting to pound. Bang, bang, bang.

"And I can see that you have your hair highlighted," she adds accusingly.

My hand automatically reaches up for my head. I hate admitting to this at the best of times. "Yes. I was feeling rather dowdy," I mutter in explanation. The truth is that I look so crap at the moment that there is a serious possibility that my child will find the placenta more aesthetically pleasing than its mother. Having my hair highlighted was an attempt to stop the rot.

"But what about the chemicals?"

"Chemicals?"

"Do you want to poison your baby? They can be born with such horrible deformities if you've highlighted your hair and injected all those horrible chemicals into your system. You might as well inject heroin into your eyeballs."

Thank you for that. Bang, bang.

"Do you swim?"

I nod, assuming this at least will earn me Brownie points and somehow distinguish me from Hannibal Lecter. All the maternity books advise gentle exercise and, while I have been forced to abandon my hour-and-a-half, high-intensity aerobic workouts (big shame that my personal trainer never forgave me for vomiting on the stationary bikes), surely the effort I make dragging myself to the baths every week or so will be regarded as a good thing.

Wrong.

There is a collective sharp intake of breath by all the women in the chemist's (all of whom, I suddenly notice, have buggies and babies and rolls of post-natal fat).

"You shouldn't be swimming, think of the damage the chlorine can do. Would you consider drinking bleach?"

Yes, if I have to listen to anymore of this nonsense.

The hammering inside my head is escalating and I really have to concentrate to hear what the bump woman is saying. I seriously doubt that it's worth the effort. She goes onto give me her qualifications for offering this advice. "It's my third. All cesareans. Look." And before I have a chance to object she whips her jumper up and trousers down and flashes her scars at me. What to say?

Nothing.

Pregnancy seems to be a rite of passage to a club, and all the other members (mums and mums-to-be) think that we've bonded naturally, just because we're in this club together. And while I concede that listening to Penny's illuminating little facts about pregnancy wasn't altogether irritating—in fact it was interesting—her information was accompanied by a roast lunch by way of an incentive. I no more want to share my gynecological details with a complete stranger than I want to go to war, which, I might add, seems to be a very close analogy for childbirth if these women are to be believed. This isn't the first time a complete stranger has taken it upon herself to share her battle scars. Last week in Café Rouge I met a woman in the queue for the loo who insisted on showing me her stretch marks, and there was another woman at the checkout in Marks & Spencer's who was determined to share more information than necessary about her problems with incontinence. Marks & Spencer's, not Netto!

It's repulsive.

On the other hand, who else am I going to play with? Sam only wants to talk about veil lengths; she and all my other childless friends and acquaintances are running ahead in their open-toed, kitten-heeled shoes, dashing into wine bars and designer-boutique changing rooms—I can't keep up. I'm not even sure if I want to. Whereas the bump woman would like nothing better than to discuss pelvic-floor exercises.

One of the grubby kids sneezes, and the bump woman slowly

bends down to dig out a tissue from her bag and then dig out the snot from the child's nose. He doesn't appreciate her devotion and starts up an almighty wail. My brain splinters with pain.

I feel my life is over.

I have two choices right now: I could cry and scream and rant and rave, I could stamp my feet and kick and scratch (a little like the snot-nosed kid is doing). Or I could call Libby.

I reach into my bag and pull out my mobile. After all, with so much commotion I'm not sure my tantrum would even be heard in the chemist's.

30

I briefly tell Libby about my day, then I start to sob down the phone that I'm sick of trying and can't try any harder and yet I don't seem to be good enough as I am. It reminds me of a conversation I had with Jessica when I was seven and stranded at Brownie camp. Confused about how to make a washing-up-bowl stand from twigs and unsure of the genuine demand for such a product, I rang her in tears and begged her to pick me up. For the record, she didn't. She believed grubbing about with creepy-crawlies and having to ration loo roll was character-building.

Luckily Libby has experience with seven-year-olds.

"I'm not sure how I'll manage. I'm fire-fighting on too many fronts. I'm sick of trying. Trying to be what Hugh wants in a partner. Trying to be what Kate and Tom want—or at least will tolerate. Trying to be a patient and good friend, which I'm failing miserably at—I recently told Sam that I didn't give a toss if marrying in August was reputed to be more fortuitous than marrying in, say, May, as per some dodgy old wives' tale. Trying to be thin is a battle I've lost. I'm also defeated in my battle to try to be attractive, witty or coherent. How am I ever going to handle this enormous pitch when I have this enormous body?"

Somehow, despite my sobbing, Libby manages to get the gist of what I'm saying. She immediately says she'll put the kettle on and that I'm to come straight around to hers. I don't need any further persuasion, but I'm delighted when she tells me that Millie is at her grandparents' for the evening.

Libby lives in Earls Court, in the top-floor flat of a Victorian terraced house, above various transient yet consistently pleasant Australian travelers. Her flat is tiny, but while there's not much space there is lots of life. She greets me with a hug, which isn't very London but is very her, and I feel better for it. I follow her through to the skinny kitchen at the back of the flat, trying not to trip on the numerous piles of stuff that litter every surface. There are magazines, Millie's shoes, comics, crayons and toys, yet-to-be-unpacked shopping, piles of washing (needs to be washed, needs to be ironed, needs to be put away). The flat is cluttered with half-completed creative endeavors (knitting, tapestry, tile mosaics—Libby's; paper-tissue butterflies, splatter-paint pictures and cardboard models of HGVs—Millie's). There are dozens of Millie's works of art pinned to the fridge, the freezer and any available cupboard door. There are colored fairy lights hung on every wall, as though Libby and Millie celebrate Christmas all year round. Then there are the books, the most impressive collection of books I've ever seen outside a library. The books are integral to their home. They crowd the shelves, tables, windowsills, the TV top and the sideboard. They are scattered randomly on the floor and are stacked neatly in piles in the loo, under the settee, on the stairs. Added to this there are the surprise stores—books in the kitchen cupboards, the cutlery drawer and on the shelf where she keeps tinned spaghetti and cornflakes. There are thousands of books, quite literally.

I'm feeling a bit shy after my histrionics, so I try to make general conversation to lighten the mood. "Have you read them all?" I ask.

"Yes," says Libby, "why else would I have them?" I don't tell her that my shelves are mostly stacked with lifestyle magazines. The books I do have are made up of: 50 percent I have read, 25 percent that I keep meaning to read, and 25 percent that I feel I should read. Libby has worthy books discussing theology, politics, history.

There are poetry books, literary books, books about music, travel, law and biology. There are dozens of novels, every Whitbread and Booker contender since the year dot, and her shelves also boast the odd sexy, trashy novel, which, I think, shows a certain amount of quirky independence.

I follow Libby through to the kitchen while she gathers up the necessities for a comfortable evening debrief. I watch her efficiently pull together teapot, mugs, biscuits, milk and sugar, and put them on a tray. Her crockery doesn't match, but is a hotch-potch of brightly colored hand-painted affairs. They look great, comfortable, inviting, which makes me wonder why I spend time combing the shops for the exact replacement cup or matching milk jug when a piece of my Conran crockery gets chipped. Would the world draw to a halt if my crockery didn't match?

The window is open a couple of inches allowing, if not fresh air, then certainly the noise of the street to seep into the flat. I can hear an irate driver rowing with a traffic warden and, in the distance, a pneumatic drill. They are digging up the Cromwell Road again. It's spring, the season of fertility and promise, but only according to the calendar. April is having an identity crisis; it thinks it is January. Everything is still extremely bleak. The rainfall has been record-breaking, the freezing temperature ball-breaking.

Libby leads me through to the sitting room, where she has set up an ironing board, surrounded by yet more piles of clothes. She doesn't seem bothered or embarrassed by the mess. Nor does she appear to be fazed by my outburst; she says nothing about my hysterical phone call. I, on the other hand, am horrified. It's hardly accepted behavior in front of someone you've met only once. I head toward the tatty, squashy settee, which is positioned close to the fireplace, and I fall into it. The clock ticks and the iron makes a swishing sound as it lets off steam. I'm here for the same purpose; despite this, I'm mute. Libby's question wasn't a difficult one. Did I enjoy Wales? It should be easy enough to answer and yet I'm struggling. The shame is overwhelming. I know I've said too much to pretend I was simply joking when I called from the chemist's. I

"Suppose," I mutter grimly. "But I was collecting the prescription when I called you, and I wasn't particularly calm then."

"You have to eat them, not keep them in your bag. It is normal, you know, to feel . . ."

While Libby is searching for the right words I beat her to it. *"Fucked off."*

"Yes," she admits.

"I'm just no good at it." And for the first time since I arrived I lock eye with Libby. She doesn't flinch, but meets my confession head on. She stays silent but her gaze oozes empathy and understanding. The tiny brown flecks in her otherwise blue eyes tell me it's O.K. to be honest. Even if honest is abominable, vulnerable or unfashionable.

I carry on. "I'm tired and emotional. I'm spotty, my hair is falling out, and I'm fat."

Libby demonstrates her integrity by not rushing to assure me that my face hasn't changed at all, or that, from the back, I don't even look pregnant.

This is undoubtedly a good thing.

Although I wouldn't have minded just a tiny smidgen of insincerity, simply to cheer me up.

"It isn't a competition," she says. I cast her a withering look. Her naiveté is unprecedented.

"It is. Everything is."

"But you are looking forward to the birth, aren't you?"

"Huffing and puffing?" I ask incredulously.

"No. I mean actually having a child, being a mother."

I could bluff. I could summon up "the voice" and repeat for the millionth time that I'm "thrilled, absolutely thrilled," but that wouldn't be the whole story. I stare at the crumpled tissue I'm gripping in my hand. It's heavy with my snot and tears, an unromantic testament and a timely reminder of my recent hysterics.

"I'm terrified," I reveal. I stir the Earl Grey and watch the leaves dance with the water in the cup.

"Of?"

Deep breath. Plunge. "All of it. The ugly pregnancy, the ugly labor and being a mother. I'm not 'thrilled, absolutely thrilled' as much as 'terrified, absolutely terrified.' "

"Ah."

"Pregnancy is too big for me. It's too much of a challenge. I don't like the small bladder, the large stomach, the vomiting, the breathlessness, or the isolation. And motherhood? More small bladders, fussy stomachs, more vomiting, breathless tantrums and isolation. I'm just not sure I'm up to it." She stays absolutely still and her inertia pushes me to add, "It scares me, being needed that much. I'm scared of the dependency."

Libby comments sensibly and gently, "They don't stay in diapers forever."

But even the sensibleness of her tone doesn't stop me pointing out, "I don't even know which diapers. Presumably you've seen the bewildering array available on supermarket shelves. Toweling, disposable, waterproof, recycled, maxi, mini, freedom, newborn, front-loaded, back-loaded, super-absorbent, elasticated legs, and all of the above come in about twenty different sizes."

I'm on a roll. All the anxiety, fear, self-doubt that I've been bottling up for weeks, no, years, comes tumbling out.

"There is no end in sight. When it finally does stop peeing and shitting, in that disgustingly dependent way, when it finally sleeps through for an entire night and perhaps even manages to say something cute, I still have to negotiate it through nursery and primary school, with all their associated horrors. Head lice, bullying, Ofsted and end-of-term reports." I fling myself back against the settee, nearly upsetting my teacup. Libby cautiously puts down the iron, but she doesn't interrupt.

"And which nursery school?" I demand. "Or should I have a nanny or a childminder? And am I damaging this child if I go back to work? If I am, tough, because I simply could not stay in with it all day every day." I glare at Libby as though she personally has insisted that I should. "Which school?" I yell, and if she were to suggest one right there and then I would take her up on it because, really, I don't have a clue. A few "helpful friends" and acquaintances have already telephoned me to say that it's too late to put my name down at any of the best prep schools, as the places are all taken for the next million years. I've only just managed to restrain myself from screaming down the telephone line, "But it's still a fetus!"

I'm exhausted.

Tired of trying to pretend everything is fine. Tired of having to pretend that it's even better than fine. "Fine" would be failure that I have to eclipse. I pause, reflect and then divulge, "I feel as though I've been exposed as the fraud I am."

"What do you mean?"

"I'm not an eight, let alone a ten. I'm a five and a half."

Libby doesn't understand, so I explain that while I appear to be the epitome of self-confidence—*appear* is the operative word—I'm not a natural at anything much.

"It isn't enough to have a good job, a lover, a lovely home, great friends and a gym membership; suddenly there's a new measure. I have to give birth without putting on weight and while repeating yoga chants, and then I have to nurture another Einstein without giving up the day job," I yell my frustration.

"I think you are too hard on yourself. Who set these unreasonable standards?"

Who, indeed? Did I? Did Hugh? Did Becca, way back in 1987? Was it Hollywood?

"Perhaps it would be wisest if you didn't worry about the school at the moment," says Libby, dragging me back to the problem in hand, or at least to the problem I'm prepared to admit to. "One step at a time."

One step at a time, what nonsense! I've always prided myself on my ability to multi-task. Although, recently, I've done nothing but drop balls. Libby unplugs the iron and starts to wind the cord around the handle. Then she moves a pile of freshly ironed clothes so that she can sit next to me. She squeezes my arm.

"The thing is, as I'm going to be a mother I want to be a good one," I plead.

"You will be," Libby assures.

I wish I could be as certain. I wonder if I can admit to Libby why my relationship with women like Penny is so complex. As much as it pains me to say so, I do admire Penny. In many ways she is exactly the type of mother I want to be. In other ways she horrifies me. Her eternal self-sacrifice is at once resplendent and repugnant. I do want to be the sort of mum that feeds her child homemade, organic, nutritionally balanced food. I want to take my child to ballet, tennis and French lessons (although not necessarily before it is three years old), yet this means that my life won't be my own. I'll simply be the chauffeur; constantly scheduling car runs to Tumble Tots and Water Babies. How will I ever have time to fit it all in? Will I ever moisturize my knees and elbows again? Then there are the teenage years when my child will hate me anyway, however much time and effort I have devoted to it. If it's a boy it will become smelly, moronic and uncommunicative, and if it's a girl it will undoubtedly be hysterical, anorexic and shrewish. Final insult to injury is that it will make me a grandmother.

As though she's reading my mind Libby says, "Motherhood is not all anxiety, uncertainty and defeat, you know. Far from it."

"What is it like, then?"

She pauses. Someone less serious would be able to answer this question very easily. They'd say "fantastic" or "awful" or "hard" or "relentless." But whatever answer they'd give would be oversimplified, one word, or perhaps one line. Or they might give me a cliché, because mums often describe motherhood by resorting to clichés. They say, "It's changed my life," or "It's like falling in love." Libby doesn't do either of these things. She picks up a KitKat, takes a bite and then stares into space; or she could be looking at the huge pile of laundry that still needs to be plowed through. She takes a deep breath.

"It is the most overwhelming experience I've ever had. It consumes my every waking moment, and, actually, a fair amount of my sleeping moments too. I have so much to say about being a mum that I am always tempted to stay silent. It's an amalgamation of a zillion squabbling emotions: joy, rapture, satisfaction, fear, guilt, wonder, relief, worry. Especially worry. I sometimes think that I might be made physically ill with worry. Am I too strict? Not strict enough? Am I teaching her wrong from right, and who am I to make the distinction? Will it matter anyway because possibly something unimaginably ugly will happen to her—"

"Libby!"

"I know it's awful just letting the thought flit into your head, never mind articulating it aloud, but it does come into every parent's head. The fear of cracked skulls, broken bones, broken hearts, and so much worse. And sometimes I want to collapse with the weight of my fears and responsibilities. I want to crawl under the duvet and let someone else take over. Of course there isn't anyone else, so I can't, and besides which I only have to look at her and I'm"—Libby searches for a particular word—"renewed. She's my reason to live, but more than that she's everybody's reason to live, even for those people who have no idea of her existence. She is the future."

I stare at Libby, wondering if she's joined some mad cult, but she looks just the same. Slightly frazzled and pretty. Does she think Millie is going to be the first female president of the U.S.A.? I mean, she's a bright enough kid and I don't want to burst the bubble, but there's the small question of the passport.

I realize that perhaps I'm on the wrong track when she adds, "Aren't they? Children? The babies we bear, not just mine or yours but all of them, they are the sum of everything and everyone that has gone before and here they are, our future. There's renewed hope and possibility in every one of them. I suppose, thinking about it, I do occasionally miss a spontaneous trip to the pub but I don't hanker after it. And if I make myself remember, then, yes, the labor was painful, the sleepless nights were irritating, but with all that I still wouldn't change a thing. Fact is, giving birth may seem crappy and disturbing now, but I can guarantee that you'll think it is the best news in the world fifteen seconds after the afterbirth slithers out. It's not orderly. It's messy and complex but it is beautiful and amazing, too." She rolls the KitKat wrapper into a ball and tosses it in the direction of the waste-paper bin; it misses. "That said, sometimes I could scream because she's asked me just once too often why she can't have another ice cream or Barbie doll and I think I might kill her, and, for a second, I hate, I'm so tired."

"You hate her?"

"Not her, I just hate. But mostly she's about joy. An indescribable, unrepeatable splash of colorful, wonderful joy."

As I walk home from Libby's her words swim around my head. She made it sound so simple. A baby being "the best news in the world." A baby being the "reason to live . . . everybody's reason to live . . . the future."

So simple and convincing.

Even though it's drizzling I've decided to walk a few Tube stops; I could do with the fresh air (or at least London's apology for fresh air), it might clear my head. I don't bother with my umbrella but let the rain fall onto me. I'm aware it's full of pollutants, but it still feels symbolic and cleansing.

I'm all mixed up. Partly because I don't understand what Libby is on about. Partly because I do. A "splash of colorful, wonderful joy." Color? Which color? Thinking about it, there's not much color in my life. Traditionally, I've always worn black; after all, I was a student in the late 1980s and my career is in advertising, so what other color is there? I did flirt with the whole brown purple gray-is-the-new-black thing—that happened toward the end of the last decade—but Hugh brought me back down to earth and reminded me that black is the one true classic. My flat used to be decorated in a dozen subtle tones of mauve but I painted it in a dozen subtle tones of brown when Hugh moved in. I couldn't expect a man to live with such girliness. To be honest, neither the sludgy mauves nor the sludgy browns could be fairly described as colors.

A huge canary-yellow street cleaner trundles past, spraying and splashing puddles left and right. Pedestrians grumble and swear as their coats are drenched, but I start to laugh. Even though I got sprayed too. I know that in the past I'd have been screaming and cursing. My blood pressure would have been soaring. I'd have already been calculating how and when I could change into another pristine outfit before anyone saw me in such a state. In fact, I keep spare clothes at work just for this type of crisis. But today I simply laugh and brush off the worst of the spray from my coat because it's not the end of the world, is it? So I'm a bit grubbier and damper than I was a few minutes ago and I don't look quite so perfect. I've lived to tell the tale.

I think I'll paint the nursery canary yellow.

Then a double-decker bus flies by too, drenching me for a second time.

Yellow and red.

31

Since Libby's description of children as our future (I'm sure I'm paraphrasing to the detriment of her beautiful speech in favor of a fairly obvious, tacky song—but you know what I'm on about), I've started to allow thoughts of what this might be like. Beyond pregnancy, to when I am a mum. A mummy. A mother. Someone's mother. My baby's mother.

And I'm so excited I can hardly think.

Yes, I'm fat, but, now that I'm so fat that I'm beyond help, I've decided to surrender and that feels good. So good. Now when I wake up on a Saturday morning and it is past midday I do not feel guilty about the depths of sluggardly behavior I have sunk to. Because sleeping is good for the baby. It makes a nice change to lie in bed and do absolutely nothing. I no longer believe that Saturdays have to be spent reading the papers to keep informed. Or visiting farm-produce market shops to buy cheese, the fishmonger's to buy bream or cod, the Italian deli to buy sun-dried tomato and rosemary bread because Hugh hates the "processed muck that all the supermarkets churn out."

I no longer feel guilty when I fail to run six miles or swim thirty lengths. Total surrender to my body shape feels like an honorable discharge. I embrace the freedom of eating what I like, because eating is good for the baby. Each mouthful of previously forbidden food feels like I'm sticking my fingers up to the blokes on the building sites who torment you if they do whistle, insult you if they don't.

Have you tasted chips with salt and vinegar, eaten from a bag? I mean, really tasted? Not just gobbled them down, guiltily, hardly allowing their fat, squishy gorgeousness to hit your taste buds. But slowly chewed them, luxuriated in the burning crispiness of the out-side and then creamy corpulence of the inside. You should do.

I've grown so large that I'm invisible. I've vanished off the fashion-despotism radar screen and I feel liberated. It no longer matters if I'm wearing the very latest shade of black, in the very latest length. As a child I always thought being the invisible man would be rather fun, and it is. It allows you to arrive late and leave early from the office, it allows you to sit out of strenuous exercise (including sex) if you so choose, and it allows you to dawdle around supermarkets.

I still have piles, which are excruciating and a humiliation, and I've got odd patches of funny-colored skin on my stomach but, as I'm invisible, only I know this.

Instead of resenting the pregnancy and regarding it as a reversal of everything I've spent almost the last fourteen years trying to achieve, I've started to consider the possibility that I was trying to achieve the wrong things. I'm beginning to accept and, on occa-sion, actively enjoy the pregnancy, because after all there's no other way to a baby, is there? And I so want this baby.

BANG.

I have turned gaga. I have become obsessed. It's happened to me. I show people the baby scan, I tell them when it kicks me, I talk about my plans to breastfeed—it's official, I am captivated. I go back to my maternity books and read them all over again. How could I ever have thought of my baby as an alien? Admittedly, its head is still a little bit out of proportion, but this is definitely a baby. I hold the book to my stomach and try to imagine that little being inside me. A tiny thing with fingers and toes, and ears, eyes, a mouth and a nose. It is gorgeous. How could I have missed the fact that it sucks its thumb from fifteen weeks onward? How adorable. Even the fact that the baby weighs approximately 200 g, "a figure that will increase more than fifteen times between now and delivery"—this doesn't faze me. I've been asking what is there to life if there are no bars, no restaurants, no shops, no massages; well, it's obvious, there's life itself. The baby has replaced my work, my gym, and my friends' infatuations. Everything. It *is* true the absolute sweetest things on this earth are the little socks that babyGap sells. The most beautiful, wondrous things on this earth are babies' hands (all babies are now lovely, although mine will obviously be the loveliest).

However, my enthusiasm for the coming baby and the fat me is possibly not shared by Hugh. I tried to ignite him in the same way as Libby had me. I encouraged him to talk about any fears or doubts he might have about the upcoming birth, but he sniggered and asked if I'd recently attended an American workshop about "sharing emotions." So I told him about the splash of colorful, wonderful joy—only I can't be quite as good an orator as Libby, because Hugh simply stared at me.

"Don't you see what she's getting at?" I persisted.

"Babes, I've told you I'm delighted about the baby," smiled Hugh. I bite my tongue and resist begging him to tell me again. "Have you seen my golf socks?"

"Third drawer down on the left."

I know he *said* he was pleased and he did send flowers to the office, and I want to believe him, but I can't help but notice that since then he's rarely mentioned the pregnancy. Well, other than to ask me where he will store his LP collection if we are going to convert the spare room into a nursery. I pointed out that we don't even have a record player anymore and suggested he sell them. We could do with the extra cash.

And I can't help but feel disappointed that Hugh didn't keep his promise to sit down with Kate and Tom in Wales and tell them our news. I'd imagined us all sitting in front of an open fire. Hugh cuddling a newly scrubbed, straight after bathtime, angelic-looking Kate and Tom (I know it's a stretch but it was a fantasy). I'd rehearsed with him how he should explain, very gently and carefully, that a new brother or sister wasn't anything for them to worry about because each baby comes with its own extra bag of love. That the love he had for them wouldn't have to be shared or spread more thinly (we'd gloss over the fact that time, however, would be at a premium). As it was, Kate caught me with my head down the loo on Sunday morning.

"Are you poorly?" she asked with what could have been mistaken for glee, if a minor hadn't delivered the question.

"No, she's pregnant," sighed the world-weary Millie. Kate stared non-comprehendingly, so Millie took her off to give her a lesson in basic biology using Barbie and Ken as props. I would have been concerned, but how much damage can a couple of eunuch dolls do? Anyway, I couldn't leave my sentry position, and where the hell was Hugh?

Hugh doesn't find the scans fascinating, nor the books frustrating, nor the biology miraculous. Admittedly, none of it is new to Hugh and it's all new to me . . . still. His attitude was best summed up in Wales when Henry asked him if he wanted a boy or girl.

"All the same to me."

I was thrilled and waited for the statutory line, "as long as it's healthy."

He surprised me. "After all, I've already got one of each flavor." Oh . . .

It's odd, but this is the first genuine difference of opinion I think we've ever had. We're normally so in sync. I can't think of anything more absorbing than talking about the baby, thinking about the baby, planning for the baby. I'm not saying that Hugh doesn't want it—I'd say he's neutral.

Quite a big difference of opinion; perhaps it would have been better if we'd started with a disagreement about which color to paint the downstairs loo.

God, I really should be thinking about this pitch.

The phone rings, giving me the perfect excuse not to think about it right now.

"Hello, darling."

"Hello, Jessica."

"What does the book say?"

Luckily, Jessica has filled Hugh's shoes in terms of being appropriately enthusiastic and excited about the coming birth, although I remain careful not to make an outright reference to the fact that the birth will make her a grandmother. She rings once a week and I read the appropriate chapter from the maternity book.

Week 21
The skin covering your baby begins growing in two layers. These layers are the epidermis, which is on the surface, and the dermis, which is the deeper layer. . . . The epidermis is arranged in four layers. One of these layers contains epidermal ridges. These are responsible for patterns on surfaces of fingertips, palms and soles of the feet. They are genetically determined.

We both fall silent in amazement.

"How can something so tiny be so intricate and perfect?" asks my mother. "To think, right from the moment of conception, it's all mapped out, what sex it will be, what color eyes it will have, even its tiny fingerprints are already forming." I normally interrupt my mother with an effervescent flow; my silence startles her. "Are you still there, Georgina? Are you all right?"

"Yes. I'm fine."

"What did Hugh think of the color that you painted the nursery?"

"He said it was fine."

And I believe him, I do. Because it has to be, hasn't it? It has to be fine. I know Hugh said I'm angry, tearful, neurotic, and before that he thought I was compliant, accommodating and comfortable, which are not the attributes I imagined our relationship would be based on. And, recently, I've begun to think that he isn't quite as considerate as I imagined. He isn't quite as interested or forgiving. But still, everything is fine. Because things really do have to be fine now. This child I'm carrying is half his. Half him. The soles of my baby's feet have been genetically destined by this man. So he can't be a disappointment. He simply can't.

32

I buy Kate and Tom Easter eggs from Thorntons. Big ones. The biggest in the shop, and I have their names iced on them. They'd possibly prefer Barbie and Bob the Builder eggs respectively, and Becca very probably will be furious that I've bought them eggs at all. I think she has a no-chocolate, no-sweets, no-fun policy, which she intends to follow until the children are at least twenty-one. However, that is not my motivation for choosing these eggs. I chose them because, when I was a child, my uncle bought me a Thorntons egg, and he had my name iced on it and I still think it was the best Easter egg I ever received. The best in the world.

On Easter Monday I am sat at home, flicking between channels. Rather disappointingly, *Jesus Christ Superstar* is not being repeated, I have to make do with *Jesus of Nazareth* with Robert Powell. And while his performance is excellent, only outdone by his amazing eyes, I'm not sure that I feel quite right about finding Jesus sexy. I switch over, but the alternatives don't interest me either. There's a western, a documentary on the Rolling Stones, or rugby.

Hugh is playing golf, which is an Easter Monday tradition. I feel that my Easter has lacked the structure that marks the holiday, or indeed distinguishes it from any other bank holiday. Surely someone (other than myself) should have bought me an Easter egg (I bought six, actually, and have them stashed in secret hidey-holes throughout the flat). And shouldn't there have been fish on Friday and hot cross buns? Shouldn't there have been a roast lamb on Sunday? Last year Becca took the kids to her parents' and Hugh and I took advantage of her absence. We played house and entertained. We had a fish supper for six on the Friday (I wore a black boob tube and bootleg trousers—Joseph). We went out for lunch with four other couples on the Saturday (I wore a black Sportmax trouser suit) and we held a roast-dinner party, for ten, on the Sunday. I wore a Prada shift dress, in gray—well, it was Easter Sunday. We drank champagne, vodka shots and highballs, and while each meal was upward of three courses, followed by coffee and petit fours, I picked at salads throughout.

Still, that was a tradition of sorts.

This year, when we are a real couple, we've marked the resurrection of Christ by arguing about whether we should visit a gallery (my choice) or go for a walk in the country (Hugh's preference). Hugh is astounded that I won't fall in line with his plan. I am too. As all I've ever wanted was Hugh, I've only ever wanted the things he wanted. Everything I have ever thought of for the last thirteen years I have thought about through a Hugh filter. Would Hugh prefer pink or red nail varnish on my toes? Would Hugh like to see this film or that film? Has he ever eaten at such and such restaurant? His answers would shape mine, blur into mine, become mine. But I don't want to go for a walk. I haven't got maternity rambling gear; besides, I really want to see the new exhibition at the National Portrait Gallery.

"No one is going to that exhibition," Hugh argued.

"I know it hasn't had much publicity, but I really want to see it."

"No one's going, Babes."

Including us, apparently.

In the end we do nothing.

Next year things will be very different, because next year we will be a family and, at the very least, our baby will be dressed as an Easter bunny, with floppy ears and a pompon tail. I'll wear various flirty little dresses with tiny flowers, in turquoise, lilac and pink.

I'll accessorize them with colorful cardigans, hemmed with sequins and frills. Hugh will wash the car. The sun will shine. We'll have a proper Easter.

The phone rings, interrupting my daydream. I winch myself out of the settee and think, not for the first time, how much I'd like a domestic crane to help me get about the flat.

"Hello." For a moment I can't place the voice. "Hello, it's Becca."

"Hugh's not here," I answer automatically. "I'll tell him you called."

I'm about to hang up when I catch Becca's garbled, "Actually, I rang for you." She coughs, clearly as surprised to find herself ringing me as I am.

I force myself to remember the conversational social niceties that get one by in awkward situations such as these. "Hello Becca. Are you having a nice Easter?" Like I care.

"Fine, fine. Very nice. And you?"

"Fine."

"Really?" The question surprises me. It's genuine.

"I've stopped being sick," I report. Becca had been right; the books were wrong, I stopped being sick nearer the six-month mark than the third. I can't bring myself to admit as much.

"That's good."

"I'm a bit spaced, not very good at remembering things for more than two minutes in a row, but I'm fine."

"This is a nice stage of pregnancy before you get too—"

"Fat."

"I was going to say, uncomfortable."

We both laugh, it amounts to the same. What am I doing having this conversation with Becca? I pause, waiting for her to enlighten me as to why she called. I wonder if the kids want new bikes.

"I rang to thank you for the Easter eggs."

"Oh. Err, that's O.K. Hugh chose them," I lie. My motivation for lying is complex. I want Becca to think Hugh is more thoughtful with regard to Kate and Tom than he is, and I also want her to think I am less so. I'm not sure why I want her to believe it's this way around; perhaps because it should be.

"Oh, I don't believe that for a second," she dismisses, and I haven't the energy to lie again. There's no point—she was married to him. "I also rang to see if you've signed up for NCT."

"Err, not yet," I confess.

"Well, you must. They fill up extremely quickly and it's invaluable."

I haven't a clue what she's talking about. NCT? Is it a union? However, I can't bring myself to confess this to Becca because a sixth sense tells me that if I do I'll show how inadequately prepared I am to be a mother because NCT is certainly something to do with being a mother.

"Give them a call tomorrow, I'd say it's imperative." I sigh, relieved at the reemergence of the bossy Becca, it's the one I feel much more at home with. Then she adds, "I always wanted a Thorntons egg when I was a child."

And the human Becca is one that terrifies me.

May

♡

33

Why, oh why, can't we have meetings in offices, like everyone else? Offices with tables and chairs, instead of in trendy boardrooms that are disguised as private bars (lots of thick cigarette smoke and big squashy leather settees). I'm sat on one of said settees; in fact, I'm drowning in it. How will I heave myself out? Why did I wear a skirt today? What are they saying?

"And that's a task for you Georgina, O.K?" asks Dean. "It's a real responsibility."

I nod. I'm not sure what I've just agreed to, I hope Julia is taking notes. Whatever it is, since it's been described as "a real responsibility," I know it's something no one else can be bothered to tackle.

"So let's meet again, say next Tuesday? We could have a working session to bang the final proposition into shape. What time's a good time?" asks Karl.

Everyone instantly reaches for their Palm Pilots; I struggle to my feet and then just about manage to bend to pick up my handbag, when I hear them agree to Tuesday at 4 P.M. I drop back onto the settee and sigh. No doubt the plan is for the meeting to run into the evening. This achieves two objectives. One, by working late the team can convince themselves and everyone else that they are very busy and, two, by working late they can avoid confronting the fact that they have no life outside the office.

"Err, actually, I have a problem with Tuesday," I say.

"Turn a problem into an opportunity, Georgina. I'm interested in solutions. Am I crystal?" Dean flashes a smile; it's designed to terrify.

"It's just that Tuesday isn't very good for me," I persist. The room stops, and everyone stares at me with a level of horror which really ought to be preserved until I announce my waters have broken. The usual form is to cancel any previous commitments. "I'm going to my parental water-conditioning class at 8 P.M. Can you guarantee that I'll be out of here by seven-thirty?"

"No, Georgina, I can't guarantee that. You'll have to reschedule. We're working to a deadline here."

We are, but it's not imminent. It's May now; by the end of June we have to have a clear strategic positioning. In July we have the actual pitch, where we'll present our proposed brand strategy and an idea for an ad (the creative concept, daaaarling). At the rate we are currently working we're in danger of hitting burn-out before the end of this month.

Dean stands up, indicating that as far as he's concerned the issue is not up for debate. He's obviously very irritated with me, but I can't bring myself to care.

"Thing is, Dean, the baby is working to a deadline too. I'm six months pregnant. I've religiously worked ten-hour days ever since you employed me in 1990, and I've regularly supplemented those hours with weekend work too. All overtime unpaid. I need some time to prepare for the baby. I only get one shot at this and I'm not going to jeopardize its health. Let's agree to meet at 2 P.M. and then we can finish by seven. O.K."

"I've a lunch on Tuesday, I won't be through by 2 P.M.," comments Karl. I stare at him. I'm pretty sure I've done Medusa proud when he mumbles, "Well, I'll see if I can rearrange."

"Yes, do that." I relaunch myself from the settee, relinquishing only a small amount of dignity. We've just spent five hours debating how we would staff the account if we win it. This information will be boiled down to only one page of an inch-thick presentation document. We'll be lucky if the client is still awake at the point when this chart is presented. If only there was an award for time-wasting meetings we'd win the golden pencil. We've spent this long on this issue because it's Karl's issue to resolve, and he wants to make it appear trickier than it is.

In an effort to finally wrap up the meeting and summarize the discussions I comment, "The way I see it, Project Zoom requires a pretty straightforward management proposition. A two-pronged attack. A very simple division between the detail of retail and—"

"I love the way you loyally stay with the small stuff," interrupts Karl, with a barely disguised snigger. "Such attention to detail is always commendable."

Ass.

In advertising, attention to detail is essential but often dismissed as myopic. I wish I had money on the fact that his next comment will be, "But where's the bigger picture? Where's the vision?"

"Have you given any thought to the bigger picture, George?" He smiles around the room but doesn't look at me.

"It's a *two*-pronged attack," I continue, not allowing him to push me off track. "A very simple division between the detail of retail and the larger brand-equity proposition. I'll jot something down and deliver it to you by this Thursday, Dean. That will give you a chance to consider it before our Tuesday meeting. This should save us some time on the day."

While my job consists of galvanizing the troops and ensuring that the strands of the pitch—the creative proposition, the finance, the staffing, the breakfast on the day—all come together in an impressive and coherent way, I often help write the deck, too. Karl's torn between being offended that I'm stepping into his territory and being relieved that he'll have less to do. For all his chat throughout the meeting, I know he hasn't given Project Zoom much thought; earlier on today I caught him drawing tits on a whiteboard—he said it was a diffusion curve.

"What do you say, Karl?" asks Dean.

"Yeah, it could work." All capital ideas are received with a degree of cynicism, as are crap ideas. No one knows the difference.

"Obviously, Karl and I have worked on this at length and very closely," I lie. It's true that in the past I would have worked alongside Karl, keeping all the guys to the strict timetable agreed months previously, liaising with the media agency, talking to the international clients to find out as much as I can about cultural differences, and generally making sure that we do our utmost to win the business. Or, at the very least, not get caught with our pants down. But nowadays Karl and I rarely discuss anything much; that's not what Dean wants to hear, he wants a cooperative team, and if I pretend we are such Karl will feel grateful. His gratitude is useful. I'd rather keep him sweet; I've seen how he deals with people who cross him.

"That's the spirit," says Dean. "There's no 'I' in team."

"But there is 'M.E.,' " laughs Karl.

"Good one, Karl," chuckles Dean.

I wonder if he really is stupid enough to think Karl is joking.

34

It turns out that NCT is not a union (oh, how Libby laughed when I asked her that one), but a sort of national educational club charity for parents-to-be, new parents and children. They run prenatal classes, which is what Becca was referring to. It's a good way to make friends with other mums-to-be. And, while only a matter of weeks ago I'd have argued that I didn't want to be friends with other hormonally unbalanced beached whales, now I can think of nothing I'd like more. I have a need and desire to learn as much as I possibly can about labor and the aftermath.

Hugh is not coming to the prenatal classes or the confidence-in-water course that I've signed up to (I'm contemplating a water birth—just because it worked for Freya, doesn't mean I have to rule it out). Libby has just called to offer to come with me to the classes, but I don't want to look like a lesbian.

"You won't," she argues.

"I will." I'm almost crying; I'm certainly whining.

"You won't," she asserts. Once again demonstrating her expertise at handling petulant children. "I bet when you get there that there'll be loads of women with their friends or their mums accompanying them."

"You think so?"

"Yes."

"Who did you go with to your prenatal classes?"

"No one."

"Oh."

"It felt very lonely," she adds quietly. "Personally, I'd have been happier to have been mistaken as a turkey-baster type."

Suddenly terrified, I'm not even embarrassed by my 180-degree U-turn. "I'll pick you up at seven-forty."

"Us. Millie will have to come too. I can't get a babysitter this late in the day."

Ah, Millie. Well, every silver lining has a cloud. Of course, Millie and Libby. Libby and Millie. Libby can't do anything without considering Millie. *Anything at all.* She can't have a night out or visit Tesco's. "Yes, see you both at seven-forty."

I put the phone down and it immediately rings again. This doesn't surprise me; my social life is now more or less restricted to telephone conversations. In my hall it doesn't matter if I sit naked except for a pair of socks. It doesn't matter if I have to hang up several times to dash the short distance to the loo, and at least I know the loo will be clean. No one can see how much ice cream I'm spooning into my mouth, or the fact that I'm combining it with Weetabix.

It's Jessica.

"How are you?"

Her imperious tones almost shock the truth out of me (fat and beginning to like it), but, just in time, I realize that my mother would regard this as a sure sign of deep depression, so instead I lie. "Fine, weight gain has stabilized." (Lie.) "Skin clear." (Lie.) "And I'm just on my way out to the gym." (Not a lie, but perhaps a misrepresentation.) Jessica seems suitably appeased; she's imagining a neater, more groomed me and I'm probably wearing low-slung white linen trousers and revealing a tanned, shapely bump. In fact, I'm in an outsize T-shirt from M&S, and I'm wearing XXL joggers that I once bought in the States for a fancy-dress party. Hugh and I went as a pair of Charlies (as in Chaplin)—we wore a leg each and we were (literally) inseparable. I'm now happily filling them on my own. I count it as a blessing that video telephones are still a figment of the imagination of the guys on *Tomorrow's World* and haven't yet gone into general circulation. I dread the day when technology will reveal the less picturesque truth. I know I should be snacking on dried fruit or wholemeal bread and I would, if only it tasted more like chocolate.

"How's the heartburn?" she asks.

The maternity book warned that "overeating and eating before going to bed at night are two major causes of heartburn. Eating five or six small, nutritious meals a day instead of three large ones may make you feel better." I took that as license to eat five or six large meals a day and really I feel much better.

"Fine. I start the third trimester in two days; I'll be twenty-seven weeks." The countdown is obsessive.

"Ah, the home stretch," laughs Jessica, excitedly. "Oh, read it to me," she urges.

Although I'm in a hurry and it's breaking the rules (we don't normally allow ourselves to look ahead in the book, I suppose it's superstition), I decide to read it to her anyway. " 'In early development the eyes are on the side of the head. They move toward the middle of the face between weeks 7 and 10 of pregnancy. Eyelids cover the eyes until about week 27, when they open.' " We both gasp in amazement. "I wonder what it can see?"

Jessica gives some instruction about what to eat to maximize iron absorption and then she hangs up.

I rush around the flat trying to locate my maternity bathing costume and a big towel, which, after some unseemly dashing, I find and push into a waterproof bag. Actually, when I say dash, I mean move around the flat in a clumsy lumber, which is as near to a dash as possible if you are carrying an extra three stone.

I start to hunt for twenty-pence pieces and pound coins for the meter and locker. At the point when I am precariously balanced on a dining room chair, reaching up to a small shelf above the door in the kitchen, the phone rings again. I know that behind the pile of old *Economist* magazines there is a tin in which I used to save twenty-pence pieces when they first came out; there's probably a fortune in there. I feel around blindly and have only just located the tin when Sam's (woeful) tones float up toward me. Bugger.

"Hi, it's me. If you're there, pick up."

It's probably just yet another crisis about the wedding, something along the lines of she can't source table linen to match the shade of Gilbert's cravat. Big tragedy. There's a pause during which I try to decide whether it's worth my while making the effort to get down off the chair. Will I accomplish this feat in time to pick up the phone before the answering machine cuts out?

"I know you're there."

It's depressing that she assumes I have no social life. We haven't seen much of each other and I'm not sure why. We've played telephone tennis for weeks, leaving messages on one another's machines, but never actually getting to talk. When we do fix up a lunch or supper Sam cancels at the last minute. She's very wrapped up in the wedding plans and I'm very wrapped up in the pregnancy. For the first time ever, our lives are moving at a different pace and in different, although not opposing, directions. This shouldn't be enough of a reason to dissolve a thirteen-year friendship, should it? I lower myself down off the chair and rush into the hall to pick up the phone; the moment I get there the line goes dead. I decide against calling her straight back. I'll ring later tonight when I have more time to talk.

I climb back on the chair and seize the tin, the contents of which are unhelpful, mostly buttons, paperclips and about £2-worth of lira. I look in all the usual change-gathering receptacles in the flat—soap dish in the downstairs loo, the fruit bowl on the hall table, a coffee mug on the breakfast bar, my desk drawer. Not a penny. In desperation, I start to hunt behind the cushions on the settee and under the bed. God, look at this, my box of old diaries!

In the past I've always been a strict and dutiful diary writer. Ever since I went to university, I've religiously made an entry every day, sharing my thoughts, experiences, hopes, dreams and fears with myself—at least this way I could guarantee a receptive and sympathetic audience. I haven't looked at my diaries for weeks. I stopped making entries shortly after I found out I was pregnant. The early days were so miserable, entry after entry describing vomit; the reading was too boring and, frankly, if your own diary is boring, then you are the last person who should remind yourself that this is the case. I may now start keeping a diary again to detail the amazing changes in my head and my body, which, I now concede, are fascinating.

I pick up a heavy brown leather diary for 1999 and hold it close to my nose to drink in the familiar creamy, warm smell. The pages are well worn on this one. I can't resist, I lower myself to my knees and then my bottom, every movement is as tricky as a three-point turn, and I sit on the floor with my back against the bed and start to read.

Oh yes, we went ballooning! God, that was terrifying! And here's a whole section on our holiday in the Maldives. That was an amazing holiday. What times we had! I can almost feel the sand between my toes, and everywhere else for that matter! Sex on the beach, sex on loungers, sex in the pool and, almost disappointingly, sex in the hotel. I'm suddenly thrust back into a world of skinny limbs and scanty underwear. I smile fondly to myself. I turn back the pages of the diary. My birthday. Sam arranged a big dinner at Titanic. Everyone came, Julia and Karl, Drew, Brett. Not Hugh. So many people; yet I remember the birthday as being excruciatingly lonely. I rush on. Christmas. The Christmas Hugh ate two dinners and didn't tell me until he was sick on Boxing Day! He was still living with Becca and he nipped to my flat for an hour or so on Christmas Day in the evening, under the pretense of walking the dog. That was good of him. Wasn't it?

Was it?

Suddenly the euphoria starts to dissolve. The hair on the back of my neck twitches then stands up and my tongue feels sticky and dry. If I didn't know better, I'd identify this feeling as guilt or, more accurately, shame. What was Becca doing on that Christmas night when Hugh was walking the dog? Was she pleased with him for getting the dog out from under her feet, or did she resent having to struggle to bathe and put two over-excited children to bed on her own? How come I've never thought about that before?

I shiver.

I can't help thinking about the fact that Becca wanted a Thorntons egg when she was a girl and although it seems unrelated to my present state of uneasiness, it isn't. If she wanted an egg, what else did she want out of life? Almost certainly not to be a single parent. Because who wants that?

It's *Becca*, for God's sake.

What am I doing feeling sorry for *Becca*?

She can look after herself. It's all history now. And we are where we are. And she did have a fling with her tennis coach. Or at least she probably did; she always denies it but Hugh is almost certain. And she's dating again now, isn't she? She's happy. I turn to another page, desperately trying to recapture the delicious feeling of euphoria that I felt when I first opened the diaries. I know which bit always cheers me up. I pick up the cream suede diary for 1998 and turn to March 5. It's a bit about a party. *The* party actually. The party when Hugh and I stepped over the boundary from "just good friends" to "*very* good friends."

It was a party to celebrate my promotion at Q&A to President of Neoteric Enterprise; I'd invited Sam and Hugh and Becca. Becca, predictably, turned the invite down, said she couldn't get a babysitter. She pretty much handed Hugh to me on a plate. Q&A had hired a limo to drive me home, anticipating that I'd drink so much I'd be incapable of getting a cab, let alone remembering my own address. I suggested Hugh share the limo home. We didn't exactly live near each other (he was north London, I was south), so by accepting the offer he was making his intentions clear. I'll never really understand where that first kiss came from. One moment we were talking about the fact that 54 percent of carbonated drinks are consumed by under-twent-four-year-olds, and the next he was kissing me. All those years wishing and wanting and waiting and sounding like a 1960s track, then suddenly it was happening and it seemed the most natural thing on the earth. As innocent as bending to tie his shoelace. Well, actually, not so innocent, as we ended up having sex in the back of the limo.

"We could barely contain our wanting. I felt so sexy that the action of crossing my legs in the back of the limo nearly sent me into orbit."

I reread the phrase. Four times.

We could barely contain our wanting.

It doesn't make me feel euphoric.

It's my handwriting and it's my diary. I assume, then, that this was my life. But I'm not certain. I don't recognize it. I flick through April, May, June. By the summer, we couldn't keep our hands off each other; every opportunity and, hey presto, knickers down. I return to the 1999 diary. We had sex in five countries before I broke my New Year's resolution not to drink more than three units in one night; now that is what I call going some. God, and what detail I went into! If I ever get fed up at Q&A I might seriously consider a career in writing hard-core Mills and Boons. I read another passage and then another. They are all the same. They either detail us having sex, or reasons why we couldn't meet and have sex. I pick up the year 2000 diary and start to make a list of the places we made love. Besides beds—in numerous hotels, mine, the spare one in Sam's flat—there was also my office, his office, my boss's office, my bathroom (shower, bath, floor), kitchen (breakfast bar, washing-machine—on top, not inside, ha, ha), sitting room (settee, chair), dining room (table, floor), and stairway. Aside from the fact that I bought this flat before the property boom, it certainly appears that I've had my money's worth from every single room. I continue with the list. In the year 2000 we made love in greenhouses, sheds, swimming pools, laundry rooms and pantries, in parks, cottages, cars, cinemas, beach huts and on beaches. On planes, trains, ships, yachts, in rowing boats and once, most uncomfortably, in a punt.

The adventurous nature of our rendezvous naturally came to a close in the middle of 2000, when Hugh moved into my flat. The urgency fell out of the relationship, although the frequency was still impressive. This year has scored pretty poorly on both counts. I snap shut my diaries and place them back in the shoebox and push the shoebox back under the bed.

I'm depressed. Not just because I can't remember when we last made love but because I can't remember when I last wanted to.

Yes, I can, it was Easter. I wanted sex with Robert Powell.

The phone rings again; this time I do get there in time. It's Hugh, who has called to tell me he's working late. I suppose that it's progress that he's called at all. He sounds really pleased that I'm going to the gym, which cheers me up somewhat. For reasons I can't explain, even to myself, I keep him on the line longer than necessary. For reasons I've never been able to explain, it does the trick—as it always has—his voice cheers and soothes me.

"Are you happy?" I ask. It's a risky, unadvisable question, but his answer heartens me.

"No, I'm Sneezy," he jokes back.

Of course it doesn't matter if we don't have acrobatic sex any-more; I certainly don't miss the carpet burns. Nor does it matter that Hugh once ate two Christmas dinners. I thought it was funny at the time. We pass five minutes more in pleasantries and then he hangs up. I place the phone back in its cradle and try very hard to hang onto the uneasy calm that the conversation has reinstated.

I check the time. I'm really going to have to get my ass in gear if I want to make it to the water-confidence class on time.

Now, what was I doing before the phone call? I know, looking for money for the meter and locker. Ah ha, Hugh's jacket pockets. I often find loose change in the pockets of his jackets when I'm taking them to the dry cleaner's. I lumber back upstairs and start to rummage through the numerous garments. We really need a sort-out. We've both got far too many clothes, and we won't have as much space when the baby comes. Nor can I imagine I'll need my extensive, exclusively black, dry-clean only wardrobe. I rum-mage through his jacket pockets. Spare office key—he can never find that when he's looking for it. Chewing gum. Condoms; God, they must have been in there for ages. Blockbuster membership card. Receipts for taxis and restaurants and clothes. I can't believe he thinks he'll get that through expenses! That's odd, we've never been to the Lucky 7 restaurant. I wonder when he went there? I must ask him what he thought of it. I've read rave reviews in all the lifestyle mags. Eventually I find two pound coins in his sports jacket. I pocket them and rush out to meet Libby.

I know what you're thinking. Condoms and a receipt for a restaurant. A bill that comes to about £80, a bill that means a meal for two. You think Hugh's having an affair.

Me too.

It's not just the baby that's opening its eyes.

35

Libby, Millie and I settle down to hot chocolates and king-size Mars bars. The beauty of going places with a seven-year-old is that I don't have to apologize for this gluttony. Despite showering, we all still smell of chlorine and disinfectant. Only Millie has bothered to blow-dry her hair; I do this as infrequently as I possibly can nowadays because it requires exhausting arm-raising. Nor have I reapplied my make-up. Why bother? It's nearly nine o'clock—we'll have to take it off again in a couple of hours. Still, I feel beautiful.

Radiant.

For the last forty-five minutes I've just floated and bobbed about in a pool with about a dozen other mums-to-be (at least four of whom were actually bigger than me!) and I feel fantastic.

"I thought I'd die laughing when the instructor told us to jump but keep our legs together, and you shouted back, 'It's a bit late for that,' " says Libby.

We both giggle uncontrollably and cackle unattractively until snot comes out of our noses and tears out of our eyes.

You had to be there.

Millie, who I now try to regard as "a splash of colorful, wonderful joy," looks at us with contempt and suggests that we've lost the plot. Then she asks, "Are you going to get married? Because then I could be your bridesmaid." Since she discovered that Kate is being one of Sam's bridesmaids it has become Millie's greatest ambition in life to be one too. I know how she feels.

"It's tricky," I comment, and stall by blotting a tissue on all the damp bits of my face.

"Why?"

Her directness no longer takes me aback. I've now realized that this is how children operate. They have a sixth sense that identifies which question you'd least like to be asked, and then they ask it.

"He's still married."

"Is he planning on getting divorced?"

"Oh yes, we've lived together for nearly two years now." I barely blush as I use Sam's technique of rounding up; in fact we've been living together barely over a year. "It's only a matter of time."

"How much time? What's the delay?" Normally Libby would step in at this point and tell Millie not to be impertinent. The fact that she doesn't suggests to me that she also wants to hear the answer.

I really don't know.

I fall back on "It's tricky" once again.

"Is Becca making things difficult?" This time it's Libby who asks the question.

"I can't honestly say she is. Her lawyer has been a bit tardy, but . . ." I don't know what else to say. I try and remember what Hugh says to me when he is explaining the delay. I can remember the words he uses. Something about minimizing the disruption for the kids, trying to coincide it with a school year. But we've had a new school year and, anyway, Tom hasn't even started school yet. Hugh goes on about financial implications and I know he wanted to wait until his grandmother passed away, but she's been pushing up daisies for eight months now. When he explains it to me it always sounds so perfectly reasonable, but repeating it back, even to myself, the delay is inexplicable. I patch together a party line from the things he's said to me in the past. Surely, if I can make Millie understand then I'll have a chance of getting it too.

"There are a lot of people to consider, that's the thing about marriage and divorce, it's not just about two people or even two people plus two kids."

"But you must have known that before you started the affair," points out Libby, with irritating reasonableness.

"Yes, I did, but no, I didn't," I sigh. "His mother is distraught—she loves Becca."

"Even after she had the affair with her tennis coach?"

I admit that I *might* have misled Libby a little bit here. Upgrading a probability into a certainty.

"Oh God, Hugh hasn't told his mother about that; it would break her heart and he is far too considerate." That's probably why Hugh is careful to minimize my visits to his mother too, just out of respect for her sensibilities. "I see quite a lot of his father," I justify. "His attitude is slightly more accepting." As I'm talking I slurp my hot chocolate. I think the conversation would have rested there; perhaps we'd have started to talk about the virtues of a crib versus a Moses basket—only I add, "Of course, there's the little matter of him having an affair."

"Another one?"

Despite Libby being one of the coolest and most liberated people I know, this does get the net curtains twitching.

"Another one," I sigh.

It was something about saying aloud that Hugh was considerate that prompted this confession. It is after all a great big fat lie. I used to think he was. But I don't believe it anymore.

I tell Libby about the restaurant receipt, the condoms, and that he has been doing unreasonably long hours in the office recently. I ask her where else could he possibly be channeling his sex drive; it's certainly not coming my way. She knows about the endless rows. I've already decided that these are not things that I'll be telling Sam or Jessica. How can I? They've listened to me worshipping Hugh for a lifetime.

"What do you think?" I ask Libby. "Do you think he's having an affair?"

"Sounds as though you do."

"Well, it's pretty conclusive evidence, isn't it?"

She moves her shoulders—it's a cross between a nod and a shrug; I'd say sixty-forty in favor of a nod.

"So, what are you going to do?"

"I don't know."

And I don't. I could confront him, ask questions, demand answers. Scream, shout, rant, rave, cut up his clothes, scratch his car. Theoretically I could leave him, although, if I'm honest with myself, this is unlikely. I mean, not only have I spent all my adult life trying to be with this man but now I'm having his baby; it hardly seems to be the optimum moment to pack up the old kit-bag. I could ignore him. I could ignore the evidence. I could wait. After the baby I'll be sexy and thin and interested and interesting. I could order another hot chocolate. I decide to do that.

It's easiest.

36

I get home at ten. Hugh is still stood in the hall, flicking through mail; it's obvious that he hasn't been home long.

"Another late night?" I ask and only just resist adding ominously, "at the office."

"Yes, but worth it, I think. We're making some progress." I don't ask what on. Hugh notices my wet hair and gym bag. He throws out a broad smile; it's not the smile of appreciation he bestowed in the old days, it's more one of relief. It's a smile, though. "You've been to the gym."

"Water-confidence classes with Libby," I remind him, even though we discussed it less than three hours ago. "In case we go in for a water birth."

He puts down the mostly brown envelopes and asks, "Have you eaten?"

"Not a thing." Well, besides the Mars Bar and the prawn-and-avocado triple-pack sandwich that I bought on the way home from the baths.

"Let's go out for dinner; you can tell me all about your evening with Lizzie."

"Libby," I correct, but he doesn't hear me—he's already on his way out of the door.

I am hungry. I'm always hungry, but what I'd like most in the world is to curl up on the settee and watch TV; yet I realize that saying so would be tantamount to a declaration of war. For weeks

I've moaned that Hugh never takes me out anymore. A dinner invite is not to be sniffed at. I'm being ungrateful. It is neglectful women who cause their partners to have affairs.

That or the male inability to control their knobs.

Hugh lets me choose the venue and I pick a noisy, trendy restaurant, which used to be a regular haunt of ours pre-pregnancy. The second we arrive I know my choice is a mistake. I'd have been wiser to pick a quieter, more intimate restaurant. London's glitterati hold little allure for me right now. I wish Hugh had given me time to put some make-up on, or at least change out of my tracksuit and into my Mamasoon shift dress; it's my "posh frock" by virtue of being my only frock. I open the door and hit a wall of cigarette smoke. I silently calculate the probability of projectile-vomiting over a waiter.

We are shown to our table. It's positioned at the back of the restaurant; the waiter pulls out a chair for me, the one facing the wall. This is the direct opposite of the etiquette that the female guest is usually shown to the seat that faces out onto the action. Am I being overly sensitive or am I being hidden? A quick glance around confirms that I probably am being hidden. The restaurant is packed to bursting with women whose breasts still stick out further than their stomachs. I hate them. It's wall to wall with toned arms and slim hips. Now that it's May, the first tentative signs of summer are finally visible in London. Not just lighter evenings and leaves on the trees, but skirts and dresses which are shorter and tighter and the occasional sighting of a color other than black. I know that this summer I am going to resemble a sumo wrestler; half an hour ago this didn't matter but, suddenly, it does matter again. The happiness that I felt at the swimming pool starts to dissolve. Libby (and even Millie, to an extent) put me at my ease; sitting opposite Hugh I suddenly feel as though I'm sat on a couple of mating hedgehogs.

He doesn't make me happy.

I'm not happy when I'm with him. That is not particularly fine, whichever way you look at it.

No, it's not true.

It can't be.

I won't let it be.

I'm unhappy because I'm surrounded by toned abs. I was happy with Libby because I was surrounded by other bumps. This is not about Hugh.

I peek over the menu and take a look at Hugh. Quite a big part of me is expecting a 666 to be tattooed onto his forehead, or perhaps when he meets mine his eyes will be bloodshot, because surely there has to be some outward manifestation of his ugliness, his evil betrayal.

His eyes are still green and sparkling merrily.

He looks confident, happy, relaxed. He does not look like a guilty man. Maybe I've been too quick to condemn. A restaurant receipt is hardly a confession signed in sperm. Look how overwrought Othello became about a handkerchief, and no good came of that. Hugh's demeanor radiates innocence.

Although he's well practiced at deceit.

A skill that I used to be grateful for.

Fool.

My brain is about to spontaneously combust. I don't know what to think. The sickness in my stomach has migrated to my head. I home in on Hugh's cuff links; they are shiny white gold, engraved with his initials. I bought them for him to celebrate his new position at R,R&S. The shiny gold cuff links, his clean, square fingernails, the sharp creases in the cuffs of his shirt, all conspire to convince me that he is the same man I said goodbye to this morning. The tiny specks of stubble that are peeking out of his chiseled jaw also want me to believe in him. His long eyelashes that gently brush his brows, putting me in mind of a horse swishing its tail, can't be wrong.

I push the hazy, scary thoughts from my mind and try to amuse myself by looking around the restaurant again.

Besides the superwaifs, there's a liberal scattering of other advertising bods and the odd dot-com nearly there millionaire, average age twenty-two. I feel ancient. Hugh looks tired but relaxed. He still fits. I'm not sure what terrifies me the most—the fact that I don't fit in, or the fact that he does.

Hugh smiles and says, "So tell me about this swimming class that you and Lizzie went to."

I do, but I know he's not listening. He keeps glancing around the room, checking out who he should be shaking hands with, who he should be waving to, who should be waving to him. I take a deep breath and resist commenting on how little of the menu's selection is appropriate; most of the dishes are soused in rich, soft cream-cheese sauces or alcohol; raw fish and rare meat make up the remainder. I choose a tuna salad. Hugh drains his martini, orders two courses and a bottle of wine. I tell him about the baby kicking like crazy when the music is pumped up at the pool and about it being still throughout the Mozart. He raises his eyebrow, which is his devilishly handsome way of expressing interest. It looks genuine enough, but then I've seen him practice it in the bathroom mirror. I know he uses it in presentations to clients. Still, I blunder on. I tell him about the legs-together joke and he does laugh.

It still feels fabulous to make him laugh.

Even though the man sitting opposite me is still married to Becca and is perhaps having an affair with yet another woman, I still adore him. I do love him. As much now in the teeth of confrontation as I do in the grip of orgasm. I can't stop myself. It still feels fabulous to hear him laugh.

"You could come if you wanted. Most of the other women there take their partners along." Unwilling often, but all the same present and correct.

"You can't suddenly uninvite Lizzie, Babes," says Hugh and he manages to sound honestly regretful.

"Libby."

O.K. The best thing is not to think about the condoms in the jacket pocket. Or the restaurant receipt. Or the late nights at the office. Hugh is mine. I've waited a long time for him and I'm not allowing an insignificant little dalliance, which is very probably a figment of my imagination anyway, to get in the way of the important stuff. And the important stuff is that Hugh lives with me now. He chose me. And I'm carrying his child.

We should get married.

Hugh married Becca, I silently lament. Never one to sit imagining the great white meringue, it surprises me that suddenly, violently, this is all I want. I want to be a wife. I need to be a wife. I want a ring on my finger. I want the guarantees. Oh, I know it's not a guarantee, but I want what she had. Even if I take it off her. Even if someone else has already taken it off me. In the car on the way home from the baths I tried to think of things from Hugh's point of view. He has been very stressed recently, very busy indeed. And I haven't really been paying any attention to that, none at all. The problem is that, however fascinating Hugh's career used to be, I can now only see it in terms of what it will provide for our child. I want him to be successful but not because I care whether he feels the buzz of being a successful man, I just need him to continue to earn a good salary. Perhaps that *is* unfair of me. In addition I know that, as far as Hugh's concerned, by becoming twice my usual size I've become half the woman I was. I don't talk to him, or about him, or about anything that interests him the way I used to. I don't watch him play rugby or cricket. I don't drink with him. I don't smoke with him. I don't have sex with him.

I do argue with him.

Perhaps he is getting a bum deal.

"I had a really great time at the pool," I smile. "At least it's big enough. Or at least it is as long as half the water jumps out when I jump in."

I pull a funny face, which hopefully conveys I'm laughing at myself, not feeling sorry for myself.

"Did you learn anything?"

"Yes. There were about a dozen women there, nine of whom had not planned to be parents; I learned not to trust the rhythm method."

Hugh laughs again. Suddenly he takes my hand. This voluntary touch is the first one I can recall for quite some time; it sends shivers up my back and into my crown—I think that even the ends of my hair are on fire.

"I can't wait until the baby is born," Hugh says.

Tears of delight spring to my eyes. God, how I've misjudged him. How quickly I moved to condemn. Hugh is by some way the kindest, most terrific man I have ever known. The most sympathetic, understanding, gentle male on the entire planet.

"Can't you?" My grin stretches from earring to earring.

"No. I can't wait to get the old you back again."

"The old me?"

"You know the—" He lets go of my hand so that he can draw a picture of an egg-timer in the air with both hands. "Although I think you're going to have your work cut out for you, the way you've been piling on the pounds. You really are going to have to stop bingeing on Mars Bars. It's not healthy."

Piling! Bingeing!

Bastard.

In the car I decided that the important thing was to stop the rot, right now. I'd planned to entertain him with amusing anecdotes about the water-confidence class and the funny things that happened at work today. I'd rehearsed these stories, carefully eradicating any trace of pain or humiliation so that we'd simply be left with pleasantries and humor. I had planned to pretend that today's work meetings had excited and lifted me the way they had always done in the past, but suddenly I can't be bothered. I can't be bothered to make my day sound better than it was. Nor can I be bothered to tell him about my actual day. I don't think I'll be bothered to fight for my former figure, either. I'm not sure I'm prepared to put the effort in again. All that skipping and running and lifting and jumping and starving. It suddenly seems pointless; besides I'll have a baby and won't have time. God, I wish I was at home, under the duvet.

Alone.

The waiter arrives with Hugh's starter. I should have ordered one as well; it would at least have given me something to do with my tongue—it's apparent I've lost the skill of biting it, because while I don't plan to say it I suddenly hear, "Jessica loves me even when I'm fat. So does Libby."

"I love you even when you're fat."

"So you think I'm fat." Hugh sighs and doesn't comment but it's an articulate sigh.

We both fall silent. He chews and looks around the restaurant. I stare at my hands and rack my brains for something to say. What was the plan? Entertain him with amusing anecdotes or stab him to death with a fish knife? I can't remember.

Hugh seems to be equally stumped for a line in witty repertoire.

"Sam called for you this evening."

"Did she? Any message?"

"No."

"I expect it was some crisis about her wedding."

"Expect so."

I had promised myself that I'd call her back tonight. I wish I'd done so, rather than come out on this pathetic excuse for a date with Hugh. We fall silent again. I pick up a knife and start to carelessly draw it along the edge of the table. I hope I'm making him feel nervous.

I'm not. Hugh rebukes me with a stare and I feel as though I am Tom or Kate. I put the knife down and fold my hands in my lap. This isn't what I had in mind when I agreed to supper out. Why aren't we laughing and chatting and making each other randy? I rack my brains for *anything* to say. Something elegant or witty or pleasing. Something entertaining that will make Hugh smile or even laugh out loud, that raucous, charming laugh that still bewitches me. I'm confounded.

"Or maybe Sam rang up to offer some advice on sterilizing bottles. Since I became pregnant none of my friends are capable of having a conversation with me without mentioning the pregnancy." I realize this wouldn't win awards for conversational brilliance, but it's all I can manage.

"Maybe that's you," comments Hugh, as he shovels another fork full of meat that's practically still mooing into his mouth.

"Me?"

"Maybe."

"Are you saying I'm boring?"

"No."

"Well, what are you saying?" Even I can hear the hysteria mounting in my voice. I no longer care whether I'm elegant or witty or amusing. And if Hugh were to laugh his supercilious, arrogant, overconfident laugh right now, I'd shove it where the sun don't shine.

"You talk about the pregnancy a lot and the er . . ."

"Baby," I prompt.

"Yeah. That's all. That's all I'm saying."

"So what's wrong with that?"

"Nothing. I didn't say anything was wrong with you talking about it a lot. I just said that maybe it's you that introduces the subject into conversations, not your friends."

"You *are* saying I'm boring."

"No."

He means yes.

Hugh is saved from elaborating because the waiter comes to take his plate away. I'm about to object and point out that Hugh has hardly touched his carpaccio but Hugh waves it away and says he's finished.

The thing is, it's quite possibly true. Since my road-to-Damascus conversion I probably have turned into one of those awful women who talk about nothing other than pregnancy and the associated horrors. But Sam talks about weddings. Doesn't she? Oh God, I can already see my friends gathering at dinner parties in years to come, their eyes glassy with boredom, as I retell the funny little stories that all begin, "Jamie/Mirabelle/Giles/Hatty (I haven't decided on a name yet) said the funniest thing today . . ."

If I'm not vigilant, I could end up being one of those ghastly women who insist on showing photos of the baby, packs and packs of them, while running a video of its first Christmas, even though the baby is sat right there. How awful! I promise myself that I can and will talk about something else. From this moment on I will not mention my aching back or swollen ankles. The word pregnancy will not pass my lips. How hard can it be? It's not as though I talk about it all the time. I do have other topics of conversation.

"So how was your day?" I ask Hugh with a bright, wide smile.

"Very interesting as it happens . . ." I don't catch exactly what's interesting because I'm considering the pros and cons of breastfeeding. Halfway through my salad and his roast wood pigeon I notice that Hugh has noticed I'm not listening. He stares coldly. In an effort to dispel his (correct) belief that I'm thinking about the pregnancy, I say the first thing that comes into my mind.

"Have you heard anything more from the solicitors about the decree nisi?" I see immediately that it would have been wiser to confess to my thoughts on whether I ought to pack bedsocks in my hospital bag; they say your feet turn to ice during labor.

"No."

"They're a bit slow, aren't they? You could have passed an act of Parliament in a more efficient time frame."

"Are you suggesting it's my fault?"

"No. But I do think you ought to know what the delay is. Is Becca stalling?"

"Why the sudden interest?" Hugh's tone is that of someone trying (desperately) not to lose his temper but (obviously) about to do so. I can hardly say, "Because Libby and I were just discussing it and, on public inspection, your excuses to date fell at the first hurdle," nor can I comment, "Because I have reason to believe you're having an affair. Another one."

Instead, I try to appear breezily efficient and cool. "Oh well, it's not important."

"Whether I'm divorced or not is unimportant to you?" It's obvious that, rather than breezily efficient and cool, I've managed to appear brutally indifferent and cold. This conversation is running down the same tract as the "love me when I'm fat" conversation. It's a lose/lose situation. Hugh mops his lips with his napkin and flings it onto his plate.

"I didn't say that," I spit.

"Yes, you did," he hisses.

"Why are you being argumentative?" I seethe, throwing my knife and fork down onto the barely touched salad.

"I'm not being argumentative." We fall silent again. Hugh lights a cigarette; I think he's being provocative. I stare my silent objection. The waiter clears our plates and he uses a small silver dustpan to clear away the crumbs and spills on the tablecloth but he can't budge the atmosphere.

Another successful evening, then.

37

"You did *what*?"

"It's not like I'm confessing to joining the Foreign Legion."

"I'd possibly be less surprised."

"Julia, it's not so heinous."

"Well, how did you hear about it?"

"Sam gave me the number."

"Yeah, it sounds just up Sam's street."

"I simply needed a change," I justify.

"Whatever," comments Julia as she drifts back to her desk, clearly mystified.

The nature of my crime is that I visited a Color Me Beautiful technician. You know, one of those women who advise you on what colors you should be wearing and what make-up tones suit you. It was fascinating. Well it was, after we got past the "Is your hair brown or blond?" question. (Answer: blond at the moment except for an inch or two at the roots. Not that I actually believe all that rubbish the bump woman in the chemist spouted, but you never can be too careful, can you? I'd never forgive myself if there was any truth in the things she said and it's not worth the risk just for a few months' vanity.) Once we'd established that I'd become a "natural" blonde again after the birth, Cecilia (my Color Me Beautiful technician) was able to advise me as to what I should be wearing. She held little duster-size pieces of material to my neck, and pulled my hair back with a series of colorful scrunchies in an effort to discover which "season" I am. It was a surprisingly good laugh. For the first time in months I felt feminine and fun. When I said as much to Cecilia she asked, "So why haven't you been feeling feminine?"

"Ha, isn't it obvious?" I pointed toward my huge stomach.

"But you're more feminine now than ever!" she gasped.

Apparently, I suit baby blue, indigo and the lightest tones of purple. I should wear mint in the summer (which I'm finding a bit hard to swallow) and when I have serious meetings where I want to influence I ought to wear jade. Which is what I'm wearing today. I haven't gone for the full-on jade suit—in fact I'm still in a long white dress (it hides a multitude of sins), but I am wearing a jade scarf around my bump, à la Nicole Appleton, and carrying a funky little green handbag. I thought I looked rather swish; Julia clearly believes that this is another aberration driven by my hormones.

She pops her head back into my office. I wait for her to continue her tirade on black being the only appropriate color for an agency, and certainly for a client meeting, but she surprises me. "Here, if you are serious about this we might as well go the whole hog." She holds out a bottle of emerald-green nail varnish, "Give me a shout when you want your toes done. I assume you'll need some help as you can't reach them anymore," she grins.

I used to spend hours, literally hours, drifting around beauty counters. My idea of Elysian Fields definitely was spending unending Saturday afternoons with my fingers in pots of buttery creams, or testing shimmery powders on the back of my hand. If Anna Sui had a new body paint out then I'd have tried it even before it was reviewed in *Vogue*. If Urban Decay brought out a new test tube of lilac glisteny stuff and a dinky puff to go with, no questions asked, I'd whip out my plastic. I can fall in love with well-presented and packaged beauty products sat in delightful temping rows as easily as other women fall in love with Brad Pitt. Boots is, unquestionably, the grown-up girl's candy store. Yet, while I really enjoyed playing "girl's world" with Cecilia and Julia (for the record I did "influence" the meeting today, insomuch as I persuaded the boys that a sushi bar was not a great venue for lunch), I realize that make-up is not the reason I was born to be female.

That thing Cecilia said about me being more feminine now than ever—I think she's right. I lie awake at night and rest my hand on my stomach. On *my baby*, and it doesn't feel ugly. It isn't just a protruding mass of fatness. It feels entirely womanly and breathtakingly beautiful. And I know, absolutely know, that this is the most important thing I can ever do. At the risk of sounding too American, it's a privilege that a baby is growing in my body.

I think I might dissolve with excitement.

June

38

Suddenly in June as I hit month seven I become Herculean. I brim with energy and anticipation. And while I have shaken off my lethargy, I know I am still being held to ransom by my hormones. Instead of avidly consuming *Campaign* and *Marketing*, or even shopping, I decide that the most useful way to channel my energy is to wash skirting boards, paint walls and polish floors. Then I start to plant window boxes, grow herbs, and hoover behind the settee. Libby is delighted. She insists I'm "nesting."

I dismiss this as the idiocy that it surely is. "I am not nesting," I yell. "I simply want everything to be clean and comfortable and . . . ready."

"You're right. How could I have muddled that up with nesting?" she asks with a grin.

"I'm simply doing it to avoid being seen in public," I defend, taking care to cross my fingers.

It's eight o'clock in the evening, I am bent double over a steaming bucket of water, plunging my rubber-gloved hands into the mass of soap suds when, suddenly, I catch my reflection in the long bathroom mirror. Except it can't be me. Can it? Because the woman scrubbing floors, well, for a start she's scrubbing floors, secondly she's wearing paint-splattered non-designer jeans, which aren't fastened but held up with a scarf. Her hair has dark roots showing through, it needs a wash and so is pulled back into a severe knot. She's rotund. More alarming yet, she is half-smiling to herself as though she is gaining some satisfaction out of scrubbing floors and being inventive enough to use the small scouring pad to really get at the dirt in the grout between the tiles. Surely that isn't my reflection. That woman looks familiar, but she doesn't look like me . . . she looks more like . . . Penny or Becca. I peel off my rubber gloves and cast them aside. They slap against the bucket and the scourer.

In panic I call Sam to ask her if I'm turning into Becca. I can ask this, safe in the knowledge that Sam would rather lie to me than hurt my feelings and therefore will deny it vociferously, making us both feel good.

Surprisingly, she's in.

"At last, we speak," I say. Our answering-machine-message trail has continued recently and besides grabbing a quick coffee last month I haven't seen her since we went to Wales. The coffee meeting was unsatisfactory. Sam was glowing and giggly one moment and then took a call from her seamstress. There was some problem about veil length that totally broke the mood. Sam became distracted and jittery. I don't think she's eating enough.

"I'm desperate to see you," she says.

"I don't suppose you're free now, are you?"

"Yes, brilliant, I'll come over."

I pause and look around the flat; it's in an amazing state of disarray. Before I started scrubbing the floor I had been tidying my wardrobes. I'd just got to the point of emptying the entire contents—jackets, suits, tops, trousers, handbags, shoes, hat boxes and false boobs (which look a bit like chicken giblets)—onto every available surface, when I noticed that the bathroom floor needed scrubbing. I've had the Klimt posters reframed. They look better in gold frames after all, but I haven't had a chance to hang them in the bedroom so they are propped against the skirting board in the living room. I went to Tesco's yesterday and did a big shop, only half of which has been unpacked. I can see about three piles of ironing and any remaining floor space is decorated with open maternity books and magazines. My flat looks like Libby's home. It's light years away from the serene, *feng shuied* abode that I used to keep. "No, let's go out. I'm a bit stir-crazy myself."

Sam is more successful than she'd have you believe. You have to be very tough and very good to be a management consultant, and she's an exemplary management consultant. She's accustomed to fancy restaurants as she dines with clients most lunchtimes and evenings. I've arrived at the restaurant before her, and from my seat I watch her as she efficiently drops off her jacket, expertly touches up her lipstick and orders vodka before she sits down. As the crisp white napkin is settling on her lap I ask, "So what news?" This question comes at enormous personal expense, as I put my own concerns on hold (Am I turning into Becca? And names— does she like Jack or Toby if it's a boy? Ellen, if it's a girl?).

I allow Sam to dive in first. "Oh, nothing special. I just thought it would be nice to meet up, just the two of us," she mutters. I'm not convinced for a nanosecond. Sam's vodka and orange arrives with surprising speed and she drinks it equally smartly, then she orders another. I can spot them at a hundred-mile radius; Sam is a woman on a mission.

"I'll have a still mineral water with a twist of lime," I instruct the waiter loudly. Recently, I've reveled in my virtue and no longer hanker after a glass of champagne. "So, how are the wedding plans?" Over the last five months I've started every conversation I've had with Sam like this. Indeed, I occasionally used it as conversational filler with her even before she'd met Gilbert.

Normally her response is both enthusiastic and verbose; today she is surprisingly reticent. "Fine."

"That's it? Fine?"

"Yes. What else do you want me to say?"

"Well, isn't there some minor catastrophe? Like being unable to match the ribbons on the bridesmaids' dresses with the exact shade of the roses in the church floral displays? Or maybe something really serious is happening, like you've timed the car route from your flat to the church three times, and now have to decide how to find an average journey length. Should it be the mean, the mode or the medium?"

"Oh, it's all one big laugh to you, isn't it?" snaps Sam.

This is absolutely unprecedented. I have never, ever, in all the years I've known Sam, heard her snap at anyone. She is the absolute epitome of kindness, appeasement and tact. She would rather walk a tightrope without a safety net than appear confrontational. I've often wondered how this gentleness and occasionally giddy attitude accomplished anything at work. But it does.

"I'm a big laugh, a big joke," she hisses, downing her second vodka and immediately ordering a bottle of Chablis.

I cautiously sip my mineral water and, on putting it down, I reach across the table and squeeze Sam's hand. "You are not a joke, Babes. I never laugh at you." And while this isn't absolutely 100 percent truthful, it is the reassurance Sam needs. "Have I done something wrong?" I ask.

"No, this is nothing to do with you."

Relieved, I encourage Sam to look at the menu. However, I notice that while I mentally devour every dish and get an enormous amount of entertainment just imagining what everything will taste like, Sam can't seem to concentrate on the delicacies that ought to tempt her. For all the interest she takes in red peppers stuffed with codfish mousse, or the creamed gazpacho with cured ham, we might as well have been at McDonald's and ordered two cheeseburgers with fries. I order an oriental salad with delights such as crispy duck and an orange and cashew nut dressing, then baked turbot with calamari. I ask the waiter to replenish the bread basket and comment to Sam that I think I'll have room for pudding. She's in a bad way—she doesn't show even a flicker of surprise at the amount I'm ordering. I'm in a bad way. I think that even after eating this lot I could still happily devour a cheeseburger and fries. Sam looks desperate and can't seem to make a choice. I presume she's still on a calorie-, fat- and taste-control diet for the wedding, so I point out a couple of the least artery-hardening options; after all, this used to be one of the most essential dinner-party skills I possessed. She nods, mutely accepting my suggestions; obviously she couldn't care less what she eats.

I wonder what can be throwing her equilibrium so completely.

"I've kissed James."

Ah.

"With tongues, and I enjoyed it," she confesses in a rush. I don't know if she's expecting to be struck by lightning or handed a cigar.

"James, as in . . ."

"My future brother-in-law, yes," she adds impatiently.

With depressing regularity in the past, Sam and a number of my other friends have come to me with confessions of this kind. Normally, I defuse the situation by yelling out something flip like, "Scores out of ten?" because that's what girl friends are born for. Today I'm wary of saying anything before I've had a chance to weigh up exactly what this means.

"Just the once?" I try to establish the extent of the indiscretion.

Sam nods ferociously, but then after a couple of whole-hearted declarations of, "Yes, of course, just the once," the nod dissolves into a shake.

"Twice?"

Shake of the head.

"On an on-going basis?"

Nodding again.

Ah.

"Sober?"

More nodding.

"Just kissed him?"

Shaking head again. I feel like a Victorian dentist trying to extract teeth with a cumbersome and painful pair of four-foot-long tweezers.

"We're having an"—she pauses and checks who is sitting at the tables nearby—"an affair, for want of a better word," and then more bravely and firmly she repeats, "We're having an affair."

I check my reflection in the mirror on the wall; I'm searching for something priestly in my face that prompts or demands confessions such as these. I try and fail to appear unfazed. An affair, Sam! Sam, an affair! What's the world coming to? I grab another roll covered in pumpkin seeds and start to butter it vigorously.

"Since when?"

"Since Wales."

Now that I count my life in weeks I'm quickly able to calculate. "This has been going on for fourteen weeks, over three months?"

"Yes."

"But you've been so happy in the past few months."

"Yes."

"I thought it was Gilbert making you happy, and the wedding preparations."

"No."

Sam is in agony. It's obvious. I quickly try to assess the situation. James is fun, extremely charming, intelligent, and he has a quite overwhelming physical presence. He is definitely a horn, even I noticed as much in my near-eunuch state.

"Is it just sex?" And I almost want her answer to be in the affirmative. It will be easier for her in the long run.

But she shakes her head. "I think I'm in love with him. I didn't want it to happen, but the moment I met him I knew it was going to. He's all the things I like about Gilbert except that he's younger and spunkier and more"—she searches for the word in the bottom of her wine glass—"more alive. At first I thought it was just sex. It is true to say that there is an unprecedented sexual attraction between us. The air was crackling on the drive down to Wales, I was certain that Gilbert would pick up, but he didn't."

Poor trusting Gilbert.

Silly sod Gilbert.

"After the rounders game and the fish pie—"

"A well-known aphrodisiac."

"It seemed inevitable. We went walking in the woods—"

"In the dead of night?" She nods reluctantly. "Oh, Sam you

went for a PISS!" I'm not referring to the bodily function here, but to a Potential Illicit Snog Situation. Sam nods unwillingly. After all, you don't just happen to find yourself in a situation like that, you have to put yourself there. Sometimes you go for a PISS with no intention of letting things get out of hand, and sometimes you desperately want them to.

"And there was this moment. You know, The Moment. When you know you are going to kiss each other and you know you shouldn't, but you know you are going to anyway. You look at the floor and then at his eyes and then back at the floor again."

"Sam, no one does that except in films."

"I do. I did. He's not like a film, George, everyone else was but he's not."

And despite my gruffness I do know. I remember that moment exactly. She's talking about the sort of moment when Hugh and I first kissed in the limo. I, too, had put myself in a Potential Illicit Snog Situation; in fact I'd been putting myself in one for years, and eventually Hugh noticed he was there too. I drag myself back to Sam.

"And did you have sex with him then and there in the woods?"

"No, of course not." Sam's shocked at my presumption, which is unfair. After all, she's the one that's shagging her brother-in-law to be. It's not so odd that I should inquire whether there was a bit of action in the woods à la Titania and Bottom.

"We've been seeing each other and trying not to sleep with each other ever since."

Oh, that old one.

"Until last week."

"When I presume . . ."

"You presume correctly. You told me to be nice," she justifies.

"Do you sleep with every man you are nice to? Don't answer that."

Our food arrives. Sam leaves hers untouched and, while I know I am running the risk of looking insensitive, I am thirty-one weeks pregnant, nearly full-term, so I dive in.

"Go on." I encourage her to finish her story, not least because it gives me the opportunity to eat my food uninterrupted.

Sam doesn't need much prompting. "He's it. He's the One. My teapot's lid."

How romantic. Despite the seriousness of the situation, it takes every ounce of my willpower to suppress my giggles.

"He makes me feel I can be entirely myself. He makes me feel that I can be *more* than I am. He is potential. He's realization. I'm in love with him." She smiles so broadly I think her face will split. Her huge brown eyes radiate unreserved delight. "He is the first man that I have ever been with where I feel I can confidently be me. You know what I mean."

Of course I do.

I think I do.

I should do. I stay silent and allow her to fall into a stream of gibberish.

"I don't have to adapt myself, edit, mold or change myself in any way. I don't have to fake an interest in his hobbies or quash any passions of my own. We can talk about anything, our childhood, work, ambitions, travel and friends. And he *listens* to me. It's not just me doing all the polite inquiring and sympathetic nodding of the head. He doesn't seem to need me as an emotional crutch or as a hostess or for money, like all the other men I've dated have done, but he does seem to really want me."

I think it's time I injected a bit of caution, a smattering of reality. "Sam, you have said similar stuff before."

"I know," she admits. "I've said it before because I've wanted it to be true. But this really is different. He really is different."

I've heard this before, too.

"What should I do?"

I sigh. "What do you want me to say, Sam? Do you want me to tell you to call it all off, draw a halt? Or full steam ahead?" In my experience these confessions are never shared in the hope that the story teller will get some genuine advice, but more so they can tell you what they are going to do and square it with their own conscience. Sam looks at me with fear and despair, and love and hope, but she doesn't answer my question. "How does James feel?"

"The same," she replies confidently.

"You're sure?"

"Certain."

"No fifty-fifty, do you want to ask the audience? Call a friend?" She glares at me. I know I'm being flip but actually I'm relieved. This is difficult but not a disaster. So she loves her fiancé's brother; that's not the most convenient scenario, I admit. But if he loves her too then it's not an irretrievable situation. She hasn't been seeing Gilbert that long, less than a year. Yes, there will be a lot of heartbreak and embarrassment in the short term, but providing they both have the courage of their convictions then they will pull through. I say as much to Sam.

"You're suggesting we tell Gilbert and weather the storm?" She's incredulous.

"Yes, I am. You're lucky you've discovered how you feel about one another before the wedding."

"I can't do that."

This surprises me enough to make me put my fork down, possibly the first time in months that I have voluntarily done so rather than had it wrestled from my hand.

"Why can't you?"

"Because I'm marrying Gilbert."

"But you love James."

"Yes."

"And he loves you."

She nods.

"So?"

Sam becomes impatient. "Aren't you listening? I'm *marrying* Gilbert. *Marrying* him. James hasn't mentioned marriage."

I'm astounded.

Sam sees as much and tries to explain.

"Some people, no, to be accurate, most people think my obsession with getting married is sad and pathetic." Yes. "Outdated and restrictive." Yes. "But it's not." Oh yes, it is. The pantomime is in my head. "Those people misunderstand me. They assume I need a man to define me. It's not true. I know who I am. What I like. What I want from life. So how can I be sad?" I assume it's a rhetorical question, so I don't jump in with my response that marrying one man while loving his brother seems pretty sad to me. "The career thing has never done it for me. I admit there is a certain excitement to foreign travel, managing a team of twelve people, and I'm definitely not knocking the terrific salary, but . . ."

The "but" hovers in the air like an annoying mosquito. The "but" represents all that fails to keep her warm at night.

"But my greatest ambition, what I really want, always wanted, all I've *ever* wanted is to be married."

This is hardly breaking news.

"But surely *who* you marry is of vital importance?" I probe.

"Not really. Not any more."

I think this is the most honest thing I have ever heard anyone say. It's also the most pitiful.

"Oh Sam," I murmur, for want of anything more articulate to say.

"Look, Gilbert is a firm offer."

"You're not selling a house!" I almost scream. I notice that a number of other diners have now abandoned their conversations, preferring instead to listen to ours. I can hardly blame them; this is better than Jerry Springer.

"Better the devil you know," shrugs Sam. I know she's trying to sound brave. I know she's not feeling it.

"But you know both James and Gilbert." It's not the first time one of her clichés has appeared woefully inadequate.

"Oh well, then, a bird in the hand is worth two in the bush." I scowl, frustrated. "I can't risk it," Sam explains. "I'm not going to repeat my past mistakes."

It is true that Sam has been known to misread the signs of the guys she's been dating, assuming they were further along the commitment chain than they obviously were. She's often entertained me with tales of misadventure and misconstruing. For example, when she was eighteen she was extremely disappointed when her boyfriend at the time failed to propose at her birthday party and, instead of giving her a ring with a precious stone, he presented her with a Culture Club video and the *Rocky Horror* soundtrack LP. Far more useful in my opinion, but not in Sam's. When she turned twenty-one she was sure all the signs were there that Terry was going to propose. She managed to ignore the fact that he'd repeatedly told her that he wanted to travel after he graduated; she thought he was teasing. He wasn't. And then there was Matt, whom she dated when she was twenty-three. He kept telling her she'd make a lovely wife. Not his, apparently. Nick (she was twenty-five) did say he wanted to demonstrate his commitment, but again this declaration failed to produce a diamond ring—just a bag of dirty laundry every Sunday evening. And then there was Steve, and then Rod and then . . .

"Nothing," Sam screeches, as though she's been following my thoughts. "Not a single proposal in over seventeen years. And I used to ask, 'Why not? Why not? Why not?' " I notice that the Chablis bottle is empty. So does Sam. She beckons to a waiter and orders another. Her starter is still untouched.

"I'm not ugly," she shouts defiantly.

"You're lovely," I confirm. I want to say more, but she's in full flow and it's fueled by alcohol; there's nothing I can do except listen and hope that none of the diners are her clients, or are related to her mother.

"I work out. I try to be pleasant and liberal and informed. I may be past my initial bloom, but, the point is, even when I was bursting with youth no one made an offer. I'm not dull or smelly and I don't have any unsocial diseases. I'm fairly good at Trivial Pursuit; I nearly always win the pie pieces. I read the *FT* every day, for God's sake. But for years there was nothing doing. I used to watch them on the Tube—married women—and they're not all that special."

I focus on the red patch of skin on her neck, which I know as well as I know my own hand. When Sam is riled or embarrassed or excited her neck blushes. Apparently, when she orgasms she looks exactly like a vine-ripened tomato.

"Yes, of course some of them look lovely but some are real hounds, and some are obviously above average intelligence but others seem to be just one up from pond life. So I'd ask myself, why not me? It's not that I was overly fussy, not a fact that I'm unduly proud of. And then, finally, there was Gilbert."

She pauses not so much for breath but to replenish her glass. I start forking up bits of her starter and shoveling them into my mouth. Well, she's barely glanced at it and I don't want to offend the chef.

"George, before Gilbert proposed I was at the stage where I didn't mind if a man was short, earned less than me or used his knife and fork incorrectly. Gilbert saved me."

I notice that Sam has stopped calling Gilbert "G." He's become Gilbert once more. Indication that she is seeing him for what he is.

Sam is blinking ferociously, because the only thing that is more embarrassing than a woman ranting in a restaurant is a woman sobbing in a restaurant. We are both glad when the waiter interrupts us to clear our plates and deposit our main course. He takes Sam's plate away, although I am still cramming her food into my mouth.

"The proposal was *so* perfect." She's trying to convince herself.

"You were drunk," I remind her.

She brushes my objections away. "He'd booked a table at the Ivy. The Ivy! Usually you have to be featured in *Hello!* at least twice before you can hope to secure a table at the Ivy."

Personally, I'm not all that gung-ho on proposals at a table in public. I find the other diners intrusive, but whatever lights your fire. I've always known that Sam is scarily starry-eyed and idealistic.

"The ring is beautiful."

But not the one she wanted.

"He thanked me for agreeing to marry him."

This almost touches me.

"Getting married is all I ever wanted and I've wanted it so desperately, for such a long time. I don't know how to want anything else." She pauses. "James isn't talking marriage."

"Are you sure?"

"Yes, I asked him." She has no shame. "It's so unfair. If we were in a film he'd propose. He'd offer me a marriage proposal to replace the one he's asking me to sacrifice. No one in a film says, 'Don't marry him, shag me,' do they?"

"What did James say when you talked about marriage?"

She waves her hand, drunkenly, "Oh, some nonsense about not ruling it out. Blah, blah. One day both of us may be ready to make that kind of commitment to each other. Etc., etc. Too big a decision to make in the heat of the moment. So on and so forth."

"Sounds pretty sensible to me."

"Sounds like a get-out clause to me."

Even I am now beginning to lose my appetite. How has this happened under my nose with my failing to notice? Sam's right. It has always been a joke that she's desperate to marry but suddenly it seems dark and deadly serious. She is prepared to marry one man while loving another rather than go through life ringless. It's as if Germaine Greer never existed. I feel irredeemably depressed. What's left for us in the twenty-first century? We have no religion, we don't believe in everlasting love, and the only comfort available is a handful of confetti and a three-tier fruitcake. I've never even met anyone who likes fruitcake. There has to be more to it than that. Doesn't there?

Sam, oblivious to my profound pondering, comments, "Men, they are like buses, aren't they? You wait forever and then two come along at once. Perhaps it's a case of the grass is always greener," she tries to comfort herself.

If I think back through our relationship, it has not been one punctuated by thoughtful pauses. The opposite is true, as we've always preferred chatter and irrelevant observation to silence. Our evenings together were a foggy mass of excited gossip, scandal, palaver and prattle. More babbling brook than still waters. So I know lots of stuff about Sam. I know when and where she had her first kiss, and who she lost her virginity to. I know that her favorite meal is jacket potato with curried baked beans and mayonnaise, although it's never been fashionable. I know the sound she makes when she orgasms. I know she "sort of" believes in God, although she only goes to church for weddings, christenings, funerals and midnight mass on Christmas Eve. I know she always believes the best of people, she invariably looks on the bright side and she doesn't even find Anthea Turner irritating. I know how many times she's been in love, and how many times she's been in lust. I know which hairspray she uses, where she buys her hosiery, what she wants to call her children. In short, I know the contents of her fridge, her bathroom cabinet and her heart. And she knows lots of stuff about me—she knows I lost my virginity to Hugh. That my taste in food, art, music and film were all formed with, through or for Hugh. Well, Hugh is pretty much all there is to me.

I also know one or two things about Sam that she's never told me; things that she's possibly oblivious to. Things like, she's the most generous, magnanimous, sweet-natured woman in the city of London. She's beautiful, talented, inimitable, and the reason she's not married isn't because no one's offered to date, but because she's too good to settle for the flotsam and jetsam that has washed up on her beach. And even the flotsam and jetsam have known this.

How has this happened? What should I do or say? I can't let her make this mistake. I've always followed a policy of non-interference; I'm there for my friends if they ask for help but I don't thrust it upon them. It's too messy. Too complex. Last time I tried to be honest with Sam was when I told her not to rush into an engagement. She's hardly going to thank me if I underline my point with a "told you so."

So she's marrying the wrong bloke. How bad can it be, spending the rest of your life paying for a mistake?

Bad. Bloody, fucking bad. I *have* to be honest. I've been

amused and indulgent for too long. I can't stand by and let her destroy her life.

"Sam, for goodness sake! You can't go on living your life by following a handful of outdated old wives' tales and clichés. It might make things appear simpler, but you're kidding yourself," I burst.

"But it is better to be safe than sorry," she whines.

"This nonsense might be useful until secondary school but grown-up life's too complex for you to retreat into *The Oxford Dictionary of English Idioms* every time you have a dilemma." Sam is silent. "You have to get yourself your own set of values and opinions," I insist. "You have to think about this very carefully. You have to think what is best for you. And being married to one man while loving another won't make you happy. You're not being fair to yourself, or to James or Gilbert for that matter. You have to think about Gilbert too."

"The way you thought about Becca?" Sam looks up and stares into my eyes.

"What's that got to do with anything?" I ask, genuinely bemused. We're talking about Sam, not me.

"Don't you see, George? Don't you know why I came to you?"

"Because I'm your friend."

"Because we're exactly alike."

Whoa, hold your horses, matey. No, we are not. Sam may be the most generous, magnanimous, sweet-natured woman in the city of London. She is beautiful, talented, inimitable, but she's also an appalling throwback as far as the cause of female independence is concerned. She thinks that being married is the only way to be happy. She believes this so strongly that she's prepared to marry the brother of the man she loves just to ensure a dual-pension policy. I'm quite different. I'm with Hugh although the wedding band is noticeably lacking.

"No, we are not. I'm with the man I love."

"Be imaginative," she spits nastily. "For Hugh, read marriage. You pursued Hugh with the same grim determination that I pursued an engagement ring. The only difference is I'm more honest with myself. You didn't allow the fact that he was married to someone else to distract you, nor the subsequent births of his daughter and son. You've hardly got the steadiest grip on reality, have you? Physician, heal thyself."

"You've got it all wrong."

"Have I? Well, as long as you're sure." I've never seen her so angry and bitter before. Where's Sam gone? Gentle Sam, lovely Sam. "George, you punched, kicked and clawed your way to where you are now. You suffered countless humiliations. For years he ignored you. He forgets your birthday, he doesn't pay any bills, and this is what you reinvented yourself for."

La, la, la, la. I'm not listening. Mentally, although not physically, I've put my fingers in my ears. La, la, la, la. It is a technique I used to use when watching horror movies as a teenager. I'd pretend to be brave, but I'd sing to myself so the scary reality didn't sink into my consciousness. I want this conversation back on track. I want to talk about Sam, Gilbert and James.

"You're marrying for the dress, the day, the fantasy," I accuse.

"And why are you with Hugh?"

"We are alike." But are we? I used to think we were, but now I'm not so sure. I push on as much to convince myself as Sam. "We have the same tastes in music and books and art."

"You don't even have tastes of your own! You imitate his tastes."

"I wanted him from the moment I saw him and I've never wanted anyone else."

"Yeah, well, sometimes we have the best sex with the worst people. It's God's April fool."

I try and be patient; after all, I've seen her knock back a fair amount to drink tonight, all on an empty stomach. She probably doesn't mean most of this. "You're twisting this, Sam. I'm not the one with the problem. You are. You're deluded."

"At least Gilbert is a nice guy to be deluded about."

"Meaning?" Actually, I'm not sure I want her to tell me.

"Hugh is a prat, George."

"He is not a prat," I counter automatically, although mentally I know the insult has already seeped into my mind and heart, and I'll haul it up for closer inspection when I'm next alone.

"He is a selfish, childish, petulant, inconsiderate prat," says Sam, who never says anything bad about anyone.

"I thought you liked him," I stutter in disbelief. "You've been his friend as long as I have."

"He's a funny enough guy to spend Rag Week with. He's pleasant company at a dinner party. But that's it. You're wasting your life." She stubs out her cigarette.

I'm beginning to think I should stay at home. I certainly should avoid restaurants. Bad karma.

Our dinner ends fairly swiftly after this outburst. Sam and I struggle through the main course, she hardly eats a thing, I hoover up everything edible in the vicinity, and then we promptly pay the bill. There's little left to be said.

39

To use a Sam phrase, "You could have knocked me over with a feather." To be more original about it, I am shattered, shocked, stabbed and (this is the hardest to admit) somewhat contrite. Sam has chucked me. My status as her best friend is no more. I haven't been seeing that much of Sam recently, but the fact that I'm unlikely to see her again sends shivers of horror bouncing up and down my spine. Another void. I used to be very good at filling gaps. I'd visit the gym, buy clothes, have a facial. In fact, these methods for filling the terrible nothingness that haunted my existence were so effective they became my life. But the pregnancy has slowed me down. I can't shop or skip, which gives me more time to think. Forces me to think.

Sam's right, of course, I didn't think about Becca. Not really. If I thought of Becca at all, I thought of her as the antithesis of me. Initially, when I had spreading hips, rats' tails hair and a limited general knowledge, she had slim hips, flowing tresses and was a serious contender for the *Krypton Factor*. I rarely thought of her except in terms of what I was not. Or, rather more accurately, what I had not got.

Hugh.

As I worked off the spare inches and devoted more and more time to the *Times* crossword, she appeared to be sliding down the slippery slope of smug marriedness, landing in a sludgy mess of mushed veg, mushed mind and mushed skin tone. It's only now that my hands are back in the rubber gloves and the steaming bucket of hot water that I consider Becca may be, *must* be, more than that which I am not.

After years and years of seeing Becca as the devil incarnate, recently, since supper with Sam, I lie awake at night thinking, "Maybe she isn't." In fact, she's beginning to look more and more like a victim in all of this. And if she's the victim, then I'm the aggressor. Which is not how I like to see myself.

It didn't work. La, la, la, la didn't work. The cruel home truths have stained my consciousness and, however hard I try, it's impossible to ignore what Sam said. *Punched, kicked and clawed my way to where I am now . . . suffered countless humiliations . . . he ignored me . . . this is what I reinvented myself for . . . Hugh is a prat, George . . . a selfish, childish, petulant, inconsiderate prat. I am wasting my life.*

The funniest thing is she doesn't even know about the suspected affair and she thinks this. Of course, I'm using funny in a post-modern, ironic sense. There's nothing funny about this situation.

It isn't news.

She thought she was telling me something I didn't know, but she was wrong. I've known it for a while. I can't exactly date it. I didn't wake up one morning and think, "*Fuck*, what a waste of fourteen years," it was a more insidious, cumulative process. It possibly started when he announced our pregnancy to our "six closest friends," and I'd never met any of them before, or, for that matter, since. I was very tired and sick and I'm not sure they were worth the effort. His endless jokes about my expanding waistline have also worn me down. Hugh has never understood that putting on weight is a necessity when producing a baby. The endless long and lonely nights haven't done much to persuade me that he's a great guy. I've added them up. I've been pregnant for 224 days, we've known I've been pregnant for 161 days, Hugh and I have spent thirty-five evenings together in that time. I know I'm anal, I'm bored. I'm desperate; it makes you anal. The condoms and the receipt didn't do much to improve my confidence in him, either. I can't name the exact moment when I realized that my issues about being pregnant were not about the discomfort of hemorrhoids, the restricted social life, the swelling stomach. I didn't fear losing my status as a goddess per se, I feared that losing that status meant I would lose Hugh. I'd like to think that he's not the type of man to walk out just because I'm the size of a house. I'd like to think that. But Sam's right, isn't she? Don't even answer that, I know the answer. I've known for quite some time that Hugh is a prat.

But he's my prat, and love is a really hard habit to kick. So, before you ask, I'm not going to leave him.

I'm staying with him because of my baby, because it deserves a father. And because of Becca's babies, because I stole their father. It's the only way I can make amends. It's possible that my actions haven't been 100 percent honorable to date. The fact that I've been blinkered by love explains it, but doesn't excuse it. I want to do the right thing. If I were to leave Hugh now I'd have ripped their lives apart for nothing and that's not fair. It doesn't seem much, but at least if our relationship works and Kate and Tom grow up believing that their father left their mother for the love of his live—as I'd always believed—then maybe they'll find it in their hearts to forgive us both. Maybe we'll all muddle along as a fairly unconventional family. And if that's too much to hope for, at the very least I can guarantee that they'll get Christmas and birthday presents. It's not much, but it's all I can offer in the way of making it up.

So I must not think about the possibility that Hugh is having an affair. It doesn't have to mean anything significant. It doesn't mean anything at all, unless I say it does. I have to get our relationship back on track because the stakes we are playing to are terrifyingly high. Two children and a fetus. Nor can I think about the fact that Sam might be marrying one man while loving another. I can't even think about the pregnancy. The thing is, the chances are, if I managed to miss the fact that my best friend is ensconced in an affair just weeks before her wedding, then there's a serious possibility that this isn't the only sail that is blowing me up shit creek. I know that recently I've been far too installed in babyville. I know that I haven't paid enough attention to Hugh or to my job. I can only fix one thing at a time, and I've decided it ought to be my job.

Because it is *my* job and Hugh is just Hugh. He's not my Hugh. Or at least not exclusively mine, which might as well mean not mine, mightn't it? I'm staying with him, but I've woken up to the fact that he's not my sun, my moon, my stars. I hope one day he will be again, when I stop being angry. In the short term it's probably wisest to concentrate on something else.

I *have* to win the Project Zoom pitch. I have to be entirely and unreservedly focused. I have to be pithy, witty, droll, keen, jocular and waggish. My knowledge base as far as cars are concerned is traditionally female: the color (interior and exterior), the presence of power-assisted steering and a CD player are important. As is not breaking down. If a car conversation gets deeper than that I find it very difficult to avoid my eyes glazing over. So my first stop is the newsagent's, where I buy ten car magazines and set about learning everything there is to know about luxury-car brands. At least that way I'd be able to appear credible at a factory visit or when I meet the dealers.

I utilize my sleepless nights studying engine sizes, understanding suspension—front, rear and standard issue—I now know what a chassis is. I can hold a plausible conversation about the wheel base and engine transmission of most luxury cars. I know about tire tread, width and grip. I know that a car with rear-wheel drive and a low center of gravity holds the road like a sports car. I am able to say things like, "Well, the straight-line speed and performance are beyond dispute on the Jaguar V6, but it sounds trouncey at high revs compared with a BMW's honeyed straight six," and I know what I mean. I know that an aluminum- rather than steel-built car is better for the environment, although "real drivers" bemoan the bastardization of the driving experience. They like to feel the car grip the road under them.

And while this might not be everyone's solution to a lack of best friend and to a philandering lover, it's the best I can come up with at short notice.

July

♡

40

I call Libby to show off my new knowledge. She's not exactly impressed, even when I tell her that a Volkswagen Golf 2.0 GTI is 3 mm shorter than a Ford Focus 2.0 Zetec, and these cars aren't even Project Zoom competitors. Her lack of enthusiasm could be something to do with the fact that it is after midnight.

"Did I disturb you?" I ask guiltily.

"Not really. I was ironing Millie's school uniform. Then I'm going to go to bed."

"It would be easier to park," I insist.

"What would?"

"The Volkswagen."

"Three millimeters, no one would notice the difference," she scoffs, betraying that while she might not be that interested in what I have to say she was at least listening to me, which is good of her. "Especially me as I'm not very good at judging lengths."

"That's because every man you've ever slept with has told you he has an eight-inch penis."

We both laugh.

"Anyway," I persist, "the Volkswagen Golf 2.0 GTI is 36 mm wider than a Ford Focus 2.0 Zetec, so it's back to the eternal short-and-fat versus long-and-thin debate."

"Well, my vote is with short and fat every time."

We giggle again and then I comment, "God, cars *are* sexy.

Really sexy. Suddenly I get it. I understand the penis-substitute thing."

"Oh-oh, your hormones are raging again," Libby comments.

"What makes you think that?"

"Every one of your conversations reverts back to sex, whatever you're talking about."

"But haven't you noticed that the vocabulary used when talking about cars is desperately provocative? All the car mags go on about is size, performance, grip, how the cars 'respond' when 'handled.' "

Libby is laughing again. "I think it's going to be Hugh's lucky night."

Not Hugh's.

"Sex is definitely the right territory for Project Zoom. Or at least passion is. It's an Italian brand. I think I'm onto something."

Libby laughs and points out that even if I was trying to sell thermal bedsocks to the old and infirm, I'd probably give it a sexy spin right now. We laugh and then hang up. She goes back to ironing Millie's uniform. I go back to lying on my bed, staring at the ceiling.

Libby is right—I do feel more randy than a fifteen-year-old schoolboy at the Playboy Mansion, but my thirty-three-week bulging stomach definitely doesn't do it for Hugh; he doesn't think my popped tummy button is in the slightest bit dinky. I think it looks great. Nor does he think the dark stretch marks that have oozed across my belly are exotic. The other day he came into the bedroom, and maybe he would have made overtures; after all I was lying naked and spreadeagled on the bed. However, he sensed that I was thus reclining due to the overwhelming, somewhat startling and sudden appearance of summer, not because I was feeling unbearably randy. Cooking a baby is hot work. Besides, he caught me scratching my boobs and I thought he was going to hoy.

Anyway, even if he were willing, I'm not sure I am. I'm staying, I'm just not playing—as yet. Not when there are so many unresolved issues swirling around. The receipt, the condoms, the late nights "working" are all still burnished on my mind. I do try to submerge the issues with thoughts of Project Zoom and, largely, I'm successful. It's only late at night when I lie awake staring at the ceiling, like this, and I find myself counting cobwebs rather than reading about throttles and clutch control, that uninvited thoughts and images charge into my mind. Like gatecrashers at a party, they are difficult to evict without a row.

As a mistress I've long since been accustomed to the thought of Hugh kissing someone else's body. Laughing at someone else's jokes, making breakfast, even making babies with someone else. I'd quickly become accustomed to the fact that anything I did with Hugh—picnics in National Trust gardens, watching fireworks in the park, making fireworks in the bedroom, selecting prams from the Mamas & Papas catalog—the chances were Becca had already done that, been there, written the book, starred in the movie. I'd got used to being the understudy, waiting to step into the lime-light. There had always been someone before me. I'd just never imagined that there would be anyone *after* me.

This woman. The other "other woman," what is she like? Is she brilliant and ballsy, or ephemeral and feminine? Is she blond or dark or a redhead? Is she skinny? What size are her feet? What perfume does she wear? What are her favorite flowers? Does she like it when he kisses that tiny groove where her back stops and her bottom starts, the place where sweat sits after energetic lovemaking? Does he suck her toes? And if he does, does it make her come? Has he ever put his tongue up her nostril just for a laugh? Do her wardrobes smell of his clothes? Of wool and sweat and stale aftershave min-gling, fusing to create a bomb that is guaranteed to blow me away.

Most nights I deal with the heebie-jeebies.

Tonight I want my mum. I grab the phone and press memory three. Hugh's mobile is memory one; I rarely use that nowadays. Sam is memory two; I never use that. A change in my telephone patterns shouldn't amount to much, but it does; I feel my life is unraveling like an old jumper.

"Out of all of Henry VIII's wives which one would you have *least* wanted to be?"

"Darling, what a philosophical question for you to put to me at—" I sense her scrabbling around for her alarm clock, even though we are miles away from one another. "Two in the morning." (That's taking the time difference into consideration.) "I'm so pleased your very expensive education wasn't entirely wasted."

I cut through her ill-humored sarcasm. "Which one?"

"The last one," she says finally.

"But she outlived him," I protest.

"Maybe so, but she had to treat his gouty feet for years, which is definitely my idea of hell on earth."

"Well, I think Anne Boleyn was the most put upon," I pronounce. And before my mother even has the chance to ask why, I tell her. "She didn't even have the dignity of being the first and she was followed by the one he loved the most."

"Oh, and here's me thinking you were going to say something conventional, like she was executed."

I stay silent for a moment, considering that I have possibly just shown my hand.

In a tone that my mother often uses, the one that suggests she knows more than I give her credit for, she adds, "Still, the Princess Elizabeth must have been great revenge."

"She was frigid and red-haired," I whine petulantly.

"The red hair was her father's and saved her from losing the head it sat on. And her decision to remain celibate was incredibly wise. I wonder if she inherited her intelligence from her mother? Is everything all right, George?" asks Jessica. She almost tricks me into being truthful; she sounds so entirely out of character, so very mum-like.

"Fine," I assert resolutely.

"It's just that it is the middle of the night."

"No, really, I'm fine." It is going to be O.K. This dalliance of Hugh's will burn out. I'll win Project Zoom. The baby will be born fit and well and we'll be O.K. Kate and Tom will continue to get their Christmas and birthday presents on time.

"Well, since you've woken me in the middle of the night you might as well read out the book."

"Good idea." I scrabble about on the floor next to my bed, the book is never far away. " 'Week 33.' It's official, it's a watermelon. How's it ever going to come out?"

"What else does it say?"

" 'Wearing rings and watches can cause circulation problems. Sometimes a ring becomes so tight on a pregnant woman's finger that it has to be cut off by a jeweler.' Well, that's one indignity Hugh has saved me," I joke. "'You might not want to wear your rings if swelling occurs. Some pregnant women purchase inexpensive rings in larger sizes to wear during pregnancy.' " I trail off as I think of Sam with her fake engagement ring, looking through bridal magazines. It shouldn't matter to me but it does. I hear a cab pull up outside. I don't want to risk another row with Hugh. "It really is very late. I'll let you get back to your beauty sleep. I'll call you in the morning," I say.

"You are O.K., aren't you?"

"Never better. Got to go, Mum."

I pull the covers around my ears. I close my eyes and pretend that I've been asleep for hours. I hope Jessica doesn't jump to the wrong conclusion because I called her Mum. Or worse, the right one.

41

I look out of my office window onto Golden Square; it is littered with groups of picnickers and pigeons. Every inch of grass and cement is taken up. The sun has decided to put in a rare appearance and, in response, Londoners have flooded out of their offices in droves. There's an abundance of trendy, Soho types who work for one of the many nearby advertising agencies or media houses or, more enigmatically, are "in film." They lie in silent, smoking huddles; their only concern is achieving an even tan as quickly as possible. There's every shop assistant, waiter and hairdresser in the West End who has been able to swing a lunch hour. There are a number of beautiful girls, long-limbed and languid, reading magazines about how to be yet more beautiful. There are tourists, relieved to be discarding their waterproofs at last. There are couriers pausing to smoke a fag, their bikes propped against them, enjoying the fleeting sensation of freedom that pretending to be Mediterranean creates. There are some oldies with gray hair and walking sticks, and they are thinking that while many things were different in their day perhaps some things were just the same. The oldies, like me, find their gazes repeatedly drawn to the lazy couples, lying on the grass, benches and each other—kissing, caressing—not caring who sees their explicit intimacy because, after all, it's London, it's summertime and they love each other.

There are no pregnant women.

So I'm glad to be tucked up in my cool air-conditioned office;

it's a relief and we are making some headway on the pitch. I'm channeling my Herculean energy injection into becoming the George of old. I have called Frank Robson, the Zoom Marketing Director, and by befriending him I have become Q&A's Trojan horse.

"Frank, it's Georgina Richardson here . . . Yes, delighted . . . Thrilled . . . It's an honor . . . Our approach is different, Frank, we're not here to tell you about your advertising, we're going to set up an integrated partnership . . . Absolutely . . . Look, ideas aren't the problem; every agency could come to you with a good idea, we're looking at the competitive advantage . . . We're looking at your bottom line . . . We want to talk to you about every aspect of your communication strategy, dealership, staff, trade marketing, event marketing, direct marketing, product placement, sponsorship, PR . . . No, BMW already owns that territory . . . You don't want to touch it. No, that's Audi's positioning, wouldn't go near it with a barge pole. The last thing you want, Frank, is another 'me too' branding. Or, worse yet, a 'me too late' . . . I'm looking forward to seeing you as well, Frank."

He bought it.

He respects me, he trusts me, he likes me and, because he hasn't seen me for several months, there's a fairly good chance that he fancies me. I think I'll limit our relationship to the telephone, until the actual pitch date and then, and only then, he can discover the truth. The fact that he's been flirting with the Michelin Man. By then it won't matter because we'll blow him away with the high standard of our work.

In all the years of trying to impress Hugh, Dean, Karl et al., I have never worked so hard on a pitch. This is the big one. Besides the massive amount of revenue that winning Project Zoom would create for the agency, there is another much more personal issue at stake. In advertising you're only as good as your last ad or, in my department, you are only as good as your last pitch win. Since my last pitch win was for odor eaters, with a net income of a few hundred thousand pounds—hardly enough to cover the cost of the team's salary and the market research—things could be better. I want to prove to Dean that I haven't "lost my edge" but, more than that, I want to prove it to myself.

Recently, I've been wondering if Hugh and I had both applied for the position as MD at Rartle, Roguel and Spirity, who would have got it?

Could I?

How good am I?

How good would I be on my own if, say, if I had to be?

Julia interrupts my thoughts by slamming an inch-thick document onto my desk; every fiber of her body is screaming resentment. She obviously feels my insistence that she deliver the research on unit shift and share of voice for every saloon, coupe, convertible and roadster that Lexus, Jaguar, Mercedes, Volvo, Audi, Saab and BMW have produced to be somewhat unnecessary. Especially as I insisted that she provide the information by today, and she's had to sacrifice her lunch hour in the sun to do so. However, my experience has always proven that Julia's "research" is rarely that; there will be more holes in it than there are in fishnet tights at a tarts and vicars' party. I do feel guilty that by missing today's sun Julia may have missed the British summer altogether, so I promise to read the research and give her feedback a.s.a.p. I'm hoping she'll see that her contribution is valuable and that the deadline I set her was an actual deadline, rather than a deadline drawn in sand.

"Whatever," sighs Julia, betraying her lack of passion about tracking car sales since 1980. I make a mental note to mention this lack of enthusiasm at her next appraisal, but I doubt that I will. When it comes to the crunch, I'll probably tell her she's doing marvelously and is a great asset; I'll then give her a pay raise even though she already earns about double what she's worth.

"Is everyone ready for the pitch practice?" I ask.

"Suppose." She barely hides her indifference.

I bite back my irritation. For the past couple of weeks I've been working around the clock. I've attended research groups as far north as Edinburgh and as far south as Hove. I've talked to Zoom marketing managers in France, Italy, Germany, Sweden and Japan. I've visited countless dealers' stores. I've masterminded a workshop with the client so that we can try to understand the brand as much as possible. I've commissioned creative briefs, vox pop interviews, and helped pull together a mood tape that represents the brand as it stands, and another to demonstrate where we'd like to take it. We've seen and understood the client's market plans, or at least one strain of them. The strain that rewrites all that's gone before and creates unrealistic expectations of what can be achieved in the future. We've studied the brand plan, the marketing strategy and the budget. Karl, Drew and I have met on a daily basis to debate the brand positioning and Brett drops in on our meetings with unprecedented regularity, demanding to see a creative brief. Everyone in the agency knows how important this pitch is to us.

I stride into the meeting room that we have commandeered for the pitch; we call it the "war room." This is blatantly an act of self-aggrandizement, but I work mostly with men so it's necessary for their egos; as are sweat rings under their armpits, the bigger the better, and to think I used to worry that my bump was disgusting. There are pieces of paper haphazardly Blu-Tacked to the walls of the war room; these are the fruits of our recent efforts. They are titled: *Future Product Line-up. Brand Personality. Brand Personality Index-linked Against the Competitors. Driver Profile. Competitive Encroachment.* There are charts showing the competitive ad spend of every car brand in this category, broken down by media type and year spend, share of voice, share of mind. There are examples of competitive ads, Web sites and communication propositions. Our job is to develop a communication strategy that is at once relevant but different. It's a struggle. All car ads are the same—they show cars speeding around the Swiss Alps. The same-color car, the same stretch of road, the same Swiss Alp.

I catch Karl reading the *Sun;* he tells me he's doing research into the minds of real people.

"It's a luxury-car brand," I argue. "You haven't got time to waste."

He closes the paper and rubs his temples. "God, George, what hormone is it that's giving you all this energy suddenly? I'm knackered. We haven't stopped for breath in weeks."

"Two weeks until we present the strategy, Karl; we both know this isn't the time to slow down."

"Suppose not," he agrees reluctantly.

Secretly I know he's thrilled that the old George has made a reappearance, and secretly I am too. O.K., so I may not have toned calves (or indeed toned anything), I may not be able to wear tailored, sexy suits (although everything I wear is clingy, this is an accident of nature), but at least I'm able to write an impressive pitch document. It's a thrill to be appreciated for my mind. It's a first.

The rest of the team join us: Drew, Brett, Julia, a pair of creatives, an Account Director and an Account Manager.

"According to the research, which brand has the benchmark status in this category, Jaguar or BMW?" I demand.

"BMW," replies the Account Manager.

"O.K., well, let's interrogate BMW then," I bark. I mean, let's understand as much as we possibly can about BMW's communication and advertising strategy, but it would be social death to be as straightforward as to say that—jargon to advertising is of equivalent importance as sun-blushed tomatoes are to the Bluebird Café.

"Have we considered this sufficiently from the consumer's point of view?" asks Drew. "Have we done enough research into current perceptions of the brand?"

"Yes. We've segmented the results of the group research and the vox pop research by age, class, sex, sexual orientation, income, religion, marital status, usage level and personality factors," assures the Account Director. The idea is that a clear understanding of the customers will mean that we can advertise to them more effectively. In reality, research is used as a post-rationalization to push through the creative endeavor, which Brett and Dean prefer.

"O.K., well, let's run through the deck then," I instruct. "We'll start with agency credentials, show them lots of ads that look pretty, then we'll go on to the agency philosophy . . ."

"Excellent concept, Brett, the boys have done good," smiles Dean; his attempt at an English idiom is proof that he's really pleased with the creative team's work.

I smile, relieved, not least because the concept is actually mine. I don't want the praise, I just wanted something that Brett, as Creative Director, signed off, and Dean, as MD, was delighted with. Not as simple a process as it sounds. For weeks, Drew, Karl and I have been arguing the positioning for the Project Zoom brand. As usual, we spent 90 percent of our time outdoing one another in the up-your-own-bum stakes.

"Our job is to communicate the brand's desire to admit to its humanity." (Drew.)

"It's a car," I reminded him, playing with the ring-pull on my can of fizzy orange.

"We must gradually move the brand tonality from clinically severe and strategic to something more congenial and charismatic. More sunrise than seascape." (Brett.)

"It's a car," I repeated, as I munched on the soft bourbon biscuits. They are my least favorite biscuits in the whole world, but I'd eaten the chocolate fingers and the custard creams, needs must.

Then we spent roughly 7 percent of our time arguing like children.

"There has to be a picture of the car." (Karl.)

"No, there doesn't." (Me.)

"But all car advertising has a picture of a car." (Karl.)

"Exactly." (Me.)

"Well, then, *we* have to have a picture of a car."

"We don't."

"Do."

"Don't."

"Do."

"Don't. Don't. Don't." I only just resisted stamping my feet.

The remaining 3 percent of our time was spent feeding the creative team ideas that we then wanted them to present back to us. The trick is that they have to think the ideas are their ideas in the first place; any creative worth his DKNY trainers will seriously oppose anything that management might actually like. Karl, Drew and I then had to pretend we believed our idea was their idea and while we "quite liked it" we "had reservations" as it was "too outlandish." The creatives then told us we were "dull tossers" and wouldn't know a good idea if "it bit our lardy fucking asses." Finally, faux-reluctantly, we agreed to use "the idea" for the pitch.

Downing Street looks decidedly un-spin in comparison.

The idea is this:

The cars look beautiful, but then you expect that; if you are spending anything upward of twenty grand on a car, it's a given it's going to look good. Karl has argued for various ads that, boiled down in a melting pot, are little more than beautiful shots of the cars. I've argued that Zoom is the master brand in terms of engineering genius, technical innovation and excellence, and this is what we have to communicate. At the risk of appearing a bit wanky, it is possible to refer to their cars as having intelligent wheels, an engine with a brain, a sequential gearbox that contributes to a unique driving experience, and functional lightweight steering. These cars are in fact the ultimate boy-toy, a Swiss Army knife on wheels, the dog's bollocks. And that's the creative solution.

There are no pictures of cars; there are no winding Alpine roads. There's a black screen. Then, first of all, there's a simple line drawing of a Swiss Army knife. The Swiss Army knife morphs into line drawings of other boy-toys such as a WAP phone and then an iPAQ. These pictures morph again into ground-breaking inventions such as the Enigma code machine, the Apollo II capsule—inventions that have, arguably, altered the course of history. The penultimate drawing is of a dog's bollocks. The final shot is of the car's badge. It's brave, it's risky, and we're all unsure as to whether the client will let a picture of dog's bollocks get into production.

However, the concept will raise a laugh in the pitch presentation and it does the necessary in terms of shock, cut-through and communication. We've tested the ad concept in six European countries and it went down a storm with the target audience of males aged twenty-five to thirty-five. Guy Ritchie has agreed to direct the ad, and Ewan McGregor has agreed to do the voice-over, providing we remain "edgy" (i.e., keep the bollocks).

I think it might work.

We've backed up this sixty-second ad with a number of shorter ads that draw attention to specific technical innovations. In addition we have a strong, efficient and differentiating media plan.

I think it might work.

By the time the rehearsal is over it's after nine o'clock in the evening.

The team has had enough. I give them my credit card and tell them to put it behind the bar at the Crown and Scepter and then go on and get slaughtered; I'll pick up the tab tomorrow. They're grateful; they don't need to be asked twice.

"Are you joining us?" asks Drew. And, while it's nice to be invited, it's been a while, I say no because I want to go home and have another read through the deck. As I turn the lights out in the war room I can smell something in the air. Not just summertime, not just the fat, creamy lilies that are scattered in vases throughout the agency, with a liberality that suggests we are expecting to host a wedding for *OK* magazine. There is a faint whiff of possibility, of power, of success. The perfumes I used to drench myself in, which have eluded me of late. And I love that smell.

42

Despite the fact that the Tube is heaving and I have to stand for the entire journey home (the age of chivalry is not only dead, it's entombed), and despite the fact that I am wedged between a cheesy armpit and a girl who is weeping into her mobile phone, I still manage to walk through my door feeling positive.

I waddle to the bathroom and start to run a cool bath. I might even paint my toenails because open-toed shoes are eternally sexy, irrespective of hip width and stomach girth. Although looking at my swollen feet I may be kidding myself.

I wish Hugh would rinse his stubby hairs away and not leave them cleaving to the porcelain; how difficult is it to swill a bit of water around a sink? I notice that he's left his empty can of shaving cream on the loo seat, too. This is his way of asking me to buy him another can. Doesn't he know that there is a Boots on every high street? Anyway, where is Hugh tonight? He must have said. I remember that he was asking for his dress shirt this morning; he must be at some awards do or client dinner. When he asked where his dress shirt was, I wanted to yell, "On the floor, in the smoky heap that you left it in last time you went to a black-tie function." But, of course, it wasn't. Because I also want to be perfectly efficient and the drive to be perfectly efficient is the one that made me pick up the shirt, wash it (with all the other white washing on a very high temperature), press it and return it to his wardrobe. Just call me the laundry fairy.

Don't think about it. Don't think about it. Don't get wound up, not after such a successful day, I instruct myself.

I slowly and carefully ease myself into the bath, enjoying the sensation of the cool water enveloping my body and the feeling of buoyancy, which temporarily releases me from my feeling of off-the-scale massiveness. I stroke the baby and start to talk to it.

"Mummy's been a ball-breaker today," I brag, and then I apologize in case "it" is a "he" and "he" is feeling intimidated. Slowly the Radox works its way into my skin and psyche and I begin to drift, mentally as well as physically. I begin to daydream about my perfect life. My perfect life is this. It's a hot summer afternoon and I'm sat in a garden under an umbrella; I'm watching my baby crawl and gurgle on a picnic rug on the grass nearby. Various friends are with me, and we're all drinking Pimm's, and there's a smell of barbecued sausages drifting toward us (although, because this is a fantasy, there's no smoke choking the guests, and I have remembered to bring my washing in off the line). There's a medley of children running around the garden; I can identify Millie, Kate and Tom, but there are others too and, again because this is a fantasy, none of them are squabbling. Libby's there, and Sam with James (go on, then, I'll throw in a wedding ring for Sam). I've won Project Zoom and therefore Dean has awarded me a generous maternity-leave package, so I know that this time of languid summer afternoons, while not endless, is at least extended.

Suddenly, I sit bolt upright in the bath, sending waves of water crashing over the edge onto the tiles.

I can't see Hugh.

The water floods past the bath mat and really has made an awful mess.

I suppose he must be doing the barbecue. Mustn't he?

After my bath I wash the bathroom floor, and as I'm on my knees I wash the kitchen floor too. Then I tidy the drawer where I keep the cookbooks and the money-off coupons. I should probably have done this before I got in the bath, but my ability to think sequentially is impaired at the moment; it's another pregnancy symptom, and not one any woman should ever confess to any man.

At 9:15 P.M. I pour myself a large glass of iced water and add a slice of lemon. I'm trying to trick my mind, my body and soul into believing that I'm enjoying a hefty G&T. It's boiling hot and the sun is streaming through the blinds, which I've pulled down because I'm naked but for a pair of Mothercare maternity knickers—although, arguably, these knickers are more modest than some of the skirts I used to wear pre-pregnancy. My thighs stick together, and when I pry them apart they make a thwack sound, not unlike a plunger relieving a sink of years of hair and dead skin.

"Who could resist me?" I ask ironically. I giggle to myself, because this doesn't horrify me as it would undoubtedly have done in the past. In fact, it makes me laugh so much that I let my thighs melt and mash together over and over again, just for the pleasure of pulling them apart and hearing the thwack sound.

The doorbell rings.

Bugger, I could ignore it. I look down at my naked state, and state is definitely the appropriate word—boobs hitting my knees, sweat running over my bump in rivers. There's no one on this earth I'd let see me dressed like this. Or, rather, undressed like this.

Except.

Sam!

Thrilled, I dash to the door and am about to fling it open to reveal my naked, corpulent self, but at the last second I'm infected with a hint of caution. I spy through the mailbox.

"James?" I yell.

"Sorry to arrive unannounced. I know it's rude of me, but—" The "but" is so desperate that I barely remember to fling a jacket on to protect my modesty and protect his sensibilities. I open the door.

"Come in."

This time his face does flicker on greeting me, but I can't kid myself—it's not appreciation, it's bewilderment.

"Er, if I've come at a bad moment . . ." he starts to apologize, as he scans my semi-nude, nearly immodest state.

"Oh, don't worry, we're not swinging from the chandeliers. I'm on my own actually. It's fantastic to see you." I realize this sounds a bit like a come-on and I'm mortified. I've obviously spent too many evenings on my own; I'm pretty hopeless at deciding what's acceptable chit-chat. I decide not to worry too much; I suspect James has more on his mind than my semi-nakedness. "Come in, fix yourself a drink, I'll go and find some clothes," I urge, pulling him over the threshold before he can run away and before the neighbors start talking.

Five minutes later, I come down the stairs again and this time I'm decently clad. James is sat in the kitchen at the breakfast bar. I'm pleased to see he has poured himself a beer—it shows he's relaxed—and I'm delighted that he's poured me a glass of milk—it shows he's thoughtful.

"You must think it's odd my coming around here like this."

"Not really." I head toward the more comfortable chairs in the living room and James follows me through.

"You've got to talk her out of marrying my brother," he splutters before he's even sat down. "You're her best friend; surely you don't think she should marry him, she loves me." James turns a bit pink as he realizes that what he's said could sound irresponsibly arrogant.

"I've tried."

"Have you?" He looks up at me with surprise and scary intensity. James has very deep brown eyes and, although my personal favorite has always been green eyes, I have to admit that his are exceptionally beautiful. They are aflame. The fire is unmistakable, unambiguous, unequivocal.

His eyes are lit up by love.

I haven't seen that for a while.

"So you don't think she should marry him?" he asks.

"Well, not if you love each other, no." I'm being cautious. Because, after all, I don't want to say anything that will compromise Sam's position. She is my best friend, albeit a best friend who can't stand being in the same room as me.

"It's such a mistake." James runs his hands through his hair and hangs his head. His pain and frustration are almost tangible. He really is delicious—what can Sam be thinking of by looking a gift horse like this in the mouth? "I don't get this obsession with being married." He suddenly looks up at me and is obviously hoping I can explain it to him. I can't, he's the wrong sex. How can I explain that Sam has come to the end of her tether? She can't bear to be the spare female at even one more cozy dinner party hosted by smug couples. She's been a bridesmaid about six times. She's woken up in her share of strange and familiar beds only to be asked to drop the latch on her way out. In short, she's seen love come and go more often than is decent and she can't risk it again.

"Well, from her point of view, you're a bit of a gamble, a wild card," I stutter. I'm trying not to offend him, because he looks genuine enough sat on my sofa with his tan and his pecs and his burning eyes; on the other hand, he is shagging his brother's fiancée, which isn't exactly the epitome of trustworthy behavior.

As though he were reading my mind, James says, "There's no reason for you to trust me, I'm behaving treacherously toward Gilbert. I'm aware of that."

"Yes."

"But you have to believe me that I've never done anything like this before."

"That doesn't necessarily make it O.K.," I comment, and after all I should know. James looks as though I've just punched him.

"I love her." He stares at me for about two weeks. I've met dozens of Sam's boyfriends in the past. I have even heard one or two say exactly the same thing. I can't look convinced, because James feels compelled to add, "I love the way she scrunches her nose up when she laughs. I love her because she is the most altruistic, forgiving, sweet-natured woman I've ever met. I love her because she is beautiful, capable and peerless. I love her because she buys at least three copies of the *Big Issue* every week even though she has a direct debit for Shelter. I love the way she can drink me under the table. I love it that she's competitive. I even love her flat feet and the fact she scratches her head when she's thinking."

I don't think I've ever heard any man say such things about any woman to a third party, not even grooms about their brides in their speeches at the many weddings I've attended. James loves Sam for the same reasons I do; well, except I could take or leave her flat feet and scratching.

"What about Africa? Aren't you supposed to be going back soon?" I can't see Sam living anywhere without there being a Chanel or Dior or Estée Lauder concession within spitting distance. He can't seriously think she'd go with him.

"I'll get a job here. I'll work in a travel agency. I'll find something. I'd do anything."

Considering that it's been difficult to persuade Sam's boyfriends to move over in bed or give her a share of the duvet in the past, I admit this is serious.

James stands up and moves toward the door. He's leaving because we both know I'm not the one he needs to convince.

"Sorry, to—er—have barged in like this. I just needed to say it."

"Don't be sorry." I sweep his embarrassment away as best I can. "Have you thought of telling Gilbert about your affair?" I ask.

"I can't do that to either of them."

"No, I suppose not." I open the front door and James starts to walk up the path. "Have you thought of proposing?" I yell.

"Not while she's engaged to my brother." He shrugs.

"No, suppose not," I repeat and then add, "Er, good luck."

I realize that my parting shot is inadequate and imperfect in the face of his pain and passion.

Oh God, being an adult is so difficult.

Hugh comes in at one-thirty in the morning. I'm at the dining room table, ostensibly reflecting on the enthusiastic, almost unearthly preoccupation the engineers and designers at Zoom have with building the ultimate driving machine; in reality I'm worrying about Sam and James and Gilbert. Hugh has been through the door for about thirty seconds and he still hasn't mentioned the shiny kitchen floor. I don't think I can forgive him.

"Where have you been?"

He doesn't answer immediately, but empties his pockets of his mobile, loose change and keys. To think I used to find this little ritual endearing, when obviously it's as irritating as someone scraping their fingernails down a blackboard.

"I told you, we went to the Unilever clients' summer ball."

"We?"

"Yes, me and the team." He seems confused.

"Why didn't you ask me to go with you? I suppose it's because I'm too fat to be seen with. Where was this ball? So who's on this team?" I know, I make those involved in the Spanish Inquisition look inadequate.

Hugh doesn't look at me, but tells the breakfast bar that no one took their partners. That the ball was at Grosvenor House. That he had mentioned it this morning, and that the team members are Mark, Tom, and Toni.

"With an 'i' or a 'y'?"

"What?"

"Toni. With an 'i' or a 'y'? Male or female Toni?"

Hugh almost grins. "Well, I suppose, strictly speaking, she's female, but not easily identifiable as such. She's a real bulldog. Good brain, though," he adds as an afterthought.

"Really," I snipe. It's not Hugh's style to comment on female intelligence. He rarely walks along the street turning to check out the pert gray matter. He's never commented, "Fantastic pair of medulla oblongata." I'm not convinced for a second. I've heard it all before. Well, at least if not first-hand then certainly second, through films and girl friends. No one ever admits to a colleague being attractive. The bulldog is undoubtedly far from being a bruiser. I can see her now—a leggy, skinny, redhead. A number of Hugh's sexual fantasies involve redheads.

"I'm telling you the truth," he insists.

"As though you'd know what it is," I mutter.

"What's that supposed to mean, George?"

I don't bother answering. I walk to the kitchen, open the fridge and hunt around for the milk.

"How many copies of the *Big Issue* do I buy a week?" I ask Hugh.

Hugh stares at me as though I've just confessed to a three-in-the-bed but doesn't answer.

"What do you love about me, Hugh?"

He loosens his tie. "Your ability to hold a sequential conversation," he mutters sarcastically.

I pour myself a glass of milk and head off to bed with my week-by-week pregnancy guidebook.

43

It's hard to say how things are going. The Managing Director, Marketing Director, the Marketing Controller, two Marketing Managers and the Brand Manager all appear rapt. But it crosses my mind that they could have learned that encouraging-nodding-of-the-head technique in a course at Tunbridge Wells.

Karl is being predictably slick and efficient.

"The health of the brand is excellent. Sales are at record levels, the product continues to improve and goodwill among consumers has never been higher. Why, then, I hear you ask, would we suggest that now is an appropriate time for a change in the communications strategy?"

Actually, none of the clients has asked any such thing, and I have a horrible feeling that one of the Marketing Managers has just started writing a shopping list on the agency-supplied notepad, with the agency-supplied pencil. Undaunted, Karl carries on, his rhino-like skin is an invaluable asset at times like this; a more sensitive man would crumble.

"Given the success of the brand, you may be inclined to simply repeat what you've already been doing. More of the same. But that's not a good idea. Why not? I'll tell you why not." Karl pauses dramatically. "The environment in which we are operating is constantly changing, and we need to change with it. After all, once you're at the top there's only one way to go." He starts to crank up the emotional pressure. If you can't impress them then depress them was not the agreed strategy. I fling him a warning look. He ignores it.

"Success is invariably followed by plummeting decline and the decline can always be traced back to the unwillingness of an old dog to learn new tricks. Think of the Roman and Soviet empires, think Thatcher. Or, more prosaically, think Spam and Red Mountain . . ." Karl continues to try to intimidate the client as he briefly touches on some media-buying issues. "There is increased competition in advertising in the car category on TV, in in-flight, in the press and on posters . . . So-called 'innovative' media ideas offer no respite as they are copied immediately . . . And we all know that TV does not deliver as it used to."

The clients are just reaching for the Prozac when I cut Karl short by pointing out that the best brands, with the appropriate communication, can always cut through the clutter.

The clients smile at me gracefully. Karl winks at me, and I realize that we have just played good cop/bad cop to perfection—without even rehearsing it. I feel a flicker of excitement dart up my calves and then explode in my stomach. We're a good team. I'd almost forgotten how good we could be.

Drew is suitably academic and incomprehensible. He asks, "Are there truly any real brands?" No one knows how to answer this, although he has been asking it at every pitch for as long as I've known him. I don't mind; it's the planner's job to be obscure. One of the uppity Marketing Managers starts to attack the segmentation chart that Drew is presenting. Drew bats back by pointing out that this is the same chart that Mars always use, and, if it's good enough for Mars, well then . . . Drew then adds, "Why keep a dog and bark yourself; after all, it's better if you stick to the knitting." No one has a clue what he's on about, least of all himself, or the uppity Marketing Manager. No one wants to admit to being ignorant, so his point is conceded.

Drew then shows over forty slides on the market-research results, sprinkling his presentation with details on continuous surveys, retail-audit presentations, consumer panels and tracking studies. He uses so many acronyms I'm beginning to think *I'm* in the wrong meeting, so I have no idea what the clients must be thinking. AGB, TGI, EPOS, DAR, EGG, NRS. I, for one, fear he's gone OTT. Even if he has a point, we're so bored that we can't be bothered to let him make it; the pitch process is fast turning into a kind of slow-water torture.

When Frank looks confused enough, I start to chip in with my thinly disguised sales pitch. It's a unique mix of: flattery—"We're all aware of the exacting standards you set;" glossing—"So what did the brand research tell us? We did credibly well against all the key dimensions of performance, engineering quality, technology and design;" and telling him how it is—"But I'm afraid the brand performed poorly against the aspirational characteristics, dynamic, sporty, contemporary and prestigious."

I can see the clients sinking into their seats; it's my job to lift them.

"But don't worry, we do have the solution."

Drum roll, and then Brett presents the creative concepts, which are all anyone is ever interested in anyway. Brett shocks us all. He's very keen and largely articulate. When questioned by Frank about why we went with this direction, he doesn't say, "because black is my favorite color," he shows an astonishing amount of acumen. "What we are trying to do is exploit the dissonance between the brand's residual association with yuppies and the 1980s, and current cultural values of anti-badge advertising. This is all about not taking yourself too seriously, about being big enough to take a pop at yourself . . ."

It's clear, they love them. The MD slaps Frank on the back, Frank beams and winks at me. The Marketing Managers are already getting excited about the prospect of meeting Guy Ritchie. Now all I have to do is draw the meeting to an accurate and memorable conclusion.

I start with a bit of reassuring good sense about knowing what their company is good at, about never underestimating the workload, nor the importance of selling the idea to the sales force—at which point Frank surprises me by stealing back the show.

"Do you mean that?"

"What?"

"The bit about the importance of selling the idea to the sales force?"

I can hardly say no. "Yes."

"Good. Let's do it. We've seen six agencies and I'd say it's down to two. You and one other." He doesn't pause to say congratulations. "You can both present to our sales force, and we'll see what they think."

This is great news.

"You can do it this afternoon."

This is bad news.

It's an unusual situation. Frank's on-the-spot decision to take advantage of a sales conference that just happens to be taking place today (I smell a rat) is unlikely to be a genuine impulse. I don't seriously believe that the decision of who will handle the advertising business will rest with the sales force. I think the MD and Frank's marketing department are just trying to keep the unions happy. My experience is that really good advertising never comes from committee approval. However, the client is god and if they want their potential agency to sweat blood and tears in front of a two-hundred-strong audience we'll do it.

And then some.

Although, as Dean, Drew, Karl, Brett and I pack up our charts and tapes (in the knowledge that we have less than fifty minutes to get to Euston station, buy our tickets and board the train for Milton Keynes), it's hard to view the "opportunity" to pitch our creative concepts to the entire sales force as quite the victory it surely is. This morning we were running on adrenaline (well, at least I was; I can't vouch for Brett, his adrenaline quite possibly comes from something a little stronger than black coffee and Pro Plus). The adrenaline rush lasted throughout the morning's presentation, and while we are all trying hard to cling onto the can-do attitude we're all feeling a bit nervy and jaded.

Thank God it's a bright sunny July day and all of London is celebrating this fact. The parks are full, the cafés are heaving, and the streets are bubbling over. The world is awash with optimism. People are actually smiling at one another in the street as though they were living in a different century. Black clothes seem to have been banished overnight as effervescent beauties and uglies dress in flirty, colorful summer dresses that are unashamedly feminine. Blokes grin their appreciation, trying but failing to pluck up the courage to strike up a conversation. There's nowhere quite like London, on a hot summer's day, to convey possibility. The smells of sweet sweat (barely disguised by designer perfumes), sun oil, lager and garlic all collide into one another to create an infusion of expectation. Even the facts that my previously toned upper arms are rubbing the edge of my maternity bra, and that the sweat is running down the chafed flesh, don't upset me.

"I think we can really do this, guys. I think we might just win it."

Karl looks doubtful, Brett looks sulky (he had a big lunch planned) and Drew is simply looking out of the cab window.

"Really. I have a good feeling," I enthuse.

Only Dean picks up my ebullience, and that's only because he's American. "You're all ready to wow them, Georgina?"

"Sure thing, Dean," I grin.

"Attagirl, go get 'em." He thumps my back and I regret my lack of pompons. Dean definitely sees me as the team cheerleader.

The pitch is perfect.

Karl is pleasantly polished and effective. Drew cuts his presentation in half, which still means it's twice as long as necessary, but it is an improvement. And, most importantly, Brett's presentation of the creative concept sends a ripple of excitement through the audience.

It's in the bag. It's in the bloody bag! I'm sure of it. All I have to do is make a careful and notable summary. No flannel, no frills, no problem.

I stand in front of the mike, which immediately squeaks irresponsibly. Rather than yell "testing, one, two, three," which is so unoriginal, I cough and realize that the sound hasn't been picked up. I glare my irritation toward the back of the hall. A scruffy individual, in jeans and square glasses, begins to panic and run around, as though there is a rocket up his boxers. If only. I turn to Dean and smile prettily, trying to convey that everything is under control. An outright lie. The mike makes another high-pitched squeaky sound; this one apparently indicates that the blip in the sound system has now been rectified. I'm meant to understand this because the geek in the jeans and glasses has stopped sweating buckets and is holding his thumbs up in the air.

I approach the mike for the second time, rehearsing my opening under my breath. "It's an unusual position you find yourselves in. You are a victim of your own success. The sheer volume of sales . . ."

Then it happens.

It starts in my shoes, or at least I think it must because it certainly builds from somewhere, and my shoes are as far away from my mouth as any other part of my anatomy. It builds in my stomach and pauses there for a fraction of time. Long enough for me to recognize it for what it is, but not long enough for me to stifle its progress. My stomach growls and rumbles. Then it rises up my esophagus; there's a moment where I can't breathe. Then the sulfurous, clamorous, ruinous BURP explodes.

I'm so pleased that the mike is working efficiently and that it picks *that* up.

Not.

A number of the more juvenile members of the audience (about three-quarters) start to titter, and, before I can quickly look around for someone to blame the bodily explosion on, the worst thing happens. I fart. A rip-roaring, resounding, wall-reverberating, ripe FART.

I'm finished.

The room erupts into riotous laughter. The members of the audience, on average, earn £30K apiece and yet their mental age is equivalent to their shoe size. I notice the odd woman in the audience trying to keep a straight and loyal face but then their solidarity breaks as they hear repeated imitation farts, which the majority are indulging in.

What can I do? I can hardly ask for everyone's understanding that the uncontrollable gases are the result of my being thirty-four weeks pregnant. Sales forces rarely do understanding. I catch Dean's eye and immediately wish I hadn't. He looks like he's just had intercourse with a cactus. His face is puce, his eyes are rolling, I think that is genuine steam emitting from his body. Surely he can't think I did that on purpose. Surely he knows I'd rather eat my own eyeballs than fart in public. Of course I've farted, and for that matter burped, in public before. Once at Christmas 1997, and another time near the turn of the millennium. But on both occasions I was at noisy parties and able to walk swiftly away before anyone attributed them to me. I'd rather curl up with agonizing stomach cramps than fart in front of Hugh, I'd rather excuse myself from bed at 3 A.M. saying I need to walk the dog than let loose, and we don't even have a dog. And now I've farted in front of two hundred potential clients, my most important colleagues, and my boss.

I see no reason to carry on living.

I stumble through the presentation, but I'm not sure anyone is listening. I battle against the tasteless gas jokes, which are heckled intermittently, and after twenty minutes I ask, "Are there any questions from the floor?" About one hundred hands shoot up.

"Can I offer you a Settler?" Snigger.

"Can you run through the budget? I do hope your claims to cost efficiencies aren't all *gas and air.*" Titter.

"I liked your ads—at least they're not a *rip off* of anything else I've seen." Chortle.

So I did have their attention.

44

The alarm clock interrupts my nightmare. I'm grateful. I was dreaming that I was presenting to a huge audience of a company's sales force, and it was a really important pitch for business, worth millions of pounds in advertising revenue. It was essential to Dean that Q&A win this high-profile, multimedia, international account, and I ruined the presentation by uncontrollably letting rip. As I mooch into consciousness I'm struck with a hideous thought—this was not a dream. This really happened. I sigh and pull the covers back over my head. I can smell Hugh's early morning body and it's some comfort; at least it is until he says, "So are you going to face up to"—he hesitates and then sniggers—"your gaffe and go into work today?"

However big the man, farts and burps are irresistible joke fodder, it's genetic.

I peek out from under the covers and scowl at him. I wish I'd never told him about the incident. It would be nice to get some sympathy, but I realize my chances are anorexic.

"Come on, George, you can't hide away for the rest of your life."

"I'm not planning to hide away for the rest of my life—just until after the pregnancy," I mutter.

Hugh shows no mercy but flings the duvet completely off the bed. I dash to the shower, not least because I don't want him to see my corpulent flesh. As I close the bathroom door he asks, "Who were you presenting to, anyway?"

I hesitate. In the past I've sometimes broken agency confidentiality and discussed with Hugh an account that Q&A were pitching for. He's often a help when bandying ideas about, but this time I have observed Dean's instructions for absolute secrecy and I haven't discussed the fact that Q&A are on this luxury-car pitch. *The* pitch that the *entire* industry is talking about. Well, at least I haven't discussed it with Hugh, although Libby does know what's going on. It's not that I don't trust Hugh to keep tight-lipped, it's just that . . . I don't trust Hugh.

I turn the shower on full blast and pretend I didn't hear his question.

The pitch is over. I've obviously blown any chance we had of winning, and, for a moment there, I thought we did have a chance. I dread to think what the consequences might be. I can't imagine Dean suddenly developing a sense of humor. He's probably already started to reconsider my severance package. His threat wasn't so decent as to be veiled.

Worse still, the pitch is over and so I no longer have an excuse to avoid thinking about the possibility that Hugh is having an affair. The possibility that he's betraying me. Because no matter how many times I tell myself that it's best to ignore the signs, I can't. Because no matter how many times I tell myself that an affair isn't significant, it is.

I'm tired. Really tired. Tired because recently I've put enormous effort into trying to win the pitch. The long hours and deep concentration were arduous. And I'm tired because I'm pregnant. My body, proficient at lifting weights and running marathons, has never endured anything quite so physically grueling and demanding as this. But mostly, I think I'm tired of Hugh.

I know, big news.

When I emerge from the shower, Hugh has already left for the gym; he still works out before going into the office and then showers at the gym. On the bed there's a breakfast tray. Tea and toast and croissants, with honey on the side (my favorite accompaniment)—not in a jar but carefully decanted into a little bowl, which looks so much better. There's also orange juice, and when I taste it I note it's freshly squeezed. There's a small vase of sweet peas that must have been cut from our garden; they are still dripping with morning dew. The tray looks beautiful. It looks just like something you'd find in the pages of a lifestyle magazine. I sit on the bed and stare at the tray. A large tear rolls down my cheek and splashes onto the toast. I'm not sure if I'm crying with relief, regret or rapture.

45

"You are a fucking genius," laughs Brett.

Have I walked into the wrong office?

"Yeah, well done, George. Fair play, who'd have thought it?" Karl shakes his head with mystified delight.

I don't react. It could be a wind up. Trust no one is closer to scripture than mantra in advertising.

"Congratulations, Georgina. Congratulations, every one of you. Well done for all your hard work. Take the rest of the day off," booms Dean.

A cheer engulfs the war room and within seconds ripples through the agency. It sounds genuine enough.

We've won.

"We've won?" I know I'm being slow—the champagne corks are already popping and it's unlikely that I've got the wrong end of the stick, but I want to be sure.

"Yes, we fucking won," laughs Karl. He sits back in his chair, putting his hands behind his head as he rests his feet on his desk. He's trying to look like a man who knew all along that Project Zoom was in the bag. Not like a man who berated me for the entire journey home from Milton Keynes for "throwing away the pitch."

"And it's all thanks to you," smiles Dean, pumping my hand.

"No, not really. Karl, Drew, Brett, the whole team . . ." I splutter modestly. I've never known the New Business Director get such direct verbal praise for winning a pitch. A bonus yes, but not so much of the glory.

"You're being modest," smiles Dean.

I am.

I wrote most of the pitch and the creative idea was mine (cleverly planted to appear to have been generated in the creative department so as not to offend anyone, but in fact mine).

"No, really, it was a team effort."

"Oh yes, the pitch document was." With a dismissive air Dean waves his cigar-holding hand and brushes away months of work.

"But then . . ." I don't grasp it.

"The gas thing, that was *yours*," Dean chuckles. I stare, uncomprehending. He tries to enlighten me. "Apparently, Frank couldn't make his mind up between the two agencies on the shortlist, but that—er—gas thing you did swung the vote. The dealers loved it. They thought it made our agency appear less poncy than the other contender. They liked our down-to-earth attitude. So we were awarded the £80 million account, and Q&A are now £8 million better off. Let me buy you lunch."

So we won.

But not because I spent hours arguing over the appropriateness of the word "intelligent" rather than "efficient" to describe an engine. Not because I trawled through endless videotapes of groups of men talking about their passion for revs. Not because our team was the most committed, thorough and creative. Not because I worked so hard that sometimes my head burned and my eyes turned fizzy. Not because I ate, drank and slept cars for weeks. But because I had wind.

"Good job you're pregnant, Georgina," adds Dean as he slaps my back. "The old George was far too sexy for gas. Far too polished to pull a stunt like that."

"Yes, it's a blessing." I try to smile.

It *is* a good thing we won the pitch. A brilliant thing. I look around the agency and everybody is laughing and smiling and joking. No doubt they've already mentally spent their bonuses dozens of times over. They radiate confidence and self-belief; nothing lifts an agency like a pitch win and a multinational, multimillion-pound win is the jackpot. Part of me really wants to join in the celebration, but part of me holds back. The office revelers appear to be at a 100-mile distance from me. It's as though I'm looking at them through a lens; a lens smeared with Vaseline, like photographers use when they are taking one of those tacky wedding shots. Take the Vaseline gimmick away and what are you left with? Inappropriately dressed people, with glued-on smiles. I did want to win this pitch, so, so much, but surely there ought to be more dignity involved in winning. Surely the actual work I do, the way I spend my day, all my days, my life, ought to mean more. I try to explain my feelings to Karl.

"Don't you think it's an odd tie-break?"

"Who can drop the biggest clanger? Who the hell cares? We won, didn't we?"

"I suppose."

He's right, I'm being churlish. We won, that's the main thing. Who'd have thought it? I was worried that my pregnancy would destroy my career; in fact, it's galvanized it. I was so sure that I no longer fit in this world now that I no longer fit into my jeans, but perhaps I do. Perhaps there is another way of doing things. I would have preferred to be appreciated for my ability to effectively position a brand rather than my ability to make trumpeting sounds, but the point is I won the pitch. I begin to smile and allow myself to feel if not proud, then at least pleased.

"We screwed the asses off Rartle, Roguel and Spirity," laughs Karl.

"Who?" The agency name is so familiar, but it's the last one I expected to hear in this context. "Rartle, Roguel and Spirity were in the pitch?" I ask. My stomach lurches, but, for once, this isn't to do with the pregnancy sickness. The lurch stubs out the flicker of pleasure at winning the pitch. Suddenly everything slams into focus and I can see the whole picture far too clearly.

"Duhhh. Yes. Keep up. They were on the shortlist. Apparently, it was down to them or us. Don't you read *Campaign*?" Karl rolls up a copy of *Campaign*, and playfully hits me over the head with it. "They leaked their involvement last week," he explains. "Quite a good publicity stunt if you are sure you're going to win, which they obviously thought they were. Bloody suicide if the client is snatched from under your nose." Karl sniggers. He leaves the magazine with me and wanders away to refill his champagne glass.

Rartle, Roguel and Spirity.

Hugh.

So this is what Hugh has been working on all this time. This might even explain the late nights. Although not the condoms. Oh my God, he'll be devastated. He must have spent months, literally months, on this pitch. Why didn't I know this? It's so obvious. How can I have been so wrapped up in the pregnancy as not to have known this? Poor, poor Hugh.

I read the article, which clearly states Rartle, Roguel and Spirity's involvement in the pitch. It gets worse. There's a picture of Hugh and a quote from him. Stupidly, arrogantly, he's quoted as saying he'd lay his job on the line that no one could come up with a more thorough response to a client brief than the one R,R&S had come up with. Surely he wouldn't have said that if he hadn't had insider information that he'd already won the pitch, even before it had taken place. Sadly, such things do happen in our business. But he hasn't won. We've won it and we've won it because I farted.

This is a disaster.

I bolt into my office and close the door behind me. I call Hugh, but his secretary says that he's in a meeting and she can't put me through. He might be, or he might just hate me. I beg her to get him to call as soon as he's free. She grunts; I'm not sure if it's in agreement.

I call Jessica and briefly fill her in on the events of the last twenty-four hours.

"But, darling, that's marvelous news," she trills.

"No, it's not, Hugh is going to be broken-hearted." I try to convey how prestigious it would have been for Hugh, as the new MD of Rartle, Roguel and Spirity, to have brought in the Zoom business.

"But, surely, as President of Neoteric Enterprise at Q&A, it's an extremely prestigious win for you. And isn't your salary dependent upon how much new business you win?"

"Well, yes," I agree.

"Hugh's isn't."

"Well, no."

"And didn't your boss make it clear that he thought you weren't up to the job now that you're pregnant?"

"He hinted as much."

"So then. From what I can see it was down to either Hugh or you being made unhappy. You're my daughter, Georgina; this is clearly the better result."

"But I won it for a stupid reason." I sigh. I'm literally banging my head on my desk; metaphorically it's against a number of brick walls.

"No, you didn't, Georgina. Get a grip." Jessica's clipped tones jolt me into taking notice. "Do you honestly think £80 million of business is awarded on a whim? It seems to me that the win being attributed to the incident"—neither of us can bring ourselves to be more graphic than this with regard to my bodily functions, God knows how we'll get through labor—"is just one of those urban myths that you advertising types are so fond of." I stop banging my head; she may have a point. "I imagine you won the pitch because of good old-fashioned hard work. You tried hard. You were successful. Just be proud of yourself."

"But I feel terrible for Hugh." How can I explain to Jessica that I'm more used to wanting what Hugh wants and what is good for Hugh than I am at even identifying what I want? "He will assume that I *knew* I was pitching against him."

"Why didn't you know? Ought you to have known?" she asks.

It's a tricky one. I don't like to admit that I didn't know that R,R&S were pitching partly because I've been neglecting the industry press and partly because I've been neglecting Hugh. My silence is very telling.

Jessica adds, "Hugh's big enough and pretty enough to look after himself, George; it's about time you realized that."

"I thought you liked him," I wail.

"I thought you loved him," she comments.

46

*H*ugh, somewhat predictably, doesn't come home from work until very late. I'm lying in bed but I'm far from asleep and that's not just to do with the growing baby pushing against my bladder.

Today should have been a perfect day. Dean insisted on taking the Project Zoom team out for lunch. Most of the team are still there, twelve hours later, scoffing and quaffing. However it was all I could do to force down a couple of mouthfuls of prawn and glass-noodle salad with sesame and ginger, and my modest portion had nothing to do with the fact that I had to pick out the prawns. For once I was glad to have a legitimate excuse to avoid champagne. I didn't want to taste that dry crackle at the back of my throat. I didn't want to feel that intrinsic headiness of bubbles zapping my brain cells that definitely signals celebration. Because I didn't feel much like celebrating.

"Cheer up, George. It's not a bloody wake, you know," laughed Karl as he ordered a double brandy and cut himself some blue cheese from the board.

I realize that it is absolutely impossible to explain to Karl or Drew or Brett why I'm sad. They can't understand that I'd rather Hugh had won Project Zoom. None of them are in a serious relationship, even Brett, and he's married. They never have "issues" or "problems" or things they "need to discuss." If a woman that they are sleeping with ever suggests that she needs to talk she is swiftly shown the door. They all had emotional lobotomies before they left prep school. It's a pity we can't have a chat because they could give me a great insight into Hugh's state of mind.

I didn't enjoy the lunch.

I wonder how many more lunches Hugh's going to ruin for me.

I can tell from listening to the sounds he makes as he closes the door and takes off his jacket that he's drunk. I hear him throw his jacket on the back of the chair and I hear it miss and fall into a crumpled mess on the floor. He stumbles upstairs, crashing from one side of the stairway to the other; I hear a picture fall off the wall. It's a good thing we haven't yet got a baby for him to wake. He swings into the bedroom and then pauses for a moment; it's obvious that he's attempting to appear sober.

I pretend to be convinced because he needs me to be so. "Hi." I smile, falsely bright. I don't ask where he's been. Or who with.

"Hello, Georgina," he articulates carefully. He sits on the end of the bed and starts to take off his shoes. He doesn't put them carefully in his wardrobe but casually throws them across the room. His shoes are unimportant now and my grandmother always said you could tell a lot by a man's shoes.

"I was just going to make a cup of tea, do you want one?" I offer with sham geniality. I know, by the way his eyes are dangerously dancing around, that he needs to sober up.

"No." He starts to take off his clothes and then wanders into the bathroom. I get out of bed and follow him.

"Hugh, I think we should talk." This is perhaps unconsidered of me; as a bloke he's never going to welcome this opener. His extreme anger, bruised pride and stupendous alcohol intake aren't likely to increase his inclination for a heart-to-heart. But we do have to talk, sooner or later. There's a lot to be said.

"What about?" He stares at his own reflection and doesn't look at me.

"I'm sorry about the pitch." It's as good as any place to start.

"Liar."

"I am."

"Oh well, if you're sorry that's that then, isn't it? Apology accepted." His tone is scathing and cruel. I'd like to blame it on the drink.

"I didn't know you were pitching for the business," I explain. He still won't look at me so I'm also talking to his reflection.

"Liar, liar, pants on fire," he sings, and then he dances a small jig around the bathroom. I take a deep breath and try to see this as great practice for when the baby is born. His juvenile behavior is exposed as astonishingly inappropriate when he stumbles and bangs into my bump. I move away from him and wrap a protective arm around the baby; he doesn't notice.

"I didn't know," I insist.

"Did."

"Didn't."

"Did."

This isn't getting us anywhere.

"Even if I had known, what could I have done? Would you have expected me to pull out of the pitch?" I try to hold his gaze and to reason with him but he looks away. Surely this has hit a nerve. He can't possibly have expected me to throw the pitch. He can't have needed me to do that.

Hugh doesn't answer for the longest time. Finally he replies, "Yes. You should have pulled out."

"Yes?" I'm astounded.

I can hear the tap in the shower dripping and the cistern of the loo is filling up, but I can't hear the words Hugh is saying. His mouth is moving but I must have got it wrong.

"Yes. You pulled out of the race for the MD position at R,R&S, didn't you? One more small sacrifice wouldn't have made any difference to you. You're about to have a baby, for Christ's sake, what do you care about Q&A's end-of-year billings? Your loyalties lie with me."

He's finally turned toward me, but I wish he hadn't. His face is just centimeters away from mine; as he shouts he sprays spittle on my cheek. I've never seen him so furious. Tiny little lines of bitterness are engraved on his forehead, small shafts of resentment run along his cheeks up to his eyes and down to his mouth. I'm sure they weren't there this morning. He looks ugly. This man, who has always appeared the epitome of beauty and fineness, is ludicrous.

I try to remain logical. "Yes, my loyalties lie with you. And yours with me. Winning this business is not about billings, Hugh, or the business-performance league tables. I'll have to go back to work after my maternity leave. We need the money. Leaving on the high of a big account win is invaluable for me. It will make such a difference to my reputation, and Dean has promised me a bonus. Think how handy that will be, what with a new baby and the money we pay Becca and the kids." I'm trying to remind him that we are a team.

The truth is we need my job with its big salary and expense account. The offer of a company car and private health-care scheme are useful too. At this precise moment I'm even feeling affectionate toward the annoying little card that I swipe in the vending machine to get a cup of watery tea.

"I'm wounded, George. I've nothing more to say to you," says Hugh. He has definitely missed his vocation and his era. He makes Oscar Wilde look underplayed.

"There *are* other things to talk about," I insist. I'm getting heartily sick of him deciding the parameters. I try to provoke a response. "I'm not sure if I even care about the bloody car account," I mutter, not really under my breath, because I do know how to flick his switches.

"What?" Suddenly I have his attention. Surprise. Surprise. "You don't care about the pitch?"

"Well, not on the scale of things, no. It's just business. It's got nothing to do with you and me. And our particular business has very little to do with anything really important."

"Really important?"

"Gear sticks versus the war-crimes tribunal and Slobodan Milosevic. Wheel girth takes on illegal immigrants suffocating in lorries. Two-tone metallic finish versus child soldiers."

No response. I go for something a little closer to home. "Leather interior over and against Tom's birthday tomorrow. You forgot to sign his birthday card even though I bought it over a week ago and left it on the dining room table all this time. I had to forge your signature."

It's as though I haven't spoken.

"You're not sure you care about the car account? So you wrecked my life for something you're not really sure about. How could you, George?"

And he's brimming, absolutely flowing, with indignation and self-righteousness. It's almost laughable. In fact, it is laughable. I can't help myself—I start to chortle. These inappropriate responses may or may not be a result of the pregnancy, but they are liberating; I do hope they last. I no longer care if R,R&S lost the pitch, I no longer feel guilty that Q&A won the pitch. In fact, I think I'm rather pleased. I don't want what Hugh wants because I no longer believe that what Hugh wants is right. His halo has slipped from his head to around his neck; a little bit of me hopes it strangles him.

"Oh Hugh, I didn't wreck your life." I giggle at his melodrama. "They haven't even sacked you. I hurt your pride. No, that's not even true. You set yourself up for a fall by doing the interview for *Campaign*, by being the big man, saying your balls were on the line and that R,R&S had an unsurpassable pitch. I didn't do this to you."

"Why didn't you tell me you were working on the pitch?" he screams, frustrated by my amused stance.

"I never realized you considered me such a threat."

Hugh snorts. I can't make out any particular words but I'm pretty sure that whatever he's saying involves plenty of blasphemy and lots of expletives.

I start to think about the films we've seen together, the meals we've eaten together, the miles we've run together, the holidays we've lazed through together. I'm thinking about the hours I've spent on StairMaster equipment, under hairdryers, in boutique changing rooms, cooking in the kitchen, body-brushing in the bathroom, loving in the bedroom, and I wonder why they don't count for more. And I wonder why it doesn't bother me that they count for so little. How did we end up here, so angry with each other and ourselves? Incapable of a civil exchange about the weather, never mind meaningful communication about our life together. Why can't he calm me like he used to? Why can't he excite me? Why can't he reach me?

Why can't I reach him?

"Why didn't you tell me you'd been to the Lucky 7 restaurant?"

I'm trying to keep my voice free of accusation, but Hugh knows me too well. I watch him in the bathroom mirror as he freezes, thinks for a second, and shouts (unnecessarily loudly, as I'm in the room), "Didn't I?" In that second his face sweeps through a rush of emotions. Initially angry, he suddenly becomes contrite, and then his contrition dissolves as a wave of irritation washes over his face and, almost instantly, disappears. If I hadn't been watching him so intently I might have missed it. But then, I'm always watching him so intently.

He puts down his toothbrush, which he's been bandying around to help him express just how indignant he is; he's oblivious to the little flecks of Colgate he's sprayed everywhere—after all, he won't be the one cleaning the bathroom tiles. He picks up a bar of soap and climbs into the shower. He turns the tap on and zillions of little particles of water whiz out of the faucet; even so I don't think he'll wash himself clean.

"Didn't I mention I'd been?"

"No, you didn't. Which is odd, don't you think? Because normally you're so keen to impress when you've been to a cutting-edge restaurant." I'm still sniggering to myself because, really, how stupid is it to show off about which restaurant you've been to? It's not as though he goes to these fancy restaurants to actually enjoy the food. The wine list—yes; the prices—yes; who else was there—yes; but not what he ate. Still, I digress.

I open the shower door. The hope is that his nakedness will

make him feel vulnerable, evening up the score—my inches of flesh make me feel very vulnerable. Not the fatness, that doesn't bother me anymore. The fact that this is a baby. I've made a little person with this man. This silly, spoiled, angry man is the father of my child. How can I retrieve this situation? What result do I want?

"George, you're getting water on the floor."

"Are you seeing someone else?" Because this matters to us more than an £80 million pitch or £8 million of revenue ever could.

"No," he says simply.

And in the past I know I'd have accepted his word, I'd have argued with myself that there could be any number of reasons that he'd eaten at Lucky 7. It could have been work. He hasn't tried to deny that he was there, has he? I'd have told myself that I was being silly and that it was wrong and unfair of me to jump to conclusions. I'd have told myself not to rock the boat, to be grateful that this man, the pinnacle of everything I ever wanted, has chosen to be with me. I'd have glossed over the fact that, in terms of adultery, this man has form.

As it is I can't.

"I'm sick of these rows, George. I've had these rows before. Now if I can just have my shower in peace and then get to bed. Is that so much to ask?" Hugh tries to push me away from the shower door and close it. I jam my foot in the door. I won't be ignored.

"When? Tell me. With Becca? Tell me. Say it. When have you had these rows before?"

"O.K., yes, I've had these rows with Becca," Hugh concedes, not getting my point.

"And she was right, wasn't she? You *were* screwing someone else. You were screwing me. So who are you screwing now?"

47

I'm desperately in need of some light relief."

"I'll send Millie around."

"I didn't mean light as in weighs less than four stone, I meant as in humorous."

"So did I," says Libby, indignantly.

Thinking about it, it is true that Libby laughs more than nearly anyone else I know. Could that be because she has a child? Well, you certainly do need a sense of humor to be with Millie twenty-four seven.

"Are you going to leave him?" she asks. Not one for beating about the bush. I've just spent thirty minutes on the phone bringing Libby up to date.

"Fourteen years. Nearly half my life. Twice Millie's," I justify.

"Suppose," she comments, instantly understanding my investment. I don't think I can explain about the fact that I feel truly guilty about splitting Becca and Hugh up. I can't find the words to clarify that it would be O.K. if we were for real, for love, forever.

"And I'm carrying his child."

"True."

"I don't *want* to be a single mother."

"Is there any other kind?"

I laugh grimly. The thing is, I still believe in the happy ending. Bloody hell, no one wanted a happy ending more than I did (well, except Sam possibly). "I think there is another kind," I answer truthfully. "I have seen concerned and conscientious fathers at the water-conditioning class. I've spotted nervous and sweating dads-to-be waiting hopefully for the scan results. There have been sightings in Tesco's and in the park on Saturday mornings. I watch them all the time."

We're both silent. It would be easier to pretend this type of man didn't exist than admit that we've made bad choices. But I know they do.

"I don't think I'm up to being a single mother. I'm not as brave as you. Not as strong. You do a brilliant job but I don't think I'd be up to it."

I have these fantasies, you see. It's Christmas Day and Hugh is carving the turkey, the flat is full of tinsel and good cheer. The baby is sat in front of a log fire opening its presents, Jessica and my father are there, even Henry and Penny and their kids have joined us.

Not that we have an open fire.

And, anyway, they are very dangerous with small children around.

O.K, another fantasy, a bit lower on the risk list of accidents in the home. Hugh and I are lying in bed on a Sunday morning and the baby is lying propped up on pillows between us, gurgling, giggling. That's not too much to ask, is it?

Although, in reality, Hugh would probably expect to continue his morning visits to the gym, even after the baby is born. I'll probably spend Sunday mornings juggling the baby and the roasting dish, because Hugh has said that he'd like to reintroduce Sunday roasts once we have the baby. Even though the baby won't be tucking into a joint and three veg for quite some time yet.

I sigh. If I'm honest with myself I know that the fantasy will always be light years away from the reality. He will never help me choose clothes in babyGap; even now I pick out Kate and Tom's pressies. I usually do that in my lunch hour. I'm the one who washes floors, I cook, I shop, I iron and take our suits to the dry cleaner's and pick them up again. I buy loo rolls and change the water filter. Hugh only need mention that he fancies the new R.E.M. album (his tastes are mainstream, but he is thirty-four; he's unlikely to express an interest in that-new-indie-revival-band-that-played-in-the-pub-in-Camden ever again). He expresses the interest and the next thing the CD appears in our stereo, as if by magic.

No, actually, as if I'd bought it and put it there.

Yet he looked horrified when I hinted that I might like a small token of his esteem as a thank you for having the baby. He said, "Don't you buy the presents now?"

I order furniture. It's me who arranges to be at home whenever there is a delivery of any kind. I arrange the payment of all bills— Barclaycard, Amex, gas, electricity, TV license, council tax, mortgage. I am the one acting as a human incubator.

Hugh goes to work.

Abruptly, it seems extremely unbalanced.

I admit I used to do all these things for myself when I lived on my own, of course I did. But then the mess was my mess. My cereal bowl, my empty yogurt carton, my clothes in the washing basket and my wet towels on the bathroom floor.

What am I saying? That I'd be better off alone? No. Of course not. I can't be saying that. I'm just saying it seems unfair.

Libby must have been thinking along the same lines because she says, "I don't know why you think you couldn't manage on your own. You have a highly paid job, you bring in massive revenues for your agency. You own your own flat, your own car. You're the one who runs marathons for fun. You lived in New York, New York, for five years; you did all that on your own." (She says New York, New York, with a twang; a bad impersonation of a U.S. accent is essential when saying those four words, however serious the discussion. I'm so pleased Libby has remembered this.)

"That was the old me," I insist.

"You'll be the old you again, after the baby is born."

The odd thing is I don't know if I want to be. For a start, I don't think I have the energy to read another article that promises

I'll banish cellulite for life, or that I'll lose fifteen pounds in a month or that I'll learn twenty-five surefire ways to increase my sexual energy. Sometimes I feel my head is bursting, it's holding so much stuff—how to be brighter, better, wiser, thinner, more fashionable. I try so hard. Too hard. I try at every aspect of life. I try to be the perfect woman for Hugh, the perfect friend, the perfect employee. I even try to be the perfect stranger, for goodness sake. I sometimes think I'm going mad. The other day I found myself wishing I were a video recorder. Right now, I could do with a rewind, fast-forward and erase button. Although, notably, there's still not much call for play or stop.

Secondly, even assuming I had the energy (and time—unlikely) I don't think I want to be the old me, because I'm not that keen on her anymore. I'm not even sure if *I* ever really existed beyond being what I thought Hugh wanted. I don't blame him for this. I blame myself. And I'm even sick of that, blaming myself. I want to fix things and move on. But what would be a "fix" in this situation? I do know that I don't want to put my considerable energy and whatever talent I might have into regaining skinny thighs because there *has* to be more to life than being a perfect size 10. I know there is; I put my hand on my stretched stomach and gently rub my bump. Besides which, trying all the time is exhausting and demoralizing because, however hard I try, I'm never quite good enough. There's always something I've forgotten to do, even if it's only applying a second coat of lipstick.

I want to articulate some of this to Libby.

"I need to fix some things."

"Such as?"

I sigh. "It was Sam's hen weekend last weekend; she didn't even invite me."

"Was it one of those outdoor-pursuits things? She probably thought it was too active at this stage in your pregnancy." Libby is already trying to find excuses.

"No, it was nothing to do with the pregnancy."

"Have you had a disagreement?"

"Sort of." I'm pretty certain that my wedding invite is invalid. Which strikes me as odd, I've been on the guest list for fourteen years and now I'm NFI. "It's complicated. I'm sorry I can't tell you the details, it would be breaking her confidence." I know Libby is itching to ask me to spill the juicy gossip and I am tempted, but I resist.

"Call her, uncomplicate it," suggests Libby, offering a solution as though she were a man.

I ache to call Sam. I miss her with such ferocity that I feel an emptiness that's as real as hunger. We haven't spoken since the evening at the restaurant when she confessed to her affair with James. I'd love for her to see the size of my bump now, it's unreal. I just keep growing and growing and when it seems impossible that I can stretch anymore without popping, then I grow some more. I'm sure she'd love to feel the baby kick. I'd like to tell her about the pitch win. But, most of all, I'd like to explain that I do understand; now I know exactly what she meant when she said getting married was all she ever wanted and she'd wanted it for such a long time she didn't know how to want anything else. I know why she compared her obsession with getting married to mine with getting Hugh. I now understand how brave I was asking her to be when I suggested she dump the fantasy. I'm not sure I can, either.

"And there's Becca," I add.

"Becca?" Libby is understandably surprised.

"I feel guilty, seriously guilty about breaking up Hugh's marriage. I'm beginning to think I owed Becca a bit more . . ." I hesitate. I know the word but don't think I can bring myself to say it. "A bit more solidarity."

"Oh, call her and say as much, I'm sure she'll understand," says Libby glibly.

"I think I might."

"I wasn't being serious!" She's horrified. "People don't just call each other and say, 'Look, I've been giving this some thought, maybe I shouldn't have run off with your husband.' People just don't do that."

"I might."

Because, for the first time in my life, not doing the done thing seems to be exactly what I ought to be doing.

August

48

Sam or Becca? Becca or Sam? Both are foul calls to have to make. Both involve eating a gag-inducing amount of humble pie. Libby says that I'm just trying to avoid the really big issue of Hugh's philandering. It's possible.

Two more weeks go by and I've done nothing. Well, I've been to work; at least there I'm still basking in the glory of the pitch win. I've edged closer and closer to my expected date of delivery. I've passed Hugh in the hallway. I've even slept in the same bed with him but I haven't called Sam or Becca and I haven't pushed Hugh on the pertinent question of who he's screwing now.

"Are we going to Sam's wedding, then?" asks Hugh.

It's the first sentence we've exchanged in over two weeks so I feel a bit of a spoilsport when I have to answer in the negative. "I don't think so."

"Christ, George, she's your best friend. I can't believe you're missing the wedding because you're too fat to fasten your strappy sandals."

I glare at him. "That is not the reason I'm not going to the wedding. For your information, as it's so obviously passed you by, Sam and I have had a falling-out."

"Really?" It's touching that he does pause to look at me before he asks, "Because she wouldn't let you be bridesmaid?" Believing that I'd cut off my best friend over something so trivial is less touching.

"No, Hugh, because we had a major disagreement about love, life and the reason we are here."

"Girls! You really overcomplicate things. Why do you talk about such stuff?"

"Because neither of us follow football," I mutter, and then I turn back to my book on breastfeeding.

Hugh leaves the room.

Even for a pregnancy outfit my wedding outfit is gorgeous, by virtue of it being a wedding outfit. I'd planned to wear a long red dress that pretty much covers everything from shoulders to ankles. The only thing it does expose is my vast cleavage, as the dress has a great plunging neckline. I know that my heaving bosoms are my best attribute at the moment (although, admittedly, the competition from the rest of my body is at an all-time low). I'm working on a theory of drawing the eye up over or down over, actually anywhere away from my expansiveness, and so have bought scarlet, shockingly high sandals and a very wide-brimmed hat. Both of which are swathed in sequins, feathers, glitter and all manner of girliness. Weeks ago, Hugh suggested I wear my black shift from Mamasoon, presumably so I'd blend in and minimize myself as much as humanly possible. I did buy black shoes and a black hat but later rejected them; I don't want to disappear. I want to be loud and proud, I want to celebrate my fertility and femininity.

And, anyway, I can no longer fasten the black number.

Not that it matters either way, as things have turned out. The hat and the sandals are still in their boxes. I haven't called Sam. Sam hasn't called me. I won't be throwing any confetti today.

It's five to eleven. Right now Sam is climbing into a cream Rolls-Royce and heading to the church. I'm lying on my bed in my bedroom. The windows are open and bright sunshine is bathing the room. I can hear next door's kids squabbling over a tennis racket; I can hear a lawnmower and I can smell the freshly cut grass. It is a beautiful August day, a perfect day for a wedding. I can't help but grin to myself because I know, absolutely know, could put money on it, that Sam will have woken up this morning and said, "Happy is the bride whom the sun shines on." I know exactly what's happening.

The bridesmaids are wearing gold. The readings are a mix of the secular and the divine. Obviously the congregation are obliged to sit through I Corinthians 13—"Love is patient and kind. . . ."—because no wedding is complete without it, but Sam has also chosen a John Donne poem, one of the raunchy ones. She'll walk down the aisle to Handel's "Arrival of the Queen of Sheba" and leave to Mendelssohn's "Wedding March." She chose all this before she completed her university finals. It's not easy finding a comfortable position at thirty-seven weeks but this thought doesn't help.

Hugh comes back into the bedroom. I spend most of my time here now, often asleep, sometimes just lying on my bed thinking. I'm working on a theory of Why stand when you can sit? Why sit when you can lie? It's not as easy as it sounds. The thinking that is, not the lying. I realize that there is a genuine possibility that I've never thought before. I've fantasized, imagined, idealized. The pitch is over and I've started to think. I've been the Dutch boy with my finger in the damaged dam wall. I've been trying to hold back a tidal wave of thoughts and now, carefully, slowly, I've dared to remove my finger. I want the flood. Hugh spends most of his time downstairs in the living room. He's taken to playing his CDs at a very high volume. I use his track selection to follow his mood. In many ways it's a more reliable form of communication than actually talking to him ever was. He's worked his way from Gloria Gaynor's "I Will Survive," to Culture Club's "Do You Really Want to Hurt Me?," which I never did like. And this morning he listened to Tom Jones singing "I (Who Have Nothing)." This, if I needed it, is absolute proof that he's not gay, and that he doesn't understand the female psyche. In situations like this you should end with Gloria.

I close my eyes. I don't want another row. I'm just not up to it.

"I thought you might like some lemonade. It's homemade." He puts the glass down on the bedside table.

I open my eyes (not least to check that this is for real and I'm not dreaming; toward the end of my pregnancy my dreams have become extremely vivid). I heave myself up to take a sip. "It's lovely, thank you." I only just resist asking, "What's brought this on?"

"Do you want a pillow for under your feet? I read that it helps with the water retention."

Call the FBI—the body-snatchers have got him! Hugh goes into the wardrobe and rummages around for the spare pillows, and then he helps me to stuff them in between my knees, under my bump and under my feet. I know I look like a stranded hippo but I don't care. After years and years of trying to be skinny, lithe and energetic for him, it's a relief to be so peaceful just being me. He can take me or leave me—what am I talking about? He already has.

Hugh sits on the edge of the bed. "I can't believe we're not at Sam's wedding.".

"No, nor can I."

"After all these years." He pauses and gazes out of the window. I half wonder what he's thinking but I'm no longer curious enough to ask. Yet, somewhat out of character, he volunteers his thoughts. "We all go back such a long way, don't we?"

"Yes."

"She's wanted this for a long time, hasn't she?"

"Yes."

"Do you remember how Sam always dressed up as a bride for all the fancy-dress parties at uni? Every Halloween party she went as Frankenstein's bride. The Tudor party, she went as all six of Henry VIII's wives. The bondage party, she went as wedlock. She always wore white gowns at the end of term ball."

"At the Christmas party she went as a fairy on the top of the tree," I defend.

"She looked like a bride."

"True, she did," I concede. It's no good; her behavior was transparent and as such difficult to defend.

"Can you name Sam's three favorite films?"

"*Four Weddings and a Funeral, My Best Friend's Wedding* and *Muriel's Wedding.*" I giggle, everyone can name Sam's three favorite movies. "*Seven Brides for Seven Brothers* comes a close fourth."

"I love playing charades with her," smiles Hugh. While it's a bit disloyal poking gentle fun, even Sam would admit that we are entitled. Hugh and I have watched all these videos on so many rainy Sunday afternoons that our tapes have worn thin. Hugh jumps up and grabs the chair from the end of the bed. He drags it toward the wardrobes and stands on it. He starts to rummage around in the cupboard space above the wardrobe. Hat boxes, shoeboxes, sacks of old clothes and bundles of old letters and cards cascade to the floor.

"What are you looking for?"

"These," he pronounces cheerfully as he carefully pulls out my photo albums from the top of the cupboard. He picks out the large black leather albums housing the photos from my university days. I'm meticulous in the categorization of my memories—black leather equals university. Blue leather for the photos from New York; there are five of those albums, one for every year. Then I have brown albums until 1998, when the albums become red. I would never have guessed that Hugh knew my code. It's odd that he can still surprise me.

Pleasantly.

I turn the pages of the album; the tissue paper between the card pages wafts gently, promising unlimited treasures.

"That was Freshers' Week," I say, pointing to a shot of Hugh stood by the table where they were recruiting rowers.

"Look at your hair on that one. It's almost brown, I'd forgotten."

"There's Sam as Frankenstein's bride." I laugh.

"God, I hope she looks better today."

"There you are with the rugby team," I comment. A young Hugh smiles his boyish smile from under his blond fringe.

"You look lovely on that one." Hugh is pointing to a picture of me in my third year. My transformation was in process. My hair is blond and I'm slim, but it's early days because I'm smiling and I look careless. I'm stood next to Sam, who looks just like Sam. Happy, hopeful and wearing a white ball dress. It's probably just my hormones, but I'm crying again.

Hugh lays his hand on my leg and says, "I'm sorry." Then he squeezes my leg and leaves the room.

I'm overwhelmed. Hugh is not prone to bouts of sentimentality. I'm moved that he cares that he's missing Sam's wedding, that he cares that I am. Isn't it the strangest thing? After countless displays of Hugh's insensitivity and neglect, as unreasonable as it sounds, it is in this moment of tenderness that I finally realize.

I don't love Hugh anymore.

I wish I could. I wish I believed that the lemonade and the pillows and the breakfast in bed the other week were motivated by genuine repentance, but I fear they are the result of an inflamed conscience. I wish I could forgive him for ignoring his growing child, for his countless examples of irritability and selfishness. I wish I could forgive myself for falling in love with an idol and ending up living with a man. I really wish I could love the man. I stroke my stomach and apologize to the baby for getting everything wrong. And while I'm still not sure how to go about getting it right, I promise, I swear to the baby that I will.

I must have fallen asleep again, because the sound of the phone ringing wakes me up. In my half-conscious state I feel around for the handset.

"George?"

"Sam!" She's rung me with a debrief! She's rung me to ask me to go along to the reception. I'm already reaching for my red frock. Oh, I love her, I love her. I just want us to be friends again. I want to un-say all the stuff I said. It wasn't worth saying, not if it meant I would lose her. Even if I was just being honest. I forgive her all the things she said. She was just telling it like it is.

"Sam, I'm so glad you called. I've missed you so much. How

was the wedding? I'm very sorry I wasn't there. I *am* glad you called," I start to repeat myself as I rush on. Excitement is mixed with self-consciousness, mixed with absolute glee. "How was it? Are you beautiful?"

"I am officially show-stopping," she laughs. Her laugh is high-pitched and hysterical. I wonder if she's been swallowing helium from the balloons. I pull myself to a sitting position and start to inch out of the massive, shapeless T-shirt that I live in. I wonder if I'll have time to wash my hair.

"Congratulations, Mrs. Crompton," I trill.

"Actually, it's congratulations, Ms. Martin."

"You're keeping your name?" I'm stunned; it's a very un-Sam thing to do.

"Well, imagine the scenario, I'm in all my finery and, oh George, I did look good."

I'm struggling to undress with one hand, hold the phone with the other and try to listen to every particular at the same time. In the end I give up dressing and pause to drink up the details. Pregnancy has left me unable to multi-task, which will be a bloody disaster after the baby is born if I'm handicapped thus.

"Did you go for a tiara in the end, or flowers?"

"Tiara."

"Hair up or down?"

"Up."

"Oh God, I bet you were gorgeous. I wish I'd been there." Sam is silent. "Go on, I want to hear everything, from start to finish." I'm now propped up against the headboard, the phone is cradled under my ear. My fingers are itching to unwrap the sandals and hat, to release them from their boxes and expose their finery. If I hurry, I might still make it in time for the first dance and maybe even the speeches.

"Well, the thing is, I'm sat in the Rolls on the way to the church . . ."

"Yes."

"And my father is telling me some funny story about his and

Mummy's wedding day, but I can't *hear* him. I'm staring right at him, and I can see his mouth opening and closing, and he's sat right next to me, but I couldn't hear him." She pauses for breath, I'm trying to catch mine too. "I could hear you," she says.

Oh God.

"I could hear you telling me to get my own set of values and opinions. *You* telling me to think very carefully. *You* saying that marrying Gilbert isn't fair to him or to James or to me. I couldn't get that stuff you said out of my head."

The hat box slips off the bed and falls to the floor.

"You—" My heart slows, almost stops.

"Yes. I thought I could ignore you, but I couldn't. I realized, you're right."

Oh no. Oh no. I mean, oh yes. Yes, I am right, but oh no.

"It's not about the dress, or the flowers, or the canapés, or the swans—"

"You had swans?" Even at this undoubted code-red moment I think swans are worth commenting on.

"Yes," says Sam with some dignity and then she continues, "it's about the man. And as nice as Gilbert is, he's not *the* man. James is."

I can't believe what I'm hearing. "You stopped the wedding?"

"Yes." Sam is trying to sound brave but I know her well enough to appreciate that she's seconds away from boohooing for an Olympic medal. "So you see that's why it's congratulations, Ms. Martin."

Sam dissolves into tears and I tell her I'll order a cab.

49

I'm sat at my desk, making a "to do" list for Julia, who is going to cover for me while I'm on maternity leave. My heart's not really in it, particularly as I know that Julia will lose this list within the first thirty minutes of being in sole charge. I am not going on maternity leave until I actually go into labor. Obviously, this isn't an ideal case scenario; all the maternity books suggest that you take at least a fortnight, if not four weeks, off work before the birth. However, Dean isn't keen to give me more than three months' leave in total, and I want to spend as much time as I possibly can with the baby. I'm still negotiating for six months, but Dean keeps insisting that Q&A needs me; suddenly, he seems to think I'm single-handedly keeping his agency afloat. This is no nearer the truth than when he thought I was losing my touch, but he, like many advertising-agency types, likes to operate in extremes. I can understand why, it makes life so much simpler. The hues and tones I've been dealing with of late are terrifically complex.

I am now just one week away from my EDD. Just seven days, or 168 hours, or 10,080 minutes, or 604,800 seconds, depending on how you look at it. And while I know that many, many babies are late and that first babies are notorious for being so, I still have my fingers crossed in the hope that mine will be on time. I know that every day after the EDD will seem like another month, because every day that's passed in the last few weeks has seemed an eon. For a while, after Sam called off her wedding, time flew past as I was genuinely immersed in her problems, all of which seemed more immediate than anything I had to worry about. Suddenly, I was in charge of the disposal of two hundred chicken drumsticks and returning several toasters. Her constant bemoaning her fate was definitely a welcome distraction; not that it was easy to see her in such a bad way. She hasn't yet plucked up the courage to face James, Gilbert, or her mother. She spent the first ten days after the non-wedding hidden in her flat with the blinds down, the answering machine on and the doors locked. I intravenously dripped pizza and gin into her system, and listened while she beat herself up for being "so cruel," "so blinkered" and, finally, after several pizzas (*ai funghi* and Fiorentina), "so fat." After she'd crawled in and out of her hair shirt I persuaded her to take a holiday (after all, she was due a honeymoon, she was waxed in all the appropriate places, and her bikini was packed). So at the moment she's soaking up the rays in the south of France, although she did promise that she'd catch the first plane home the moment my contractions start.

I can't wait.

Obviously, I have to, there's no alternative, but I'm beginning to really understand the term "expecting." I've never longed for something so much in my life; I've never anticipated, yearned, craved or dreamed for anything with such ferocity; not even Hugh. Yet I am exhausted, and I could probably do with some time resting; if the baby is late I should put my feet up. If I'm honest with myself it may be my last opportunity.

Ever.

There has been so much to organize before the birth. Over three months ago I drew up a list of jobs that I wanted to complete before the baby was born. There were forty-nine necessary jobs on the list. Fifty would have been neater.

The list was deceptive. A job such as "sort childcare" took no more space on the piece of paper than "pack hospital bag," but in fact it took an unfeasibly long time. I've visited eleven nurseries, the homes of six childminders, and interviewed twelve nannies, six of whom could actually speak English. I'm still undecided. I have my name down on two nursery waiting lists and, assuming I do negotiate six months' leave, there's an Australian nanny who is planning to come to England after Christmas; I liked the sound of her over the phone but would still have to meet her. Other things on the list included: clear out cupboard under the stairs, clear out kitchen cupboards, paint nursery wall, put up shelf in nursery, put up curtain rail in nursery, make up cot, fix video recorder, fix camera, update address list, buy announcement cards, plug hospital telephone number into my mobile phone, buy all baby equipment (as per list B), pick up pram, etc., etc., and so on and so forth. Although there seemed to be an enormous amount to accomplish, the list did give me a greater sense of control. But, then, it crossed my mind as I packed labor massage oil into my hospital bag, that I'm fooling myself. The fact that I've packed bedsocks and sanitary towels doesn't mean I'm any more prepared to be a mother. I'm still going off into the unknown with little or no relevant experience. The difference is this no longer terrifies me—it excites me.

I subdivided the job list into three categories: those jobs I reasonably thought I could tackle, those that necessitated outside labor, and those I thought Hugh could be responsible for. The split was roughly thirty-five, eleven, and three.

Three jobs are still outstanding.

Four, if you include "Make peace with Becca."

My only outstanding job.

Interestingly, it's this one that will probably prepare me best for being a mother. I want my child to be born into as much love as possible, and while it's messier and more perplexing than the traditional two-point-two-with-a-dog-family, this is the family the stork has predestined for my little bundle of joy. I don't want any jealousy or cruelty or bitterness between Kate and Tom and my baby. I mean, I know I've always found Kate and Tom ghastly, but I'm hoping that this is a stage—mine. If possible I'd like them to know each other, grow with each other and even love each other. This won't happen without Becca's support. But Becca doesn't owe me any loyalty. So, although it's a long shot, it is my only shot—I have to ring her up. I want to assure her that after the baby is born, Kate and Tom will still be as much a part of their father's life as they've ever been. I want to apologize for the fact that he's not as much a part of their life as he should have been. I'm not sure if things could ever have turned out differently. I still believe I couldn't help loving Hugh as much as I did. So, while I can't undo what's done, I can try to salvage some of the relationships and stop there being anymore human debris.

I pick up the phone and start to key in Becca's number.

Christ, Libby's right, people don't make this sort of call.

It's madness.

I hang up before I've pressed the final digit. I take a deep breath. For the last fourteen years every action, every deed, every impulse I have ever made has been driven by my passion for Hugh. I know for certain that Hugh would not approve of my making this call. He's always been very strict that I don't discuss the past with Becca, he said it was too painful for her, which I understand. Besides, he maintains that we have nothing to apologize for. He's often saying that true love operates on a higher plane than the concerns of the everyday. Which presumably includes his children, a thought that appears almost obscene now. In his more romantic moments of old, he used to say we simply couldn't help ourselves, that we were destined for one another. Besides which she was having an affair, a fact he never tires of repeating.

Even so I have to make this call. Not just for the baby. For me. It seems right to me.

I punch the numbers in.

"Hello, Becca."

"George, are you in labor?" She sounds startled, as well she might—there's not much call for us to phone each other to natter.

My hand is shaking and I reach for the glass of water that's on my desk. This is definitely the hardest thing I've ever done. But then I haven't been in labor yet. "No."

"Oh." She's stumped but too polite to ask, "So why the call?"

"Well, to be fair, I owe you one," she laughs.

"Sorry?" She *owes* me?

"An emergency dash to the maternity ward," she explains.

"Oh, of course." I now understand that she's referring to our mad dash when she went into labor with Kate. Hugh was away at a conference and I'd promised to look in on Becca as she was past her due date. I was there when her contractions started; I dashed through the traffic giving the finger to those who hindered our speedy progress across London. It was way before the affair began, of course. So much has changed since. Some things are the same, though. I mean, what was Hugh thinking of, booking a conference after his wife's due date? I work in the business, I know that it's unlikely that the cure for cancer or even for the common cold would be discovered at one of our conferences. I know "conference" is a generous euphemism for piss-up.

"I think you broke every traffic law. Speeding, U-turns, stopping on red routes," laughs Becca. It had indeed been a cinematic dash.

"I was scared," I defend.

"*You* were scared! I was petrified." We both fall silent. "You were very good about my waters breaking in your car."

"No problem," I say, as I'd said then. In fact the stench was so gross and so pungent I'd had to sell my beloved Spider at a ridiculous discount—in fact, I'd have paid someone to take it away.

"After having seen that labor I'm surprised you ever went in for a baby," adds Becca.

"I'm not going to be as stoical as you with regard to drugs. My policy is, yes please, as many as you can, as fast as you can." Becca laughs, as women who have only used gas and air throughout labor do laugh. It's an odd mix of envy and pity; there's always a smidgen of superciliousness—they are probably entitled to the superciliousness. Probably. The current "right thing" with regard to labor is to want a natural birth because "we've had natural births for centuries." My thinking is that for centuries we've thrown Christians to lions and drowned women with PMT, calling them witches, and we don't anymore—it's seen as progress. I've been held ransom to the arbitrary "right thing" for decades and now I moonie at it. Give me drugs.

I stayed with Becca for most of her labor until her mother arrived. Hugh arrived just in time to catch the froth from the champagne bottle. He missed the placenta slopping into a bucket. I'd thought at the time that this was further proof of how unsuited they were to one another. I'd even taken a certain amount of pleasure from the fact that Hugh obviously didn't feel compelled to be with his wife at that unrepeatable moment, the birth of their child. Why didn't I see it as a measure of the type of man he is? Why did I insist on believing it was a measure of their relationship? A cold film of shame drenches my entire body and simultaneously hardens my resolve. I *owe* her the apology. What sort of woman watches another woman in labor and gets pleasure from the fact her husband missed the event?

Not a very honorable sort. Not the type of woman I want my baby to be brought into the world by. I used to think that when certain things went wrong they could never be put right—what a defeatist attitude.

That said, I've no idea where to begin. The silence yawns between us.

Becca resorts to the weather. "The heat is stifling. How are you managing? Are you wearing hippie-chick floaty dresses?"

"No. The look I'm going for is more elephant man. I stay in as much as I can and if I could wear a paper bag, then I would, but they don't make them in gross size," I admit, laughing. Becca laughs too. I wonder which one of us is most surprised by my honesty.

"Nearly there," she encourages.

"My weight and blood pressure are soaring with the temperature."

"And your spirits?"

"Soaring too."

"Well, that's the main thing."

I see an opening. "Would you like me to call when I go into

labor? I would . . . you know . . . if you wanted me to," I offer hesitantly. I mean, what is the etiquette?

"Well, you needn't call me when you go into labor, but call as soon as you know anything, sex, weight, mother and baby doing fine. That sort of thing."

"Yes. I will. Because Kate and Tom will be interested," I clarify.

"Yes. Kate and Tom will be," she agrees.

"A half-brother or sister," I add cautiously.

"Indeed." She doesn't sound overjoyed, but then nor does she sound at all distressed.

"I'm sorry," I rush.

I didn't mean it to come out like that. I'm hardly being particularly clear about what I'm sorry about. I'm certainly not sorry I'm having a baby, a half-brother or sister for Kate and Tom. But I am sorry for so many other things. However, it quickly becomes clear that this is one of those unsurpassably embarrassing and painful moments in life, when you think you have just said something absolutely momentous, and the other person thinks you're making small talk about the shocking price of organic vegetables.

"I've been meaning to ask you, Georgina, it's probably a bit late now, but I have a baby bath, a Moses basket and a high chair"—she pauses—"well, I'm sure you've bought everything new."

"No, no, we haven't." That's a lie, actually we have. Or rather I have, but I want to accept Becca's offer in the spirit it was intended.

"Well, you're welcome to borrow them," Becca says generously. And then she adds, "As long as you're careful." I'm pleased to recognize the bossy perfectionist; she's less disarming. 'You never know, I might have need for them again, one day."

"What?" I know I should have made an effort to hide my astonishment.

Becca laughs. "I'm only your age, George, I haven't thrown in the towel."

"No, of course not," I rush to cover my gaffe. Becca having

more children is something I've never considered. Why does she insist on proving that there is life after Hugh?

"I made a mistake once, but I can't let that dictate my whole life, can I? Sorry, I probably shouldn't refer to Hugh as a mistake when speaking to you, but so much water has passed under the bridge that I think we can talk about it like adults, don't you?"

"Absolutely." We can talk about it, I wanted to talk about it, but this isn't the conversation I was expecting. She doesn't sound like a woman waiting for me to apologize. Apologize for wanting Hugh so much, for tempting him away, for not giving them a fair chance.

"They say one man's meat is another's poison, don't they? Or, in this case, one woman's poison is another woman's meat."

I let the cliché pass. I remember the trouble I got into last time I pulled someone up on their over-reliance on these clichés. I'm beginning to reappraise my view of the wisdom available from Garfield desk diaries; perhaps it's an important social currency.

"I always knew you'd be there to pick up the pieces. That was a great comfort to me when I threw him out. I'd long suspected that you were in love with him. I knew that he'd fallen in love again and as cruel as it sounds that's quite a relief for the conscience."

"I'm sorry? Are you referring to your affair with your tennis coach?" Suddenly I'm piqued. I'm confused. What is she saying? This isn't what happened. She didn't throw him out. She had an affair. She became sloppy and unreasonable and then Hugh left her *for me*.

Becca laughs somewhat indulgently. "Poor Hugh. I never had an affair. He never would believe me; he had to think that I threw him out for someone else because he just couldn't believe I simply didn't want him." Suddenly Becca remembers who she is talking to. "Goodness, this is hardly a cheerful conversation for you, is it? I'm not saying you got my leftovers or anything. You two seem much better suited; you always had so much more in common. I never could get excited about advertising concepts or pot-holing but you like all that, don't you?" She stops digging. "Perhaps I could give the baby stuff to Hugh next time he picks up the children?"

It is possible that she's lying, that she's trying to wind me up, but I don't think so. Oddly, I trust Becca more than I trust Hugh. Hugh never left Becca for me. He didn't *choose* me. She never even knew he was having an affair. In light of this it seems unlikely then that she begged him to stay, not even "for the sake of the children." It seems unlikely that she's spent the last fifteen months sat by the phone waiting for me to call and apologize. I don't owe her or Kate or Tom anything.

Well, that's a relief.

And it's the most shocking, galling, abominable deceit Hugh has ever thrown at me.

Julia pops her head around the door. "Dean wants to see you, George."

Oh bugger, I'm not in the mood to argue about maternity leave.

50

The flat is thick with silence. Accusations hang in the air like fine cobwebs—when you walk into them they cling, impossible to brush off.

I hear Hugh's key turn in the lock. Slowly the door opens and I hear his footsteps, normally strong, one, two, three, and he's in the sitting room; today they are hesitant. I hear him take off his jacket and the gentle clink of coat-hangers banging together as he hangs it up (unprecedented—normally his jacket stays on the back of a chair until the next use). It's obvious that he is delaying the inevitable.

I am sat on the settee, curled up into the smallest ball I can possibly make my thirty-nine-weeks pregnant body shrink into. If I could, I'd disappear altogether. To say it's been a bad day is a woeful understatement. First the call with Becca, and then Dean.

Obviously Hugh has heard about the security escort that frog-marched me out of Q&A. Every advertising agency in the city will have heard by now. Always a hotbed of gossip, such a momentous occasion could not have passed by uncommented upon. I doubt very much that electricity was needed to power the thousands of PCs in the West End this afternoon; the buzz from this scandal will have been power enough.

I've been fired. For stealing a creative concept from Rartle, Roguel and Spirity. The Project Zoom creative concept, to be accurate. From Hugh, to be explicit.

"Hello." Hugh's voice, although expected and well known is a shock, precisely because it is so familiar to me. How could he have done it? I ask myself for the millionth time that day. How could he have thought so badly of me and betrayed me so completely? Talk about Judas's kiss.

"Why did you do it?" I ask.

"You shouldn't have looked in my file."

"You think I looked in your file?"

"Well, didn't you?"

I don't bother to dignify the outrageous slur with anything more than a very articulate "you bastard." I am so splintered with fury that it takes quite a few seconds before I'm composed enough to add, "You faithless, untrusting bastard."

"Are you saying you didn't read my files?"

"Of course I didn't. I can't believe you think I would have."

"I kept telling them it was unlikely."

"Unlikely?" I yell. "Unlikely? You signed my death warrant. Why didn't you say it was impossible?"

"But it was possible, George. I did bring a paper file home. Besides that there were electronic details of the concept on my PC. You have access to that."

It takes every ounce of reasonableness I possess to resist physically evicting him from my flat there and then. I think I could do it; what with my Incredible Hulk–like proportions and rages, I'm sure I could. Instead, I take a metaphorical and literal deep breath.

"So let's get this straight. Frank Robson showed your CEO Q&A's winning creative concepts—a highly unprofessional move since they are still only in pre-production, I might add."

"My CEO and Frank are quite friendly. I think that's why my CEO was so sure we'd won the pitch."

Ah, now I understand why Hugh did the ill-advised interview with *Campaign*. How stupid of him. He, more than anyone, ought to know that personal relationships count for very little in this business.

"Then your CEO showed the concepts to you and you said that they were *your* idea." I want to get my facts right.

"Yes. I recognized them instantly." Hugh pours himself a whiskey and sits down on the sofa opposite me. He doesn't even appear concerned.

"But they weren't your idea," I splutter.

Hugh opens his briefcase and lays on the coffee table some illustrations of a penknife, a telephone, and a laptop. I have to admit the concept is oddly similar to the one we used on the Project Zoom creative pitch. I'm pleased to note, even in my wrought-up state, that they are not as good. We used a Swiss Army knife, not a penknife. We used a WAP mobile, not a land-line telephone, an iPAQ, not a laptop. Hugh's concepts have no edge. There's no Guy Ritchie, no Ewan McGregor, no suggestion that this car is the dog's bollocks.

"These were in the file that I took to Wales, a file you handled," comments Hugh snippily. "I had to report that you had access to that file."

"I've never seen these concepts before in my life," I insist.

"Well, you would say that, wouldn't you?"

"Yes, because it's true!" I yell.

"I didn't say to the board that you'd cheated for certain."

"Oh, that was good of you."

"I just said that you were very ambitious and I suggested Frank ask Q&A who came up with the winning concept."

Of course the ensuing investigation quickly threw up the fact that I had planted the idea in the creative department. Not so long ago Brett had been only too happy for his team to accept the glory of winning the pitch; however he dropped all ownership as though it were a particularly angry python the moment the idea became immersed in controversy. I don't blame him. He was simply telling the truth; I did plant the idea in the creative department. However, I was aggrieved when he went so far as to suggest it was *peculiar* that I should "hide my light under a bushel," and that the circuitous route of bringing my idea to the table was *suspect*. He implied that my planting a creative idea in his department was the most bewildering and treacherous act of industrial espionage ever. No one is prepared to admit that this is how it always works in advertising if the account management or the new business department have a creative idea. If we admitted as much, the bottom would fall out of the industry. The client has taken a dim view of the "skulduggery" and is threatening to take the account away from Q&A. Dean fired me in an attempt to appease the client. A complex chain of events, but, if I trace it back, Hugh's lack of faith in me is the catalyst.

But it was *my* idea. I did not copy it. "It has to be a coincidence. Things like this do happen. We live together, we talk together, we have similar tastes, we've been thinking along the same lines. That must be it." It must be. Suddenly, I see a glimmer of hope. "You have to vouch for me, Hugh. You have to say I wouldn't look in your file. You have to tell them, your CEO, Frank, Dean, everyone, you have to tell them that you believe we both could have come up with this idea independently."

The glimmer of hope is a mirage.

"No can do, Babes," says Hugh, lying back to stare at the ceiling with his hands behind his head. There isn't an iota in his tone to suggest he's regretful. "They wouldn't believe me. They'd think I was trying to protect you."

Not if they know him.

We sit in silence, the unmistakable sound of a relationship cracking. Pain, shock and disbelief have left indelible stains.

"There's no need for any histrionics, George; I can forgive you."

I'll never be able to forgive myself. I say nothing, and reasonably enough Hugh takes this to be agreement.

"Do you fancy a whiskey, then? No, of course not. Sorry. Well, I'll have another if it's all the same to you," he adds.

And it is.

That's just it.

It's the same to me. Being with Hugh has lost its color and

sparkle, and it's all the same to me. Hugh sits back down with his tumbler of whiskey and reaches for the remote; he starts to flick through the channels. Obviously he considers the conversation closed. I gaze at the TV but can't make out the words. Even the noise of the traffic, drifting up from the high street, normally so intrusive and vibrant a hullabaloo, seems muffled and distant. I turn to study Hugh. In many ways he looks just the same as when I first met him fourteen years ago. He is divine. His height is imposing. His eyes are still huge, sparkling, green, still dramatically offset by long lashes and perfectly arched eyebrows. He's still blond; I can't imagine a gray hair ever having the nerve to find its way onto Hugh's glorious crown. His features remain chiseled; if anything, age has worked for him, he hasn't piled on the pounds, he's become leaner, sharper. His jutting cheekbones and square jaw are indisputably, classically handsome.

But do you know what? Up close, he's a crashing off-the-scale disappointment.

I stand up and walk to the bathroom. Pulling a handful of tissue paper from the roll, I blow my nose. It's a loud, guttural sound; it's hardly attractive. I hardly care. I stare into the bathroom mirror. I don't look anything like I looked when I met Hugh—I was plump and cheerful then. Nor do I look anything like I did this time last year—I was lean and nervous then. An obese, ringless, pregnant woman stares back at me from the mirror. For a moment I feel so dreadfully sorry for her. In the last nine months she's lost her sex drive, her ambition, her job, her body shape. She's just realized that she never had an identity, she doesn't want her lover, and nor does she want to live in a world where you might as well be dead than be bigger than a size 4. Fleetingly she looks pitiful. She looks tired. She is a great swelling, not much more than a mass of hormones, punctuated by blood-red eyes and acne. She even has a downy upper lip. The obvious thing to do now is to get pissed, but it's not an option for her. Nor is having a cigarette, or even a water biscuit with a spot of Brie. She can't descend into pizza-box frenzy as she has nutritional values for her baby to think of. She realizes she doesn't have another line in disaster management.

"Did you pitch the penknife concepts?" I yell through to Hugh.

"No, we dumped them. We went with some beautiful shots of the car racing around—"

"The Swiss Alps."

"Yes," he shouts back.

"Bad call," I mutter.

And I smile at the pregnant hormonal woman and she smiles back. She also thinks it's funny. She's in on the joke. Hers is a wide, life-seizing grin that almost splits her face.

And do you know what? On a scale of one to ten, she's an eleven.

I'm an eleven.

It strikes me that Hugh isn't very good at his job. He should have recognized that car on a winding road on the Swiss Alps has been done to death. For the first time, I really believe that Q&A won the pitch because we had the better concept, not because I had wind. I'll get another job, if I want one, because I am good at my job. I'll get another job with a huge salary and an expense account and a company car and private health care. I'll even get another annoying little card for the vending machine.

Hugh, by contrast, isn't very good at his job. Or, indeed, any of his jobs, MD, father, husband or lover.

I walk back into the sitting room.

"Hugh?"

"Yes, Babes?"

"Get out, Hugh."

"What?"

"Get out."

He nearly chokes on his whiskey; spluttering, he asks, "You're throwing me out because of a pitch?"

He can't believe what I've just said. I can't believe it's taken me so long.

I'm not throwing him out because of a pitch. I'm throwing him out because he's selfish and faithless. I'm throwing him out because he lied to me about how he and Becca broke up, because he's probably having another affair, because he forgot Tom's birthday, because he didn't come to the water-confidence classes, because he's never massaged my aching back, not once in nine months. I'm throwing him out because fourteen years is long enough to pay for an error of judgment.

Epilogue

Sam was right about being in love. It's not about worshipping from afar. It's not about adapting yourself, editing yourself, molding yourself or changing yourself.

He makes me feel I can be entirely myself. He makes me feel that I can be *more* than I am. He is potential. He is realization. I'm in love with him.

He needs his diaper changing.

I scoop him up and take him upstairs. I do the necessary, which isn't pleasant but it isn't as awful as I'd imagined it would be. It's made bearable by the fact that he coos and gurgles and smiles at me throughout. Flashing his sparkly eyes, which are beautiful, although they are not green like Hugh's, but blue, like Jessica's. I kiss his stomach, letting my lips dissolve into his luscious skin, which is as soft and creamy as melting butter. I drink in his smell, more delicious than freshly baked bread or recently brewed coffee and sweeter, purer, clearer than a spring morning or new Egyptian-cotton sheets.

My son, Samuel (obviously named after Sam) arrived exactly on the expected date of delivery. Only days after I had finally reconciled myself to trading my Chanel LBD for a backless, paper hospital gown. While the labor hurt more than even I'd feared, I can't really remember precisely what the pain was like. On the other hand, I won't ever forget that giving birth is the most exquisite, enriching, material and substantive thing I have ever done.

I could have picked my darling splash of color's christening to give some insight into our life together. He was christened on Christmas Eve. It was bitterly cold and wet. There was no sign of romantic snow; however, there were candles, and carols, and choirboys and choirgirls. Hugh came with his new bint and his best intentions. At this distance I can see his best intentions for what they are, largely inadequate. But with this amount of space and time between us I can forgive him his mistakes and I can forgive myself mine. After all, we produced an adorable baby boy between us, which means something. It means everything.

Libby is Samuel's godmother. She's going to fit this duty in around restraining Millie from rushing into her teens, and retraining as a doctor. Sam and James came too; they are currently blissfully unmarried, although James did accept my offer to become Samuel's godfather, which suggested (to Sam at least) that he plans to stay the duration. I think he does. Becca and the kids were there. Becca brought a date, Miles; he's not a tennis player. Jessica and my dad traveled in from Cape Town. The big surprise is that one and all now know Jessica as "Grandma." Although some things never change, her hat was bigger than mine, her waist smaller. Still, I didn't feel inadequate, I felt proud of her and content with myself.

After the baptism all the guests came back to my flat and we drank masses of champagne and took scores of photos of Samuel. This day does give an insight into our lives because it was a day full of fun and promise and love and laughter, but then it was his christening and as such was biased toward being a successful day.

It's perhaps fairest to describe any old ordinary day. Today, for instance. It's an icy cold January afternoon. After I've changed Samuel's diaper, I pack his (huge) day bag, put him in the car and drive across town to Hyde Park. We park and then walk. And walk. And walk. Stopping only to shelter from the rain showers or buy a cup of hot chocolate for me. We walk past the Serpentine, which looks austere but grand. We walk past the deserted bandstand and I think it looks rather charming and other-worldly; it makes me want to rush home and read some Jane Austen. This is an extremely unrealistic expectation; nowadays I rarely have the time to read the bus timetable, let alone the opportunity to pick up a book. Any spare time I do stumble across I use to sleep.

We walk around the Round Pond and I chatter constantly to Samuel, pointing out ducks and pigeons to him, although he's really too young to be aware. I promise him that I'll bring him back to Hyde Park in the summer when it's heaving with happy revelers. He smiles and gurgles but then he's not particularly discerning, he smiles and gurgles at almost anything I say; he'd probably have had the same response if I'd offered to take him to Oxford Street in rush hour. I walk up and down. I circle. I walk so much that I'm actually warm even though it's freezing and late.

I pause near a park bench, check for bird excrement and chewing gum, then sit down to watch the city relinquish the day to the onslaught of twilight. Even though Samuel hasn't been fed in the last two hours and I haven't thrown him up into the air recently, I notice that he's dribbling sick. I scrabble about in my handbag and locate some tissues with which I wipe his mouth, sick-splattered coat and blanket. There's hardly a soul around, except for the occasional tramp and office clerk. I smile and nod but don't get a response. This shouldn't surprise me but it does. My life is so changed I often have to remind myself that others haven't gone through this transformation. That woman in the Burberry raincoat, for instance, she can't see me. I have a pram; I'm beneath her notice. But then she probably doesn't know what chips taste like either. The occasional mother rushes by with her toddler in a pushchair. The kids are invariably ugly, tired and dirty. At least they are to me. Their mothers probably think they ought to be models in Huggies commercials. All the mothers nod and smile at me. Some even stop and ask me how old my baby is. Sometimes I meet a mum in a park and I think we could become really good friends, if I had the time to go for a coffee and a chat. I don't often have the time, but it's nice to know it's a possibility. I'm sure that in the spring, when Samuel is sleeping through and is in a better routine, my social life will pick up again. It will be different, more Play-Doh than pantyhose, certainly more gooey than Gucci, but I'm really looking forward to long hours rolling on picnic rugs and eating strawberries with cream. I'm also looking forward to starting my new job. In the spring I'm going back to work four days a week at a market-research company in Battersea.

Samuel starts to scream. It's a really loud, unforgiving, piercing scream, which tells me in no uncertain terms that I've missed the slot when he expects me to whip out my boob and supply supper. I sometimes do miss this slot but now, at least, I recognize the scream that communicates as much. I pick him up and try but fail to pacify him with cuddles. I consider, should I rush him back to the car and suffer his ear-splitting cries until we get there, or should I feed him here? Samuel is five months old but I still make mistakes, I know I always will. Progress is that I now realize that the mistakes I make are unlikely to be irrevocably harmful. I'm not perfect, I am good enough. I start to fiddle with my coat buttons, wondering if it is possible to get across to my breast without forfeiting all my modesty. For the record, my boobs have changed shape. But I'm pleased and relieved to note that they still defy gravity.

Although they no longer defy belief.

As Samuel starts to feed his wails subside. I look up and catch the eye of another new mum rushing by with her pram. She smiles proudly, first at her baby and then at me. I smile back. The smile we've exchanged is the secret smile of the initiated. It's a smile that conveys a unique mix of total exhaustion with unquashable exhilaration; it combines bewilderment and wonderment. It's a smile that acknowledges that our days are seemingly endless battles against soiled diapers, sticky hands and spew, yet, as each day passes by we feel cleaner, more dignified, more elevated than ever before.

I am good enough.

Thank-Yous

First and foremost, the biggest thank-you goes to my parents, especially as I now have some idea how hard your job has been (and arguably still is!). Thank you, Louise Moore and all at Penguin for being professionals and for being pals throughout. Thank you, Jonny Geller, Carol Jackson and all at Curtis Brown for your love, support and enthusiasm at home and abroad. Thank you, Deborah Schneider, Louise Burke and Amy Pierpont for your passion, faith and spirit. Thank you to all at Pocket Books who have taken this book from manuscript to the bookshelves in American homes. Thank you, Camilla Harrison, for your insight into new business deals. Bob McBrain, for being a long-suffering mate and letting me use your office. Nicole Ingram, for your big smile that broke through writer's block. Alex King, for your eternal friendship and for editing genius at the last moment. Elaine Donoghue, for believing in my dream before I did. Marian Keyes, for sending the most wonderful letter.

And thank you, my readers, without whom this would be pointless.

Up Close and Personal with the Author

IS THIS BOOK AUTOBIOGRAPHICAL?

When I first handed in the manuscript of *Larger Than Life* to my British publisher, she read it and then immediately telephoned me; she was very concerned. She wanted to know if everything was "OK at home?" I remember being grateful for her concern but laughing and assuring her that *Larger Than Life* was, "just a story."

"Are you sure?" she persisted. "It's just I can't imagine how any one could have written so convincingly about a break up of a relationship without having been through it."

I laughed and assured her my husband and I were "extremely happy." We split up less than two months later. I was stunned at the time. It wasn't that I had been lying to my editor friend, the truth is stranger than that. I, like George, had been deluding myself. I believed everything was OK in my relationship because I wanted to believe it.

GEORGE WAS OBSESSIVE ABOUT READING ABOUT HER PREGNANCY. DID YOU FIND BOOKS ABOUT PREGNANCY HELPFUL? DO YOU HAVE ANY RECOMMENDATIONS?

My experience was very similar to George's in this respect. At first I found the books superficial, inaccurate, euphemistic, or depressing. Later I came to find them fascinating and couldn't get enough of them. But that's just to do with my personality. I like being well read on subjects, for example if I am visiting a foreign country I will read a guide book and carry a phrase book. Being pregnant was like visiting a foreign galaxy, never mind a foreign country! It helped me to be prepared. After my son was born I did use a book to help me guide him into sleeping routines. I try not to be evangelical about the right way to deal with pregnancy and parenting because I think there is such a thing as advice and information overload. Do what suits you. If you are the sort of person who normally reads around a subject do so, if you think ignorance is bliss, it might be. Above all, keep a prospective.

AS A WORKING SINGLE MOTHER, ARE YOU MANAGING TO STRIKE A BALANCE BETWEEN LOOKING AFTER YOUR CHILD AND YOUR CAREER?

I am in an extremely privileged position that I am able to work from home and therefore have a career that I love as well as being able to be mum, with little or no guilt. As I say, this is a privilege. I know mums that work out of the home, mums that work in the home and mums that are not paid for the work they do. Nearly all of them are wracked with guilt as to whether they are neglecting their children, their careers, or both. There is no easy answer but it is worth pointing out that all these women *work*.

You made your heroine "the other woman" and initially she appears rather vain and cold, why did you chose to do that? Why - didn't you make your heroine more traditionally nice, and therefore easier to like?

Because I like a challenge and because I like to think my books tackle life's realities. Life is not "yes or no," it's a scramble of "maybes, what-ifs, and good intentions." George is an obsessive. Her personality disorder clearly comes from a lack of inner confidence. Unfortunately one sexual experience, when she was very young and naïve, has formed her outlook for her entire adult life. She is wrong to have an affair with a married man but she is so convinced that she is in love and "meant for" Hugh that she justifies her unfair actions. Equally she is wrong to place so much emphasis on outward appearances, again she justifies this by saying her passion is motive enough. Some people actively dislike George initially, I just felt sorry for her—but then I've a very forgiving nature. By the end of the book readers are always cheering for her, which is important to me. It was essential that George came to understand the unreasonableness of her actions and that she repents and puts right as much as she can so that she can go on to live a more worthwhile life. I guess that makes me a moralist or at least a believer in happy endings.

YOUR OTHER BOOKS, *PLAYING AWAY* AND *GAME OVER*, ARE ABOUT INFIDELITY AND CLEARLY IN *LARGER THAN LIFE* INFIDELITY IS STILL AN IMPORTANT THEME TO YOU. WHY?

Because being unfaithful is so damaging and painful to everyone involved, and whilst everybody knows this, infidelity still thrives. This fact bemuses and fascinates me. And I'm not just talking about sexual infidelity, although that is clearly the most cut and dried permutation of infidelity. I'm talking about broken promises, lies, and the lack of trust between any two people. The world would be so much simpler if we were all more faithful in our actions and words. Yet the reality is so far from that. It's a pity, but a reality, that nice people sometimes do not very nice things. I find that unsettling. In *Larger Than Life*, Sam and James have an affair. They are both lovely characters and yet one is cheating on her fiancé, the other on his brother, why? Passion's a strange one! I think I'll keep writing about it forever, as I'll never understand it.

ARE YOU SAYING YOU WRITE TO HELP YOU UNDERSTAND THINGS?

Yes I suppose I do. I write to explore and explain the mysteries, misunderstandings, and mistakes in my own life as much as anything else. I've always found writing very therapeutic. It was always an automatic reaction to any type of excitement or trauma for me. I was never disciplined enough to keep a diary but ever since I was a child if ever I wanted to understand something, or express my self clearly, I wrote it down. I've been fascinated, and somewhat overwhelmed, by the power of my subconscious. It is now clear to me that when I wrote *Larger Than Life* I was preparing myself for admitting that my relationship wasn't a happy one although I'd always insisted it was.

DO YOU THINK ABOUT YOUR READER WHEN YOU ARE WRITING?

It sounds rude to say not much but in fact I don't. I dare not. I think as soon as a writer starts to wonder, "What would they like to read about?" then he/she will tie themselves into knots. If I do imagine my readers I always imagine them as sympathetic friends who are cheering me on, which may not always be accurate but it is a comfort! I absolutely love hearing from my readers. I'm still utterly thrilled and astonished when someone tells me that they've read one of my books and that they enjoyed it or that it even made them laugh or cry. I think this is an honor.

WHAT NEXT? MORE BABIES OR MORE BOOKS?

My baby is perfect, I can't improve on him but maybe my books could still do with a bit of work!

Like what you just read?

IRISH GIRLS ABOUT TOWN
Maeve Binchy, Marian Keyes, Cathy Kelly, et al.
Get ready to paint the town green. . . .

THE MAN I SHOULD HAVE MARRIED
Pamela Redmond Satran
Love him. Leave him. Lure him back.

GETTING OVER JACK WAGNER
Elise Juska
Love is nothing like an '80s song.

THE SONG READER
Lisa Tucker
Can the lyrics to a song reveal the secrets of the heart?

THE HEAT SEEKERS
Zane
Real love can be measured by degrees. . . .

I DO (BUT I DON'T)
Cara Lockwood
She has everyone's love life under control . . . except her own.
(Available June 2003)

Great storytelling just got a new address.
Published by Pocket Books

Then don't miss these other great books from Downtown Press!

HOW TO PEE STANDING UP
Anna Skinner
Survival Tips for Hip Chicks.
(Available June 2003)

WHY GIRLS ARE WEIRD
Pamela Ribon
Sometimes life is stranger than you are.
(Available July 2003)

LARGER THAN LIFE
Adele Parks
She's got the perfect man. But real love is predictably unpredictable. . . .
(Available August 2003)

ELIOT'S BANANA
Heather Swain
She's tempted by the fruit of another . . . literally.
(available September 2003)

BITE
C.J. Tosh
Life is short. Bite off more than you can chew.
(Hardcover available September 2003)

Look for them wherever books are sold
or visit us online at www.downtownpress.com.